Born in Lancashire and  Alexandra Connor has h... including photographic m... PA to a world famous he... novelist that she has foun... writing over twenty acclaimed sagas she has also written thrillers and non-fiction art books. When she isn't busy writing, Alexandra is a highly accomplished painter and presents programmes on television and BBC radio. She is also a Fellow of the Royal Society of Arts.

By Alexandra Connor

The Witchmark
Thomas
The Hour of the Angel
The Mask of Fortune
The Well of Dreams
The Green Bay Tree
Winter Women; Midsummer Men
The Moon Is My Witness
Midnight's Smiling
Green Baize Road
An Angel Passing Over
Hunter's Moon
The Sixpenny Winner
The Face In The Locket
The Turn Of The Tide
The Tailor's Wife
The Lydgate Widow
The Watchman's Daughter
The Soldier's Woman

The Soldier's Woman

ALEXANDRA CONNOR

headline

First published in 2008
by HEADLINE PUBLISHING GROUP

First published in paperback in 2009
by HEADLINE PUBLISHING GROUP

1

Cataloguing in Publication Data is available from the British Library

ISBN 978 0 7553 4114 6

Typeset in Sabon by Avon DataSet Ltd,
Bidford-on-Avon, Warwickshire

Printed in the UK by CPI Mackays, Chatham, ME5 8TD

Headline's policy is to use papers that are natural, renewable and
recyclable products and made from wood grown in sustainable forests.
The logging and manufacturing processes are expected to conform to
the environmental regulations of the country of origin.

HEADLINE PUBLISHING GROUP
An Hachette Livre UK Company
338 Euston Road
London NW1 3BH

www.headline.co.uk
www.hachettelivre.co.uk

To all the women of this generation –
And generations past –
Who have fought against the odds.
And won.

PROLOGUE

I was never a real girl. Not the kind that loves clothes and gossip and dolls. In fact, I was horrified by anything in baby clothes, breathing or not. When my parents bought me a doll's house for my sixth birthday I was mortified. I had wanted a toy gun, like my brother James. I think in all honesty that James and I got mixed up. He was by nature a pacifist, I was a fighter in my pram. It did no one any good to try and dress me up. Or to try and correct my diction. We did, after all, live in Oldham and it wasn't – even in a child's eyes – grand.

But then a child sees everything differently. I didn't think it was strange that James and I were brought up by my mother's sister. It was just the way it was. We knew that our father had been killed in a tram accident, and unfortunately my mother passed on soon after. To hear my aunt tell it, she was bloody selfish, dying like that . . . Of course now I realise how impossible Agnes's situation had become. She had been left with two children to bring up, and although there was some small amount of money to help her out, it was always a struggle. Especially as she was on her own. Widowed. And not likely to be married again, with two kids in tow.

But James and I didn't recognise our aunt's misfortune then. I just played her up a lot and hung around our maternal grandparents' shop, the City Photographic Studio. Underneath, in smaller letters, the sign proclaimed: Portraits Are Our Speciality. Sounded grand, but in fact it was a basement in David Street, the Jewish rag trade quarter of Manchester. Every day my grandparents went to work in the city, and then came home at night to their house on Hardy Street, Oldham. As for me and my brother, we lived with Agnes in the next street, Gladstone Street, in a cramped, narrow house, scrunched in the middle of a sullen terrace. I slept with Agnes, and James had a room no bigger than a rabbit hutch. As for a bathroom, we bathed once a week in an old tub, hung on the back of the shed door. The lavatory was in the yard, and at night you used a potty, whether you liked it or not.

Agnes always had pretensions to gentility, egged on by my grandmother, who – when she had the devil in her – could make trouble in an empty house. As for my grandfather, Sid, he was as languid as an Eastern concubine and eager for James to take over the family business so he could retire at the age of sixty.

And what of my brother? Well, James was as sweet as I was mischievous. As charming as I was outspoken. He was patient, caring and thoughtful. He didn't steal pies or get his new clothes torn. He tried at school and was polite to our neighbours on Gladstone Street. He was fun and affectionate and half the time I couldn't stand the sight of him. Too perfect by half, he made me look all the worse by comparison, and by the time I was eight I had given him a nickname that stuck for life – Angel James.

For all our differences, we had one thing in common. He might have been five years older than me, but I remember one afternoon not long after our mother's death very well. Our grandfather had been developing a photograph of a prominent Manchester butcher (due to marry) and my brother and I were sitting outside the darkroom.

I can still smell the aroma of the chemicals leaking under the door, and hear the sound of papers being dipped and sloshed about in the liquid.

And then Angel James said: 'Who d'you think you'll marry?'

I snorted. 'I might not marry!'

'Yes, you will,' he replied patiently, dreamily. 'I'm in love.'

And then I looked at him and there was something so extraordinary in his face I caught my breath. Some infusion of life, of happiness. It was so palpable that I could almost have touched it. It was one of the few moments in my childhood, I'm ashamed to admit, when I didn't sneer. Instead, some longing opened up inside me.

'In love?' I echoed. 'Really?'

He nodded. 'Yeah . . . and you'll be in love too one day.'

My curiosity flared. 'Does it hurt?'

He grinned. 'No . . . but it can ache a bit.'

Normally a fifteen-year-old boy wouldn't confide in his ten-year-old sister, but we were always close. And besides, I think he knew how much I wanted to hear what he had to say.

'Her name . . .' he said, pausing for emphasis, 'is Gracie.'

Oh Gracie, what happened to you? I look back now – all these years later – and wonder if you still have the spark to light a man's fantasy. Or are you fat and sour in a city back street somewhere? But for that moment – as Angel James confided her name – she epitomised an aura of tingling, breathless romance. And of hope. Of something that could make a person glorious.

God, we were such romantics. In the blood, it must have been, because our aunt and grandparents certainly didn't encourage fanciful thoughts. But that winter afternoon, listening to the noises coming from the darkroom on David Street, I looked at Angel James and envied him. I wanted to be older. Out of school. Out of lisle stockings. And most of all, in love . . .

'I think I could love a soldier,' I said at last.

James burst out laughing. 'A soldier!'

'Well,' I said, mortified, 'why not? I think I'd make a good soldier's woman.'

PART ONE

CHAPTER ONE

Oldham, Lancashire, 1901
The temperature in the room was cool, the curtains drawn. Faith hung back at the door. Laid on the dining table was a coffin, the lid removed and laid up against the wall of the front room. Small for her age, Faith could only see the upper part of her mother's folded hands, the tip of her nose, and a little of her thick dark hair. She knew that if she walked closer she might see more, and if she climbed on one of the dining chairs she could see all of her mother – but she couldn't face that. Couldn't face the reality that this was her mother – the widow Ivy Farnsworth, dead at thirty-six.

Gripping her brother's hand, Faith stood rigidly by James's side, her gaze locked on the open coffin.

'Should we get close?' she asked timidly.

'We don't . . . we don't have to.'

Faith nodded, and kept staring at the tuft of her mother's hair. 'What if they're wrong?' she whispered. 'What if she's not dead?'

'She's dead,' James replied, squeezing Faith's hand tightly. 'Sorry, love, but she is.'

Unnerved, Faith looked at the coffin. How could her mother really be dead? How could the loving, lively Ivy be reduced to a still figure, with all the animation of a ghost? She had been so much fun, hiding behind the kitchen door to surprise Faith when she came in, laughing with James when he told her about his exploits on the football field, the dirt patch behind the Methodist chapel. Even after their father had been killed so unexpectedly, Ivy had somehow managed to keep her family together, maintaining her spirit and her sense of humour. She had been a wonderful mother, never allowing her own grief to ruin her children's lives; never wanting bad luck to become a habit. She had been brave, witty and good, Faith thought desperately. How could that much life, that much energy, be gone?

'I don't want them to put that over her!' Faith said suddenly, her voice echoing with panic as she noticed the coffin lid leaning against the wall. 'I don't think she'd like it. And it's cold in here. It's too cold for her.' Suddenly letting go of her brother's hand, she walked over to the table and pulled out a chair. Climbing on to it, she stared down at the dead body of her mother. For a moment she willed the chest to rise, for her mother to breathe, for her to awaken. Her eyes closing, Faith prayed for the intake of breath, for the return of warmth and life into the waxen figure. She prayed with her eyes closed to any god that was listening. She tried to make a bargain: she would be good if her mother would only wake up. She would work hard at school, do the chores, even have her hair plaited, if only Ivy would come back to life. Please, please, God, she begged, please . . .

At last Faith reopened her eyes. For one glistening moment she expected a miracle. But when she touched her mother's hand there was no response. Instead, its coldness shocked her and she gasped, jumping off the chair and running out of the front room. Away from the smell of damp. Away from the table with the coffin on it. Away from the coldness of death and her unmoving, unwaking mother.

CHAPTER TWO

Agnes Todd was wearing the checked apron she put on for cooking – and that meant trouble. Not a natural chef, she wrestled with the culinary basics and made gravy that could bend a fork. But she persisted. She had to, because there was no one else to look after the children she was due to inherit. The death of her brother-in-law, Stanley Farnsworth, had been a shocking accident, but the demise of his widow Ivy only a year later had been tumultuous.

It was no good the neighbours on Gladstone Street commiserating with Agnes about the sad loss of her sister. In Agnes's eyes, Ivy had committed the worst possible sin: she had ducked out of her responsibilities. And the result of that dramatic ducking was that two children were about to land, unneeded and unwelcome, on her doorstep. A lad of fifteen and a girl of ten were not what Agnes had anticipated. After all, hadn't she had her own troubles? Lost her own husband only two years after they had married? Some life hers had turned out to be. Mind you, Bernard Todd *had* left her the house, and that made Agnes one of the few around who owned their own property, but it didn't make up for being a widow . . . In Agnes's daydreams of snagging a well-to-do widower, she had toyed with the possibility that there might be children involved, then consoled herself with the fact that they would be grown up and unlikely to impinge on her life. Agnes did not like children, nor had she ever wanted to give birth to her own, so the imminent invasion of her sister's offspring was something of a shock to her.

And shock takes different people in different ways. In Agnes's case – when she had recovered from the knowledge that she was about to become an unmarried surrogate mother – the reality of her position hit her as hard as the tram that had carried off poor Stanley. She was thirty-nine, and her chances for getting married again had depended on her snaffling a middle-aged widower. But how likely was it that she could ever get a man like that with two kids in tow? And besides, her house on Gladstone Street didn't lend itself to children. Over the years Agnes had accumulated an impressive collection of ornaments. Turning round in the Gladstone Street house required the skill and dexterity of an acrobat. On the eve of the children's arrival, she toyed with the possibility of moving her knick-knacks, but dismissed the idea out of hand. The children, she decided, would have to fit in with her, not the other way around.

It might have made more sense if the children had

gone to live with their grandparents in the next street. But, as Beryl Bentley said repeatedly, it was not a good thing to have two children rattling around the house when she was out at work all day with her husband in Manchester.

All Agnes's protestations had been stonewalled. And continued to be dodged as the day of the children's arrival came around.

'I don't understand, Mother,' Agnes said, pushing aside the flour and the basin and putting her hands on her hips. 'I've stopped working at the bakery. Why do you *have* to carry on at the studio?'

Beryl's steely expression focused on her daughter. She knew that Agnes was hoping she would give up work in Manchester and help her with what were after all her own grandchildren. But Beryl had no intention of leaving the business to her husband's devices. At only five foot six, Sidney Bentley lacked height, but not charisma. His eyes were delphinium blue, his skin smooth and unlined, his hair glossy as coal. One look at Sid and a person thought of Welsh choirs and hills, of soft rain and hard winters in the valleys. He might have no accent, but he had a slow-moving charm that he could use to devastating effect. Sid also loved his clothes. No man in Manchester was more of a dandy. Having been running the City Photographic Studio for many years, Sid had numerous friends among the men working in the neighbourhood, and would recommend their services – particularly those of Mort Ruben and Laurence Goldbladt – to his customers. 'After all,' he would say, 'you want to look good in your photograph, and a new suit will do the trick . . .' In return, Mort or Laurence would let Sid have a suit for himself, cut price. Or an overcoat. If Sid had found them a lot of business, he might get an extra pair of summer trousers. But that didn't happen often. After all, no one had money to throw around.

'Well?' Agnes said, breaking into her mother's thoughts. 'Why *do* you have to keep working in Manchester when you could help me out with Ivy's children? I don't understand why I have to get lumbered with them. I don't even like children, and I didn't get on with Ivy. You could help me, Mother. Together it wouldn't be difficult.'

'I have to keep an eye on the business.'

'On Father, more like.'

'Agnes,' Beryl said warningly. 'That tongue of yours will get you into trouble.'

'I'm only speaking the truth!' Agnes snapped back, slumping on to a kitchen chair and gazing morosely into the unlit grate.

For a fleeting moment her mother had sympathy for her, but it didn't last. Beryl knew only too well that she had to keep an eye on the Manchester photographic shop. Sid wasn't to be trusted with business matters. Or with the accounts. Or with women. Mind you, she thought, he *was* a good photographer. Could make a prince out of a pig's backside if it was called for. And some of their customers certainly needed the help. Like the woman who had come in the previous month with an older man, asking for a portrait. Pocket-sized, she had said, so my uncle can carry it with him. Within thirty seconds Beryl had summed up the situation: a mistress with her married lover. She even considered – momentarily – throwing them out, but decided that she would increase the fee instead. The 'uncle', delighted with the result, paid. And the following week, another set of unlikely relatives followed.

'It won't be that hard, Agnes,' Beryl said, taking a seat next to her daughter. 'We have to pull together.'

'Seems like I'm doing most of the pulling.'

'Your dad and I will have the children at the weekends.'

Agnes's face lit up. 'You will?'

'Of course,' Beryl replied, feeling magnanimous. 'When I get home from the studio on Saturday dinner time, you can send them over. And they can stay with us until Sunday night. That'll give you some time off.'

'To clean up after them,' Agnes replied, then decided not to antagonise her mother any further in case she withdrew the offer. 'I don't know anything about children.'

'Oh, they look after themselves,' Beryl said lightly. 'Anyway, James is fifteen, grown up—'

'So why is he still at school? He should have a job by now.'

'His mother wanted him to be a teacher.'

'Hah!' Agnes retorted. 'Well, there's no money for that, despite Ivy's big ideas. James will have to work.'

It was true, Beryl realised. Even when her daughter was alive there hadn't really been enough money to pay for further education. James would have to learn the family trade and take over the photographic business. She knew it was what Sid wanted. He was already talking to Laurence about his grandson coming to work for him. Bragging about how James had been clever enough to be a teacher, if things hadn't gone so bad for the family.

'Whatever you say about James being nearly grown up,' Agnes went on, 'the girl is only ten.'

Beryl glanced at her daughter. 'What?'

'Faith is only ten years old. She's still a child.'

'Not for long.'

'And I have to share my bedroom with her.'

'Oh, for pity's sake!' Beryl snapped. 'The kid's a bloody orphan, have a heart!'

'*You* have a heart, Mother! It's not you that's looking after them!'

Annoyed, Beryl picked at the cuff of her blouse, thinking about Ivy. The daughter she had got on so well with. The daughter she had laughed with, joked with, talked to. Not that she didn't love Agnes, but she had never been as close to her elder daughter. There was always a distance, a remoteness. Still, Beryl thought, pulling herself together, this was no time for grieving. She did enough of that at night, when it was dark and quiet. When she came downstairs in the house on Hardy Street and sat thinking about Ivy. Thinking about how strange life was; how nothing turned out the way it was supposed to. She knew that Sid had been hit hard by the loss of their daughter. But Sid was Sid, and his temperament was elastic and bounced back from trauma. Hers didn't. Not that anyone knew that. Beryl kept her feelings to herself: weakness was no good in a family that relied on her.

'You'll manage,' she said at last, glancing over to her elder daughter.

Sighing, Agnes got to her feet, straightened her apron, and looked into the glass over the mantelpiece. It was said that she had one of the finest heads of hair in Oldham, and it was true. Piled up softly in the current fashion, the auburn waves framed an oval face with piercing, intelligent eyes. Her forehead was high and smooth, like her father's, her cheeks full, only her chin showing the determination that had daunted many a man. But although Agnes wanted to marry again some day, she was in no hurry. Instead she had glided like a galleon through her thirties, watching her friends and other workers at the bakery marry and begin families, without a twinge of envy. In Agnes's own eyes, she was waiting to make her choice. Nothing more. She wasn't on the shelf, she was in the running – and determined to run the right man to ground as soon as he arrived on her track.

Unwavering, she gazed steadily at her reflection in the mirror. She had done all the moaning she was going to do, she decided. She was stuck with the situation, so she might as well make the best of it. Her nephew could help her around the house, doing the heavy work, and as for her niece . . . maybe Agnes could become a mentor to Faith? The thought was a soothing one, and when Agnes turned back to her mother she was brisk and composed again.

'I'm learning to cook.'

Beryl nodded, trying not to show her surprise. Agnes's cooking could fell an army.

'My niece will have to learn about cooking herself. And how to keep a house. I can teach her that.'

Keen to encourage her, Beryl nodded. 'No one better.'

'Girls like housework and keeping things tidy, don't they?'

'Most do.'

'Maybe she'll be good at sewing,' Agnes went on, eyeing a basket full to the brim with mending. 'And in the school holidays we could go shopping together, and she could help me in the garden . . .'

Beryl nodded again, not daring to mention the fact that Agnes's garden was a back yard with a selection of flowerpots in it. This was not the time to dissuade her daughter from anything, even her ludicrous pretensions. Dear Agnes, so keen to be one up on her neighbours that she had developed selective eyesight. Her yard was a garden, her clumps of flowers sagging under the north-west downpours an oasis of beauty. She didn't see the outside privy, or the coal hole. She didn't see the brick wall with the weeds sprouting out of the top of it, or hear the collier's wife screaming for her brats to come in at night. Agnes saw what she wanted to see. So when the smog came down, choking, restricting visibility to three feet, Agnes talked about 'mists' as though she was in Devon, not ground under the mill chimneys of the industrialised north.

'Of course people will think she's my sister,' Agnes went on, glancing in the mirror again and liking what she saw. Her niece might turn out to be a godsend after all. A pet slave. A grateful little mouse she could impress. 'Maybe it won't be so bad . . .' she said dreamily, noting her mother's sly glance and adding deftly, 'Who knows? We might even turn out to be friends.'

CHAPTER THREE

'It won't be that bad,' James said, stopping for the third time at the end of Gladstone Street. 'We might be happy here.'

'We *won't* be happy!' Faith replied, kicking at the dust around her feet.

It was a warm spring day, too warm for March, the sky high and densely blue. Birds, singing intermittently, collected on the chimney stacks of the terrace on Gladstone Street, a cat slinking up a steep roof towards them. At the last moment the cat charged, the birds making for freedom and the high sky above. Defiantly Faith stared ahead, her ankle-length serge dress topped off with a white apron, her hair tied away from her face and decorated with a large white bow. Rather too large for her little face, it fluttered in the sullen spring air like a giant moth.

'Aunt Agnes could turn out to be nice to live with.'

'You know she won't be!' Faith replied, sitting down on the edge of the pavement.

'Get up!' James said hurriedly, glancing round. 'What are you doing?'

'I'm not going another step,' his sister replied. 'I'm never going in that house. I'm never going to live with Aunt Agnes and I'm never going to be happy again.'

She fell silent, her expression determined as she crossed her arms. Sighing, James sat down next to her. A curious passer-by glanced at the two of them, then walked on.

'I miss Mum too.'

'I don't see why she had to die.'

'She didn't mean to. She didn't mean to leave us here,' James explained, stretching out his legs and crossing his ankles. At the end of the street a cart passed, pulled by a shire horse and stacked high with coal. In the driver's seat, a man held the horse's reins and clicked his tongue softly. 'She didn't die deliberately.'

'Mum didn't even like Aunt Agnes, so why are we going to live with her? Why can't we go on living with our grandparents?'

It was a good question, but James knew the answer only too well – their grandparents ran the photographic studio in Manchester full time, their grandmother the driving force. Beryl neither wished, nor could afford, to give up work. She had looked after them for the previous few weeks, but now it was time to move on. James understood that his grandmother had to work. The money his father had left behind had been disappearing far too quickly, despite their mother's very best efforts at conserving it. Now what was left would have to be supplemented by the City Photographic Studio to pay the rent on the Gladstone Street house and other necessary expenditure. Given the circumstances, it was obvious that Agnes would draw the short straw and have to take them in.

Expressionless, James looked down the terrace, his gaze settling on the front door of his aunt's house. It was painted black, like a big gaping mouth just waiting to take a snap at them. Even the sunlight seemed to favour the other side of the street. Agnes's house was in the shade, her neighbours hunched up around her like a row of gloomy pigeons on a washing line.

'She might not be as bad as we think—'

'She will be!' Faith interrupted. 'Remember what Mum told us about her when they were young? About how Agnes borrowed her communion dress and spilled dandelion and burdock all over it?'

'But—'

'And then she told everyone that Mum wasn't her real sister and that she was adopted.'

James raised his dark eyebrows. 'Agnes was only six at the time.'

'Still . . .'

He gazed at his little sister, amused but not daring to show it. Faith was small for her age, but her feet promised an incipient growth spurt and he realised that she might, in the end, be tall. Her face was oval, her eyes long-lashed and intensely dark. As for her hair, it was the colour of liquorice and shiny like ebony. She looked delicate, he thought, but was immune to illness. Cold winters that had other children – including himself – coughing and wheezing didn't faze his sister. The choking peasouper fogs, with their sulphurous smoke coming thick from the sooty chimneys, might hobble a grown man, but not Faith. Even childhood ailments she dodged. James might have suffered from chicken pox and measles, but his sister had ducked the diseases' blows with the alacrity of a boxer.

Her physical constitution was amazing, and in keeping with her character. Faith was feisty, opinionated and brave, even at ten. She might be a girl, but she could punch her weight. Which was why James was so in awe of her. So impressed by this scrap of humanity who had endured the loss of their parents and now faced the alarming prospect of life in Gladstone Street. James knew that Faith cried for their dead parents, but in the morning she would deny it, even if her eyes were puffy. He knew that she missed them, as he did – but he was fifteen, not ten. It was easier for him.

Or was it? He would have to leave school now, he had been told as much. Go and work for his grandparents instead. Which wasn't what he wanted. Or what his parents had wanted . . . But then the handsome James had an equable temperament, and his character was flexible, adaptable. He knew that despite his reservations he would do what was asked of him – he just wasn't certain that he could say the same for his sister.

'Come on,' he urged, nudging Faith's arm. 'We said we'd be there for tea.'

'Our aunt can't cook.'

'Well, that's true,' he agreed, thinking of the occasional sodden Sunday lunch they had endured over the years. 'But she might make more of an effort now.'

Faith gave him a quizzical look.

'Can't we run away?' She turned to him, pleading. 'Please, James, think about it. We could run off now. Never go to that horrible house. We could make for Manchester, Liverpool, even London. No one would find us . . .'

'We have no money.'

'We could make money!' she wailed. 'We could work.'

'Faith, you're ten years old. You're still a child.'

'No, I'm not!' she replied hotly, all self-pity gone. 'I bet I could survive on my own.'

James had a feeling she just might.

'But you're not going to,' he told her. 'We're going to live with our aunt, whether we like it or not. And we're going to make the best of it, Faith.'

She could tell from the tone of his voice that her brother had made up his mind and wasn't about to budge. James was usually adaptable, but not in this.

'For how long?'

'Not for long,' he told her, helping her to her feet. 'Time passes quickly. Soon we'll have our own lives. It's not for ever.'

'Nah,' she said curtly. 'It'll just seem like it.'

CHAPTER FOUR

David Street, Manchester

At the same moment that James and Faith were plucking up courage to enter Agnes's house, Sid was watching the back of his wife's head as she counted the takings. Her hair was pulled away from her face and wrapped into a tidy bun at the back of her neck. Nice hair, but not luxuriant like Agnes's. Carefully he studied his wife, knowing that she was unaware of the scrutiny. Beryl was fifty-nine years old, a bit on the stout side, her corsets holding her spreading waistline in check. But the elegant ankles he had fallen in love with, she had retained. He smiled as he looked at the inch of black lisle stockings and the dainty tight-laced boots. Almost a girl's feet. His gaze travelled up over the sombre navy dress with its white apron, a gold watch pinned at her left breast. And around her wrists the detachable white cuffs she always wore in the studio.

When they married, no one had given them much of a chance. Tommy Bentley's son was bound to be like his father, and would soon be chasing skirt. But although Sid had a lot of Tommy in him, he was more of a flirt than a seducer. His charm was devastating when in full flow, but the follow-through would have been too exhausting for him. He liked women, but not enough to risk the home life that Beryl had made so easy for him. And when they moved into the house on Hardy Street and the birth of their two daughters followed, Sid luxuriated in the downy centre of a nest of females. Spoiled, he spoiled his girls in return, and when Ivy married he was equally tolerant of his grandchildren, James and Faith.

In fact, Sid thought, puffing on his black Turkish cigarette, his had been a cushy life so far, until the shocking death of Ivy . . . Sighing, he looked around him. The light in the basement was never that good, and on grey afternoons the lamps were lit virtually all day. But the photographic studio was in a good spot, David Street being close to St Peter's Square and the rag trade area of the city. Not as fashionable as St Anne's Square certainly, but the rents there were huge and way out of Sid's reach. Besides, being in a basement had some advantages, like a dark-room that really was dark at the back of the shop, and a cool place to store film plates and chemicals in the summer. In the winter, though, it could be unbearably cold, the thick brick walls getting damp unless you kept the stove lit. Sid stored the kindling in the poky yard outside. The same yard he shared with the other six businesses on the David Street premises.

'What are you doing standing there?' Beryl asked, turning and catching her husband's eye.

He smiled at her. Sharp tongue, acid sense of humour, but feisty – and he liked that.

'I was thinking about this place.'

'What about it?'

'About how it all started . . .' Sid replied, lighting up another of his black cigarettes, an affectation he had picked up from his friend, Laurence Goldbladt, who swore blind that women found the smokes irresistible. The cigarettes were a luxury and damn near ripped the skin off your lips, but the tobacco was the best, and besides, if it improved your flirting with the ladies, so much the better. 'D'you remember the first sign that was hung here?'

Beryl nodded, seeing it clearly in her mind's eye. It had been a large dark green sign, with the lettering in gold – City Photographic Studio – and it had hung over the basement steps until one winter's day it had fallen on a customer and broken his collar bone.

'Green was always an unlucky colour,' she said dismissively, turning back to the books.

Sid wasn't convinced that green was unlucky, and thought the broken collar bone was due to shoddy carpentry rather than divine intervention. Besides, whatever Beryl might say, the sign had attracted customers – photographs still being something of a novelty back in the 1890s. A fresh, exciting new medium, becoming available for the general public. People were suddenly able to have themselves immortalised, photographs becoming landmarks in their lives. They could map out their existences in prints; marriages, births, old age were all processed and put into family albums. Fixed on photographic paper for the generations to come. In fact, photography offered a kind of immortality for the average person. A marker of what they had looked like and achieved. For many northerners, money was tight, but most could stump up a shilling for a photograph, and – if they saved up – a decent frame off Tommyfields Market.

Sid had taken over the studio from his father, the frequently inebriated Tommy Bentley. Memories of Tommy were sketchy; he hadn't been the family type. More the womanising, rambling, roaming tom-cat type . . . Sid smiled, thinking fondly of his roguish father. It was true that Tommy had been a bastard, but he'd been a cheerful bastard. And besides, if he wasn't happy with his common-law wife, why shouldn't he change? Once, twice, even three times? Ah yes, Tommy Bentley was a hell-raiser all right.

After one long weekend away from home, he had come back to make noisy love to his latest wife – Sid's mother – and introduce his son to the wonders of photography. With a cigarette hanging out of the side of his mouth – bugger the fire precautions in the lab – Tommy had squinted his way through the developing process in the David Street basement. Often clumsy from the drink, he had reeled around the enclosed darkroom, hanging slopping prints from pieces of string above his head, the liquid dripping on to his collar and marking his shirt. Barking orders that no one should enter, he emerged much later waving a series of photographs that should by rights have been dismal. But they were great. Always great.

Sid smiled to himself, leaning against the wall and looking at his hands. There was only one thing he didn't like about the photography business, and that was the mess it made of your nails. Thoughtfully he picked under his index fingernail. It had certainly been an exciting business to inherit. Tommy Bentley had got the best of it, when photography was just beginning, but Sid had been in pretty close to the start. The initial novelty of the studio had caused quite a stir in Manchester. Even in a basement in David Street. But like Tommy would say when he was sober: 'You start in a basement, then it's a ground-floor studio, then it's a string across the north-west.'

Pity was that Tommy, for all his natural artistic skill, was totally feckless. All the money he made he poured down his neck, or down the necks of the women he picked up. Or photographed. Crouched down, his head under the black sleeve of the camera, he would stare at his clients. His appeals to 'relax' and 'smile, please' soon gave way to 'You look marvellous' and 'What a picture this will make for the lucky man in your life!' Women who could never have afforded to have their portrait painted could suddenly see their likeness in a photograph. And what a photograph. Although he had plenty of competition in the new profession, Tommy Bentley had the skill in posing a person – and the best backgrounds in the north-west. Whilst other photographers were content to place their subjects on a chair with a painted curtain behind, or leaning against a painted column, Tommy Bentley created his own backdrops. They turned out to be as flamboyant as he was. In the Manchester basement, clients found themselves transported to Ancient Egypt (complete with pyramids) or a sheikh's tent – a backdrop particularly popular with middle-aged women.

'What the hell are you smiling at?' Beryl asked suddenly, cutting into her husband's thoughts.

'My father.'

'Oh, that sod,' she replied, her tone resigned.

'You remember his backgrounds? The backdrops he painted for the photographs?'

'Remember them? We've still got a couple,' Beryl replied, jerking her head towards the storeroom. 'The mice got Blackpool Tower and the Pleasure Beach, but that tropical paradise is still going. Lost its colour, of course, but who'd know in black and white?'

Another memory stirred in Sid's head. His mother had surprised her husband once, finding him on the chaise longue with the wife of the Mayor of Salford. Outraged, Gertie threw him – and the Mayor's wife – out. She never got over the fact that they had broken the back castor.

Gertie's tolerance of Tommy Bentley's flirting was legendary, but she wasn't the jealous type. In fact, that was the only thing his mother had in common with Beryl. Not that he would ever know, but Beryl had set her sights on Sidney Bentley the night they had first met. Undaunted, she had brushed aside all the grim predictions of her heart being broken, because she knew what she wanted: Sidney Bentley – and Sidney Bentley's photographic studio.

'I'll never know why your mother stayed with Tommy Bentley,' Beryl said suddenly. 'I mean, it's not as if they were married—'

'Sssh!' Sid hissed, his wife raising her eyebrows.

'Who can hear? They're both dead.'

'My mother was very sensitive about the matter,' Sid replied, pulling down the front of his silk waistcoat. A little thank-you from Laurence Goldbladt. 'She didn't want anyone to find out.'

'Your father had had two common-law wives before he took up with her! Which was worse – that she wasn't really married to him, or that he was a bastard?' Beryl smiled wryly at her husband. 'At least my people were respectable.'

'Not respectable enough to stop me marrying you,' Sid replied, walking over to his wife and looking over her shoulder. 'So, how are we doing?'

'We can pay the rents, pay the bills and put a bit in the Post Office for a holiday later in the year.'

'I could take it down to the Post Office for you.'

Beryl snorted. 'I could throw the money in the Manchester Ship Canal too. But I'll not waste it.

There's two pubs and a betting shop on the way to the Post Office.' She tapped Sid affectionately on the cheek. 'You develop those pictures of the Ramsbottom brat instead.'

'There won't be one good one amongst them. The bloody kid couldn't keep his head still for a minute. And when he finally did, he stuck his tongue out.'

Laughing, Beryl gathered up the account books and placed them in the desk drawer, locking it with a flourish and pocketing the key.

'I'll go straight home after I've been to the Post Office.' Sid raised his eyebrows; Beryl never went home early. 'I need to call in on Agnes and see how the kids are settling in.'

Putting out his black cigarette, Sid avoided his wife's gaze and wondered if he should utter the next words. The loss of Ivy had been a blow to him, and he knew how much it had rocked Beryl. Just as he knew that one part of his wife wanted to take over the care of their grandchildren.

'You think we're doing the right thing?'

She stiffened by the basement door. Rigid in her long brown coat, still adjusting her hat.

'About what?'

'You know, Beryl. The kids.' He moved on quickly. 'Agnes has never had children. She doesn't know about them. You do. You're their grand-mother—'

Beryl turned, her face flame red. 'And I'm working! I'm the one that keeps this family afloat, and let's not forget it. Without me, you'd have run this business into the ground and there would have been no chance of anyone supporting Ivy's kids.' Her voice was metallic with fury. 'I've lost my daughter. I know Ivy was your daughter too, Sid, but I was closest to her. Not like Agnes. We just rub along. I love her, but not like I loved Ivy. But that's the past. Our girl's dead and her children have come under our care. Now I accept that. They're family, it's right that they come to us, but I can't stay home and mind them. Agnes might not be used to children, or to looking after someone else's family, but she'll have to learn how to cope.'

'Beryl, calm down—'

'I don't want to calm down, Sidney! I can't give up work, because if I do, the whole family will come crashing down around our ears.'

He drew himself up to his full height. 'I'm not a fool.'

'You're not a fool in some ways, that's true enough. But you're a fool with money, and money is what we need now.' Jamming in her hatpin to secure her hat, Beryl flounced out, her boots clicking on the basement's stone steps as she made for the street.

CHAPTER FIVE

Mr Perry Braithwaite was watching through his kitchen window, which looked out on to Gladstone Street, wondering if he should say something to the two kids hanging around outside. He had heard about the death of their parents – who hadn't? – but his interest was more than passing curiosity. The fact that Mrs Agnes Todd had been kind enough to offer them a home had filled him with both admiration and horror. Perry had been married once; his wife had died a long time ago, leaving him to a quiet and unassuming life. Working at the town hall as a clerk, he filled his regular days with his regular ways, and went out weekly with his male friends for a drink at the Lion and Bugle pub. Never too much, just enough to make him merry, but not silly. Perry didn't like silliness in women or men. He didn't like anything that was childish. It unnerved him.

Having been brought up by older parents, Perry's life as an only child had been comfortable but controlled. No one in his family showed their emotions. In fact, when his father caught his arm in the machinery at Platts factory, people commented on his stoicism as the firemen struggled for three hours to free him, cutting through his bicep in the attempt. As for Perry's mother, she was allergic to excess. So it came as no surprise to anyone that Perry Braithwaite, slim, grey-suited, short-haired and quietly spoken, was the epitome of respectability. He was the living example of a man who could be taken anywhere. He would have died rather than offend.

When his wife passed on, Perry continued working at the town hall and kept the house neat, and if he regretted having no children, he never said. Instead he attended church on Sundays, caught the tram to Union Street at 7.16 every morning, and was so reliable people could set their clocks by him: 'Perry Braithwaite's in his winter coat. Must be the first of October'; 'Perry Braithwaite's drawn his front room curtains. Tonight will be cold.'

He became a walking metronome for neighbourhood trivia, and only escaped being despised by his sheer niceness. But Perry did harbour the odd secret. Not many, in all his fifty-plus years, but a couple of big, aching ones. Like being in love with Agnes Todd.

Sighing, Perry stared at the kids in the street outside. He wondered fleetingly why the little girl's hair bow was so large and if a sudden wind might carry her over to Rochdale faster than any tram. But mostly he was thinking that he shouldn't have been so nice for so long. That, in short, he should have spoken out. It was all right thinking there would be a perfect time, but that perfect time was running out before his very eyes. In a matter of minutes, two children would arrive on Agnes Todd's doorstep and life would change for ever. She would cease to be a widow, and become a woman with two charges. A family . . . Perry sighed again, then wondered if perhaps he should count himself lucky. What if he *had* expressed his feelings and he and Mrs Todd had become attached? He would have been landed then . . . His ignoble thoughts shamed him. How *could* he think in those terms? These children were Agnes Todd's niece and nephew, they were her blood. So how could they be anything other than acceptable?

But then again . . . Perry turned from the window. He would bide his time a little longer, see how the situation worked out. When the children had settled down with his beloved Agnes, he would declare himself. But not yet. For a while he had to be content to watch the object of his affection in silence, certain that time and opportunity would bring them together. That was what a nice man did, after all.

'What,' Agnes asked pointedly, 'is that?'

Automatically Faith touched the bow in her hair. 'James put it in for me.'

'Couldn't you get a bigger one?' Agnes replied sarcastically. 'There must be a yard of ribbon there.'

'I like big—'

Jabbing his sister in the ribs, James stood in the kitchen doorway. Both of them had dressed themselves up: he in his three-quarter-length breeches, wool jacket and cap, his sister in her mid-calf-length black dress and boots. And the bow he had struggled to tie that morning. Perhaps not that well; certainly too big, he could see that now. But he had just tried to copy what he had seen their mother do so many times in the past.

'We shall all have to get on and be happy together,' Agnes said, gesturing to the table. A plate of baleful scones and a flattened piece of sponge leered up at the three of them. 'I baked for you.'

'Thank you,' James said, smiling and nudging his sister.

'I don't like scones.'

Agnes's expression went from tolerance to irritation in an instant.

'You have to watch your mouth, young lady! No one likes cheek, and I won't tolerate it in my house.'

Really, she thought, outraged, what a nerve! Faith might be only ten, but she looked like hard work, Agnes realised with a shudder, then tried to console herself. They had just lost their mother; it was a trying time for everyone. She would be patient if it killed her. And besides, it was only during the week; Beryl would have the children at the week-end . . . But suddenly, that Wednesday afternoon, the weekend seemed to be aeons away.

'I got your things dropped off here and put yours,

Faith, in my bedroom. We'll be sharing.' She stared at the stern little figure in front of her and dreaded the invasion of her privacy. 'As for you, James, you'll have your own room. It's not big, but . . .' She moved to the stairs, the children following obediently as she carried on. 'We have to cope with limited space. Of course, I have some house rules.'

She paused, flinging open the door of James's room. It was hardly more than a large cupboard, with a narrow bed and a chair beside it and a large floral potty underneath. Stunned, Faith was about to speak, when James stopped her with a warning look.

'It'll do fine, Aunt. Thank you.'

Mollified, Agnes thought that she could grow to like this lanky, dark-haired boy with his good manners.

'Like I said, it's not big. I used to use it as a storeroom, and God knows it was a job to clear it out when I knew you were coming.'

'Thank you for going to all that trouble.'

Tugging at his sister's sleeve, James forced a response out of her. 'It's very nice.'

'Huh,' Agnes replied, crossing the tiny landing and flinging open the door of her own bedroom. Following her, James and Faith looked round the room, taking in the heavy Victorian furniture, the washstand, and what looked to be a camp bed in the corner, with another, smaller potty underneath.

'You'll sleep there, Faith.'

'But—'

Surreptitiously, James tugged on his sister's sleeve again. Faith moderated her tone and smiled at her aunt half-heartedly.

'Thank you.'

Pleased by her niece's appreciation, Agnes looked around the bedroom. Even to her selective eyes it seemed cramped, and the camp bed looked as inviting as a grave. But – as she had said to Beryl repeatedly – what could she do? She couldn't afford to buy a proper bed, even a second-hand one. So the camp bed had been purchased for a few bob off Tommyfields Market. It was in good condition, army surplus, the kind a soldier might sleep on. When Beryl had looked at it askance, Agnes had reminded her that money was short – Ivy having left very limited savings behind.

'We have to *keep* the children, Mother!' she had snapped. 'Clothe them and feed them. I think a bed comes second after that.'

Still staring at the camp bed, Agnes continued, 'I'm sure you'll find it very comfortable.' Her conscience suddenly pricked her. 'Look, you can have my eiderdown.'

'Thank you,' Faith replied.

She was desperately homesick and missing her mother. Missing their old life, their old home. Even the sadness after their father had died wasn't as bad as this empty feeling, standing unwelcome in the Gladstone Street house. As for her aunt . . . Faith stole a glance at Agnes as she fussed around the room. She couldn't be that old, but she seemed it.

Her dress was long and funereal, her face stern. There was only one soft feature about her: the amazing hair . . . Overwhelmed, Faith choked back a sob. How was she going to sleep in this room, with this relative stranger? The woman none of them had ever really got on with. Hadn't she heard her mother talk about Agnes? About how selfish her sister was? How set in her ways? How she didn't like children? And yet they had come to live with *her*. Not their grandparents.

Faith resented that bitterly. Both she and James loved their maternal grandparents, and after their mother died they had presumed they would go and live in Hardy Street. In fact the thought of being taken in by the Bentleys had made losing their parents less traumatic. Sid was indulgent and Beryl – even with her sharp tongue – good-hearted . . . Staring at her boots, Faith tried not to cry. James was talking to their aunt, but Faith wasn't listening. She was thinking how unfair it was that her father had had no family. That there had been no Farnsworth grandparents to turn to. Instead they had ended up with Agnes.

Sadly, she looked around at the bedroom and the scuffed boxes holding her possessions. Their parents hadn't been well off and had rented their home, so their belongings were few. Besides, it had been made quite clear that Agnes didn't want her home overrun with other people's possessions – even if those possessions were the only things that offered comfort. Desperately, Faith thought of the worn brown toy monkey she had crammed at the bottom of one of her boxes. She was too old to play with it, but she had clung to that toy when her father died and cried into its worn fur when her mother passed on. And every night she tucked the monkey in the crook of her left arm and talked to it, very quietly, telling it all her secrets. She glanced at her aunt. No more talking to the monkey now. Not out loud, at least. Not when Agnes would be sleeping in the same room.

'I'll leave you two to unpack your things,' Agnes said suddenly, making for the stairs and hurrying down to the kitchen.

Solemnly, Faith looked at her brother. Even Angel James looked despondent, ill at ease.

'Are you *sure* we can't run away?'

He gave her a slow look. 'It'll get better.'

'But your room is so small.'

'Lucky I've stopped growing,' he said, trying to smile. 'Will you be all right in here?'

He glanced over to the narrow camp bed and wanted – for an instant – to kick it over. All his life James had been protective of his little sister. When their father died he had willingly taken over the man's role in the household and looked after his mother and Faith. But no one – least of all him – had expected their mother to die so soon afterwards. As a result, his protective streak was now focused entirely on Faith. She was his responsibility, his tiny family. He might have grandparents and an aunt, but in James's eyes, he was his sister's guardian and would defend her against anything.

'It won't be so bad when we get used to it.'

'How d'you know that?' Faith replied, going over to her boxes and rummaging in the largest one. 'How d'you know it won't be horrible here?'

'We have to make the best of it.' He paused, watching as his sister pulled out the old worn monkey and hugged it to her tightly. 'You see what I mean? It's getting more like home already.'

'But you'll be away so much – now that you have to go and work in Manchester at the studio.'

'I'll be home at night. And besides, you'll be at school in the daytime,' James replied, trying to make light of the situation. 'You'll have your friends there.'

'I can't bring them back here, though, can I? Not to Agnes.'

'Well, not if she's cooked,' he agreed wickedly. 'Did you see those scones? You could choke a horse with one of them.' He squeezed her arm reassuringly. 'Don't worry, it'll be OK. I'm with you, remember? Nothing bad can happen whilst I'm around.'

He was wrong. The first week, Faith threw a ball over the wall and it smashed the window of Mrs Fletcher's next door – and she had an invalid husband to look after. Agnes, discomforted, found herself apologising to a woman she had never liked, whose 'invalid' husband was the biggest sponger in Oldham. A bad back, bad neck, bad legs and a bad temper kept Mr Fletcher off work. On the rare occasions he had got a job, his phantom illnesses soon rendered him useless, the excuses inexhaustible. 'The only thing he hasn't claimed is being pregnant,' some wag said archly. But for all of that, Faith still got into trouble for breaking the window.

The second week was even worse. Faith was sent home from school for being disruptive and Agnes had the unpleasant and uncomfortable task of having to talk to her teacher, giving an account of Faith's behaviour, and her home life. Which, the teacher implied, was obviously unhappy. For two days afterwards a mortified Agnes could hardly speak to her niece. But the third week went better. Faith was at school in the daytime, and when she came back to Gladstone Street she did her homework on the kitchen table in silence. When James returned from Manchester – full of stories about the photographic studio – Faith came back to life, chatting and joking. He told her about their grandparents, about the customers and their sittings, and about the strange lad who was Sidney's odd-job boy. Poor Lennie Hellier, James told his sister, he had a club foot and had apparently arrived out of nowhere some years before, without a history or a family. Sid and Beryl had tried repeatedly to get close to him, but Lennie had stayed wary and withdrawn. It was a shame, James told Faith, going on to tell her about the newly opened secretarial college across the road. Eager to listen to her brother's tales, Faith's animation lasted until bedtime. But as soon as James moved into his rabbit hutch, she became withdrawn, and the sight of her aunt's corsets as she undressed had her scurrying under the sheets on the camp bed.

The nights dragged for Faith. Across the hall she could hear her brother settling down, then silence as he fell asleep. In her room, she heard her aunt brush her astonishing hair, blow her nose, plump up her pillows and then sigh expansively before going to sleep. And then the snoring began. Sometimes it was light, intermittent. Other times it was full-bodied, almost a pig's snort, until Agnes rolled over and started breathing normally again. And then there was the nocturnal usage of the chamber pot . . . Somehow every action Agnes performed grated on Faith. She was everything her mother *hadn't* been. And to be stuck with her in the gloomy Gladstone Street house was insufferable.

Within a month, Faith's work at school had begun to deteriorate. A few times she had fallen asleep at her desk, but allowances had been made for her. Everyone wanted to give her time to adjust. But time wasn't what Faith needed. She needed what every ten-year-old needed: her own parents, her own home and her own bed. Grief, unexpressed and controlled, made her little body rigid. Her nature dampened into a squib of her previous fire, her feistiness curtailed by her homesickness.

Even James couldn't rouse her out of her despondency. And to her shame, Faith realised she was jealous of his happiness. His hopes for a career as a teacher had been set aside, but James had adjusted well. He might not brag about working with his grandparents, but Faith could see that he was contented. Why shouldn't he be? she asked herself. Why shouldn't her brother make a new life? But try as she might, she couldn't find her own new start.

Instead she clung desperately to the old toy monkey and felt out of place and desperate as only a lonely child can be.

CHAPTER SIX

With the arrival of the new king, Edward VII, England seemed to alter. The austerity of Victoria's reign had lapsed and the pleasure-loving king and his beautiful wife, Alexandra, gave a more approachable face to royalty. One of the strangest anomalies was how many weddings were planned for the summer of 1901 – something Sid was delighted about. He was also delighted at how his grandson had taken to his new role as apprentice. Although his parents had dreamed of their only son becoming a teacher, James readily understood that he had to earn his keep and couldn't squander nonexistent money on further education. And so he took his work at the City Photographic Studio seriously.

Of course James didn't start as a photographer. He was more of a general dogsbody, taking over the role from Lennie Hellier. Always soft-hearted, Sid had taken pity on Hellier from the moment he had arrived, unannounced, on the back steps. Over the following years, he had given Lennie odd jobs and a place to sleep. But Lennie had never slept on the couch he had been offered; instead he had found a space under the back stairs, huddled up like a dog. Unable to make him change his mind and use the sofa, Beryl had made sure that Lennie was fed well and had good bedding in return for his graft. But despite all their efforts, he remained distant, emotionally closed off, and their repeated attempts to draw him into the family had been summarily rebuffed.

So when James came to work for them, Sid made sure that Lennie wasn't overlooked and found him similar employment over at Laurence Goldbladt's. Laurence, unusually tall and stout, was a heavy smoker with bad circulation, and a reasonably successful fur and rag trade business. Trading cheaper skins to the top Manchester fashion houses, he made a good cut for himself and ploughed the profit into his own showroom on David Street. There were rumours that he dyed rabbit fur and sold it on as chinchilla, but no one could ever prove it, and Laurence was too clever to get caught out. Living and working on the first floor of the building – above the basement photographic studio – Laurence worked long hours sewing his furs and even longer hours with Mrs Miriam Newman, a widow who sometimes modelled his collection for him.

As soon as James had come to work at the studio, he had been introduced to Laurence and to a simpering Miriam. Then Sid had taken him up three storeys to the top floor, rapping on an arched wooden door and winking at his grandson.

'Come in!' came a high-pitched cry. Sid ushered James into an attic room which was crammed with sewing machines, material and women. In the centre of this mêlée, a tiny figure bobbed up, screwdriver in one hand and oil can in the other. He wore a brown leather patch over his left eye. 'Sid!' he said delightedly. 'And the grandson!'

'James, this is Mr Mort Ruben.'

'Oh, call me Mort,' the diminutive figure replied, putting down the oil can and wringing James's hand, his one eye fixed on the visitor. 'So you're the lad? You're the lad. Nice boy, nice boy. He'll do well here.'

Around them several women laughed. Mort wiggled his fingers good-naturedly at them and hurried Sid and his grandson into a back room. Throwing several bales of material off an old horsehair sofa, he gestured for them to sit down, then poured them a glass of sherry each.

'I don't drink—'

Mort silenced James immediately. 'Everyone drinks to good fortune. You make money, you hear? Make money and help your grandparents.' He turned back to Sid. 'Handsome boy, is he courting?'

As James flushed, Sid laughed. 'He's only fifteen, Mort! Only a boy.'

'Maybe, but a good-looking boy like that could find a nice girl. What with his grandfather's business to inherit.'

Sipping his sherry, Mort studied James, beaming at him. The little man's hands were small, almost as delicate as a child's, his feet minute in spats.

'I suppose your grandfather told you all about me?'

James hesitated. 'Well . . .'

'I once made a dress for Princess Alice.'

'You did?'

Mort nodded. 'I keep it quiet, of course, but it's true. My rivals . . . I have a lot of rivals around here. Manchester *seethes* with rivals.' He paused, his tone dark. 'Jealousy is what does it, jealous people who can't bear to see someone with real talent.' His anger evaporated in an instant. 'It was pale georgette.'

'Sorry, what was?' asked James, frowning.

'Princess Alice's dress,' Mort replied, downing his sherry. 'People tried to steal the pattern. I had to keep a dog on guard in here, day and night. And the animal wouldn't go in the lift. Oh no, I had to take it down three flights of stairs – and up again – when it went for a walk.' He smiled, putting his head on one side. 'You'll do well, I can feel it. He'll do well, Sidney, as sure as I'm sitting here, the boy will do well.'

As they walked back downstairs, Sid was trying not to laugh, a bemused James looking at his grandfather in bewilderment.

'Is Mr Ruben a bit . . . crazy?'

Sid laughed again. 'No! He's eccentric, that's all. Everyone knows Mort. A more kindly man you'll never meet. He might not be the most successful trader around here, but he's popular. And he has a good business sense. Doesn't do too much tailoring for men any more, but he's a dab hand with women's clothes. And crafty too, if he needs to be. If one of his seamstresses slips up, or her work isn't quite up to par, Mort doesn't get rid of the dress, he sells it on cheaply. You go down to Tommyfields Market on a Thursday night and you'll see the rejects – high fashion in the middle of Oldham! And they're snapped up by women who pretend they paid Manchester showroom prices.' He laughed again. 'Mind you, you see a lot around here – but you say nothing, you understand, James? My father knew the value of keeping his mouth shut, even when he was three sheets to the wind. It's a very close community. Most of the merchants are Jewish, but I've been welcomed into their homes for years – as you will be. I've even gone to break bread with them on the Sabbath, and that's Friday night for them.'

James ran this piece of information over in his mind carefully. 'Does Gran know about that?'

'Would I still be breathing if she did?'

Smiling, James studied his grandfather. 'What happened to Mr Ruben's eye?'

'It was an accident. Apparently he caught it on a thorn bush on one of his jaunts to the country. Said he was trying to watch a lark through his binoculars and tripped. The scratch went septic and he lost the sight in his eye.' Sid paused, opening the door to the basement studio. 'Mind you, he can still see more with one eye than most can with two.' He winked. 'Not a word about taking Sabbath with Mort, OK?'

James nodded conspiratorially, walking into the studio behind his grandfather. Beryl was in the front room, talking to a customer, and beckoned impatiently for her husband to come in. A moment later she joined James in the back room, clutching her grandson's arm and signalling for him to be quiet as they eavesdropped on the conversation.

'What kind of portrait were you looking for?' Sid asked, his figure visible through a narrow gap in the door. His figure, and the portly stomach of his customer.

'Well now,' the client began, 'I'm celebrating the opening of my new draper's shop in Moss Side and need some kind of marker. My wife says a picture's the thing, so a picture I've come for. Something classy.'

'I can do something very classy.'

'How much?'

'The prices vary . . .'

'How much for a good-sized print I can hang on the wall of the shop?'

'Two shillings and ninepence.'

'By hell, that's steep!'

Still watching through the crack in the door, Beryl hissed through her teeth to James, 'I'd have asked three shillings. You can tell from his coat he's got a bob or two.'

Squinting through the doorway, James could just make out the Abercrombie coat and bowler the customer was wearing – and see his grandfather smile winningly.

'We charge a little extra because the customer gets a little extra.' Sid moved to the door and pointed up the steps to the sign above. 'Did you read what it said?'

'City Photographic Studio . . .'

'Portraits Are Our Speciality,' Sid added. 'I can guarantee you won't be disappointed. And we can offer an exceptional background.'

The client frowned, caught off guard. 'What's that when it's at home?'

'The background,' Sid said, his tone charming and persuasive, 'makes the photograph live.'

On cue, Beryl left her hiding place and moved into the front room of the studio. In contrast to her husband, she was professional, offering the client a seat and then setting an album in front of him. Curious, the stout man leaned forward as Beryl turned the pages.

'My husband's reference to the background refers to the quality of our painted scenes. This,' she said, pointing to one study, 'represents Rome.'

'My shop's in Moss Side.'

Beryl never missed a beat as she turned the page. 'This represents a boating scene. But this . . .' she turned the next page over with a flourish, 'is for you, Mr . . . ?'

'Shawcross.'

'Mr Shawcross.'

Still watching through the crack in the door, James studied the scene, noticing how his grandparents worked together. How Sid provided the easy charm, and Beryl the professional touch. Interested, he continued to watch as Mr Shawcross leaned closer to the photographic album and peered at the plate.

'I've not got my glasses with me.'

'Sidney!' Beryl ordered. 'The magnifying glass, if you would.'

Obediently, her husband passed the lens to Mr Shawcross, his eye suddenly huge behind the glass as he bent towards the photograph and studied it. The image was of a handsome man leaning against a pillar, an illusion of a grand room behind. The fact that Mr Shawcross was twenty years older and fifty pounds heavier escaped him; he was seduced by the image of prosperity on offer. At once he could see his customers coming to the draper's shop and gazing, rapt, at his image. What a successful man, they would say. And he lives in a house with pillars.

'Oh, I like this.'

'Indeed you would. I knew you would,' Beryl went on. 'It is natural for you.'

'And it's two shillings and ninepence?'

'Three shillings.'

Mr Shawcross huffed in his seat. 'Three shillings!'

'Isn't it worth the difference for a background of

this quality? To prove to everyone that *you* are a man of quality?'

Beguiled, Mr Shawcross made his appointment there and then. When he left, Beryl turned to Sid and beckoned for James to join them.

'You see that?'

Her grandson nodded.

'That was salesmanship,' Beryl concluded. 'The photograph will cost us one shilling and ninepence to take and develop, so we'll make a nice profit there. And unless I miss my guess, Mr Shawcross is the type to want a silver frame to go with his portrait.'

Kissing his wife on the cheek, Sid winked at James. 'See why I love her, lad? With a wife like this, a man can only prosper.'

She brushed him off impatiently. 'Ah well, be that as it may, there's no time to stand around chatting. James, come with me now and I'll show you how to clean out the darkroom and explain about the chemicals. As for you, Sid, you could do worse than pop down to Sullivan's and get us a meat pie for dinner. Oh, and get some extra gravy this time. That Mary Sullivan short-changed me last week.'

Hanging back under the shadow of the staircase, Lennie Hellier watched Faith as she entered the front door of the David Street premises. She was hurrying, slightly out of breath, and he was entranced. All his life Lennie had avoided intimacy. He had never been shown kindness until he came to

David Street, and by that time he had grown used to living without it. In fact it embarrassed him, made him sweat with unease. He didn't know how to accept concern, or how to respond to a compassionate word. Instead he had closed down inside – until he had first caught sight of Faith.

Her brother's unexpected arrival at the photographic studio and Lennie's sudden move to Laurence Goldbladt's had unnerved him. He had been used to Sidney and Beryl, but then he had realised that along with James came Faith – and that was worth any unsettling changes. Fascinated, he had watched her. And when she had spoken to him he had been caught off balance. A few days later she had given him a sweet – which he put under his pillow. Every night from then onwards, he had dreamed of her. In his dreams he wasn't crippled or withdrawn; he talked to Faith freely and even offered her his arm when they walked down David Street. People who had never given him the time of day suddenly watched him and realised that he was someone – because otherwise how could he be out walking with Sidney Bentley's granddaughter?

When Lennie woke up he was flushed with embarrassment, but he couldn't stop thinking about Faith. He knew that she was only eleven, but there was something safe about her. Even though she was not yet grown, she had a powerful character and a promise of good looks that had not yet fully blossomed and taken her out of his reach. In fact, Lennie had thought at first that Faith was more like fourteen, she seemed so mature. The growth spurt James had anticipated had seemed to happen overnight, putting inches on Faith's height and beginning the slow curving of her previously boyish frame. James had noticed the difference in his sister – and so had Lennie. For the former, Faith's transformation was welcome. For the latter, it was exciting and depressing at the same time. Soon Lennie Hellier knew she would be grown up; but just as soon, she would be as distant as a winter comet.

Unless he could impress her in some way. Unless he could tell her how he felt . . . He had been given some decent clothes and had always kept himself tidy and clean, but he could see only too easily how Faith saw him – an outcast, someone to be pitied. Shrinking further into the shadow of the staircase, Lennie could hear Faith's feet running quickly down the basement stairs. And in that instant he imagined that one day she would be hurrying not to see her grandparents, but to see him.

As gregarious as her grandfather, Faith had always found it easy to make friends. But her closest ally was Ellie Walker, a pale-skinned redhead with freckles she hated and a widowed mother who was convinced that her daughter would end up on the stage. The fact that Ellie had no talent for acting, singing or dancing did not deter her besotted mother in any way. Everyone else was blind and deaf, unable to appreciate a talent Mrs Walker was convinced would take them from Hardcastle Street,

Oldham, to Paris. Even at eight, Ellie had known her mother was wrong. By the time she had reached ten, she was getting sick of being trailed around Manchester theatrical agencies and told that she didn't have the necessary requirements. But, undeterred, Mrs Walker went out to work extra hours at Riley's Milliner's to pay for singing and dancing lessons that – she was certain – would lead to their later financial abundance.

'I was almost crying with embarrassment,' Ellie was saying now, leaning against the school wall, her hair plaited, her eyes fixed on Faith. Both of them were bundled up against the January cold, snow on the distant moors and the sky pressing down with an imminent freeze. 'The agent told Mother I was the worst act he had ever seen.'

Uneasy, Faith didn't know what to say.

'He said that not only could I not carry a tune, he doubted that I could even drag one.'

Faith blew out her cheeks and rubbed her mittened hands together.

'Mother was reading about . . .' Ellie struggled with the pronunciation, 'the Moulin Rouge in Paris.'

'Paris! Isn't that in France?'

Ellie nodded. 'The capital. And the Moulin Rouge is a place where they have dancing girls. Mother thinks my future might lie there, and that in time I might be the top act on the bill.'

'Crikey.'

'She's mad, of course,' Ellie said dismissively. 'I mean, I have no talent at all. And whether I stay in

England or she takes me to France, I *still* won't have any talent.'

Watching her friend pick at her nails, Faith thought longingly of her own mother and of the time they had spent together. On shopping trips to Oldham, and, when they were flush, visits to Manchester. They would catch the tram and go round the city, then stop off at St Peter's Square and call at the City Photographic Studio for dinner. Then they would either go on to St Anne's Square to window-shop, or wait for Beryl and catch the tram home. At Christmas, her father would bring home the little bonus he had earned and they would buy presents together, Ivy, Stanley, James and her. The Farnsworth family, walking down Tibb Street where the pet shops were. Faith looking in at the puppies and kittens up for sale and begging her father to buy her one.

'When we've moved, love, then we'll buy a dog.'

'But Daddy . . .'

He had pinched her cheek affectionately. 'Not yet, but in time we will. I promise . . .'

I *promise* . . . Faith winced at the memory, almost feeling her father's hand in her own, her mother looking on. Ivy's memory had not faded one jot in her daughter's mind. Faith could remember her mother's voice, her face, even the scent of her skin. All the innumerable kindnesses that had punctuated her childhood seemed to taunt her now. Not that Agnes was cruel, merely cold. Not aggressive, just distant. Not involved, but remote.

There were no more whispered conversations with her mother in bed about the future and about Angel James, how he would be a teacher some day. As for Faith, her mother had promised her a future not of professional promise, but emotional bliss.

'One day you'll marry a handsome man and have pretty children.'

'What will he be called?'

'Derek, or Reginald.'

Faith had laughed. 'I don't like the name Reginald!'

'What about Cecil, then?' her mother had teased her. 'Or Nigel?'

'Ugh, not Nigel!'

Her mother had paused then and stroked her forehead. Stanley Farnsworth had only been dead for a few months and Ivy was still raw from his loss, but trying to cope. Trying so hard.

'It won't matter what your husband's called, Faith. Only that he loves you. Remember that. All that matters is that your man loves you.'

Faith's thoughts came back to earth with a jolt as another pupil bumped into her. Suddenly she realised where she was. That her mother was dead and she was living with Agnes Todd. That the day trips and whispered conversations were over, and the long, bleak winter of her childhood had set in and was going to last.

'Are you feeling all right?' Ellie asked suddenly.

Faith shook off her unease. She had to act

normally. As normally as any homesick eleven-year-old *could* act.

'Yes, I'm fine . . . Is your mother *really* going to take you to France?'

Ellie sighed, fiddling with her plaits. 'She says so. But nothing can come of it, thank God. We haven't the money. Mother says she'll save up, but I can't see how she can. Even making hats on the side won't bring in enough money to pay for the boat fare over there. And anyway, I don't want to go. I keep telling my mother that she should stop day-dreaming, but she says that I'm only a child and what do I know about it?'

Faith considered the information for a long moment before speaking again. 'It would be exciting if you did go. I mean, Paris would be such an adventure.'

'Not if it's a waste of time. Mother can be so silly,' Ellie retorted, changing the subject. 'How's your aunt?'

Faith glanced away. 'She snores.'

'She's a woman!'

'She still snores. And I have to sleep in the same bedroom as her and it keeps me awake. I cough, but she doesn't take any notice, and even if I get up and bang about on the floor, she doesn't wake up.'

Ellie laughed, but Faith didn't see the joke and sighed, wondering how much she should confide.

'We've been living there for months now, but it doesn't get any better.'

'It's not that long.'

'But it feels it! I know James is happy at the studio in Manchester, and I'm pleased for him, really I am. But I don't fit in, Ellie.'

Her friend shrugged. 'You will in time.'

'But in how *much* time? It's been ten months and it feels as strange living in Gladstone Street as it was the day we moved there. I help out in the house, and I try and keep quiet, but somehow I *still* get under Agnes's feet, or break one of her ornaments – and she thinks I do it deliberately.'

'Tell her you don't.'

'I do tell her! But she doesn't believe me,' Faith replied, her tone heated. 'I miss home so much. It's nothing like it was there. Even after Dad died and Mum was so sad . . . To be honest, I don't think Agnes likes us very much. Or rather she doesn't like me. I think she's getting quite fond of James. But then he's a boy.'

'What's that got to do with it?'

'James does all the odd jobs around the house, and he's always so nice to her.' Faith sighed again. 'It's my own fault. I should be kind to my aunt, try and make friends with her, but I don't like her . . . I can't believe they were sisters. She's not a bit like Mum was. I can't bear her. I can't bear living there.'

Ellie touched her shoulder sympathetically. 'You have to get used to it. There's nowhere else you can go. It'll get better.'

'But what if it doesn't?' Faith replied, her tone bleak. 'What if it doesn't?'

The ringing of the school bell broke into their

conversation. Reluctantly, Ellie ran to the side door, Faith following her and then pausing in the middle of the playground. Her eyes were unfocused, her homesickness an aching gulf in the pit of her gut.

CHAPTER SEVEN

Still wearing her cooking apron, Agnes pulled her coat round her shoulders and ran to the end of the street. Irritated, she peered into the soggy winter darkness, hardly punctuated by the gas lamps. Where was she? Agnes thought angrily. It was a quarter to six; Faith was always home from school around four thirty. Where on earth could she be? Looking round, Agnes began to walk to the corner of Mulberry Street. She could hear a tram in the distance, and just make out its sulphur-coloured headlamps as it passed nearby. But it didn't stop, and no one got off.

Perhaps her niece had gone to a friend's house? Agnes thought, trying to calm herself. Or maybe she had been in a fight? That wouldn't surprise her; the girl was always cheeking someone. Although, to be fair, Faith had been very polite with her. Very polite – but clumsy for a slim girl. Only last week she had broken the little china bowl, and the week before it had been one of the candlesticks Agnes had been given by a male admirer. She hadn't been fond of the man, but she'd liked the pair of candlesticks and now there was only one. And what good was that? Everyone knew candlesticks came in pairs. Of course Faith had apologised, said it had been an accident, but Agnes wasn't sure. There was a sullen resentment about the girl that was uncalled for. It wasn't Agnes's fault that Faith's parents had died. It wasn't *her* choosing that her niece had come to live in Gladstone Street. It was just the way life had turned out, and they had to make the best of it.

'Mrs Todd?'

Agnes jumped, startled as the figure materialised in front of her through the fog. 'Oh, Mr Braithwaite, you gave me such a shock.'

The words weren't exactly welcoming, but he wasn't about to be put off. The opportunity he had trusted to luck had never materialised. Indeed, it seemed that every time he left his house he bumped into either Faith or James, but never Agnes Todd. Even at Christmas, when he took around a card, James had answered the door. In fact, in the ten months since the children had arrived in Gladstone Street, he had seen so little of the object of his affection that he might have been living on another continent. But here, finally, was his chance.

Concerned, he took in Agnes's distracted air. 'Are you all right?'

'Faith's not home. She should have been back a while ago, but there's no sign of her.'

Agnes peered into the smog blindly, her voice rising. Dear God, what had she done to deserve all this responsibility? Faith wasn't even her own child! She had known something like this would happen. Hadn't she told her mother that she wasn't experienced enough? It was too much, all too much for her to bear. She might have been able to cope with James, but Faith was another matter.

'Mrs Todd . . .'

'I don't know what the girl thinks she's playing at,' Agnes went on blindly, panic rising. 'She might be lying dead somewhere!'

'Good Lord, I don't think so.'

'Or kidnapped!'

Eager to show his male stoicism, Perry kept calm. 'Maybe she was delayed at school?'

Agnes paused. 'At school?' Having put himself into the role of pacifier, Perry felt a happy glow as Agnes touched his arm gratefully. 'Oh, do you think it's possible?'

Perry could feel the warmth of her hand and felt mildly dizzy. 'I imagine she's been kept back for detention.'

'Detention?' Agnes repeated, then smiled and clutched at Perry's arm tightly.

'Of course,' he croaked. 'It's the only explanation.'

'Do you *really* think it's possible?'

Standing in front of him was the woman he admired, and had not seen for months. And she was holding on to his arm and thanking him for his help.

Reason deserted Perry Braithwaite. 'Is *what* possible?'

'That Faith might be delayed at school?'

He could feel the pressure on his arm increase and lost all power of thought.

'Why?'

'For detention,' Agnes repeated, confused. 'Isn't that what you said?'

Giddy as a kipper, Perry made his move.

'Dear Mrs Todd, you mustn't stand outside in this fog getting cold. Please allow me to walk you home, where you can wait in comfort for your niece's return.'

'But I have to look for her!'

'Stop worrying, my dear lady,' Perry replied. Then, boldly, he slid his arm through Agnes's, proudly propelling her back down Gladstone Street. 'You can stop worrying now and lean on me.'

Huddled in the back seat of the number 19 tram, Faith looked around her. On her left was a middle-aged woman in an elaborate hat, her young son beside her in a sailor suit, kicking his feet into the back of the seat in front. The mother, obviously deep in thought, was staring at a letter in her hand. Faith couldn't help but notice that she was dressed entirely in black, with a small mourning brooch pinned to her jacket. Glancing away, Faith looked out of the window. The fog was lifting a little, although the gas lamps were still glowing sulphurously into the crowding darkness. The smell of the lamps mixed with the industrial odour of coal fumes struck a chord in her. When her parents had been alive they had rented a house near a colliery – her father had been out of work at the time and the rental was cheap there. At night Faith would sometimes wake and hear the distant sounds of the last men leaving and the first day's workers coming on.

They hadn't stayed in that house for long. Her father had found another job and they had moved somewhere better. But Faith's memories of that first house – although it had been poor – were achingly sweet. Her mother hadn't had any ornaments. Those had been luxuries, and whilst times had been hard, luxuries had gone by the board. Instead she had a great copper kettle that she polished as another woman would have polished a diamond. The kettle was always boiling, or just set on to boil. So shiny you could see your face in it, and the distorted image of the kitchen beyond. It was in that kitchen that Faith had practised her writing, Ivy painstakingly redoing her letters until she was word perfect. And if her mother was busy, there was always Angel James, ready to help. Patient, taking the chalk out of his sister's hand and carefully writing a letter on her slate.

'Copy that, Faith.'

She had pulled a face. 'I can't. I can't do Ds.'

'Of course you can,' he had replied, nudging her. 'Look at the shape of the letter. It's a man in profile with a big beer belly.'

Sighing, Faith gazed out of the tram window again, just making out an advertisement for

Colman's Mustard, with a picture of the cricketer W. G. Grace on it. It was strange, Faith thought, but everything in the poster seemed to be yellow, like it had been painted entirely from mustard. On the wall next to it was another poster. This one depicted a woman on a bicycle, her long skirt elegantly lifted above the wheels, her bustle smaller and more compact than they had been previously. But the white leg-of-mutton sleeves were unchanged, and her large picture hat struck an incongruous note. Faith had heard about women riding bicycles, had seen it in the paper, but not dressed like this. And the local woman who had been seen in Alexandra Park riding a bicycle had fallen off by the stone lions and been reprimanded by the park-keeper. Bikes were for boys, Faith thought. Everyone knew that.

But then running away from home was for boys too . . . Automatically she felt for the bag next to her. The one she had put a change of clothes into, along with a half-used tablet of soap and her Sunday-best outfit. She was wondering why she had done that now. Why her best outfit? She would hardly be going to church. Runaways didn't go to church. And besides, hadn't Miss Violet, the religious studies teacher, told the class that bad children went to hell? Faith's mind went back to their last scripture lesson. Ellie had been told off for talking and Miss Violet had rapped her over the knuckles with her ruler. Which must have hurt, but Ellie wasn't going to show it. Instead she glowered at the teacher. In fact, they both did, taking in her long dark dress, which covered her from her neck to her ankles, with no ornament on it, only a cameo at the neck with the profile of a girl's face. Someone once said that the image was of Miss Violet when she was young, but Faith and Ellie both knew that she had never been *that* young. There was another rumour about Miss Violet – that she had been engaged to marry a soldier, but he had been killed at the fall of Khartoum, fighting with General Gordon, and she had never got over it . . . It had been a hard story for the two girls to believe. After all, Miss Violet was sour-faced, bespectacled and had to be over forty – how could she ever have been in love? Besides, she didn't preach love. Christianity according to their teacher seemed steeped in blood and fire. There was no turning of the other cheek; her reading of the Bible was selective. And simple. If you did wrong, you were damned.

Well, thought Faith, she was certainly damned, because you couldn't get worse than leaving home – and stealing a pie as you sneaked out. It was the pie that would do for her, Faith realised. Agnes might forgive her for running away, but the apple pie had been a triumph – and everyone knew Agnes couldn't cook. Because she had stolen it, no one would ever get to see the culinary masterpiece. And worse, she had already eaten half of it. So if she *had* been thinking about going back, she couldn't now that most of the filling was gone and there were teeth marks on the crust . . . Faith gazed down at her hands, small in their knitted gloves. Angel James –

for all his kindness – would be so angry with her. So she had no choice; she had to keep running. The only question was where?

All the places Faith remembered from happier times were off limits to her. The flat her parents had once taken would be rented by someone else. There was no point going there. As to her father's old office at the town hall, who would take her in? She meant nothing to those people. They would have forgotten the little girl who had called by once or twice and sneaked over to her father's desk, wriggling on to his knee. Anyway, they – like her father – would have gone by now. Been replaced. Just like his battered desk, ink-marked, and his pens in their holder next to the glass bottle of Stephens Ink . . . Breathing in, Faith could smell the aroma of that ink. She would watch him dip his pen into the enamel well, then hear the sound of the nib being tapped lightly against the side to make sure that there wasn't too much ink, which would blot on the page . . . Overcome, she looked out of the tram window again, biting the end of the glove on her index finger. Where was she going to go? Where?

And then it occurred to her. She would go over to Manchester, to the City Photographic Studio. Sid would be kind, and although Beryl would kick up a fuss, she wouldn't force her to go back to live with Agnes. Or would she? Misery made Faith uneasy. Misery, and the realisation that she actually had nowhere to go. She had no money either. Only enough to go ten stops on the tram, and that

70

wouldn't get her to Manchester, or even close. She had been stupid running off ill prepared, without giving the matter any real thought. And now what was she going to do?

'Oi.'

She looked up to see the conductor staring at her. 'Where are yer going?'

'I paid my fare.'

'Did I ask yer if yer'd paid yer fare?' he replied, holding on to the hand strap as the tram took a corner. 'I asked where yer were going.'

'I . . . I . . .'

Out of the corner of her eye, Faith could see the middle-aged woman glancing over at her. Her expression was sympathetic.

'She's with me.'

Faith took in a breath, and the conductor turned to the passenger. 'How can she be? She didn't get on with yer!'

'Are you doubting my word?' the composed woman replied evenly, the boy in the sailor suit beside her now silent.

'Well, it were—'

'I told you when we got on that you should sit with me, my dear,' the woman said gently, beckoning for Faith to join her. Defiantly, the woman then looked back to the conductor. 'As I said, she's with me.'

Waiting until the conductor had walked off, the woman dropped her voice and turned to Faith. Her expression was calm, but wistful. Like someone who had experienced a great deal and learned to cope – not from desire, but necessity.

'So, where *are* you going?'

Faith shrugged. 'I dunno.'

'I see,' the woman said softly. 'My name's Caroline. This is my son, Leonard.'

Smiling awkwardly, Faith nodded to the boy and then looked back to the woman.

'I'm Faith.'

'Pretty name. But a young girl shouldn't be out alone in the evening. Especially not when there's a fog,' Caroline went on. 'Unless of course she doesn't want to be at home . . . Is that the problem?'

Faith hesitated for a moment before answering. 'I've run away.'

'Cor!' Leonard replied, his mother silencing him immediately, then turning back to Faith.

'Why?'

'I'm unhappy.'

'I see . . . Why?'

Faith paused again. 'My parents died. We – my brother and me – had to go and live with my aunt. I hate it there. I hate her!'

As though she was giving the matter great thought, Caroline was silent for a long moment, then sighed.

'Is your aunt married?'

'She's a widow.'

'Does she have her own children?'

'No.'

'So she's taken in you and your brother on her own?'

Faith could see the way the conversation was going and said heatedly, 'She didn't want to take us in!'

'But she did . . . Is she cruel to you?'

'Oh, no!'

'Does she beat you?'

'No!'

'Make you work too hard?'

'No . . .'

'Perhaps she doesn't feed you enough? Or give you anything to drink?'

Faith thought of the half-eaten pie in her bag and shook her head.

'No, she can't cook, but she feeds us, looks after us. She just isn't . . .'

'Your mother.'

Faith's eyes filled. 'Yes, that's right. She isn't my mother.'

Taking her hand, Caroline studied Faith's upturned face. She had never seen the girl before and probably never would again, but she knew how important her next words were.

'Faith, we can't blame other people because they aren't what we want them to be. Your aunt can't be your mother, because she *isn't* your mother. Stop blaming her for not being enough.' She squeezed Faith's hand sympathetically. 'Go home. There's no shame in turning back. You'll find that out in life. Just as you'll find out that there are some things you can't alter by running away from them.'

'But . . .'

73

'Go home and make the best of it.'

Faith hung her head, but she already knew what she had to do. 'I don't want to go back!'

'I know you don't. But you have to. You can't change things now – you can only do that when you're grown up.'

'When I'm grown up I'll leave for good!'

'Yes, you probably will. And when you're grown up, Faith, you won't want to look back and feel badly because of the way you treated your aunt.' Caroline smiled kindly, but her eyes were serious. 'You don't think so now, but before long you'll have your own life, and you'll live it your own way. *Then* is the time to fight for what you want. And *then* is the time you don't let anyone change your mind.'

CHAPTER EIGHT

As she walked through the back door, Faith's collar was grabbed in a vice-like grip.

'Where the hell have you been? We've all been out looking for you for the last hour and a half. Mr Braithwaite too.' Beryl turned Faith round, still holding on to her collar as her granddaughter tried to wriggle free. 'Your aunt thought you'd been kidnapped. Your grandfather wanted to call the police. Your brother thought you might have been killed. As for me – you're lucky I don't kill you now.'

And with that, Beryl let go of Faith's collar. Sheepishly, she glanced around the kitchen: Angel James was by the door, Sid was sitting on the sofa next to a red-eyed Agnes, and a tall, angular man was propping up the mantelpiece, staring at her as though she had run a sword through his guts.

'Your aunt was in a terrible state because of you,' Perry said, his tone admonishing.

Faith rubbed the back of her neck where her grandmother had grabbed her collar. Imploringly she glanced over to James, but he wasn't going to let her off so easily.

'Where were you going?'

'Nowhere.'

'You must have been going somewhere!' Beryl hollered.

Sid's tone was more reasonable. 'Are you unhappy here, love?'

'Unhappy! Unhappy!' Agnes shrieked suddenly. 'No one asked me if *I* was unhappy. Wicked girl, running off like that. I told you – I've told all of you – she'll come to a bad end.'

'Now, now,' Perry Braithwaite said, trying to soothe her. 'She's just a child.' It should have sounded patient, but somehow he managed to put a quiet distaste into the words.

'Just a child! There's more guile in that one than there is in a basketful of monkeys!' Agnes retorted hotly, tears beginning again. 'She's no good! She's a thief who stole my apple pie!'

Perry glanced at Faith, seeing her vices mounting like bricks in a hellish wall as Agnes went on.

'She's a thoughtless, cruel child.'

Nonplussed, Faith said the first thing that came into her head. 'Well, I don't know what all the fuss is about. I came back.'

'And I'm supposed to be grateful!' Agnes hissed. 'I suppose I should be glad you're not lying dead in a gutter somewhere, with your throat cut.'

Sid coughed; Beryl gave him a look that said, *Crikey, she's overcooking this.*

'To think I've given you a roof over your ungrateful head, and this is how you repay me! There's many a child who would be glad of my home—'

'There's many a child who's welcome to it.'

Immediately a hand descended again on Faith's collar as Beryl propelled her granddaughter ignominiously towards the stairs.

'Go to bed and think on what trouble you've caused! Have the whole neighbourhood running around after you, will you? Well, you can stop those antics now. You'll have to mend your ways.' She turned away, then shouted up the stairs, 'And you can go without your supper!'

'I've already eaten,' Faith said defiantly, running upstairs out of the reach of her grandmother's backhand.

In the end, Faith apologised to Agnes, and then she apologised to Mr Braithwaite, whilst she was secretly damning him to hell. After that, she said sorry to her grandmother and was about to repeat the performance with Sid when he waved her words aside.

'Oh, go away with you, love! I ran away from home myself – and if I was living with your aunt, no doubt I'd do the same again.' He dropped his voice, making sure that Beryl couldn't hear. 'My father was an independent spirit. You get it from my side of the family. Tommy Bentley was a hell-raiser.'

Intrigued, Faith sat down on one of the velvet

button-backed chairs in the front room of the City Photographic Studio. It was dinner time, and the sign on the door read CLOSED, as a gaggle of hurrying feet rushed past on the street above. Shopkeepers, clerks, seamstresses, all going out for their break, the light winter rain not stopping them. Glancing up, Faith could see the feet passing. Men's shoes, an occasional pair of spats, and black ankle boots for the women. The shoes reminded Faith of something Beryl had been talking about. Apparently, at the end of David Street, they had opened a typing school where young women could learn office skills – and how to be independent. Faith had read about it in the local paper and listened in on Beryl's conversation with Miss Emma Abbot, who had set up the school.

'Not everyone wants to work in service, Beryl. I tell you, those days of domestic drudgery are coming to an end. Before long, women will go out to work in respectable office jobs.'

'Fancy,' Beryl had replied, unimpressed. She had been running a business for years.

'And we teach some of the girls how to work a telephone exchange. There's plenty of work there, you know. International calls, too. I was talking to someone in Paris the other day and it sounded as though it was next door.'

Paris, Faith thought longingly. Ellie's mother was still working extra hours at the milliner's to make enough to take her untalented child over to the Moulin Rouge . . .

'He went all over the world.'

Faith blinked, her thoughts refocusing on her grandfather. 'What?'

'My father went all round the world. Australia, Italy, France . . .'

'What's it like?'

Sid smiled. He was glad to talk about his father, always liked to have an excuse to reminisce about the appalling Tommy Bentley.

'My father said that France was wonderful. Cafés, people sitting at tables on the street, chatting. And all kinds of marvellous buildings. The Arc de Triomphe, the Louvre . . .' He paused, having run out of place names. 'And the women are beautiful, so my father said. Not that they're all respectable.' He lowered his voice. 'Very saucy, French ladies.'

'Ellie's mother wants to take her to Paris to see if she can work at the Moulin Rouge.'

Sid's face coloured as though he had just been slapped. He had heard plenty about the Moulin Rouge, and none of it tallied with Faith's schoolfriend's aspirations.

'Oh, that can't be right, love. It's not a respectable place.'

'Her mother wants her to top the bill there.'

'Has . . . has her mother ever been there?' Sid asked, trying to sound nonchalant.

'No . . . but she says that Ellie would be famous if she went over there.'

Infamous, more like, Sid thought, turning to see the back door open and a slight figure walk in. The lad was about the same age as James, but there the similarity ended. This boy was achingly thin, his body bearing the evidence of childhood neglect, his club foot twisted in a clumsy boot. Seeing Faith, Lennie Hellier flushed and hovered in the doorway, because although she had always been kind to him, he was awkward around her.

And for some reason Lennie made Faith feel uneasy too, and no amount of kindness on Faith's part could absolve the faint guilty repugnance she felt towards him.

'Come in, come in, Lennie!' Sid said kindly, beckoning to the lad as he stood uncertainly by the door. 'You look cold. Hasn't Mr Goldbladt got the stove working up there?'

Nodding, Lennie's pale eyes fixed on Faith and then glanced away, embarrassed. Although Sid had given him clothes and fed him, and Laurence now gave him work, Lennie always looked down-at-heel. His hands and feet, too big for the bony body, gave him a clumsy look, and the dusting of hairs on his chin made him seem not like a lad on the edge of manhood, but like a creature hovering between childhood and some maturity out of his reach. And always around him hung the odour of fur skins and Laurence Goldbladt's tobacco.

'Mr Goldbladt wondered if yer'd like to come up and have tea with 'im,' Lennie said uncertainly. 'Mr Goldbladt said he'd like yer to come up – with yer granddaughter.'

'That sounds like a fine idea,' Sid replied. 'I heard

you've been a great help to Mr Goldbladt, Lennie. He talks very well of you. Said he'd seen you reading.'

Lennie flushed. 'I can read a little. Not much. I never had much learning.'

Tactfully Sid continued, 'Reading's a very useful ability to have, Lennie. If you want to advance. I could lend you some books.' He turned to Faith. 'Couldn't we lend Lennie some books of yours?'

She nodded, but avoided Lennie's eyes. 'Of course. I'll bring some when I next come over.'

'I'd take care of anything yer lent me,' Lennie said at last, his head bowed, his eyes fixed on the showroom floor in an agony of confusion.

Pleased by the boy's uncharacteristic forth-comingness, Sid encouraged him. 'Mr Goldbladt said that in time he might train you in the business. That would be good, hey? Not just beating and stretching the fur skins any more. Hard work that,' Sid went on, thinking of the gruelling task of the skin preparation.

Laurence hired in workers – mostly Poles and Russians – to tackle the fur bales when the main deliveries came in via the Manchester Ship Canal. All his staff were men who had worked the fur trade in their own countries, skilled, experienced hands. But they were transient and few stayed more than months, sending in cousins and other relatives to take over their duties. Never a man to pry into unnecessary details when the work was being done, Laurence paid the wages to whoever did the labour.

And if the faces changed frequently, he accepted it. But over the previous few months he had found himself relieved to have one face that never changed: Lennie Hellier's. He might be a lame, nervous boy, but he was part of the Goldbladt business, and as such, he was becoming slowly more important to Laurence. His very shyness was Lennie's best asset. Everyone in David Street knew that he hardly ever left the premises voluntarily. If he had to, he would run errands and get shopping in, but left to his own devices, Lennie kept himself to himself. Gratitude kept him at David Street. And gratitude kept him loyal.

'I reckon,' Sid went on magnanimously, 'that you've earned a break, Lennie. You work hard for Mr Goldbladt. And you can tell him that we would love to come up,' he said cheerfully, turning as Beryl walked in. 'Laurence's asked us to tea.'

'I've no time for tea!' she replied, taking off her coat and turning the sign on the door to OPEN. 'We've work to do.'

'We could take another half an hour on our dinner time,' Sid remonstrated. 'Oh come on, Beryl, how often does our granddaughter come to the studio?'

Shrugging, she studied them both. 'Well, all right, you two go, but I'll stay here. James will be back soon and he can help me.'

Before she could change her mind, Sid winked at Faith and they followed Lennie up the back stairs to Laurence's place. Hurriedly Lennie opened the side door and showed them into a room hung with skins of all sizes. The smell turned Faith's stomach as she was hurried through the hanging furs and into the showroom beyond. Just before she moved through the adjoining doorway, she noticed a huddle of blankets in a corner and was about to say something when a loud, confident voice welcomed her.

'My God, Faith, you're growing up! Isn't she growing up, Sidney? You're going to be a pretty woman.'

Unmoved, Faith smiled politely. She might be developing, but she wasn't in a hurry to enter a female world that seemed restricted by appearance and difficult-to-wear clothes. Like corsets . . .

Moving over to his visitors, Laurence Goldbladt glowed like the inside of a jewellery box. His high collar was starched white, his cuffs also, his suit cut in the latest style, the gold-rimmed buttons flashing like fireflies. As to his waistcoat, it was brocade, plush as a Persian carpet. Topping off the whole ensemble, Laurence wore a smoking cap in velvet, with a gold tassel that hung, perfectly in line, against his left eyebrow. Aware of the impressive figure he cut, he ushered his guests over to a small circle of gilded chairs, surrounding a small walnut table like Red Indians around an ambushed stagecoach.

Curious, Faith looked for Lennie, but he had disappeared and she took a seat between the two men.

'Have some tea,' Laurence said, passing her a dainty china cup filled with amber liquid. 'Best tea in Manchester. I have my contacts.'

'You *always* have your contacts,' Sid replied, taking the cup offered to him.

'I wanted to have a chat with you about some work,' Laurence continued, his tone booming. 'Mrs Miriam Newman would like to have her portrait taken. By you.'

'Oh,' said Sid, thinking of the simpering Mrs Newman, Laurence's long-term mistress – although no one was supposed to know. 'I could do a fine photograph of the lady.'

Laurence nodded, rubbing his left leg. 'I want something special, Sidney. Something classy. I'd want a frame, too.'

Now Sid was really interested. Apart from a couple of run-of-the-mill portraits and a wedding, money had been a bit tight that month. A portrait, and a silver frame, would help the takings no end.

'Silver, of course?'

'Well,' Laurence replied, slightly hesitant. 'Silver's dear.'

'You want the best, though. A man with your taste. It would be wrong for you to go for anything less.' Sid dropped his voice, Laurence leaning across Faith as he bent to listen. 'I could do a special price for you.'

'It would need to be special. I know I look like I've got a fortune, but it's all show, Sidney, I think you know that. Times aren't what they were. Even in winter, when trade's brisk, I'm not making what I used to. The skins are getting dearer – more than ten per cent up on last season. Of course, I can trust you to keep your counsel.' He paused, glancing briefly at Faith, who had leaned back in her seat between the two of them. 'You're a good girl, aren't you?'

She nodded.

'You'll not repeat a word of what you hear, will you?'

'Oh no.'

'Good, good,' Laurence replied, looking back at Sid. 'Mrs Miriam Newman and I are betrothed.'

Sid was genuinely pleased. 'My word, that's good news.'

'She's a fine woman, a very fine woman,' Laurence went on, dropping his blasting voice to little more than a murmur. 'And she's inherited a handy sum from her late father. I told you he'd passed, didn't I?'

'No, I'm sorry about that.'

'Well, he was a pig, if the truth be known,' Laurence went on, Faith listening avidly as the two men talked across her. 'A miser. Never wasted a penny on anyone. Kept it all for himself. But then again, it's an ill wind that doesn't blow someone some good, and now Miriam has inherited a nice sum. Of course, the money's not important to me. I've been fond of Miriam for years—'

Sidney cut his friend off immediately, worried that Laurence might make some remark about their relationship that he didn't want his granddaughter to hear. Smiling, Sid looked at Faith.

'Can you run me an errand, my dear?'

'Of course I can, Grandad. What d'you want?'

'Go down to the square, to Wilson's, and get me some Turkish tobacco, will you? I think Laurence and I might like a bit of smoke.'

Nodding, Faith took the money offered to her and made her way from the showroom to the back workroom. Ducking under some of the hanging furs, she winced at the smell again and then paused to look at the bundle of blankets in the corner. She didn't remember Laurence having a dog, and then she thought about what she had once heard her grandfather say – that Lennie Hellier had slept under their stairs at the studio and was now sleeping next to the Goldbladt showroom. So this was Lennie's bed? she thought, her own camp bed now seeming luxurious by comparison. She had asked Sid why Lennie slept under the stairs in the studio and had been told that it was because there he could keep his back to the wall and be near the door. What he was afraid of, no one ever asked. And because Lennie wasn't forthcoming, he was taken for granted. Not mistreated, just in the background of David Street life. A fixture, but remote. As Beryl said, he didn't seem to want or need intimacy.

Holding her nose, Faith passed by the next stack of fur skins, the money in her right hand, only pausing for breath when she reached the back stairs and looked out into the city below. The winter afternoon was fading fast, the day dimming, a man lighting the lamps on David Street, his figure illuminated gradually as he moved to the corner. But on the back stairs it was gloomy, and Faith held on to the handrail as she began her descent. Beside her the wrought-iron lift moved suddenly, creaking past and stopping at Mort Ruben's floor, someone getting out and ringing the brass bell of Mort's showroom. Watching her step in the gloom, Faith continued downwards, then stopped as a shadow moved towards her.

'God!'

'I didn't mean to frighten you,' Lennie said, his voice wavering. 'I were just going up the steps.'

She breathed in to steady herself. 'You didn't frighten me, Lennie. I'm just going out to Wilson's for my grandad.' Pausing, she studied the slight, nervy figure and felt sorry for the lad. 'D'you want to come?'

Without replying, he stared at her. Lennie had never been invited anywhere with anyone before. Least of all the girl he had been fantasising about for months. Embarrassed, he shuffled his feet.

'You don't have to,' Faith said, misreading his hesitation and moving to pass him.

To her surprise, he put out his arm to block her way. Laughing, Faith tried to push past, but then realised he wasn't joking and felt suddenly irritated.

'Lennie! Let me pass!'

'I just wanted . . .'

He trailed off but kept his arm up, blocking her exit. All he knew for certain was that he wanted to keep her there. Only to talk to her, to be close to her, nothing more. He had never been so close to a female, and he could smell the soap on Faith's skin and hear her breathing. In that moment he knew he should step back and let her go, but he was driven on by some kind of insanity, some desperate desire to touch her.

Reaching out, he rested his hand on her shoulder.

'Get off!' Faith snapped, brushing his hand away angrily. 'Honestly, Lennie, don't be such an ass.'

She was used to having an older brother, used to being teased by James, her grandfather and the likes of Laurence and Mort. Not for one moment did she realise she was under threat. To her, Lennie was just a lad who was kidding around.

'Come on, move over, I have to get Grandad's tobacco.'

Without warning, Lennie lunged towards her, putting his hand on her breast. Gasping, Faith fell backwards, off balance. Her right elbow hit the step with a crack, the money flying out of her hand and rolling down the stairwell into the hallway below. Frightened, she tried to shove Lennie off, but he was pushing her back on to the hard stairs, groping under her skirt, his face pressed against hers, his skin clammy.

It was only the sound of a door opening on the floor above that made him stop. Then, as though suddenly coming to his senses, he jumped back and pressed himself against the wall of the stairwell as Faith struggled to her feet. Her feet clattered on the steps as she took them two at a time, the sound of the lift's descent following her downwards into the darkness below.

*

'Whatever's keeping Faith?' Sid asked suddenly, looking round. He couldn't stay talking to Laurence for much longer without Beryl calling upstairs; he and his granddaughter should have been back a while ago.

'Of course,' Laurence went on, immune to his friend's preoccupation, 'I grieved with Miriam when her husband died and now we've been friends for a long while.'

'Very close friends,' Sid added, 'from what I hear.'

'You don't want to go believing gossip,' Laurence replied, secretly delighted to have the reputation of a Lothario. 'Miriam and I are going to be a proper couple. Now's the time for us to put the past behind us and get married. No point being lonely, is there?'

No point being short of money when it fell in your lap either, Sid thought wryly, toasting Laurence with his tea cup.

'So now you see why I want a special photograph of my Miriam,' Laurence said, beaming. 'A memento.'

In a big, expensive silver frame, Sid decided, thinking of Miriam's lucky inheritance. After all, why not? Laurence wouldn't be paying for it . . . Hearing the door of the showroom open behind them, Sid turned round smiling.

'Hello there, stranger, where have you been for so long?'

Faith wanted to tell him, to rush over to her grandfather and sob into his shoulder, but two things stopped her. Laurence Goldbladt for one. How could she tell Sid what had happened with an audience listening in? And besides, if she *did* tell, Lennie would be punished, maybe thrown out on to the streets. After all, his only home was David Street. Another thought followed on. How would everyone judge her if they knew? What would Laurence Goldbladt think of her? And her grand-parents? Could she really stand the embarrassment?

So she lied.

'I was talking to a friend on the street,' she explained after a pause, handing over the tobacco and taking a seat a little way off from the men.

Watching her grandfather, Faith tried to calm herself by observing the usual prolonged ritual of smoking. But whereas before it had been comfort-ing, now it was changed, spoiled somehow. Mute, she watched the rolling-up of the tobacco in the papers, the tapping of the ends, before her grandfather passed the first smoke to Laurence and then made himself another. In the quiet of the showroom, she hardly understood what Laurence was saying; his words just a dull rumble of noise, the smoke from the Turkish tobacco catching in her throat when they lit up. Once she had loved the smell, but Faith knew that from now onwards it would be forever connected with what had happened on the back stairs.

And what had happened? she asked herself. Inexperienced, she didn't fully understand that it had been a sexual attack, only that something unpleasant and sordid had taken place. Something that might have been her own fault . . . Which was another reason why she couldn't tell anyone. Had she encouraged Lennie? Done something to make him behave like that? He was a bit simple, people had said that for years, but harmless, so his actions had been out of character. What had she done that had caused him to behave that way?

Uncomfortable, Faith turned away and stared at the stove, the heat from it warming her face. Lennie's skin had felt clammy, his smell was unfamiliar, and the look in his eyes had been something she didn't understand. And didn't want to. Faith decided there and then that boys were dangerous. They weren't like her brother, not at all like Angel James. They were frightening, and from now onwards she would avoid them. Make sure she wasn't kind to a boy again. No more giving anyone sweets, or asking them to walk with her to the shops. No, she would ignore them, keep her distance. Keep safe. And keep quiet. Above all, keep quiet.

It was the end of childhood.

CHAPTER NINE

Summer heat was making Manchester intolerable. Even the basement in David Street was warming up, the front door of the City Photograph Studio left open, the sounds of carriages and horses coming down from the street outside. From higher up, other sounds floated down from Laurence Goldbladt's showroom on the hot air. He had bought a gramophone and was playing – over and over again – Enrico Caruso, the Italian tenor's top notes clattering amongst the brickwork and the iron fire escapes of the city street. And from the very top of the building, the noise of sewing machines chattered through the open windows of the attic floor. Every few hours Mort Ruben scuttled down the back steps to sit in the shade of the yard. There, beside the outdoor pipes, he fanned himself with a copy of the *Manchester Evening News* and mopped the sweat from under his eye patch. It was, everyone agreed, as hot as hell.

Which was why, on 19 July, Beryl, Sid, James, Faith and Agnes went to Blackpool for the day.

They had, like everyone else in Manchester, seen the posters and read about how popular day trips were becoming. So much so that Beryl put their names down for one of the jaunts by charabanc – ignoring Agnes's protestations that Blackpool was vulgar and they should go to Southport.

'Southport costs more,' Beryl riposted with typical candour.

'But it's refined,' Agnes replied, adding for good measure, 'Mr Braithwaite tells me that Lord Street is very elegant.'

'We want to have a paddle, not parade about the shops!' Beryl admonished her daughter. 'I've had enough of shops. I want to relax, see some sea for a change.'

Of course she won the day and they all set off in the rickety charabanc for Blackpool. The journey was lengthy and the seats uncomfortable, but they had started very early, along with a couple of dozen other people, and it was only noon when they reached the resort. Beryl was at home instantly, breathing in the salty air and taking off her hat. Sid pointed to the pier and suggested a walk. Arm in arm, they moved along, James paying for deckchairs and setting four out in a row.

'I couldn't afford another sixpence,' he told Faith. 'We'll have to take turns.'

Faith wasn't bothered. She never was when she was with her brother. With James, she was safe and happy. Always safe and happy . . . Taking off her shoes and stockings, she raised her skirt to mid-calf and paddled in the cool water, waving to her grandparents in the distance. Behind Faith and James, a row of bathing huts sported their summer colours, a man in a straw hat holding his girlfriend's hand as she came down the steps to the beach. Fascinated, Faith watched her, taking in the daring swimming outfit: the silk pantaloons under the short dress with its elbow-length sleeves, the large cap covering the woman's hair. The Blackpool Venus paused confidently, knowing that everyone on the beach was watching her.

'Crikey.' Faith stared. 'She looks wonderful. Like something in one of Laurence Goldbladt's catalogues.'

Nodding, James stood next to his sister, both of them up to their calves in the sea. Together they watched the woman's poised saunter towards the water, her companion glowing with pride as she stepped into the surf.

'Crikey,' agreed James.

Faith gazed at the woman with rapt attention. She had never been interested in fashion. Even visiting Laurence Goldbladt and Mort Ruben, she had remained immune to the siren call of clothes. And after her unpleasant run-in with Lennie, she had become even more reluctant to draw attention to her appearance. Flattery had no effect on her either. She was growing up, so what? But suddenly, as she watched the fashionable woman in the bathing suit, Faith felt a stab of envy. It was painful, and unexpected.

'Is she beautiful?'

James looked at his sister and nodded. 'Yes, she's beautiful.'

'Why?'

He shrugged. Only seventeen himself, he wasn't confident around females, but he was learning fast. After all, he had Sid's example to follow. Struggling, he tried to put his thoughts into words.

'Because she looks so . . . right.'

'Right?' Faith echoed. 'Is that it?'

'No, it's because . . . because . . . she looks glamorous.'

And that was it.

The word 'glamorous' galvanised Faith. It was a mirage of something beyond city streets and Oldham terraces. Something that spelled power and a potent demand for attention. The woman in the bathing suit had that most ephemeral of talents – glamour. And even though Faith was only eleven, she knew then the advantage it gave her. But at what cost? Confused by her own emerging sexuality, and hampered by the sordid episode with Lennie Hellier, Faith stared at the woman, fascinated and critical in the same instant. The bather was so confident, so certain of her own allure. So welcoming of the attention she was provoking. For a moment, in Faith's eyes, she seemed almost brave.

Faith was still watching the bather when James nudged her arm and pointed towards another hut. Huddled behind the striped door curtain stood Agnes; her head, with a mob cap perched precariously upon it, was the only part of her body on show.

'What *is* she doing?' Faith asked, staring.

Putting his head on one side, James watched as the apparition released the curtain and began to walk very slowly down the beach hut steps. But where the other woman had triumphed, Agnes looked ridiculous. And she knew it. Her bathing suit was too large, the pantaloons dangling around her calves, the sleeves too long, and the bathing hat slipped over to one side as she reached the bottom of the steps. Where the first woman had been a goddess, a sexual siren, Agnes looked gauche, sexless. Ignominiously she tried to rearrange herself. James flushed with pity as his aunt staggered forwards, tripping over the laces of one of her bathing shoes. Aghast, Faith watched her. Then she noticed that the glamorous bather had turned and was sniggering at the plain, middle-aged pretender. Before long, she was laughing outright, her companion joining in, and several lads pointing at the absurd spectacle. Mortified, Agnes stopped walking, her face crimson. She seemed confused, unable to move forward, or return to the safety of the beach hut. She looked lost, almost afraid.

And then, without thinking, Faith ran over to her aunt. Kissing her cheek, she took Agnes's arm, walking her proudly down to the water as though she was accompanying an empress.

That day I realised two things — that glamour can make a person beautiful. Even cruel. As the years passed, I never forgot that woman in her expensive, fashionable outfit. But although I hated her for her spite, she managed to effect a change that I would never have believed possible. An understanding between myself and my aunt.

That hot day I learned another painful lesson about growing up. And I saw Agnes Todd for what she was — not a tyrant, but an uncertain human being who could feel as humiliated and lost as a child. And when I realised that, I understood her, because we weren't really that different. In many ways she was as unsure as the children she had taken in. So when we got back from Blackpool I didn't run away again. I didn't even want to. Because Agnes was doing her best — and besides, it would have been mean.

Such little occurrences change lives.

I look back and remember those days, and I realise that although we had lost a great deal, James and I were still protected. We had a family, a home. It might not have been the one we would have chosen, but it wasn't bad. So I settled down, enjoyed my friends, my school (although I was never academically bright), my visits to my grandparents, and I watched James turn from a boy into an impressive young man in the space of four years.

Lennie Hellier stayed on at David Street, because I said nothing. When I was old enough to understand what he had done, it was too late. Besides, he never came close to me again and scurried away if he saw me coming. But the damage had been done. Emotionally I was remote, uninterested in boys. I avoided any male attention other than that of my brother.

We saw the seasons come and go on Gladstone Street. We watched the city change with the passing of the years, and the City Photographic Studio got a new sign. In those four short years Laurence Goldbladt married Miriam and got fatter, his legs taking more strain. Mort Ruben had a couple of successful seasons and asked me to model for him when one of his own girls let him down. He told me that I was pretty and looked stylish. I had certainly grown tall and the clothes looked good on me – even I could see that. But I never developed the glamour I had seen that day. The bathing woman remained an enigma to me, envied and feared at the same time. She was a barometer, a measure, the gold standard of what the ideal woman should be. And yet her appeal – potent as it was – was not accessible. And though I thought of her often, she kept her secret out of my reach.

I would see that power again many years later. And it would cost me dear.

PART TWO

CHAPTER TEN

October 1906

Putting cold cream on her cheeks, Agnes yelped as she saw a face at the kitchen window: Perry Braithwaite doffing his hat to her on his way home from work at the town hall. Hurriedly wiping off the cream, Agnes let him in, taking his coat and putting it over the back of a chair.

'You're early today, Perry,' she said, patting her hair, newly washed and perfectly coiffed.

Of course she wouldn't let anyone know why she had changed her style and drawn her hair down further over her brow, but the truth was that Agnes was going grey. Her amazing hair, her one perfect feature, was showing its age. Although a small matter to most, the grey invasion had concentrated Agnes's mind perfectly. Perry Braithwaite and she had been courting for years, Perry suggesting that they wait until James and Faith had grown up before they . . . before they . . . Well, he hadn't proposed, but Agnes had known what he meant. When she finally turfed out her niece and nephew, she would be free to marry. Perry didn't want children around, and frankly, Agnes herself had never wanted children around. She did her duty, relieved to see James out at work in Manchester and Faith at school most of the time, but now there had been a real advance, and the finishing line was in sight. Beryl had just confided something to her and Agnes was luminous with hope.

Smiling, she beamed at Perry. 'I just washed my hair.'

'And beautiful it looks,' he said admiringly, stretching out to touch it as Agnes ducked out of his way, laughing like a geisha. No letting him into any unpleasant secrets until she had him nailed.

Luckily Perry was a gentleman and didn't take it as a rebuff. Besides, Agnes's vanity amused him.

'You have the most wonderful hair in Oldham.'

Her face set. 'Oldham?'

'The whole north-west,' Perry replied, correcting his mistake and seeing Agnes relax in response.

'Oh, you do flatter me,' she crooned, going to the meat safe and bringing out a plate.

It was a matter of some luck – and not a little amusement to Beryl – that Perry Braithwaite had no sense of taste. It was, Beryl said mercilessly, the only reason his courtship with Agnes had lasted. If he could actually have tasted her cooking, he would have been long gone.

'I made a little sandwich for you,' Agnes twinkled. 'Just in case you popped by.'

'No better place to pop by to,' he replied, smiling

and reaching for a sandwich. He took a bite and chewed it slowly. He could have been eating one of Agnes's corsets and not known it.

'Delicious.'

She smiled again, sitting beside him and staring admiringly into his eyes. Middle age having also gone to work on Agnes's eyesight, Perry's lean, plain features were smoothed out, making him almost appealing.

'Did you mean it when you said we could go boating on Saturday?'

He nodded.

'I love the water,' Agnes continued. 'I was reading about the big liners, how vast they are, like floating towns.'

'Much more rain and we'll have our own private liner,' Perry joked. 'I was thinking about us. About you and me. And I thought . . .'

Her breath caught. 'Yes, my dear?'

'Well, James being out at work, and now Faith growing up . . .'

'Yes, my dear?'

'Made me think about us.'

Her smile was encouraging. 'What about us, my dear?'

'I would say we got on well enough, wouldn't you?'

Thank God, Agnes thought. At last Perry Braithwaite was going to propose – and then she could wear her hair any way she liked.

'We get on very nicely, my dear.'

'And perhaps we could continue to get on well.'

Realising she was holding her breath, Agnes took in a sly gasp.

'What are saying to me, my dear?'

'That we should—'

The kitchen door opened in that instant, Faith walking in with a look of resignation. At once Perry leaned back in his seat, Agnes shooting her niece a look that could have broken glass. But Faith was immune, putting down her school books and flopping on to the sofa in the corner.

'I failed scripture! I can't believe it. I missed passing the exam by just one mark.' She sighed. 'Missed it by the skin of my teeth.'

Agnes knew exactly how she felt.

The afternoon had been a slow one in David Street. Slow enough to make James worry when he looked at the account book. Having worked with his grandparents for several years, he was used to Sid's easy way, and Beryl's absorption with cash. Not hoarding it, merely earning enough to get by. And although the summer had been scorching – resulting in a number of holiday snaps – an unlucky accident had meant that the camera had been damaged. Although gifted as a photographer, Sid had no skill as a technician, and so a specialist was called in. Mr Archibald Truscott was tall, pale and dour. He was also around a hundred, give or take a month. Dressed from head to toe in faded grey, he told James about the first photographs ever taken, the daguerreotypes, and how skilful the photographer had to be developing the plates.

'They were . . .' he paused, 'delicate.'

'Can you mend it?' James asked. Beryl was hovering in the background, Sid staring at the visitor as though he was afraid that taking his eyes off Mr Truscott would make him disappear.

'What?' Mr Truscott replied, cupping one hand around his left ear. 'What?'

'Can you mend the camera?'

'Always in a hurry.'

Sid blinked. 'Pardon?'

'Young people today, always in a hurry,' Mr Truscott replied, pausing to blow his nose. 'In my day, you took time over things. Didn't hurry. What's all the hurry for? You die anyway.'

Nonplussed, Beryl signalled for James to go with her into the back room. There she closed the door and pulled a face.

'Where *does* your grandfather find these people? That man looks like he's been dead a week.'

'He's supposed to be good.'

'At what? Scaring children?' She sighed, hands on her hips. 'I bet it'll be expensive fixing that camera. I told your grandfather to extend the tripod legs fully. Fully, I said. But no, he has to do it his way, and now look – the camera's broken.'

Anxious to change the subject, James picked up the afternoon paper, glancing at the headlines. 'There are looters on the streets of San Francisco after the earthquake,' he commented, reading on.

'Over a thousand people have been killed and a firestorm followed, burning down houses and businesses. The police have been shooting looters on sight . . .'

Sighing, Beryl slumped into a chair. Through the crack in the door she could see Sid watching the lugubrious Archibald Truscott, and sighed again. Her feet were killing her.

'And there's more about the suffragettes . . .'

'Oh, spare me.'

Frowning, James turned to her. 'I would have thought you were all for votes for women.'

'It's not the principle, it's the way they're going about it. Getting all heated up and tying themselves to railings, it's not going to work.' She paused, thinking of her granddaughter. 'I'm surprised Faith hasn't got involved. She's just the type to march for a cause.'

Without replying, James returned to his paper. He didn't want Beryl to catch his expression or she would read his thoughts. She always could pick into his mind and scoop out his secrets. Smiling to himself, James thought about his first girlfriend, Gracie. They had met at a Co-op dance and had got on well. Until her father had caught them kissing in the porch . . . It had taken some effort to explain away the black eye James had come home with. But it hadn't put him off girls. He was too much like his grandfather and Tommy Bentley for that. But as for his sister . . . she didn't seem interested in any lad.

James mused to himself, wondering why he

hadn't noticed Faith's reluctance before. Certainly he couldn't miss it now. Not after she had refused his friend in no uncertain terms. And poor Freddy had only been asking her out for a walk in the park. James knew that if he mentioned it to his grandmother, Beryl would be delighted. One thing fewer to worry about. After all, Faith could turn heads, and if she had been that way inclined, she could have caused many a sleepless night for her family. But there was never anything like that. James wondered if he would like Faith having a boyfriend – and decided that he wasn't keen on that idea one bit. It was all right for boys to fool around, but not females. They got a name for behaving like that. Almost as soon as the thought came into his mind, James realised he could stop worrying: his sister had a good cool head on her shoulders. She might love hearing about his exploits and his girlfriends, but fifteen-year-old Faith had yet to lose her head over anyone.

Stealing a glance at his grandmother, James turned back to the paper, thinking of Peter Dodds. Poor Peter, he thought, smiling. Faith had been visiting Mort Ruben at David Street when they first met. She had become very fond of the strange little man upstairs, and it was there she had met Peter. Apparently he was the son of a friend of Mort's and wanted to get some experience in the rag trade, and so he had ended up in David Street. His skills were limited, his grasp of the business rudimentary – a lack of interest explained by his longing to go on the stage.

Apparently he had told Faith all about how some actors in London had been prosecuted for appearing in Bernard Shaw's play *Mrs Warren's Profession*. They had been had up on a charge of affronting human decency. Yet the thought had seemed to spur Peter on; his renditions of *Hamlet* and *King Lear* reported back to James by a bemused Faith. Obviously she liked Peter, thought he was amusing – but she wasn't in love. And although he had asked her out several times, she had never accepted.

Which was fine by James. When his little sister fell in love, he would want it to be with someone with a bit more about them than some dopey lad with a hankering for the boards. Someone with a bit of money, a business of their own . . . At once James's thoughts turned to the photographic studio. He had such good ideas, ways of making the business more viable. Offering special rates, or family shots that would work out cheaper than single portrait sittings. After all, hadn't Eastman recently brought out a camera that everyone could buy and use? If they weren't careful, the business could be badly affected by such innovations. And it was no good Beryl pooh-poohing it, or Sid talking about how people liked proper studio portraits. It might be true, but James was of a generation that welcomed progress. If he could choose to take his own pictures when he was out and about, he would jump at the chance. And there were many others who would think the same.

Not that James could convince his grandparents.

They were happy coasting along, and glad that James was shouldering more of the running of the premises for them. Times were not easy, though not as hard as they had been, and their ambitions were limited. James's skill as a photographer was slight, but improving. He had an eye for a picture, though not that wayward little flirt of skill that set Tommy and Sid Bentley apart. But he was a steady pair of hands, a reliable, honest man, devoted to the business, and to making it prosper. If only they could just get the camera up and working again . . .

'So who is he?'

James frowned, dragged away from his thoughts. 'Who?'

'This lad that Faith is seeing.'

Jesus, he thought, she really could read minds. 'She isn't seeing anyone. He likes her, but Faith isn't interested.'

'Good thing too, what with her only being fifteen.'

'Nearly sixteen.'

'Nearly sixteen's still too young.'

'For what?' James asked, his tone arch.

'My God, there's more than a bit of your grandfather in you,' Beryl replied. 'I don't want her getting mixed up with the wrong sort, or marrying too soon.'

'I've told you, Faith's not interested in anyone.'

'She's starting work.'

James raised his eyebrows. 'She is?'

'She doesn't know it yet, but her grandad's fixed up a real nice job for her.'

Putting down the paper, James looked at Beryl curiously. '*He* did, or *you* did?'

'Does it matter?' she replied shortly. 'All that matters is that Faith is happy, around people she's fond of. And safe. Your sister might not be interested in boys, but she's already getting attention and I want her where I can keep an eye on her. Where we can *all* keep an eye on her.' Beryl paused, savouring the moment. 'Laurence Goldbladt's circulation isn't as good as it should be. Mind you, he's overweight, what do you expect? They gave it some fancy name at the hospital – intermittent claudication . . .'

'Good Lord.'

'Means he limps,' Beryl replied curtly. 'Anyway, what with Laurence marrying Moneyed Miriam and she being lazy as a church cat, there's work to be done at the showroom upstairs. Light work, nothing heavy – that wouldn't suit a girl. But Laurence said they had been asking around, looking for an attractive young lady who could greet the customers and do a little tidying. Oh, and sometimes model the furs.'

James grinned. 'And you thought of Faith?'

'Well, I ask you, who better? The girl's pretty, capable, and although I think the world of her, not scholarly, so there's no point wasting money on more education. Besides, there are a few rich men who come into Laurence Goldbladt's showroom; she might find herself a good husband.'

'Have you told her about her new job?'

Beryl shook her head. 'No, not yet. I told your aunt because I saw her this morning when I was on the way to catch the tram. I was late, you remember? Well, anyway, that was when I saw Agnes. Her hair was down over her forehead for some reason . . .' Beryl frowned, then hurried on. 'I reckoned she deserved to know that she'll soon have both of you out from under her feet.'

'What did she say?'

'I don't know. She looked like she'd been frozen, she was so surprised. Then she started babbling about how nice it would be to have the house to herself – not that it will be for long.'

'Her and Perry Braithwaite?'

'Nothing gets past you, does it?'

'Oh, come on!' James teased his grandmother. 'Mr Braithwaite's been hanging around since the night Faith ran away.'

'And came back, which no doubt disappointed Agnes.' Beryl caught the shocked look on James's face and hurried on. 'You know your aunt. She always was a reluctant nursemaid. You never troubled her, and she even got close to Faith after a while, but she doesn't like responsibility. She'd rather be looked after than have to do the looking after. And besides, now she's not so young and the opportunity's all but passed by, she wants to get married again. Perry Braithwaite's her last chance.'

'And if Faith goes to work for Laurence Goldbladt, she can travel into Manchester with us in the mornings and not get back until the evening.'

113

James nodded. 'We'll still be there in the evenings, though.'

Beryl paused. The idea had been playing in her mind for a while and now, finally, she was prepared to give it a voice. After all, James was twenty-one, more than capable, and very protective of his sister. As for Faith, she would have a job, and a safe home. And Agnes could get married at last.

'Gran?' James prompted her. 'What are you plotting?'

'I've been talking to your grandad, and we both thought it might be a good idea for you and your sister to live here, at the back of the photographic studio. As you well know, there's a kitchen and outside lav, and on the mezzanine there's a small box room that would do as a bedroom for Faith. As for you, James, you could sleep on a sofa in the studio. I reckon it'll be a hell of a sight more comfortable than that cupboard you call a bedroom at Agnes's.'

Excitement surged through James, excitement and power. He would have his own little kingdom, the only caveat being that he would have to look after Faith. And that was no trouble. He had always loved his sister and they were good companions. In fact, he would enjoy her company. During the daytime his grandparents would be there, but at night . . . He sighed. No more creeping in to Agnes's when he had been out for a drink with his friends. No more remembering not to laugh too loud. No more ridiculous curfews at absurd hours. He was

going to be his own man. The thought was intox-
icating. If another male had been left in sole charge
of his younger sister, he might have resented it. But
this was James, and James had been protective of
Faith for years.

'You mean it?'

Beryl nodded firmly. 'Yes, I mean it. But you look
after your sister, you hear me? I know you will, but
I'm warning you, take care of her. I'm trusting you,
James. Trusting you with my precious granddaughter.'

'I won't let you down.'

'I know that,' she replied briskly. 'And it'll be
good for you to have your independence. Everyone
should live their own life, and you're old enough
now. As for Faith, we can keep an eye on her in
Manchester.' Beryl beamed at her own clever
planning. 'She'll like working for Laurence
Goldbladt. She'll feel right at home; she's known the
man since she was a kid. Liked him too. And above
all, she'll be safe there. Safe as houses.'

No one mentioned Lennie Hellier. No one even
thought about him. No one remembered that he
worked for Laurence Goldbladt and slept on a
bundle of blankets by the back door . . . Far from
keeping her granddaughter safe, Beryl had
unknowingly thrown her into a maelstrom.

CHAPTER ELEVEN

After oiling the large underside wheel of one of the sewing machines, Mort Ruben hauled himself to his feet and stretched. A trickle of oil dripped from the end of the can spout and fell unceremoniously on to his spats.

'Oh my! Oh my!' he exclaimed, leaping from foot to foot, the oil spotting the floor indiscriminately.

Smiling patiently, one of the sewing women came to his aid. She took the oil can off Mort and then glanced at his spats.

'If you take them off, Mr Ruben, I think I can get them clean.'

He stared at the spats with a look of almost childish anguish, then bent down and unfastened them. Almost apologetically he passed them to the woman.

'Excuse handling my shoes, Mrs Shaw,' he said, embarrassed. 'I trust it won't be too unpleasant for you.'

In his socks, Mort wandered up the row of seamstresses, trying to look efficient. Nodding encouragement, he praised a couple of middle-aged women, then hovered uncertainly over a young girl who was obviously nervous.

'I think . . .' He made a tiny clicking sound with his tongue, as though he was mortified to have to pass judgement. 'I think the stitches could be smaller. Could they be smaller, my dear?'

The girl looked up, her expression apologetic. She had been widowed unexpectedly and had two children to provide for. If she lost the sewing job, she would also lose the roof over their heads.

'I'm sorry, it won't happen again,' she said hurriedly, staring at the seam. 'I can make the stitches smaller, honestly I can . . .'

Conscious of her nervousness, Mort rubbed his hands, his tone placating. 'It's not that the stitches are big. In another place, they would be considered quite fine. But I think . . . I think for here, my dear, a little smaller. Perhaps?'

Nodding, she returned to her work, a larger woman glancing up at Mort as he passed.

'Lloyd George's coming down on alcohol,' she said emphatically, teasing her long-time employer, whom she knew loved a secret tipple. 'Our prime minister reckons the demon drink will do the country in.'

Mort pursed his lips. 'Such a very . . . *forceful* gentleman, Mr Lloyd George . . .' Gently he rubbed his eye patch, a mannerism he usually employed when he was uncomfortable.

'He said that drink would send us all to the devil.'

117

Mort frowned. 'Very Welsh turn of phrase.'

'And he also said that it were harmful to health.'

'I myself,' Mort said lightly, 'don't care for alcohol.'

'You don't know what you're missing,' the woman went on. 'A drink can cheer you up when times are hard.' She looked around at her fellow workers. 'Aren't I right, girls? A drink can help get you by sometimes.'

Several of them nodded in agreement. The seamstress decided that she had teased her employer enough and changed the subject. 'So, what about our new tenants? I hear Mr Bentley's grandchildren are coming to live here.'

Mort beamed, on more comfortable ground. 'Oh yes, James is going to be working and living here full time, and his wonderful sister, Faith . . .' He drifted off for a moment. 'Such a pretty girl. And she can carry clothes very well, very well indeed.'

'I wonder the landlord allows it,' another woman piped up spitefully from the back of the room. 'God knows, they usually come down hard enough on anyone else that breaks the rules.'

'I think that the matter of habitation and rental will have been taken care of,' Mort replied, trying to sound firm, but failing.

Honour, the woman who had spoken, was one of his oldest and best seamstresses. She had the hands of an angel and the tongue of a cobra, but he kept her on because she could sew faster and neater than anyone. And because he knew that Laurence

Goldbladt was always ready to offer her a job. The two men had been friends for many years, but business was business, and along with the friendship went a robust rivalry. Avoiding her critical gaze, Mort glanced around his workroom, studying his other employees. It was true that he was a kind man, too kind in reality, and a sucker for a hard-luck story. But, like Sid always said, there had to be someone with a soft heart in business. It made up for all the villains . . . Attentively, Mort walked between the murmuring sewing machines, watching the women's feet peeking out from under their long skirts as they pressed the pedals. Mort had never stinted on the machinery. He firmly believed that you got good work from good tools – hence the ever-present oil can. He was convinced that oil – in prodigious quantities – helped to keep the machines running smoothly. Not that he ever allowed any oil on the work surfaces.

Deep in thought, he fingered a half-completed leg-of-mutton sleeve, wondering which buttons would work best. Mort Ruben's button collection was legendary. He had – as had his father and his grandfather before him, in the old country – amassed thousands of them. Some were tiny, for children's garments and underwear; some silk-covered for evening wear; some so old and fragile they were unusable. But all of them were treasured. Clicking his tongue, Mort padded over to the shelf where they were kept. Holding the jacket sleeve, his one good eye scanned the bottles of buttons and the numerous cards. Mother-of-pearl, boring. Ivory, not right for the garment. Smoked pearl, dull. Silver, too flashy. Mort's small left hand ran along the cards, with their glamorous names – Molyneux, House of Paris – and came to rest on an old one, slightly yellowed. Gold buttons, carved with the emblem of a swan's head, glowed at him. Perfect! Mort thought with pleasure, absolutely perfect. Taking down the card, he remembered the photographs he had seen of the Paris designs. Very extravagant, very hard to wear for some women. But easy for a young woman with height, like Faith Farnsworth.

It would be very pleasant – and very useful – to have Sid's granddaughter on the premises full time. After all, Mort knew that Faith was very fond of him and she would be bound to tell him what was going on in Laurence's showroom. Add to that the fact that she could model his clothes . . . Mort paused. He would pay her, of course. Give her a little money to pop in her pocket for herself. Not that he wanted her to think it was charity. Times might be a little tough for the City Photographic Studio, but no one wanted to be made to feel small. Another, giddy thought entered his head at that moment. What if Peter Dodds and Faith were to fall in love? Mort sighed at the notion. He had been in love once, with the girl he married. But when she died, all his romantic ambitions seemed to die with her, and his thoughts turned to buttons . . . He considered Peter Dodds again. Not a bad lad, but then again, not interested in the business, and if he would insist on becoming an actor, not the reliable type.

'Mr Ruben?'

Surprised, he jumped, then noticed his spats in the woman's hands.

'Oh, my dear!' he enthused, taking them from her and studying them from every angle. 'There's not a mark on them! How clever of you. How clever!'

Delighted, he sat down and put the spats back on, then extended his legs and admired them, happy as a child with a new toy.

CHAPTER TWELVE

Brushing her hair, Faith stared at her reflection, her mouth dry. Of course Beryl would never have put her in such a position deliberately; how could her grandmother know about Lennie Hellier if she had never confided in her? Pausing, Faith pulled her thick hair over her shoulder and began to plait it. The next day she was moving to David Street, to live there and work for Laurence Goldbladt. Closing her eyes for an instant, Faith composed herself. Everyone could see how happy James was about the arrangement. He would have a place of his own, at night in sole charge of the City Photographic Studio. How could she spoil it for him? Say she wasn't coming and explain why . . . how could she? She couldn't – and she knew it.

So even though Faith had been stunned when Beryl confided her plan, she had kept quiet.

'Are you pleased, luv?'

She had nodded, trying to make her tone light. 'So Mr Goldbladt is happy for me to work for him?'

'More than happy. Delighted!' Beryl had replied. 'As well he might be. And you'll get a wage, Faith. I'm afraid it'll have to go into the pot, you know how things are, we need every penny we can get. But there'll be a little over for you. And you can get your clothes cheap, what with Mort being so fond of you, and Laurence said he would let a couple of sample copies come your way.'

At any other time Faith would have been impressed. Samples were originals made for the collections, usually all hand-stitched and very well finished. But after they had been modelled and worn, they couldn't be sold at full price, and usually, being small sizes, their market was limited. To have samples of the latest fashions was really something. Something Ellie would be jealous about . . .

'You'll be happy with Laurence. He thinks of you as his own daughter. As for that floppy wife of his, Miriam's never there.'

'Never?' Faith had asked hurriedly.

'Not now, she's too idle. Wants to stay home in Didsbury with her feet up,' Beryl had replied, scoffing. 'She won't be around, luv. You'll have the place to yourself a lot of the time. What with Laurence going out and about two days a week.'

It was all working out perfectly for everyone. Laurence Goldbladt, now he had a full-time receptionist, would be free to leave the showroom to Faith. And Lennie Hellier . . . Faith's eyes fixed on her reflection, then she turned away and continued to pack her bag. Her time living with Agnes had not been without difficulties, but to leave like this, to be going from safety to . . . what? Shaking her head, she tried to keep calm. She would cope somehow. Certainly keep out of Lennie Hellier's way. After all, they had avoided each other for years. But it had been easy to stay out of his way when Faith could make sure she never went upstairs alone. Easy to dodge him when she saw him in the back yard, or on the street outside. Easy to visit when Laurence was there. But now she would have to be there full time. And on her own two days a week . . .

Shaken, Faith sat down on the side of the bed. She had to tell someone. But she should have spoken up earlier, not left it so long, now that everything was arranged. Then again, Beryl had gone ahead with the arrangements long before she had told her granddaughter . . . But it was no good making excuses, Faith thought. She should have spoken out when the incident with Lennie Hellier took place. Or at least when Beryl first mooted the plan for them to move to David Street. But she hadn't said a word. Instead she had watched the pleasure in her brother's face and listened to Beryl talking about the wage Laurence was going to pay her. How much it would help. And then it had seemed imperative that Faith stay silent. Her grandparents, her aunt, her brother had done so much for her – how could she, in all honesty, speak out?

She would have to handle the matter herself. She wasn't a child any more, Faith thought impatiently, she would have to sort out Lennie Hellier on her own. If there was a problem, she would deal with it. And if he touched her again, God help him.

Ellie Walker's mother counted the money three times and then smiled to herself in a smug, vaguely triumphant way. It might have taken her years, but she had finally saved up enough cash to get her and her daughter to Paris. Once there, she would take Ellie to the Moulin Rouge and the rest would be history. Of course some people had intimated that the Moulin Rouge was hardly the place for a sixteen-year-old. But, as Sybil Walker replied, *she* had been a dancer at that age. Not in Paris, admittedly, but she had trodden the boards at Blackpool and later Brighton. She knew what it was all about. She might have become a respectable widow, but in her youth she had kicked up her heels with the best of them. And she wanted the same chance for Ellie – but without repercussions. Respectable people might talk about stage-door Johnnies and bad reputations, but Sybil had instilled the fear of God into Ellie about sex. She had driven home every detail of men, of what they did, how they did it, and how a girl never drank alone with a man. Or went to his hotel. Or gave him anything other than a kiss on the cheek in return for his gifts.

People might look askance at girls who danced semi-clothed for a living, but Sybil knew that a clever woman could play the punters at their own game. Lead them on, get what she could out of them, and *not* be stupid enough to get seduced. Or pregnant . . . Staring at the money in her hands, Sybil thought of her daughter. Of course she would have liked an easier ride for Ellie, but working-class girls didn't marry millionaires; they married miners, mill hands, coalmen. Working-class *dancers*, however, stood a better chance at landing a catch. As for her daughter's talent, Sybil had finally realised that Ellie had the dancing and singing ability of a grasshopper. But her ethereal, ghostly beauty was fascinating. And at the Moulin Rouge, some of the girls hardly moved, just stood in a kind of sensual tableau, to be looked at, admired, wanted. And *that* Ellie could do.

All that remained was for Sybil to buy two tickets to Paris. The rest was down to Ellie and to fate. It was a journey that would decide whether Ellie Walker got lucky – or came back to Oldham to live forever under the shadow of the mills.

Turning over repeatedly, Lennie Hellier moved under his blankets in his space outside Laurence Goldbladt's showroom. An eerie, unwelcome moon shone down into David Street and leered into the windows of Mort Ruben's on the upper floor, then moved into the furrier's rooms before finally its waxy beam slid, like a winter snake, down into the cold yard of the basement and the studio below. The street was deserted. A little earlier a few men – drunk from the city pubs – had staggered along the pavement singing a Marie Lloyd song, but now it was silent. Unbreathing. Threatening.

Sitting upright, Lennie hugged his knees, his head down, his mind replaying the day he had touched Faith. He had been so ashamed afterwards, so certain she would report him. For weeks he had waited to be hauled into Mr Goldbladt's office, or Sidney Bentley's studio, to be threatened, even beaten, then thrown out. He had wondered often about where he would go, whether he could find work washing up at one of Manchester's hotels. Nothing better: he wasn't qualified and would have no reference, no recommendation as to his character. He had ruined his chances at David Street, wrecked the advancement Laurence Goldbladt had hinted at, all through his own reckless stupidity. Without his safe haven, he would drown . . . But aside from the worry of retribution, Lennie had genuinely regretted what he had done. More times than he could remember he had wanted to talk to Faith, to explain, apologise. He would have sent her a note, but his writing was poor, his vocabulary sketchy – and besides, what would have happened if the letter had fallen into the wrong hands? He would have waited by the door when he knew she was visiting, but he didn't dare. There was nothing he could say, and if she saw him it might remind her. Make her finally act, when she had been silent for so long.

So the apology was never made. The note never written. The meeting never undertaken. Instead, Lennie had spent weeks preparing to be turned out, had even wondered if James would come and take him to task. Beat him up for what he had done to his sister. Then, finally, he began to realise that Faith wasn't going to tell. That she hadn't confided in anyone. That no one knew. And eventually he convinced himself that nothing bad *had* happened. Or if it had, it had only been a quick peck on the cheek. So real did the fantasy become that he could imagine himself irate if ever challenged. It was only when he saw Faith that he remembered the truth, and knew that what he had done was wrong. And always would be.

He had been so stimulated by Faith, so frightened by his actions and so terrified of his exile that time appeared to stall for Lennie Hellier. He never moved on – mentally or sexually – from that seventeen-year-old boy. Women terrified him, men bullied him, and he spent his life moving close to walls and huddled under nocturnal blankets. Only in David Street was he safe. After a long time, his detachment effected a kind of peace within him, and his world – sad and small as it was – became secure.

But no more. Tomorrow, Faith Farnsworth was moving into David Street. Lennie's actions, his sins, would come back to haunt him. When he saw her, he would remember. When he heard her voice, he would remember. His temporary pocket of peace was about to be turned out.

'How do there, Lennie!' Laurence Goldbladt said cheerfully, poking the lad's shoulder with his forefinger. 'Wakey wakey!'

Jerking upright, Lennie stared at his boss and then struggled to his feet. For once he had overslept. Hurriedly he folded his blankets and tucked them into the corner, watching Laurence Goldbladt move across the workroom and pull down a bundle of fur tails. Pouring out a little water in a washing bowl, Lennie splashed his face and hands, then pulled on his work overalls, a gift from Sid long ago. He had hardly outgrown them, remaining the same slight, malnourished figure he had always been.

'You're late today, lad.'

'It won't 'appen again,' Lennie said hurriedly, his shoulders stooped as though expecting a blow, though such a thing had never come from anyone in David Street. 'I were 'aving a bad night.'

'Well, it happens to the best of us,' Laurence said, his thoughts concentrated on the fur tails. Slowly he let his hand run over the mink, then he held it up to his eyes and studied it avidly. 'Good quality, no breaks or tears in the skin,' he muttered to himself, pleased that the previously substandard deliveries had returned to their former high quality. 'No doubt you've heard all about it, but we've a new lady starting tomorrow. Miss Faith Farnsworth.'

Hurriedly Lennie nodded, turning away and scurrying under the hanging furs towards the back kitchen.

'Would yer like a cup of tea, Mr Goldbladt?'

'Three sugars, and strong,' Laurence replied, thinking excitedly of his new employee.

Faith was a good-looking girl, and very capable

for her sixteen years. And with her grandparents downstairs and James on hand, she would cope very nicely. Besides, Laurence thought, when he was away, Lennie could do any of the heavy work if the traders and fur workers weren't about.

'I'm off downstairs, Lennie,' he called out. 'I'll be in the back yard; someone said they'd left a package down there. Back in a minute.'

Preoccupied, Laurence left the showroom, walking down the back stairs, deep in thought about the last delivery. He had tugged sharply at the fur tails and they hadn't split. That was good, he thought happily; good-quality merchandise always made him happy.

Pushing open the back door, he froze on the spot. Only yards away, a large dog rose up from the corner of the yard, moving threateningly towards him. Startled, Laurence fell backwards, accidentally slamming the door shut behind him.

'Back!' he shouted, as the animal crouched. 'BACK!'

But the dog wasn't listening. It was showing the whites of its eyes instead, its hackles raised. Terrified of dogs, Laurence stared fearfully at the stray. When he moved his hand towards the latch of the back door, the animal snarled warningly.

'God . . .' Laurence said helplessly under his breath. 'Oh God . . .'

Bracing himself, he prepared to move again, but found himself transfixed, waiting for the dog to attack. Sweat pooling under his armpits, he tried desperately to reach for the latch again. The animal resumed its snarling, creeping inch by inch towards him. Taking in a breath, Laurence was bracing himself for certain attack when the door opened suddenly and he felt himself pulled inside.

In the semi-darkness of the lobby, he stared at his rescuer gratefully.

'Oh, dear God! Thank you, Lennie, thank you. That dog . . . that dog was going to bite me.' He wiped the sweat off his face, staring at the straggly lad. 'God knows what would have happened to me if you hadn't come down.'

'It's the neighbour's dog, but I don't know what it's doing in our yard.' Concerned, Lennie looked his employer up and down. 'Are you all right? I were worried for you there, sir. Right worried.'

But Laurence was recovering fast. Indeed, on the way back up to the showroom, he was thinking about his lucky break and wondering how unpleasant the day might have turned out if Lennie Hellier hadn't rescued him. He was also thinking about rewarding his employee in some way. After all, things could have been very nasty . . . Laurence Goldbladt might not be as tender-hearted as Mort Ruben, but he had feelings and he found himself thinking of the vague promises he had made about the lad's advancement. Promises he had repeated for years. Promises that so far had come to nothing.

Walking into the showroom, Laurence sat down, watching as Lennie moved into the back kitchen and put the kettle on to boil. His shambolic gait, hampered by his club foot, had improved over the years, but his body was little changed from when Sidney had first brought him up to see Laurence.

'He's not a big lad, it's true, but he's willing.' Sid had dropped his voice so that Lennie wouldn't overhear. 'Not very educated, but honest as the day is long.'

'Where did he come from?'

Sid had shrugged. 'I dunno. He just fetched up one day. In the back yard, huddled against the wall, half starved. Never said much, never offered any confidences, and after a while you don't like to pry. Poor lad.'

'How old is he?' Laurence had bellowed, Sid motioning for him to keep his voice low.

'Who knows? Twelve? Thirteen? It's hard to tell with Lennie.'

Looking at him now, Laurence realised that Lennie must be at least eighteen, and possibly even older. The thought came as a shock to him. Hadn't he thought of Lennie as a boy, not a man? Curious, he continued to watch his rescuer through the kitchen door. Lennie had been very honest, that was true, and not as stupid as they had first thought. He could read quite well now, and after years of solitary studying had managed some decent handwriting. He might well be nervous around people, but he wasn't rude, and although his accent was heavy Mancunian, he could be coached. In fact, there were a few ways in which Lennie Hellier might make himself more useful around the place . . . Bending a fur tail in his hands, Laurence considered the matter in depth. Miriam was – he had to admit – as lazy as a snail. She loved eating, gossiping and shopping. There wasn't a department store in the north-west that hadn't benefited from her largesse. Which was all fine and good with Laurence – after all, it was Miriam's money to spend as she wished – but his workload was becoming less and less agreeable to him. Watching his wife idle away her time, Laurence had begun to envy such sloth and had gradually shortened his working hours. He now had two days off a week. Days he spent ambling around Manchester with his new wife. Days on which her money could be spent. Preferably not entirely on herself. After all, he kept her in furs, so if she wanted to press new shoes and an ebony walking stick on him, why should he protest?

Gradually Miriam's greed for plenty had expanded overseas. Only the previous week she had mentioned going to Egypt and what a wonderful time they could have visiting the pyramids. Or Athens. Or Russia. Laurence wasn't too keen on the idea of Russia, but the thought of travelling on a luxury liner was, albeit somewhat adventurous, very enticing. More than that, Miriam had mentioned that they could buy a car. Indeed, she had been sent details about the Rover model that had been shown at the Motor Show in Olympia only the previous year. Laurence could see himself driving a vehicle like that. Something sleek, something that would make all his friends and business associates jealous.

And if he had a car like that, what was the point of just driving it to work? You wanted to go into the country with it, drive with the top down and good fresh air in your lungs.

His fantasy of countryside bliss was cut short by the sound of coughing. Walking to the kitchen door, he looked at Lennie as though he was sizing up a skin to make into a coat. Was there enough to go round? Was the quality there? If it was moulded, brushed, polished and styled, could common musquash pass for mink? After all, didn't Lennie deserve a break?

'Lennie, I want to talk to you.'

He spun round, guilty. 'I won't sleep in again, sir, I swear—'

'No, no, lad, it's not that.' Laurence waved one groomed hand towards the kitchen table, gesturing for Lennie to sit with him. Surprised, Lennie perched on the edge of the furthest seat. 'When did I last give you a rise?'

'What?'

Laurence winced, looking pained. 'Not *what*, it's pardon.'

Chastened, Lennie looked down. 'Pardon, sir . . .'

'Well, when *did* I last give you a rise?'

'Yer didn't.'

'Since when?'

'Since ever,' Lennie mumbled, sure that it was his fault and that at any moment he was going to be thrown out. Surely Mr Goldbladt was just teasing him, torturing him?

'I've never given you a rise in your wages?' Laurence leaned back in his seat, studying his glorious waistcoat. 'That won't do.'

'I don't mind, sir! I don't mind!' Lennie replied, almost hysterical.

'Well, I mind,' his employer retorted, getting to his feet and studying Lennie closely. 'Stand up, lad, stand up.'

He did so.

'Straighten up too!'

'I can't do no more straightening,' Lennie replied apologetically. 'M'foot keeps me bent over a bit.'

To his horror, Laurence realised that he hadn't really thought about Lennie's club foot before. He knew about it, knew that the lad limped, but it hadn't made an impression on him. Suddenly aware of the gap between his lame employee and himself, Laurence Goldbladt felt something akin to shame and – aware of his own burgeoning good fortune – wanted to make amends.

'How old are you, Lennie?'

'Twenty-two.'

'Twenty-two!' Laurence bellowed back, then moderated his tone. 'I thought you were . . . You've no beef on your bones, that's what's held you back. I should have noticed before.'

Uneasy and suspicious, Lennie stared at his employer. Why the interest after years of hints? Why now? Just because he had saved him from the dog? Uncomfortable, Lennie watched his employer walk around him, studying him like an executioner measuring him for the drop.

'Have I done summat, sir? I'm sorry if I have, it weren't meant.'

Laurence wasn't listening; he was thinking that he had an opportunity right under his nose, and he should grab it. Taking Lennie's arm, he propelled him up the next flight of stairs and rapped brusquely on Mort Ruben's door. A moment later, Mort opened it, looking from Laurence to Lennie.

'Good morning, gentlemen,' he said, covering up any surprise he felt. 'Come in, do come in.'

'I need a word with you, Mort,' Laurence said firmly. 'In private.'

Leaving Lennie in the workroom, they moved into Mort's office and closed the door. Behind Lennie, the first seamstresses were already at work, the pretty young widow glancing up only momentarily before returning to her sewing. Flushing, Lennie avoided all the women's eyes and kept his own lowered. Having never been upstairs before, and having assiduously avoided any of the seamstresses either coming to or leaving work, he now found himself burning with panic. His club foot, in its worn, overlarge boot, seemed to grow in size every time one of the women looked at it, until he could feel it weighing down on the floor where he stood and threatening to burst through the rafters. Clumsily he tried to cover his lame foot with his other one, but no one was fooled, the sewing machines buzzing like wasps around him.

For the first time in many years he thought of his past. Of finding himself abandoned in Manchester to fend for himself. Of scrambling in bins and behind kitchens for scraps, and even stealing some bread off a dog once when the hunger had made him half crazy. Then he thought of Sidney Bentley, of his kindness, how he had taken him in and fed him and clothed him. Lennie could, if he had trusted the photographer, have made himself more appealing. But hard times had turned him and he couldn't trust anyone. So by the time he was ready to talk, Sid had grown used to his employee's reserve and curbed his curiosity. And that was the way Lennie's life had continued. He was remote, and people left him to his own devices. Until now.

As Lennie waited outside, Mort stared through the upper glass pane of his office door, Laurence looking on.

'Well, what d'you think?'

'You said he was twenty-two? My, my, hardly looks more than a boy,' Mort said sympathetically. 'Poor lad.'

'Poor man,' Laurence corrected him, returning to his previous theme. 'Can you fit him out with a set of clothes?'

'But why?'

'Because Lennie saved me from some mad slavering dog in the back yard, that's why! He saved my life.'

'A dog? In the yard?'

'Apparently it belongs to next door.'

Mort sucked on his teeth. 'My word, I hear it's a nasty animal . . . And Lennie came to your rescue?'

'Indeed he did,' Laurence agreed. 'And I'm going to reward him. It's made me think, Mort – I'm changing my life, and not before time. Miriam and I want to travel, see something of the world . . .'

'Oh my.'

'And now I've employed Faith to be my receptionist, I've a feeling that before long that girl will be more than capable of running the showroom. When I've trained her up, of course.'

'Oh my.'

'She'll need a while, but she's very sharp. And very presentable. And besides, the Bentleys need as much money coming in as possible. Well now, Mort, you don't have to be a genius to work out the possibility that's here, under my very nose.'

Confused, the little man looked up at his tall friend. 'You don't?'

'I'll be training Faith to take care of the showroom in my absence – a day at a time, at first, slowly building the responsibility up – but it's obvious that she will need assistance. And I have the very man outside.'

Mort stared at him, glassy-eyed. 'Lennie?'

'Look at him!'

'I am, Laurence,' Mort replied, turning to gaze out of the window again and wondering if Miriam's money hadn't gone to his friend's usually wily business head. 'But he's . . . he's . . . not very prepossessing.'

'Clothes maketh the man.'

'Well, yes,' Mort replied timidly, trying hard not to be unkind. 'But then again, no clothes can make a silk purse out of a sow's ear.'

'Fine feathers make fine birds.'

'A frog is a frog even if it's wearing a gold waistcoat.'

Wrong-footed, Laurence stared down at his friend. 'You just made that up!'

'Well, even if I did,' Mort replied, 'it's true. You can't make someone into something they're not.'

'I disagree,' Laurence responded, determined to make his point. He had an opportunity and he was damned if he was going to miss it. 'We could teach—'

'We!'

'All right, *I* could teach Lennie how to speak properly and greet people. He would be very useful in that way. He could also do the heavy work and help out. Sid always said he was honest, and I've never had a moment's worry that way. Besides, he's very loyal to me. And if I reward him, he'll be even more grateful, and that's the kind of good will you can't get easily.'

'But . . .'

'Think about it, Mort! I've been hinting for long enough that I would advance the lad; well, now's the time. Anyway, you're the one who's always saying that everyone should have a chance.'

'Well, yes, but . . .' Trailing off, Mort stared out at the uncomfortable man waiting in the workroom outside. It was true, Mort always wanted people to do their best, and if he could help them, he would. But for all Lennie Hellier's discomfort, for all his apparent reserve, there was something about the man Mort didn't like – and that was rare in itself.

'Sid will encourage me to do it,' Laurence went on. 'He always thought it was a good idea to make the most of Lennie. He thinks he's not been given a chance in life.'

'Are you sure you're the one who should give him that chance?' Mort asked carefully, turning from the window and looking at his friend. 'Are you sure?'

But he didn't need to hear Laurence's reply; he already knew what it would be. Having been a clever businessman and a lucky husband, Laurence Goldbladt was not a man to argue with. When he made his mind up about anything, he stuck to his opinion. And he was usually proved right in his judgement. Besides, Laurence had discovered something even more enticing than business – good living. And he wanted it in a hurry.

Startled, Lennie jumped when Mort's door opened again and the two men walked out. Putting his head on one side, Mort studied Lennie and then went into a back room. A few moments later he returned with a man's suit, holding it out to Lennie.

'Try it on, lad,' Mort said kindly, ignoring the curious looks from the workers. 'In the back room, of course.'

Instead of taking it, Lennie backed off. 'What's it fer?'

'For you,' Laurence replied, hustling the young man through to the back room and into a cramped cubicle. Studying his nails, Laurence leaned against the outside wall, offering encouragement. 'Have you got it on yet?'

'I can't . . . I can't . . .'

'Come on, let's have a look at you,' Laurence urged him.

But Lennie wasn't coming out, at least not for a moment. He was staring at the man in the mirror, who was looking back at him. The tall, slim man who wasn't slum fodder. The kind of man who didn't sleep on blankets on the floor. A man who could walk down David Street and look like he might have a little business there. The trousers were too long, but Lennie didn't mind that; in fact, the material covered his ugly boot and made him forget he was lame. Self-consciously he touched his hair and then smoothed it back with his hands. He needed a shirt, of course, otherwise people could see his scrawny chest, but with a shirt and tie he could pass for a respectable man . . .

'Lennie! Come out of there!' Laurence barked good-naturedly, watching as the curtain was drawn back. Slowly Lennie emerged and stood uncertainly in front of him.

A low whistle of disbelief escaped Laurence's lips as he heard Mort walk up behind them.

'What were you saying about how fine feather don't make fine birds?'

Mort was all business. 'I'd have to get the

trousers shortened, and a little off the jacket sleeves. We need a shirt and a tie. Oh, and a couple of starched collars.' He paused, eyeing Lennie and feeling the shift in the man's demeanour. 'You look very . . . different.'

'You look smart,' Laurence added. 'But you need a good haircut. And some cologne.'

'Cologne?' Mort asked, horrified. 'Are you sure?'

'Anyone who works for me must be smart and smell good,' Laurence replied. 'I can't have scrubbers in the showroom.'

'The showroom?' Lennie echoed disbelievingly. 'I'm going in the showroom?'

'Well, we'll have to see how you shape up, Lennie,' his employer replied, 'but if it all works out all right, you'll be making progress soon. I'm grooming your career, young man.' He winked. 'I've got my eye on the future, and I don't mean just mine. There's going to be changes at Goldbladt's. Young blood. And I've taken it into my head that your loyalty and bravery and hard work should be rewarded. You've a long way to go, but I'm counting on you.'

Lennie's mouth opened as though he was going to speak, but he didn't say a word. Instead he closed his mouth and listened. Listened to the future: that twinkling place that Laurence Goldbladt had mapped out for him. That spectacular advance from dogsbody to trusted employee. Lennie might not be academically clever, but he was survival smart and he knew an opportunity when it was presented to him. Although he had never expected such a chance to come his way, he grabbed it like a fox would snatch a chicken. Instinctively he knew it was his only way to get out of the mire. To advance, to become someone. Someone who could achieve something. Someone who would be working alongside Miss Faith Farnsworth. Not as a slum cripple, but as a success in waiting.

In that moment, ambition gnawed at Lennie Hellier's gut like hunger had once done.

CHAPTER THIRTEEN

'Of course you'll have to keep an eye on the damp,' Beryl said firmly, Sid winking at Faith as they walked around. Amused, Faith watched her grandmother as she gave her a tour of the living accommodation on David Street as though she was a stranger. Patiently she allowed Beryl to take her around the narrow back bedroom – which would be hers – then lead her into the larger back room, where the family ate – out of sight of the studio. An overstuffed horsehair sofa had been borrowed from Mort upstairs and pushed up against the wall next to the fire grate. 'James can sleep there. It'll be comfortable and warm and you'll have the bedroom to yourself. Mind you, I want you both to promise me that you'll lock the door at night. Both doors. You never know who's around in the city late on.' Beryl frowned, glancing over to her husband. 'Is this really a good idea? I mean, Faith's only sixteen, and living in Manchester on her own.'

'No she isn't. She's living with James,' Sid reminded her, rolling his eyes. 'Our grandson is six feet two – who the hell would take him on? Faith can't come to any harm with James here.'

Beryl still wasn't convinced. Even though the whole move had been her idea, now that the day had come, she was having second thoughts.

'Maybe I should stay with them for a while, sleep over, check they can cope.'

'They can cope,' Sid replied, taking his wife's arm and guiding her to the door. 'Come on, Beryl, it's time to go home.'

'Oh, not yet!' she snapped. 'It can't be that time already.'

'Well it is,' Sid replied, picking up Beryl's coat and passing it to her. 'Time for us to get the tram back to Oldham and leave the studio in very capable hands.'

'We've never left them here before . . .'

'No, we locked the place up and left it alone before. And nothing happened to it then, so nothing's going to happen to it now.'

Sid's patience was being stretched. From the first he had taken to the idea of the grandchildren living at the studio. Independence was a good thing, and besides, in the long run it might mean that he could begin to move closer to retirement. And then, perhaps, Beryl would stay home more. The thought appealed to Sid. He would like to stop working every day, like to sit with his wife and read the morning paper in a comfortable chair, rather than a rickety tram seat. He would appreciate getting up later in the mornings, and not having to leave home in the winter dark, when the fogs were down. It had been a routine that had worked for him and Beryl for decades. Leaving home whilst the street lamps were still lit, often passing the knocker-up on his way round, tapping at the windows to raise people for work. Whether they had had a quarrel or were relaxed, they always walked arm in arm. Sometimes with heads down, mouths covered against the fog. Other times – in summer – they would swing their arms together and watch the morning begin as they passed the Methodist chapel. The commute had been so much a part of their lives that they had accepted it, but Sid was finding it more difficult to work the long hours, and he knew – even if Beryl wouldn't admit it – that his wife was often tired. Perhaps they could spend more time at home now, in Hardy Street instead of David Street. Perhaps he could have more hours holding a paintbrush instead of a camera plate. Going for a walk in the park rather than spending his afternoons in a darkroom, with the smell of chemicals and the suspended ghostly images developing like spirit bodies around him.

'Come on, Beryl, let's go home,' he urged her.

She paused, then caught his eye, nodded, and followed him out.

Later that evening, when the unpacking had been done and Faith had organised what little possessions they had, she paused, glancing over to her brother. James was sitting in the back room with his head down over the account books, his hands resting on the green baize that covered the work table. For an instant she remembered him the day they had gone to live with Agnes, and the way he had consoled her then, jollied her into their new life. But this time was different. She was older and had learned to keep secrets. Old secrets, which Faith had never thought would trouble her again. After all, how could she have foreseen the spiteful turn of fate that would land her in David Street?

As though he suddenly sensed he was being observed, James looked up.

'Are you OK?'

Faith nodded. 'Course I am.'

'You just looked a bit odd, that was all.'

'I always look odd,' she replied lightly, taking a seat next to him.

'Who would have believed the way things have turned out, hey?'

'Yeah, who would have thought it.'

'I should tell you something,' James began, watching as Faith leaned towards him, just as she had always done when she knew he was about to confide. 'I won't take any nonsense.'

Outraged, she slapped the top of his head lightly. 'Flaming cheek! Don't even think of telling me what to do.'

Grinning, he leaned back in his seat. 'How long?'

'How long what?'

'How long before Agnes marries Perry Braithwaite?'

Faith thought for a moment. 'Six months.'

'I say three months.'

'Never!'

'Pound on it?'

'A pound! Who the hell are you? Mr Rothschild?' Faith replied drily. 'A shilling.'

'OK, a shilling.' He reached into his pocket and put the coin on the table. 'Let's see the colour of your money.'

'Copper, usually,' Faith replied, taking out a shilling and laying it beside her brother's. 'Winner gets all.'

Nodding, he put the shillings into a tin on the mantelpiece and then locked the front door of the studio, pulling down the blind and turning the card to CLOSED.

'Sorry you have to sleep on the couch,' Faith said.

James grinned. 'Well, it's my turn to suffer now. You had a camp bed for ages at Agnes's.' He glanced upwards as he heard footsteps on the stairs. 'Can you hear that?'

'Can I hear it! Can I miss it?'

They both listened to the footsteps descending, watching Laurence Goldbladt's expensively shod feet pass by the basement window, followed by the feet of the seamstresses who had been working late. Above them, other noises echoed. Evening noises. Like the sound of the old lift rattling downwards, and the far-off echo of a newsboy calling the headlines at the top of the street. From close by came the sound of a horse's hooves, and the voice of a Chinese washerwoman gabbled incoherently as she shuffled past on the pavement above.

Faith raised her eyebrows. 'Not like Oldham, is it?'

'No,' agreed James. 'There's life here.'

'And girls?'

'I doubt it. Remember, I have to set you a good example,' he replied, teasing her. Then he became serious again, studying his sister's face. 'Are you really all right? I mean, you can tell me.'

'I'm fine, honestly.'

'You've seemed a bit nervy about this move,' James continued, not ready to let it go. 'I mean, I can't think that you wanted to stay with Agnes, but it seemed like you weren't too pleased to come here. Why is that?'

Knowing how well he could read her thoughts, Faith glanced away.

'You imagine things.'

'No, I don't. *Is* there something on your mind?'

'Like what?'

'Like this place? Like there's something wrong here?'

Unwilling to let him cross-question her any further, Faith began to busy herself in the kitchen.

James followed her and stood by the door. 'I should have said something sooner. In fact, I'd thought for a while that you weren't as keen to visit the studio. But I like it so much here, I supposed you did too. But it's *not* as comfortable for you, is it, Faith?'

'James, you talk rubbish!'

He ignored her. 'Maybe I should have asked you about us living here before now—'

'There's nothing wrong with this place!' Faith replied heatedly. Then she calmed herself, talked more steadily to cover her anxiety. 'I grew up visiting the studio. We spent so much time with our grandparents in this building. We've been coming to David Street most of our lives. Why *shouldn't* I feel at ease here?'

'I don't know,' James said, frowning. 'Why don't you?'

CHAPTER FOURTEEN

'Jesus, Mary and Joseph!' Sybil Walker screamed at the top of her voice. 'JESUS, MARY AND JOSEPH!'

Jerked from sleep, Ellie ran downstairs to find her mother pacing the kitchen with a letter in her hand. Excitedly she waved it at her daughter, her eyes brilliant, almost crazed.

'You'll never believe it!'

'What?' Ellie asked, bemused, as she reached for the letter. Reading it, she paused, then screamed, grabbing hold of her mother, both of them careering round the cramped kitchen.

'Keep the noise down!' the Irish next-door neighbour hollered, banging on the wall. 'You've no place making such a row unless yer being murdered! Are yer being murdered in there?'

Moving over to the window, Sybil looked out, her neighbour leaning out of his own window at the same time.

'What's the racket?'

'I've won a trip to Paris!' Sybil replied.

'So yer not being murdered?'

'No, I've won a trip to Paris!' Sybil repeated.

The neighbour snorted. 'Well, take care yer don't get murdered there,' he replied, closing the window. 'It's a terrible place fer killing.'

Bright-eyed, Sybil turned back to her daughter, her voice lowered.

'Would you believe it? I've just saved enough money to pay for a trip over there and I've *won* a trip! It's God-given, that's what it is. God wants us to go.'

'God doesn't want us to go!' Ellie replied. 'I doubt if God approves of dancers.'

'Doesn't He watch over me?' Sybil retorted. 'We've got money, my girl. For the first time in our lives, we've got money.'

Chewing her lip, Ellie regarded her mother. So the day had come, had it? It was finally here, the flaming day that was going to make the French trip possible. Over the years Ellie had tried to hint, then tell her mother that she didn't want to go. That it would be a waste of time and money. But Sybil had been resolute. The Moulin Rouge was their route to riches. All they had to do was get there . . .

'Mum, it's just an idea, but . . .'

'Yes, love?'

'You could sell the trip *and* the tickets and then we could move somewhere nice.'

'Are you mad!' Sybil exploded, then dropped her voice again. 'This is what we've been working for.

Only now we can go in some style. Buy new outfits so that when you get to the Moulin Rouge you'll look like something.'

'A new outfit won't make me sing or dance any better.'

Irritated, Sybil brushed aside the objections. 'You'd think you didn't want to go!'

'I've never wanted to go!'

'But . . . but we've planned for this.'

'*You've* planned for it,' Ellie replied. 'I just went along with it, because I never thought we'd have the money to go.'

Confused, Sybil stared at her daughter. 'But I told you I was saving up.'

'You work in a milliner's, Mum! How long was it going to take to save enough?'

Stunned, Sybil took in a breath. It might have been gruelling, but she *had* saved enough. And not only that, some kind god had doubled her luck. But apparently her daughter had never believed in the Paris trip. It had been Sybil's dream, not Ellie's. A dream that had been tolerated because it was unlikely ever to come true.

'I thought you were just pretending not to be excited,' Sybil explained brokenly. 'You know, so I wouldn't feel so badly if I didn't make enough money for the trip.'

Seeing the hurt look on her mother's face, Ellie tried to soften the blow.

'It would be a waste of money, Mum.'

'But it's *my* money,' Sybil replied. 'Even if it didn't

work out over there, it wouldn't be a waste. Please, Ellie, please give it a try.'

'I've not got any talent.'

'You're beautiful,' Sybil replied, taking her daughter's delicate hand. 'Please, Ellie.'

'You could do so much more with the money.'

'I don't want to do anything else with it.'

'Mum, it's pointless,' Ellie replied, shaking her head. 'I'd just make a fool of myself.'

A sudden thought came into Sybil head. A bribe. 'It's quite a lot of money, Ellie. In fact, we could afford another ticket to Paris.'

'What?'

'We could take someone with us.'

'Have you got a boyfriend?'

Sybil sighed. Delicate as her daughter, she might look as though a feather would bruise her, but she was very determined. Ellie was going to Paris, whatever it took. She stared at the letter in her hand. Two ready-paid train tickets, and hotel accommodation. She thought of the money she had saved, which would no longer be needed to pay travel expenses.

'Why don't we take Faith with us?'

Ellie cheered up immediately, just as her mother had hoped she would. 'Faith?'

'Why not? She's your best friend and I'm sure she'd jump at the opportunity of a lifetime.' Sybil paused, weighing up her proposition. Faith Farnsworth was good-looking, but had no interest in show-business. Then again, she wasn't taking any chances. 'Faith can come with us – but she doesn't come with us to the Moulin Rouge.'

Ellie agreed at once. 'Fine.'

'You have to shine on your own, sweetheart. We don't want anyone stealing your thunder at the eleventh hour.'

Unaware of the good fortune in the Walker house, Faith had spent her first fitful night in David Street. Although James was sleeping on the sofa next door, she felt oddly lonely. Having got used to the accompaniment of Agnes's snoring, and the cramped confines of the camp bed, to have a room of her own was strangely unnerving. Finally, at six, she had risen, gone into the kitchen and made breakfast, then woken James. As usual, he was moody in the mornings, so she ate quickly and then dressed, before turning the City Photographic Studio sign to OPEN and making for the back door.

'I'm off now.'

By this time fully awake, James turned to her. 'Your first day at work. Are you excited?'

She nodded, trying to hold her hands steady.

Seeing her tremble, James put it down to nerves and hugged his sister quickly. 'See you later, all right?'

Nodding, she moved off.

'Oh, Faith . . .'

She turned back. 'What?'

'If anyone says anything to upset you, you send them to me, OK?' James told her. 'Remember that.

You have anyone giving you trouble – send them to me.'

The words were still echoing in her head when Faith reached the door of Laurence Goldbladt's showroom. After knocking, she walked in to find the place empty. Surprised, Faith glanced at her watch, then studied her reflection in the cheval glass. Sid had always told her that Laurence had had the mirror especially made, slightly distorted so that the customer looked a little taller and a little slimmer than they actually were. Faith didn't doubt it as she checked her long black dress with its starched white cuffs and wide collar, well fitted to show off her small waist and narrow back. Corsets, the bane of her life, were a necessary evil, although she often stuffed cotton wool alongside the whalebones to stop them jabbing into her skin. As usual, her hair was drawn back to the nape of her neck, and the only jewellery she wore was a watch, given to her the previous evening by Agnes. Of all people.

'My dear girl,' her aunt had said, taking Faith's hand as someone does when they are relieved to be seeing the last of the other person. 'You start your new life tomorrow and I want to give you something to remember me by.'

'I thought I would call and see you at the weekend, Aunt.'

Agnes didn't want to dwell on that. If she was lucky, she would be accepting Perry's proposal and engaged by Sunday night.

'You know how I want us to stay close,' Agnes had gone on, 'but the days of you living here with me in Gladstone Street are over. So I want you to have this.'

Proudly she had then taken out the watch and fixed it around Faith's wrist. It was a good one. A piece of jewellery Agnes had saved long and hard for, a piece she knew Faith would appreciate. Because despite her criticisms, Agnes had grown fond of her niece, and there had even been a few cosy chats between them. Moments of intimacy, that – surprisingly – had not been forced.

Touched, Faith had looked at the watch and then kissed Agnes on the cheek. 'I'll miss you.'

'And I'll miss you,' Agnes had replied, startled as the words left her mouth.

Faith's mind returned to the present as she pulled her cuff down over the watch. Walking around the showroom, she studied everything, although each object was so familiar to her she could have drawn them from memory. But this was different. This day was the first day of her work life, the first day of her employment. She was Laurence Goldbladt's receptionist, she told herself, remembering how grand it had sounded when she had first told Ellie. In fact she had built it up a little, talked about how thrilling it was going to be living in Manchester with James. She hadn't mentioned any anxiety about the move. After all, she had never told Ellie about Lennie Hellier. And it was too late now.

Hearing a noise outside the door, Faith turned,

startled, a shadow moving behind the glass pane. All thoughts of Ellie disappeared. This was reality, the present. Her confidence splintered. She was suddenly a child again, on the back stairs, Lennie pressing down on her.

'Morning, morning!' Laurence boomed, walking in and looking her up and down. 'You look marvellous! I have the most beautiful receptionist in Manchester.'

Flushing, Faith looked away. But not before she noticed a slight figure hovering by the doorway. Following her glance, Laurence laughed and beckoned for the young man to enter.

'Yes, it's quite a surprise, isn't it?' he said, seeing Faith's shocked expression. 'You know Lennie. This is the same young man we had under our noses all this time. Come in, come in, Lennie,' he called out. 'Come and shake hands with Faith. If I recall, you had a bit of a crush on her once.'

Putting out his hand, Lennie held Faith's gaze. A shirt, a tie, a starched collar and a good haircut had finished the transformation, and he was even walking slowly enough to cover his limp. All Faith's misgivings came back in that moment. She had reasoned with herself that the past was the past. That she could keep all contact with Lennie Hellier to a minimum. That he was in the back rooms, out of her way most of the time. And besides, she was still visualising him as a boy, a lame boy, a bit slow. Not harmless, but not a real threat . . . But now, looking at the polished Lennie Hellier, Faith realised what she was seeing. Not just a man being given a chance, but someone out for advancement. A man who – if he was ever given power – would use it slyly. A man most people would mistakenly underestimate and think harmless – just as she had once done.

Slowly she took his hand, felt his dry palm brush hers, Laurence watching them, then moving away.

'Welcome,' Lennie said simply.

He was confident, flexing his muscles. He knew he had unnerved her and was pleased by the reaction. Who was Faith Farnsworth anyway? he thought. Not out of his league for much longer. Not the adored granddaughter downstairs and the petted visitor in the Goldbladt showroom. No, now she was going to have to earn her living. And she would earn it within his sight and range.

'Looks like we'll be working together,' he went on. 'I hope we can be friends.'

Checking that Laurence couldn't overhear them, Faith leaned slightly towards Lennie. Pleased at her apparent friendliness, he moved towards her to catch her words.

'I haven't forgotten,' Faith said coldly, her hand grasping his tighter for an instant. 'I just want you to know that. And if you ever touch me again, you'll live to regret it.'

CHAPTER FIFTEEN

It was almost four thirty when the doorbell rang up in the Goldbladt showroom. Taking a breath, Faith lifted the heavy Bakelite intercom and said, 'Good afternoon, Laurence Goldbladt's showroom, may I help you?'

'It's me!' Ellie said excitedly. 'I want to ask you something.'

'Can you speak up?' Faith asked, anxious not to be overheard talking to a friend.

'I can't hear you!' Ellie shrieked. 'I'm downstairs, outside the studio. Can you come down?'

Faith could see Laurence's tall figure through the glass partition. 'Ellie, I can't come now,' she whispered.

'Well, when you can. I'll wait.'

Hooking the handset back into its cradle, Faith realised that she was being watched. But not by Laurence; by Lennie Hellier, who was standing by the door of the workroom, fiddling with his starched cuffs. Ignoring him, Faith turned away.

'You shouldn't be chatting to friends,' Lennie

said, trying to suppress his broad accent. 'But I won't tell on you.'

Before she could answer, Laurence walked in, accompanied by a stout woman in an overlarge picture hat. Glancing back to the doorway, Faith saw that Lennie had already disappeared; evaporated in an instant. Unsettled, she turned back to her employer, smiling at his companion. The customer was obviously a friend of Laurence's, a slightly imperious woman who was feeling the heat.

At once Faith offered her a glass of water, the woman holding up her eyeglass to scrutinise her.

'And who are you?'

'This is my receptionist, Miss Faith Farnsworth,' Laurence said, pleased with Faith's solicitous attentions. 'I have high hopes for her.'

'She's a pretty girl,' the woman replied, drinking the water as Laurence jerked his head towards the back room.

Faith picked up her cue fast, moving into the cramped changing area and pulling on an extravagant mink stole. The fur felt hot in the warm afternoon, but it looked luxurious, especially on someone of Faith's height and bearing. Elegantly, she moved back into the showroom, Laurence beaming as he saw her.

'Look at this, Mrs Bell. This is the very latest design from London. And as we know, London has the most excellent furs.'

Holding her eyeglass up again, Mrs Bell studied the mink, grabbing at the stole as Faith passed.

Jerked to a standstill, she paused, watching the woman's plump hands run over the pelt.

'What kind of a stole is that, Mrs Bell? I'll tell you. It's the kind of a stole that tells your husband's clients that he is a man of means. That he is a rich man. You know how it goes, Mrs Bell: the family is the businessman's shop window. Dress your wife in the best and she will advertise your success.'

Turning slowly, Faith walked up and down the showroom, surprised at how comfortable she felt. Although it was warm, she was at ease, and she found smiling and moving in front of an audience – albeit a small one – effortless. Watching her, Laurence realised that he had played a blinder in hiring Faith. Not only did he like the girl, and her family, but she could show off his designs to perfection. Sighing, he leaned against the window ledge and watched his new employee, knowing that he had already made the sale to Mrs Bell. The client would never be as tall, or as young, or as attractive as Faith, but in her mind Mrs Bell believed that in buying the stole she was buying the glamour. That some form of fashion transformation would occur, stretching her from five foot one to five foot seven, and wiping off the decades. She would buy the fur because she would buy hope. And Laurence Goldbladt knew it.

When Mrs Bell left half an hour later, Laurence walked over to Faith and touched her shoulder.

'You did well.'

She smiled, genuinely pleased. 'I didn't look like it was my first day?'

'No,' Laurence replied. 'You looked as though you were born to it.'

Tired of waiting, Ellie was just making her way down the basement steps, the studio bell ringing as she walked in. At once James rose to his feet to greet her, smiling automatically. The light from the basement windows fell on Ellie's hair and bleached it to the colour of autumn leaves, her skin pale as an alabaster bowl. Delicate as a willow, she stood in the dark studio, as James lit the gas lamps and then turned back to her.

'It's getting dark. Probably going to rain.'

Ellie smiled, unnervingly fragile in the gaslight. One of the lamps popped behind them. Surprised, she jumped, then laughed.

'I've come to see Faith. I'm Ellie. Ellie Walker. Don't you remember me?'

'Ellie!' James replied, astonished. He could see hardly anything of his sister's childhood friend in this vision. Having not set eyes on Ellie for three years, James realised that she was no longer a schoolgirl with freckles, but a young woman of sixteen.

Unusually nervous, he stuttered, 'I didn't recognise you, sorry.'

'I've changed.'

'You certainly have,' he agreed, pulling out a chair for her. 'Does Faith know you're here?'

Ellie nodded. 'She said she would be down. It is all right if I wait here?'

He wouldn't have had it any other way. 'Would you like a cup of tea?'

Pleased, Ellie nodded, then watched James as he moved into the kitchen beyond. Goodness, she thought, he had changed too. Not at all the lanky boy she had first met at Gladstone Street. But then again . . . Ellie frowned, trying to work out the mental arithmetic, James must be twenty-one . . . Twenty-one, she mused, his attractiveness growing by the instant. Twenty-one was very mature. Very grown up for a girl of sixteen. Not of course that he would look at a sixteen-year-old. Unless . . .

'Tea,' James said, passing her a cup and sitting down opposite her. Intrigued, he watched her pull off her gloves, not noticing the darn in the thumb, but delighted by the way her small white teeth grasped the forefinger and pulled. Transfixed, James snapped out of his reverie and assumed a professional air.

'So, why are you in Manchester?'

'To do some shopping. And to see Faith,' she replied, smiling sweetly.

'You didn't buy anything?'

'Sorry?'

He looked around her feet for bags. 'You didn't buy anything today?'

'Oh,' she smiled, suddenly understanding him, 'my mother has the bags. She's going to meet up with me at the station. You see . . .' Ellie dropped her voice, James leaning closer to listen. She smelled of cachous. 'We have a surprise for Faith.'

He nodded slowly, still leaning towards her, not wanting to move. Of course she was too young for him. What twenty-one-year-old man courted a sixteen-year-old girl? But then again, how many sixteen-year-old girls looked like this?

'A surprise?' he said at last, noting the fine hairs at her temple, and the hardly discernible freckles under the bloom of her skin. 'What kind of a surprise?'

'Oh, silly!' Ellie replied, laughing, James laughing too without knowing why. 'How could it be a surprise if I told you!'

Leaning back, she sipped at her tea, admiring James over the rim of the cup. All thoughts of Paris had gone from her mind. All thoughts of her mother had gone. All thoughts of Faith had gone. All that was occupying Ellie Walker's head was the handsome man sitting opposite her, with hair the colour of coal and eyes that made you forget your own name.

'Oh, do give over worrying,' Sid said for the hundredth time that evening. 'I've told you, they'll be all right. Faith will have had a good day and James will be hard at work, like he always is.'

'We should have gone in . . .'

'They needed a day to settle in,' Sid replied. 'You have to let them have a little time to adjust.'

'D'you think they slept?'

'Yes, Beryl.'

'I told Faith to air the bed.'

'I'm sure she did.'

'And that couch isn't the most comfortable place for a lad to sleep.'

'I've slept on it once or twice. It's bigger than most beds.'

'You're not over six foot.'

'I'm not twenty-one either,' Sid replied. 'Anyway, we'll hear all about it tomorrow when we go in.'

Beryl turned to her husband, fretful with worry. 'We should have—'

'Beryl, let it go,' Sid replied firmly. 'Our grandchildren can cope. It was Faith's first day working, and James will have had his hands full. I tell you, those kids will be fit for nothing by this time. Fit for nothing.'

In a vague, dreamlike state, Faith ran into the studio, flinging her arms around Ellie's neck and then kissing James on the cheek. 'You should have seen me! I was so confident.' She picked up James's jacket and slung it over one shoulder, walking up and down the studio, the jacket sleeves flying out behind her as she turned. 'I was elegant. Mr Goldbladt said it looked like I'd been doing it all my life.'

'What?' James teased her. 'Acting like a clown?'

Pulling a face, Faith sat down, glancing over to Ellie. 'So what did you want to ask me? I mean, you shouldn't have called on the intercom, I could have been found out. Mr Goldbladt might have caught me. As it was—'

'Oh, be quiet!' Ellie said admonishingly, smiling at James before she turned back to her friend. 'Don't you want to know why I came to see you?'

'Course I do.'

'My mother won a trip to Paris.'

Faith's expression was a study. Ellie threw her head back and laughed. It took her a few moments to compose herself again, her voice light with mischief.

'Can you imagine? All those years of saving up to go to Paris, and then she goes and *wins* a trip there?'

'Paris,' James said, the word conjuring up images of the demi-monde. 'What photographs you could take in Paris.'

'I'm not going to take photographs,' Ellie told him, her voice serious. 'My mother wants me to be a dancer. At the Moulin Rouge.'

James wasn't Tommy Bentley's great-grandson for nothing. Even at twenty-one he knew about the Moulin Rouge. And its reputation.

'You want to be a dancer?'

Ellie paused, suddenly ashamed. The whole scenario had been going on for so long and had seemed so out of reach that she had never really thought about the reality. But the look on James Farnsworth's face said what everyone else would think: it wasn't respectable.

'It's what my mother wants for me.'

'Your *mother*?'

She nodded. 'Mum thinks I'll do well there.'

Faith glanced from Ellie to her brother and then paused. Slowly she looked from one to the other again and realised what she was seeing. No, she thought, it *couldn't* be. But it was. There was a connection between her best friend and her adored Angel James.

'Are you going?' Faith said suddenly. Ellie turned back to her.

'Well, that's what I wanted to talk to you about – we want you to come with us.'

'Like hell,' James said flatly, his infatuation taking second place to his common sense. 'You're not going to the Moulin Rouge!'

'Oh, Faith can't come to the Moulin Rouge. Mother wants us to go there alone,' Ellie said hurriedly. 'But we want her to come to Paris with us.'

'God . . .'

They both looked at Faith.

'So?'

'I . . . I don't . . .'

James interrupted her. 'You're not going!'

'Why not?' Faith replied defiantly. 'It's perfectly respectable.'

'The train fares and the hotel rooms are all booked,' Ellie dived in, passing Faith a sheaf of papers. 'I can show you the information. It's all very nice. Laid on by a firm called Dexter's. You can read it if you want to. Look at the photographs of the hotel: not very big, but it looks nice.'

James's attention was still fixed on his sister. 'You can't go to Paris alone.'

'I won't *be* alone. I'll be with Ellie and Mrs Walker.'

'Three women alone!'

'What about it?' Faith retorted. 'Mrs Walker is a widow, I'm her daughter's best friend. Widows do travel, you know. The world isn't entirely run by men.'

'It wouldn't look right,' James said emphatically. 'The Moulin Rouge! What if anyone saw you? You'd be the talk of the bloody city.'

A quick gasp came from between Ellie's lips and she stood up, blushing as she hurried to the door. Giving her brother a hard look, Faith ran after her, catching up when she reached the corner of David Street.

'Don't mind him,' she told Ellie. 'He's over-protective, that's all.'

'But he's right! People will think it's a disgrace.'

'If you were accepted, you'd be a dancer, Ellie. Nothing else. If people want to talk, let them.'

'But I don't *want* to be a dancer!' she responded, her tone heated, her face flushed. 'Just because my mother used to dance . . .'

Faith raised her eyebrows. 'I didn't know that.'

'She keeps it quiet. She wasn't very successful, thought she should have done better. That's why she wants me to go to work in Paris.' Ellie paused and took in a deep breath. 'Mum thinks that I'll meet some rich man there and make a good marriage.'

The words were out of Faith's mouth before she had time to check them.

'But *she* didn't.'

'That's the point, Mum *had* a chance, and she didn't take it. She came home instead to marry her childhood sweetheart.' Ellie shook her head. 'And after all that, it didn't even work out. Long before my father was killed, my parents had been rowing. Mum doesn't talk about him, because in the end she was relieved he was dead. Not that she'd ever admit it.'

'You never told me about this before.'

Ellie caught her gaze. 'Oh, come on, Faith, everyone has secrets. You know that. And besides, it wasn't something I wanted to brag about.'

Touched, Faith studied Ellie's face and realised how alike the two Walker women were. Perhaps it wasn't so incredible to think of Sybil performing. Both she and Ellie were small-boned, with dancers' long necks and natural poise. But if Sybil had had ability her daughter did not. Any trip to Paris was doomed to failure.

'Tell your mother how you feel,' Faith said gently. 'After all, if you went to the Moulin Rouge and you weren't accepted . . .'

'I don't give a damn about that!' Ellie replied. 'I *want* them to turn me down. I don't want to hang around like a dummy in some stupid costume on some stage, being stared at by strange men.'

'You never thought of saying anything before?'

'But that's the point! All these years of Mum

scrimping and saving . . . well, I never thought the trip would come to anything. I never thought she'd save enough money – never mind win a trip to Paris!'

Putting her arm around Ellie's shoulder, Faith gave her a sympathetic squeeze.

'You should tell her how you feel.'

'And break her heart?' Ellie responded helplessly. After another moment she spoke again. 'I have to go to Paris. But it will only be bearable if you come with us. Please come. Honestly, I couldn't bear to be rejected *and* have to deal with Mum's disappointment on my own.'

'Ellie, I can't . . .'

'You can, you can!' she pleaded. 'You're my best friend. Please help me out here.'

After she had seen Ellie to the tram, Faith retraced her steps to David Street. The air was changing, the softness of late summer fading into a sudden underbelly of cool. She knew that before long the cold would begin, that the long northern winter would set in; the snows made the tram journey from Oldham to Manchester long and uncomfortable. It was all right for her and James, now they lived on the premises, but Faith didn't like to think of her grandparents struggling to work. It was time Sid thought seriously about retiring, and Beryl took some time off. Deep in thought, Faith hurried back down the basement steps. James was standing in the studio waiting for her with his hands on his hips.

'I thought maybe you'd already left for Paris. Where have you been?'

'Walking with Ellie,' Faith replied, shivering and pulling a shawl around her shoulders. 'I think it might be a bad winter, James. I hate to think of our grandparents doing all that travelling in the cold. They should start cutting back on their hours.'

The same thought had occurred to him, but he was still too preoccupied with the trip to change the subject.

'You can't go to France.'

'What?'

'You can't go.'

She shrugged. 'James, don't be a bore. Of course I can go.'

'You're sixteen!'

'But Mrs Walker isn't. Ellie and I would be accompanied by a respectable middle-aged lady. Chaperoned, in fact.'

'Chaperoned to the Moulin Rouge?' he asked drily. 'That woman can't be serious, taking her daughter to work there. I mean, a little thing like Ellie.'

Smiling, Faith held her brother's gaze. 'I thought you'd taken a shine to her.'

'I have not!'

'I think you have,' Faith replied, unable to stop teasing him. 'So what were you two talking about before I arrived?'

'Nothing in particular.'

'*Nothing in particular.*' She mimicked him, her

hands on her hips, then laughed. 'Oh James, she's far too young for you.'

'She's the same age as you!' he replied, then realised what he had said and turned away. 'I'm not interested in Ellie Walker.'

'I can see how uninterested you are,' Faith replied, moving over to her brother and nudging his arm. 'You can't tell Gran, you know that, don't you?'

'I'm not going to say anything about Ellie Walker!'

'Not that! About the trip. I can tell her that I've been invited to Paris by the Walkers, but I can't mention the Moulin Rouge. Gran would have a fit if she knew.'

'You're not going.'

'James,' Faith said curtly, 'this is a big opportunity for me. I might never get out of Manchester again. This might be my only chance to travel – and here you are, trying to stop me going. Why can't I see another country when I have the chance? I could come back with wonderful ideas for your photographs. We could get some new backdrops of the Arc de Triomphe—'

'Oh for God's sake, Faith!' he snapped. 'This has nothing to do with photographs or backdrops. You want to go to France, it's as simple as that.'

'Well, wouldn't you want to go if it was you? Especially if it was with Ellie Walker.' She smiled slyly, teasing him. 'Come on, Angel James, help me with this. If you back me up, Gran will go along with it.'

'What about Grandad?'

'Oh, he listens to Beryl, you know that. If she agrees, he'll follow her lead. Anyway, I think our grandfather would be keen enough to get to Paris himself.' She paused, remembering. 'I told him about Ellie's mother and the Moulin Rouge years ago, and he looked horrified. Then he told me all about Tommy Bentley when he went to Paris.'

James laughed, shaking his head. 'It's the Tommy Bentleys of life I'm worried about.'

Trying to mollify him, Faith was all practicality. 'We'll be perfectly safe! Three women together, how much safer could we be? Ellie showed me the papers and it looks fine. It's a small but respectable hotel and it's only for three days. Come on, James, I want to do this. I *really* do.' She paused, putting her head on one side. 'You're always having fun, so it's time I had an adventure. I want a chance to get out of Manchester for a bit. I want to go somewhere people talk about, a place that's glamorous. I want to see a new country, new people, new ways of life – before I get married and old and dull.' She nudged him playfully with her elbow. 'I'm going to go to France, James. Because if I don't, I might never get the chance again.'

CHAPTER SIXTEEN

To Faith's surprise, Beryl seemed to accept the idea with equanimity.

'Well, why not?' she said blithely. 'Your grandad and me went on a trip to Brussels years ago.'

'You did?' Faith asked, surprised. 'You never said.'

'We didn't like it,' Beryl replied, her tone curt. 'Saved up for ages and we were really disappointed. As for you, I reckon you should go on this trip. Take the opportunity. But I want to know more.'

Thoughtful, she listened as Faith told her about the trip, then she read the information leaflets, clucking her tongue when she saw the hotel room rates. In silence, she then passed the booklets over to Sid, who had just come out of the darkroom. Taking off his rubber gauntlets, he picked up his glasses and read the papers. In the background, putting together a wooden photograph frame, James was pretending not to listen.

'My word,' Sid said finally. 'They've invited you to go with them, love?'

Faith nodded. 'Mrs Walker said—'

'I don't much care what Mrs Walker said,' Beryl interrupted them. 'You can't go taking charity.'

James turned round, watching the exchange.

'It wouldn't be charity,' Faith began. 'Mrs Walker won the trip.'

'She won a trip for *two*,' Beryl replied, 'so she would have to pay extra for you. And that's charity. Charity we don't take from anyone. We never have, and we never will.'

Catching his granddaughter's eye, Sid took off his glasses and stared at his wife. 'We had a good week last week. That extra wedding studio photograph was a real turn-up. And they had prints done.'

'God knows why,' Beryl replied shortly. 'That was the ugliest bride I ever saw.'

'The point I'm making—'

'Is obvious,' Beryl finished for him. 'That we have a bit more cash in the kitty than we thought, and that we could put some money towards Faith's trip.'

'I would work for you, do errands, anything I could for free. I could pay you back that way,' Faith replied, eager to win her grandmother over. 'And Mr Goldbladt said that he was going away soon and would pay me a bit more for longer hours.'

'I daresay that big oaf will be away more and more now he's got you working for him,' Beryl responded, turning back to the leaflets. 'Paris. France . . . It's a long way away.'

'Only across the English Channel.'

'Aye, but it's a long way from Manchester to the Channel.'

'We go by train,' Faith went on, repeating what she had been told. 'Then catch a ferry at Dover.'

'I get sick on boats,' Sid said suddenly, everyone turning to him. 'Well, I can't go on the park lake any more. You may laugh, James, but when I last went on it I was violently ill.'

'That was because you'd had too much ice cream in the refreshment tent,' Beryl reminded him, turning back to her grandchildren. 'There was a concert on, some orchestra in the bandstand. It was a lovely day – until your grandfather got overheated and ate nearly a gallon of ice cream. Which, I might add, was chocolate flavoured. I warned him at the time, but would he listen? No, just like he is now. A law to himself.'

Exchanging a glance, James smiled at Faith as Beryl tapped her husband on the back of his hand. 'How many prints did that ugly bride order?'

'Four.'

'Four,' Beryl repeated, impressed. 'Four prints, frames and a studio study. More money than we expected this week, and that's a fact.' Pausing for effect, she turned to James. 'So, what d'you think about this trip to Paris?'

Faith's mouth fell open, her eyes imploring her brother to back her.

'Well . . .' James began, pretending to consider the matter. 'It would be educational.'

'Educational – is that what they call it now?'

Beryl teased him, turning back to her grand-daughter. 'Mrs Walker is a widow, isn't she?'

Faith nodded.

'I suppose the poor lady has to work?'

Again Faith nodded. 'She works in a milliner's.'

'At least she'll have a nice hat for the trip,' Beryl replied, James avoiding Faith's gaze and the subject of Sybil Walker's show-business past. 'I suppose you'll be safe enough. But no going out at night, unless you're with Mrs Walker. And no playing her up either. I know what you can be like sometimes, Faith. You have to promise to behave or you'll not be going.'

'I promise,' Faith said honestly. 'So, can I go?'

'Well, it's the chance of a lifetime, a trip to France,' her grandmother replied. 'If you don't go, you'll live to regret it.'

It was Perry Braithwaite who was most against the trip, remonstrating with Agnes about how three women should not go abroad alone. Agnes, not caring if the three women in question were moving permanently to Egypt, nodded, then tried to change the subject.

'We could go for a walk . . .'

It was the first of October, she realised. Time for Perry Braithwaite's winter coat to go on. Regular as clockwork. She liked that in a man.

'My dear, do you know that they have been in the paper?'

Agnes sighed. She had seen the *Oldham Chronicle*

article and the accompanying photograph but had hidden them before Perry had arrived. Under the caption LOCAL WIDOW WINS PARIS TRIP, there was a picture of the two delicate Walker women, Faith tall and dark beside them. All of them smiling, radiant. The piece went on to say:

> A widow who works for a local Oldham milliner's was the lucky winner of a prize trip to Paris, all expenses paid. She is taking her daughter, Miss Eleanor Walker, and their family friend, Miss Faith Farnsworth, of David Street, Manchester. Readers will be familiar with Faith's family, the Bentleys, as they have the City Photographic Studio, and her grandparents are long-time residents of Hardy Street, Oldham.

'There wasn't a word about you, my dear,' Perry replied, bringing Agnes's attention back to him.

'I don't mind,' she said, more patiently than she felt.

The weeks had passed and Perry Braithwaite, although a more frequent visitor, had yet to nail his matrimonial colours to Agnes's mast. What the hell was holding him back? she had wondered repeatedly. There was no excuse any more. Her niece and nephew had left Gladstone Street, so what was the problem? As time had gone on, and Perry had become no more forthcoming, Agnes had begun to feel a clammy unease – which was not helped by her mother's constant enquiries into her romantic life. Just how long Agnes was expected to wait for Perry to speak out – let alone disguise her grey hair – was becoming irksome to her.

Bored to the back teeth of the whole Paris trip, she said crisply, 'Could we go for a walk now?'

But Perry had spotted the half-hidden newspaper and reached for it, looking at the piece again. 'I must say that Faith has changed a great deal since she first lived here with you, my dear.'

Agnes saw her chance and grabbed it. 'Luckily time has moved on and she now has her own life.'

'But I feel you might have objected to her going abroad.'

At that precise moment, Agnes wouldn't have objected if Faith had emigrated.

'As I say, she's grown up now. She might only be sixteen, but she looks and acts very mature.' Sliding on to the kitchen couch beside Perry, Agnes took hold of the edge of the paper, her tone skittish. 'Do stop reading, my dear.'

He paused, looking at her. For a moment Agnes thought he might kiss her – but Perry had other things on his mind.

'They could have taken you with them.'

'What?'

'It would have been nice for you, my dear.'

'Nice for me!' she hissed between clenched teeth.

'Yes, it would have been a change of air.'

Agnes's eyes blazed, her patience snapping like an

overstretched garter. 'So you want to get rid of me, do you!'

Blinking, he leaned away from her. 'I didn't mean that.'

But Agnes was irritated and determined not to be placated. 'I don't want to go on a holiday!'

'My dear . . .'

'I don't want a change of air!'

'My dear Agnes . . .'

'I don't want to go to blasted Paris! I want,' she said angrily, poking Perry in the lapel, 'to go out for a walk.'

Stunned, Perry stared at her. Well, this was a turn-up, he thought. Agnes had been so good-natured and amusing before, and yet here she was, angry. Very angry indeed. Almost fiery . . . Picking up his coat, Perry stared at this new, sparky Agnes – who was suddenly wondering if she had ruined her chances once and for all.

'Well, goodness me . . .'

Her voice faltered. 'Perry, I . . .'

'Yes, goodness me,' he repeated, flushing with animation, then suddenly offered her his arm. 'You *can* be a little exuberant, and no mistake.'

By the time they arrived in Dover, Faith was very excited. Both Ellie and her mother were seasick, however, and any attempts by Faith to lighten the mood were repulsed. Finally she escaped to the top deck. Her own stomach was rolling, but she had to get some air. On deck, she wandered round watching the other passengers: a woman with twins, and a couple sitting together, oblivious to everything. The wind was pretty high, and Faith held on to her hat as she circled the top deck, her skirt flipping up around her calves. As she smoothed it down with her hands, her hat blew off, tumbling like an acrobat as she ran after it. Finally, out of breath, she caught it against the railings, her gaze moving towards the horizon and far-off France.

Although she had been keen to go on the trip from the first, Faith had found herself enthralled by the whole journey. Even the dirty extended train haul to London; the change for the next leg of the trip; and the cramped confines of the boarding ramp had not dented her enthusiasm. And when the ferry left the English coast, she felt a surge of something close to euphoria. This was an adventure, she told herself. A real adventure. The first time she had been away from home – although from the look of Ellie and Sybil, they would not be joining her on the deck any time soon. Breathing in the ozone-filled air, Faith put her head back and let the October breeze flush her skin. She fantasised suddenly that she was a woman with a past, on her way to meet her lover. Then she imagined herself older, rich, able to go anywhere in the world, whenever she chose.

Free from the confines of an industrial city, her spirits soared. Under a high, wide sky she forgot the cramped streets of Oldham and the Goldbladt studio. Out on the English Channel, Lennie Hellier seemed insignificant. In fact, everything seemed insignificant. Faith was feeling young, healthy, her life open, full of promise. She stayed on the top deck for another half an hour, then moved back to the cabin, where Ellie was being sick into a bowl.

'Oh God, I want to go home,' she moaned.

Sybil lay on the bed beside her daughter with her eyes closed.

'Stop moaning.'

'I can't stop moaning!' Ellie retorted. 'I can't stop being sick!'

Taking her hand, Faith sat down beside the bed. 'It won't be long now. Only about another half an hour.'

'God . . .'

'It will be worth it,' Faith went on. 'Think about it – tonight we'll be in Paris.'

'I don't care,' Ellie replied. 'I don't care if Paris sinks into the sea.'

Rolling her head very gently, Sybil looked at her daughter. 'This could be your big break.'

'If I live long enough,' Ellie replied, throwing up again.

But by the time they had reached the hotel, booked in, eaten a light supper and had a good night's sleep, Paris seemed suddenly to come into her own. Back to normal, Sybil bought a street map and then walked the girls over to the Moulin Rouge, standing outside on the pavement and looking at the gaudy exterior. Her eyes wide, Faith stared at the edifice and at the men who were just walking out. Men who looked all three Englishwomen up and down.

Uncomfortable, Faith hung back. 'I should wait for you here.'

Sybil, having finally reached her place of pilgrimage, seemed overawed. 'It's . . . it's . . .'

'Mum, let's not go in,' Ellie said, grabbing Sybil's arm.

'Not go in?' she replied. 'Are you crazy? After all these years, we're finally here – and you ask me that?' Annoyed, she glanced over to Faith, taking in the girl's good looks and height and reminding herself that she could be a real threat to Ellie. 'Will you wait for us outside, dear?'

Faith was all for that. 'Oh, yes.'

'You could wait in that little café over there,' Sybil volunteered, pointing to a small place where a gaggle of other women were sitting talking. 'It looks very safe, very respectable. We won't be long. You know how to ask for a cup of tea, don't you?'

Faith nodded, having been primed for the occasion.

'Good girl,' Sybil replied, taking in a long, slow breath. In fact, everything about her seemed to slow down. Her actions, her movements. Like someone gesturing underwater, Sybil Walker took her daughter's arm. 'Well, this is it.'

'I know, Mum.'

'You're beautiful,' Sybil said proudly. As Faith watched her, she realised that she was witnessing Sybil's dream becoming reality. Her hard work, the years of planning, had come finally to their fruition, and it was almost overwhelming her. 'You do your best, Ellie, you hear me? You just show them how lovely you are.'

'I know, Mum.'

'If I had had this chance . . .'

'But you can dance, Mum.'

'But *you* are beautiful, Eleanor,' Sybil said tenderly. Then she paused, smiled at Faith, and propelled her reluctant daughter towards the lurid entrance of the Moulin Rouge.

For the first ten minutes Faith wandered up the street, looking in shop windows, then she doubled back and entered the café, taking a seat by the door. Having perfected *A cup of tea, please* in French, she ordered and then glanced around at the customers. To her surprise they were an oddly assorted bunch of matrons, old men – and, at the back of the café, a few attractive women in make-up, their theatrical costumes mostly hidden under their coats. Obviously dancers dropping in for a coffee at the nearest café. The effect of the stage make-up in the daylight and their flirtatious glances at the waiter made Faith wonder how Ellie – if she was ever to work at the Moulin Rouge – would fit in . . . Over the previous week, Faith had watched the sweet tenderness between her brother and Ellie Walker; their attraction obvious, their love affectionate and teasing. But under all the playfulness there was a depth to their relationship. Oh, Ellie might be very young, but she was also very much in love with James. As for James, he was devoted, anyone could see that. Faith glanced at the dancers again, noticing how blatant they were in speech and manner. How louche. How unlike Ellie. Then her attention was taken by a man entering from the back of the café. A heavily built man with a large gold signet ring and slicked-back hair, who made a beeline for the girls and sat down between them, looping his arms around their shoulders. Faith glanced away, anxious not to be seen staring, but thinking of dainty little Ellie sitting with a man like that . . .

As though he knew she was watching, the man glanced over to Faith, and for an instant she saw the coarseness in his face – and something else. A memory of a hungry look she had seen before. In Lenny Hellier's eyes.

CHAPTER SEVENTEEN

Preoccupied, Laurence Goldbladt signalled to Lennie, beckoning for him to approach. 'I need some samples. Get me the ones from the back. The chinchilla.'

Nodding, Lennie moved into the workshop, his gaze coming to rest on the furs hung up in rows. Slowly he moved along the first row, then the next, thinking of what Laurence had said the previous day. It had been a chance remark, but one Lennie had caught. And treasured. An old customer had come to see Laurence, and the new designs for the autumn. They seemed to have known each other for a long time and laughed frequently, the visitor well dressed, with a diamond tie pin. Lennie liked the tie pin, thought it gave the man a worldly air. Thought that, in time, he might like to wear one. Well why not? Wasn't he being groomed for better things? Perhaps, in time, to manage the Goldbladt showroom? And a man with such responsibilities could carry off a diamond tie pin.

Still thinking of the pin, Lennie remembered the

conversation he had then heard. Or rather, overheard.

'Oh, that's Lennie. A good help to me. I'm training him up.'

The man had replied with a laugh. 'For what, Laurence?'

'You'll see. I have a splendid girl in my employment, and now Lennie . . . You'll see, I have plans for them. In fact my receptionist, Miss Farnsworth, is at present in Paris, looking at the new fashions for me . . .'

The words had punched into Lennie's subconscious and made an imprint that was permanent. Lennie was being groomed. Laurence also had 'a splendid girl . . . You'll see, I have plans for them . . .' *I have plans for them.* Biting his fist, Lennie fought a desire to laugh. His world – which had been so bleak and ugly – was being transformed. Not only was he being trained in the business, but – could he believe it? – he was being groomed as a future partner for Faith. And if so, a future heir for the Goldbladt business. God was being kind to him at last. All the years of grubbing about, of being a lame outcast, were over. His star was finally in the ascendant. And when he rose, he would rise with Faith.

Still staring at the furs, Lennie tried to remain calm. His desire overrode his common sense, and within twenty-four hours a chance remark had become a prediction. Faith was to be his. The business was to be his. All he had to do was work hard and wait. But then the true nature of Lennie Hellier stepped forward. He had been almost feral, turned out to fend for himself, and the terror of those years had left an indelible mark on him. His luck was turning – but for how long? How long before it turned again? Maybe went bad? The thought was undermining, shattering, and Lennie realised then that he had to protect himself. That he had to take steps to prevent his destiny being threatened. It was all right trusting to fate and man's kindness, but unless Lennie had some hold on Laurence Goldbladt he could end up back on the streets. Without work, without a roof over his head. Without power. Without Faith.

'Lennie!' Laurence bellowed from the showroom. 'Bring that chinchilla in now, will you?'

Grabbing the chinchilla, he hurried out with it, passing it to Laurence and then standing waiting for his next order. The man's wife was a small woman, but when Laurence draped her in the fur she glowed, turning from a stout matron into a strutting courtesan. Proudly her husband watched her, the woman glowing like a twenty-year-old.

And whilst he watched the customer, Lennie Hellier thought about the times Laurence had passed off rabbit as chinchilla, and musquash as mink. About the hard cases who brought in the furs: men who came from Russia and the northern territories; formidable men who had come over on ships, ready to trade. Men who Laurence did business with, but was wary of. It occurred to

Lennie in that moment that it would be very dangerous if any of the traders knew they were being cheated. Of course, they did enough cheating themselves, but if they discovered that Laurence Goldbladt was making an extra profit whilst they worked the ice flows and Canadian fur traps . . .

'Sorry,' Laurence said, turning to see Lennie waiting for him. 'I forgot you were standing there.' He patted the young man affectionately on the shoulder. 'You're a good help to me, Lennie. I don't know what I would do without you. God knows, a man needs to know that he has someone around he can trust.'

Smiling, Lennie nodded his thanks. 'I like working for you.'

'And you're good for the business,' Laurence replied. 'Honest to God, you sound more posh than I am now. As for your appearance – I always said clothes can make a man. But then again, some men can't wear them well. You can, Lennie. You're like Faith in that.'

Lennie could feel his heart speed up. 'She comes back from Paris today.'

'With news of all the fashions, I hope,' Laurence replied, picking up the chinchilla and looking at it closely. 'Was this the Canadian fur?'

'Russian.'

'I thought so,' Laurence said, 'thicker fur. Better quality.'

'Faith will model it very well.'

Nodding, Laurence glanced back to Lennie. He

knew that the young man had a crush on Faith, but what harm could it do? Lennie might stand watching Faith with rapt admiration, but she was a pretty woman, she was bound to attract interest. Besides, Laurence thought, it was a good thing for the business. With Faith around, Lennie would want to work at his job even harder, his loyalty unquestioned. He wouldn't want to be fired, unable to see Faith any more. Without appearing to do so, Laurence studied his protégé and wondered how Lennie would take it when Faith began courting. It would be a hard blow, but then again, Faith Farnsworth would make someone a fine wife. As for Lennie, he wasn't husband material. Not the kind of man any girl dreamed of. If he married at all, Lennie would be lucky to land one of the seamstresses. One of the plainer girls he could control. Because there was something of the bully about Lennie Hellier. It had never been expressed, but Laurence was sure it was a part of his nature.

Still, Laurence decided, he had made an excellent choice professionally. Lennie was learning fast and now possessed the demeanour of a civil servant in his dark suit and stiff collar. As for the bundle of a bed he had once had, that had gone. Now Lennie slept on a cot in the workroom, with a new blanket and a bolster for his head. Laurence knew that the seamstresses laughed at Lennie, and that some thought he had risen above his station. Too far, too fast. Lucky for him he had saved Mr Goldbladt from that dog, they said. Wouldn't put it past

Hellier to have planted the animal there himself, someone else replied bitterly. But Laurence wasn't concerned. Lennie had taken the opportunity he had been given and was making the best of it. On such promising beginnings good futures were built.

'Is there anything else, sir?'

Laurence shook his head. 'Not tonight, Lennie. You can go now. Oh, there is one more thing . . .'

'Yes, sir?'

'When you see Miss Farnsworth in the morning, tell her I want a word, will you?'

Lennie nodded, his tone even, controlled. 'Of course. It will be a pleasure.'

Waiting in the studio, James gestured to his grandparents to hide with him as the sound of footsteps came down the basement steps. After a moment, the key turned in the lock and Faith walked in. Surprised, she paused in the doorway, putting down her case and taking off her hat and coat.

'Hello?'

Silence.

'Hello? Is there anyone there?' Sighing, she moved towards the kitchen, disappointed that there was no one to greet her and hear her news. Then, just as she reached the door, James caught her hand. 'Oh my God!' she exclaimed, punching his arm and then kissing her grandparents. 'I thought there was no one here.'

'We waited, thought we'd get the late tram home

so we'd see you when you got back,' Beryl replied, putting on the kettle and then coming back to her granddaughter. 'So, what was it like?'

'Busy, full of people. Women dressed so well. Long, full skirts, not like ours, loads of material, and the hats . . .' Faith rolled her eyes. 'And not one pair of laced-up boots. They were all button-up, and I even saw a red pair.' She hurried over to her suitcase, opened it and passed Beryl some chocolates, Sid some tobacco and James a set of postcard views. 'I couldn't afford much, but I wanted you all to have a memento.'

'You didn't have to do that, love,' Beryl replied, secretly delighted by her gift. Moving off, she made the tea and then brought it back to the table.

'Did you get to see any of the sights?' Sid asked, winking. Faith knew immediately that he was referring to the Moulin Rouge.

'Oh yes, *all* the sights.'

'What about Ellie?' James asked, dying to question his sister alone and knowing that he would have to wait.

If the truth be told, he was annoyed about the whole matter of Eleanor Walker. Annoyed that a sixteen year old scrap of pale, ethereal beauty had press-ganged his dreams. He was infuriated that he was so interested in her. She was too young for him, too light, too silly in a way. After all, to make a career out of being a dancer, in Paris of all places! But then James corrected himself. It wasn't Ellie who wanted to be a dancer, it was her mother's wish. And that was something completely different. In fact, he believed that Ellie – left alone – would simply carry on working at the bakery in Oldham.

Of course he wouldn't tell anyone about what he had done on his day off. It would seem too ridiculous, even to Faith, his usual confidante. In secret, he had caught the tram over to Oldham and walked up Park Road, turning into Bailey Street and then pausing outside the bakery, Pilstone's. There had been a small queue of men waiting for their dinner. Hot meat pies and home-made gravy, poured out of an enamel jug. Good value for money, considering that Mrs Pilstone made the pies on the premises, and the gravy. A hearty woman, she worked from four in the morning getting the dinners ready for her regulars, while in the back of the shop her husband baked the bread the housewives would buy later. Big hunks of crusty loaves, brown-topped in their tins, the smell drifting through the smoky Oldham air. No one went short. If a regular customer hadn't got his wages, Mrs Pilstone sold him a pie with a broken crust, cheap. And no gravy. The working men knew she was a fair woman and when they were flush they would buy pies to take home after work. Sometimes even a rabbit stew if it was the weekend. Big pitmen, carters and navvies would come to Bailey Street, and if they were working too far away the youngest of the Pilstone boys, Derek, would take the food over on his bike.

James was thinking about this as he stood watching the shop – and the motherly Mrs Pilstone.

He was trying to imagine how pretty Ellie would look behind the counter, her apron dusted with flour, her reddish hair piled on top of her head. Would the working men tease her? Try and make a play for her? The thought rocked James – then he remembered the four Pilstone sons, all except Derek over seventeen. They would surely be interested in the delicate girl working for their parents. What a pretty morsel to have at their fingertips . . . The jealousy caught James off guard. He had never been prone to envy before, but now he was feeling the creeping unease that had unmanned many people.

He would have to get over it, he told himself, suddenly realising that Faith was looking at him expectantly.

'James? Gran and Grandad are off home now.'

He smiled, got to his feet. 'See you in the morning then.'

Nodding, Sid helped Beryl on with her coat, Faith walking to the door with them. At the bottom of the basement steps, Beryl turned.

'I'm glad you went abroad, Faith. It looks like it's done you good. You have to take opportunities in life. You never know if they'll come along again.'

'I enjoyed it,' Faith admitted. 'See you tomorrow.'

'See you tomorrow, love,' her grandparents chorused.

As Faith walked back into the studio, James grabbed her arm.

'So?'

'So what?'

'So what happened?'

'We had a lovely trip,' she teased him. 'And you could have taken some wonderful photographs.'

'I mean what happened with Ellie? Did she go to the Moulin Rouge?'

'Oh yes.'

'And?'

'She didn't get in. They said—'

'She was no good?'

'That she was a bad dancer and a lousy singer, but that she was very beautiful on stage.'

James didn't like that. 'But they didn't take her on?'

'They told her to come back in eighteen months' time. When she's eighteen. They said they would reconsider her then.'

'Good God!' James exploded. 'She can't go back.'

'Well actually she can,' Faith replied, taking her bag into the bedroom and putting it on the bed. 'Sybil was disappointed at first, but when she realised they were asking her to go back, she was over the moon.'

James walked to the door and leaned against it, watching his sister unpack. 'You didn't go with them?'

'No, I was a very good girl and stayed outside, having a cup of tea in a café. Very English of me,' she said mockingly. 'Ellie was surprised, I can tell you that. She wasn't thrilled about the whole Moulin Rouge thing, but after she saw the place and talked to them . . . I think she might have a go.' Faith paused, thinking of her own reservations in the café, but although she might be uncertain, she had decided that she had no right to interfere in her best friend's decision.

'It's immoral.'

'Oh, James, since when have you been a prude?' Faith asked, laughing, then pausing as she caught the look on her brother's face. 'Are you all right? I mean . . . Oh my Lord, you're *really* keen on Ellie, aren't you?'

He hung his head, mortally embarrassed. 'I never noticed her before. I know she came to Gladstone Street a few times, but Agnes didn't care for her, so I never got a chance to talk to her. Besides, she was a kid.'

'But not so much a kid now?' Faith ventured.

'No, not so much a kid now,' James replied, sitting down at the bottom of the bed.

'I'd already guessed about you two.'

'You had?'

Faith laughed. 'Well, Ellie stares at you like she can't drag her eyes away. And you stare at her as though looking away might kill you.'

'I thought we were hiding it.'

'Only from the blind,' Faith replied, putting her head on her brother's shoulder. 'Ellie's very young.'

'I know that.'

'So are you.'

'Hark at you! Hardly Methuselah yourself, are you?'

Sighing, Faith sat up again. 'You'll get over it. You're always going out with different girls.'

'I don't want to go out with anyone else. I want to get to know Ellie Walker,' he said, his tone serious. 'I really have taken a fancy to her. I can't stop thinking about her, and, well, she's a respectable girl from a respectable home – if I can get all thoughts of the Moulin Rouge out of her mind.'

Faith raised her eyebrows. 'You sound like you're going to marry her.'

'I could do worse. Well, I think I could. I need to take her out properly, get to see what she's really like.'

Stunned, Faith tried to sound noncommittal. 'It would be a good idea. I mean, Ellie might not be thinking of even getting a serious boyfriend.'

'Has she got someone?'

'No. I just mean, well, she's young . . .'

'Our grandparents were married when Beryl was only eighteen.'

Making a low whistle, Faith frowned. She had seen the attraction between the two of them, and Ellie had asked a lot of questions about James whilst they had been away. But talk of marriage! For a guilty instant Faith felt a twinge of envy. It would be hard to think of anyone else coming first with Angel James. After all, he had been her protector and champion all her life. How would she take to having her place usurped? Ashamed at the thought, Faith tried to make light of the situation, but the die was cast. One day – whether it be Ellie or another woman – James would marry. Which was exactly what he should do, Faith realised. So why didn't she feel better about it?

'What did her father do for a living?'

'Huh?'

'Ellie's father, what did he do for a living?'

'He was a bookkeeper.'

'Good job,' James replied, nodding. 'And Ellie has a job at Pilstone's, which is nice enough.'

'You *are* interested, aren't you?' Faith replied, trying to keep her voice cheerful.

'Oh yes, I'm interested. But I have to get to know her first. Have to really get to know her, see if she's the right one.' He turned to his sister, holding her gaze. 'Will you help me?'

She wanted to say no. No, I won't help you. I'll tell Ellie that you're a pig, a selfish, womanising pig like Tommy Bentley. I'll tell her that you have a dozen girls on a string and that she shouldn't go near you unless she wants to have her heart broken. I'll tell her that she could do better for herself, that she should reject you out of hand . . . But Faith knew she wouldn't, because she loved her brother. And if loving him meant that she would lose him, so be it. She really had no choice.

'Yeah, I'll help you with Ellie.'

'Put in a good word for me?'

'Put in several.'

He kissed her cheek. 'You really are the best sister in the world, you know. And one day I'll do the same for you.'

CHAPTER EIGHTEEN

1908

Peter Dodds's dreams of a future on the stage had come to nothing. He wasn't even asked back for review, like Ellie. Instead, after a long year's trying, he realised that he was never going to be Rudolph Valentino, and that he had better follow an ambition that was easier to achieve. So his father told Mort Ruben on a visit to the latter's showroom. It had been a long, warm summer, and now the autumn had arrived the city was balmy, dusty shadows falling along Deansgate and hitting the spire of St Anne's church. In Mort's eyrie of an office, Desmond Dodds looked around at the drawings of the new women's fashions. Very Ziegfeld, he thought, not without a trace of alarm. The suffragettes were to blame, of course; once you gave women their heads there would be no stopping them.

'Peter needs another job, Mort,' Desmond went on, pulling his gaze away from the advertisement for Pears soap on the wall opposite. 'The lad's settled down. He's twenty-four now, and not a child. He's ready to make a trade in the city.'

'I have nothing to offer,' Mort replied. 'Well, nothing permanent.' It was true. Mort's business was run on a shoestring. He hired help when he needed it, like his accountant, twice yearly, and he answered the door to his clients himself. There was nothing left over to support another employee. 'Have you asked Laurence Goldbladt?'

'He's not looking for anyone either,' Desmond replied. 'What about the studio in the basement? Are they hiring?'

'My, my, I thought Peter wanted to work in the rag trade?'

'Well, beggars can't be choosers,' his father replied. 'Besides, photography is an up-and-coming business. What about it? Are they looking for help?'

'Well, actually . . .' Mort dropped his voice, although no one could hear their conversation over the buzz of sewing machines in the workshop outside. 'Poor Sidney Bentley's not well. Been poorly for a while, and I know his wife wants a bit more time to look after him. She looked exhausted the other day, dear soul, but she wouldn't complain. Just said that Sid needed nursing.'

'So?'

Mort hadn't finished. 'I asked why she didn't let Faith – you remember her granddaughter? – look after Sid. But Beryl said it was a wife's duty.' His eyes watered with sympathy. 'Between you and me, Faith needs to keep bringing in her wage from

Laurence or the family would be really struggling.'

Desmond stared hard at his friend. 'So, where does this leave Peter?'

'James is running the studio now – most of the time since his grandad's been taken bad. But although he's a wonderful young man, and very conscientious, he's not a good photographer.' Mort leaned towards Desmond confidentially. 'And I happen to remember that your Peter has a real liking for photography.'

'It's a hobby of his, yes.'

'So you see where I'm heading, Desmond?' Mort went on, his eyebrows raised. 'Why shouldn't a hobby become a job? Beryl will need time off to look after Sid, Faith already has a job, and James certainly can't manage the studio premises on his own. He can do the general running and the accounts – no one better – but as for the picture-taking . . . Well, he's not that good.' Mort sighed, as though he was mortally sorry to have to be honest. 'Not bad, but not good. Not Tommy Bentley, not Sidney. Nothing like them.'

'Ah,' said Desmond. 'So they could do with our Peter?'

Mort nodded. 'But another thing.' He looked around as though to make sure that no one could overhear their conversation. 'There's not a lot of money to throw around downstairs. Sid's had to have the doctor, and what with one thing and another, well . . . They'd pay a wage, but it'd not be much.'

Desmond wasn't too concerned about the salary. He just wanted his feckless son to be nailed down into a regular job. And a job in the City Photographic Studio might be just the ticket. It would keep Peter occupied, and give him less time to brood about his artistic failure. In fact, it was just what his son needed.

'He'll take it.'

Mort raised his eyebrows again. 'Oh, I can't settle it with you! You have to have a word with James. But if you go downstairs now, I think you can catch him.'

James was, at that moment, struggling with a tray of chemicals. Being a good deal taller than his great-grandfather and his grandfather, he found the darkroom cramped to the point of claustrophobic. Turning round, he knocked off another tray of rinsing chemical and swore violently. Mort's timid voice came softly through the door.

'Are you in there, James?'

'I am. Wait a minute, Mr Ruben, will you?' James answered as patiently as he could.

Hung on a clothes line above him to dry, several developing prints wiped themselves on the top of James's hair as he turned, pulling off his gauntlets, and squeezed himself out of the narrow doorway. Once outside, he sighed and pulled on his jacket.

'It's like working in a bloody rabbit warren,' he said without preamble.

Mort smiled sympathetically. 'You need help.'

'I certainly do,' James agreed, looking around. 'I

never realised how much it took to run this studio *and* develop the photographs. And to be honest, I don't think the ones I took yesterday will be up to scratch. God, and if the customer doesn't pay me, we're sunk.'

He thought back to the engaged couple who had booked a session at the studio. Explaining that Sid was not available, James had reassured them that he could take the photograph. But when he had found himself under the black hood of the camera, looking at the couple's reversed image, he had done as he always did. He panicked. Nothing made sense to James upside down. He couldn't imagine their expressions the right way round, and the man's repeated enquiries were grating on him.

'Do we smile?'

'Please, sir, stand still.'

'Do we smile now?'

'Stand still! Please . . .'

Finally James had taken the photograph, but he was certain the woman had moved at the last moment – and equally certain that her image would be little more than sepia candyfloss.

'Jesus,' James said, sitting down. 'I'm not cut out for this taking photographs lark.'

'You remember Peter? Peter Dodds?'

James looked up. 'Oh yes, I remember him. He liked Faith, didn't he? Worked for you for a while.'

Smiling, Mort took a seat. 'I have his father outside.'

'Oh God, not for a photograph.'

'No, he's desperate for Peter to find a job. And if you recall, his son was always good with a camera. Took lots of pictures of the theatre.'

'Oh yeah, he used to bore Faith with them,' James replied, hope dawning. 'You mean . . . ?'

Mort nodded. 'Yes, why don't you hire Peter Dodds? You know him, and I know for a fact that his father's keen for him to have a decent job. You won't have to pay a big wage; Desmond's not short of money, but he *is* short of patience – and he wants his son employed. And you,' Mort said, twinkling with the pleasure of his plan, 'need someone to take the photographs until your grandfather comes back.'

Neither of them wondered aloud *if* Sid would come back. He had longed for his retirement, but being ill hadn't been the way he had pictured it. Maybe he would be too sick to return, too worn down to do the commuting. But then again, no one wanted to think of that. So in the meantime, the solution was in front of them.

'Peter Dodds,' James said thoughtfully. 'Thanks, Mort, I owe you.'

Fiddling with her hair nervously, Ellie sat down on the tram next to James. Both of them were anxious and lost for words, as James suddenly reached out and took Ellie's hand. For a second she wanted to resist, but she didn't, and instead found the action oddly comforting. Ellie was always nervous around boys, her mother having indoctrinated her with stories of men being only out for one thing. Apparently if they got that one thing, the inevitable would happen; *You'll be ruined, your chances over. You never trust a man, you hear me, Ellie? Never trust a man.* So Ellie had grown up keeping her distance from males, terrified of sex and any intimacy. Having no father or brothers around, she had become timid in male company. Her prettiness attracted men, but her diffidence kept her removed. Until she met James.

Ellie knew he had a reputation and had been out with a number of girls, but there had been no unpleasant rumours about James Farnsworth, no grubby secrets. And the fact that he was so attractive made Ellie feel even more special in his company. He had chosen to go out with her . . . But then another thought followed: what would he expect from her? How could she hold his attention? How could she, Ellie Walker, live up to James Farnsworth?

Suddenly James squeezed her hand. 'Are you all right?'

She nodded.

'You seem quiet,' he said.

They got off the tram at the next stop. On the empty street they stood together, James pinching Ellie's cheek. 'You are the prettiest little thing I've ever seen . . .'

She smiled awkwardly.

'And I want to get to know you, Ellie. I mean *properly* get to know you. I've made up my mind, and now I mean to make it my duty to find out about you,' he went on, looking into her eyes, which were suddenly moist with tears. 'What's the matter?'

'I don't know,' she stammered. 'I don't know much about boys. I'm not . . . I'm not . . .'

'You're perfect,' James replied, his protective streak clicking into action as he threaded his arm through hers. 'We'll just take this nice and slow, shall we? See how we get to like each other? No rushing about; just be friends first and then see how we go. How's that?'

Her heart shifted. He had read her mind! Reassured her, made her feel safe. Made her feel that her mother might be wrong – that perhaps there was *one* man who could be trusted.

Approaching eighteen, Faith had spent the previous year and a half learning everything she could about the business. Diligent and careful, she had been promoted, her duties increased. Nothing too taxing, but she modelled when needed, tidied up when required, and was courteous to the customers. With her looks and poise, Laurence found the business attracting more custom. Existing clients, having been given an honest opinion by Faith, sent their friends. Before long Laurence had shortened his hours, so that he could take off three days a week, as he had planned. He left the Goldbladt showroom in safe hands, he told Miriam: there were no worries with Faith, and she always had Lennie to fall back on.

And as he watched her rise in status, Lennie Hellier rose also. But although his plan for advancement was working out entirely to his satisfaction, he found Faith dismissive to the point of rudeness. Any attempt to be polite was met with frigid indifference. His offers of getting her lunch or making her a drink were ignored. At first he had thought it was only a matter of time before she relented, but as time had progressed it became very clear that she loathed him. And that there was no chance of her changing her mind. The memory of what had occurred so long before stood between them like a barbed-wire fence. Any attempt to surmount it was impossible. She was immune to his success, too. Any praise that Laurence gave out did not impress her, and she only spoke to Lennie if it was unavoidable.

If he had been privy to her thoughts, Lennie would have shrivelled under the power of her dislike. But he was seduced by the words he had heard Laurence utter – *I have plans for them*. Blinded to the obvious, Lennie believed that he had only to wait for his dream to be brought about. Laurence Goldbladt had picked them, and he had plans for them. Lennie might want to move things along, but he told himself to be patient. The future was being prepared for him, and all he had to do was make sure that nothing threw it off track. So he took even better care of his appearance, buffing his nails, using pomade on his hair and practising his diction in the mirror at night, when the showroom

208

was empty. He even sat in Laurence's chair and pretended to be the owner, with money in the bank and Faith as his wife. She wouldn't be so high and mighty then, he thought. No woman was indifferent to a powerful man. She might think he was still some runt, but he wasn't anything like the boy he had been – and she would come to realise that. Come to see that he was light years away from the runt who could hardly talk and slept on the floor at night.

But she had liked him then, he thought suddenly. She had been kind to him. And then he had ruined it . . . but he would make it up to her. Oh yes, in time Lennie would make it up to Faith. He would prove how much he thought of her, and show her how far he had come. There was only one flaw in his plotting, and it had come out of the blue.

Throwing him off balance and making him dangerous.

Whistling under her breath, Faith walked through the entrance of the studio and stopped dead. In front of her stood a smiling James, and a stocky young man she remembered well.

'Peter!' she said, moving over to him and letting him kiss her cheek. 'It's good to see you.'

'You too,' he said genuinely, his well-modulated if slightly artificial voice welcoming. No trace of any Mancunian accent in Peter's vowels. 'I'm going to be working here, taking photographs. How's that for a laugh?'

Peter had put on weight since the last time Faith had seen him, and for some reason he had grown a beard, but he was as cheerful and open as she remembered him. Perhaps his actions *were* a little mannered from his acting days, and maybe his expressions would have been better directed at a theatre gallery, but he was easy company. And after working daily with the sly Lennie Hellier, Peter Dodds struck her as a very welcome contrast.

'I remember how much you used to love taking photographs,' Faith said, going into the kitchen and starting to prepare a plate of meat sandwiches. Calling through the door, she asked: 'You heard about Grandad, then?'

'Yes, sorry about that,' Peter replied. 'Is it serious?'

'He got a cold about a month ago and couldn't shake it. Gran's worried it will turn into pneumonia, so she's put him to bed.'

Moving back into the studio, Faith laid the food on the table and turned the sign to CLOSED.

'You'll have to remember to do that at lunchtime, Peter. James always forgets.' She winked. 'Last week we were just in the middle of one of Sullivan's meat pies when a customer walked in.'

'He's coming back this afternoon,' James told Peter. 'You can book him in. He wants a full photograph shot, with the Nile background.'

Peter's eyebrows rose. 'The Nile?'

'The man wants to impress his girlfriend,' James replied, laughing.

'What about you – are you impressing anyone in particular?' Peter asked, noting the glance that passed between brother and sister. 'Sorry, I didn't mean to pry.'

'You weren't prying,' James replied. 'I'm courting, yes. What about you?'

Under his beard, Peter coloured. James raised his eyebrows at Faith. She knew exactly what was going on, that her brother would be delighted if she and Peter became close. What could be nicer? He and Ellie, she and Peter. They could all go out together in a foursome. Maybe to the music hall or a concert. Faith knew precisely how James's mind was working. And to her surprise, the thought wasn't an unpleasant one.

'I . . . I . . .' stammered Peter. Faith offered him another sandwich as she shot James a warning look.

'No actress take your fancy, then?'

'No, no one,' Peter blurted out, coughing as some crumbs went down the wrong way. 'No one,' he squeaked again.

'What a shame,' James went on mercilessly. 'I would have thought you would have had your pick of all the glamorous actresses.'

'No, no,' Peter replied, putting down his sandwich and taking a sip of water. 'No one caught my eye.'

'Well, you never know what might happen,' James went on. 'Love could be just around the corner for you.'

For the remainder of the afternoon, Peter

remained in the darkroom, trying to salvage a print from the six James had ruined the previous day. Being shorter and a smaller build than James, Peter found the working conditions perfectly satisfactory, and even ended up reorganising the chemicals on the shelves to make them easier to reach. Of course, when Sid Bentley came back, he would move them again. But that was *if* Sid came back. And no one was taking bets on that. In fact Peter was praying that Sidney Bentley wouldn't return. It wasn't that he wished the man ill; it was just that Peter didn't want him back in David Street. Not when he now had a job, and access to Miss Farnsworth.

Who was, Peter had to admit, even better looking than he remembered.

CHAPTER NINETEEN

Waving the letter under Faith's nose, Ellie looked at her friend. 'It's from Paris! They really *do* want to see me again,' she explained. 'Mum's delighted. She keeps going on and on about how it's meant and how God is making it all happen – as though God would have anything to do with the Moulin Rouge.'

Although pleased, Faith was actually dying to tell Ellie about Peter. About how he had asked her out the previous night, and how she had gone. And then how they had talked and how Peter had made her laugh. And above all, how she was finally interested in a man. In Peter Dodds, to be exact.

But she obviously wasn't going to get the chance to confide. Not for a while, at least. Faith looked at Ellie indulgently. The romance between James and her friend had deepened. She might be very young, but James adored her. And his feelings had grown as time went on. He would laugh about what an ass he was, tell Faith that he needed to be shaken. But in reality he was happy and determined to have Eleanor Walker.

Sybil wasn't a problem, because Ellie's brilliant future had been put on hold. Paris was something in the future, so she wasn't too concerned about her daughter seeing the handsome James in the meantime. It was just a flirtation, Sybil told Faith, nothing else. In reality, Ellie's life was only on hold until they heard from Paris . . . But they *didn't* hear from Paris, and after a year Sybil was beginning to get nervous. She was even more nervous when she realised just how fond James was getting of her daughter – and how attached Ellie was becoming to him. It wouldn't do. It wasn't what she had wanted for her only child. Her attempts to break the hold between them resulted in them going behind her back. Resorting to crafty measures, Ellie told her mother she was visiting Faith or working late when she was really seeing James. She didn't actually say that they had finished their relationship; she just let her mother believe that it wasn't important any longer.

As the days passed, all thoughts of Paris faded. Ellie was happy that no word had come. She wasn't interested in being a dancer. She wanted to marry James and he wanted to marry her. But Sybil kept talking about Ellie's career. Waiting for the chance to sever any link between her daughter and James Farnsworth. Waiting, waiting for the letter that didn't come.

But finally it had. And now Ellie was holding it in her hands, her voice breaking,

'What do I do?'

Faith took a breath. 'You have to be straight with your mother.'

'And tell her that I don't want to go back to Paris? That I want to marry James?'

'If that's what you do want, yes,' Faith replied evenly. 'You have to stand up for what you want in life.'

'It isn't that easy!' Ellie retaliated. 'There's only ever been my mum and me; we live for each other. And who's lived all her life waiting for me to be a success. You should have seen her this morning when the letter came; she was almost crazy with excitement—'

'But it's your life, Ellie, not hers.'

'I know, I know,' she replied, her voice failing. 'But how can I smash it all to pieces now? All her old dreams came back and she was going on about how I was going to be a star and marry some rich man.'

Some man, Faith realised, who was not working in a basement in David Street. 'You can't let your mother take over your life.'

'My mother *is* my life,' Ellie replied, looking at the letter in her hand. 'I have to talk to James, tell him that I'm going to go over to Paris and see them again.'

'What!'

'I'll fail the test, Faith,' Ellie said, her little face earnest, her plan already prepared. 'I've worked it all out. Listen to me, this will work. I'll go over and make sure they don't want me. That's the only way

Mum will ever accept this. Then I can come home and marry James.' She took Faith's hands and squeezed them. 'Nothing will keep us apart. Nothing. Not Paris, not my mother. Trust me, Faith, I love your brother too much to lose him.'

Nodding off in the chair at her husband's bedside, Beryl could feel the cold draught on her neck and pulled her shawl up around her shoulders. Soon it would be winter again. So soon it hardly seemed as though summer had put in an appearance. Leaning forward, she studied Sid's sleeping face. He was breathing more regularly now, but Beryl wasn't reassured. Of course she wouldn't tell the grand-children she was anxious, not until it was really necessary. No one else had to be worried; they had lives of their own to lead. However, she *was* relieved to know that Peter Dodds was working at the studio. James had needed the help and Peter was a natural. Not as good as Tommy or Sid, but then who was? They only came along now and again, the real naturals. But Peter Dodds was a competent photographer, and besides, he was young enough and ambitious enough to want to make a go of it.

Smiling to herself, Beryl thought of what James had told her about Faith and Peter courting. Now that *was* good news, she thought. And Beryl had a pretty fair idea that James would soon be marrying Ellie Walker. Before long both her grandchildren would be married and then they would be having children of their own. After all, wasn't that the way life usually went?

'Beryl,' Sid said quietly.

'Oh, hello, love. I thought you were asleep.'

'I was thinking . . .'

'Well, don't overdo it.'

'About things.' Sid paused, becoming serious. 'I've left the business to you.'

'What the hell are you going on about?'

'About matters we should be considering,' he said more firmly. 'You and I both know I'm not well. We know my heart's weak.'

'You'll outlive me, Sid Bentley.'

'Oh love,' he said gently. 'That's not likely now, is it?'

Suddenly overwhelmed, Beryl laid her head down on the bed next to his hand. He touched her hair, stroked it, as he continued to talk.

'I don't intend going anywhere just yet.'

Her voice was muffled against the blankets. 'You better not, you hear me? You leave me and I'll never forgive you.'

'I wouldn't leave you unless it was really necessary. You know that. I love you too much. So if you love me too, Beryl, listen to me carefully, I'm an idiot with money . . .'

'You can say that again.'

'. . . but I've signed over the Manchester studio to you, and then you can do what you want with it. Pass it on to James, or whatever. There's a bit of money in my life insurance. Ask Mort Ruben about that.'

Her head lifted, her eyes surprised. 'You never said a word about that!'

'Maybe I'm not such an idiot with money as you think. I wanted to make sure you were all right. Like I said, if anything happens to me, talk to Mort.'

'What if he dies before you?' she teased him.

'Then talk to his next of kin,' Sid replied, taking her hand. 'I want to live long enough to see both of our grandchildren married.'

'James is stuck on that Walker girl,' Beryl said, blowing her nose and glad to be talking of less emotional matters. 'As for Faith, well, I reckon she and Peter Dodds will make a match.'

Pleased, Sid raised his eyebrows. 'Not a bad match. Mind you, Faith deserves someone worthy of her.'

'Is there anyone worthy of her in your eyes?' Beryl countered, kissing the back of his hand tenderly. 'I love you, Sidney Bentley. Mind you, we didn't have it easy, did we? No one was very pleased when I married you. Who can blame them? Your father was awful, and he *would* smoke in the darkroom. It's a miracle he never blew himself and half of Manchester up.'

Sid laughed wheezily. 'He was a cracking photographer, though.'

'He was that. Even though he never took a photograph when he was sober. I don't think he knew how to work the camera unless he was drunk.'

'Remember when he tripped over the tripod when

he was photographing those soldiers and broke the sergeant's nose?'

She laughed loudly. 'And your mother, that poor woman, what she put up with.'

'But she loved him.'

'She did that, silly cow.'

'And you love me, don't you?'

She kissed his hand again, her voice a whisper. 'I love you like a bird loves to fly, Sid. Like a bird loves to fly.'

Perry Braithwaite was on one knee, staring at Agnes and wondering suddenly why she had parted her hair so far over to the left . . . Bringing his thoughts back to the matter in hand, he had to admit that she was an extraordinary woman. High-spirited and opinionated, certainly – and maybe a little pretentious – but she amused him vastly. In fact Perry had come to realise that his love for Agnes was directly related to her ability to make life comical. Not that she saw it that way. Often she fell into one of her diatribes and didn't realise how amusing she was being. But that, Perry decided, made her all the more adorable.

'Perry!' Agnes said suddenly, seeing him kneeling on the floor in the front room. 'What are you doing?'

Earlier she had dropped an earring, but she was sure she had told him that she had found it, and besides, there were other things on her mind now – like the Chinese laundry expanding. 'Is there something the matter?'

'Agnes, my love . . .'

Her eyebrows rose in irritation. 'Has your knee locked again?'

Patiently, Perry sighed. 'Agnes . . .'

'Look, my dear, just get yourself into the chair and we'll rub your knee with some comfrey oil.' Baffled, Perry winced, changing knees, and Agnes raised her voice shrilly. 'Oh *do* get up, Perry! God knows, I've suffered with a weak ankle for years, but you don't see me begging for sympathy—'

'Will you marry me?'

'A bit of pain never killed anyone, Perry—' Suddenly she stopped, staring down at him. 'What did you say?'

'I said,' he winced, his knee cracking painfully as it took his weight, 'will you marry me?'

'Yes, yes!' she almost screamed.

Bad knees and all, she had finally run Perry Braithwaite to ground.

Preoccupied, Faith stared ahead as Peter sat on the bench beside her. He had just kissed her for the second time that night, and she was feeling confused and not a little excited. Giddy almost. And now he was taking her hand and it felt very comfortable, but more than that, thrilling. Gently she laid her head on his shoulder, watching the reflection of the moon on the rooftops of St Anne's Square. Behind them, the old clock of St Anne's church sounded the hour, a city pigeon making for the dusky sky and the night beyond. She could feel Peter's beard against her forehead and wondered whether – in time – she could persuade him to shave it off.

'What are you thinking?'

She started, smiling to herself. 'I was thinking that it's nice here. With you.'

'Anywhere on earth would be perfect if you were with me.'

'That's a lovely thing to say!'

He sighed happily. 'You know, I was really disappointed when I found out I would never be a successful actor. But now I'm glad I failed. If I hadn't, I wouldn't have met you.'

Faith thought of Ellie in that instant. Her friend was due back from Paris tonight. She had been there ruining her own chances so that she could be with the man she loved. Strange, Faith realised, how life works out.

'James says you're a great help.'

'I like it at the studio.'

'You know Grandad isn't coming back, don't you?'

'James told me this morning. Said his heart was bad,' Peter replied, squeezing her hand again. 'Sorry, I know how much you love him.'

'He might not die for a while.'

'Of course not.'

'Then again, he might die suddenly,' she said, sitting up again and looking ahead. She could hardly bear to think of her grandfather's death, and changed the subject. 'Did I tell you I lost a bet today?'

He blinked, surprised. 'You didn't tell me you had placed a bet.'

'James and I laid a bet a long time ago that Agnes would pin Perry Braithwaite down within months. We were both wrong. No one won the bet. She and Perry are getting married next year.' Faith shook her head, laughing. 'Mrs Perry Braithwaite! God, she'll be impossible. And I just know it will be a big wedding, even if they can't really afford it. Just like I know she will want me to be a bridesmaid.' She turned to Peter. 'Can you imagine me in some uncomfortable formal confection?'

'I can imagine you in some uncomfortable formal confection easily,' Peter replied.

Faith changed the subject deftly. 'Can we really go to the music hall on Saturday? I'd love that,' she said hurriedly. 'We could ask James and Ellie too. She's back tomorrow.'

'Faith . . .'

She could see the look in his eye and wanted to avoid anything too serious for the moment. Faith liked Peter, indeed was getting fond of him, but she didn't want to rush things. Better to be sure of her feelings first, before she committed herself.

'Come on, it's getting cold.'

Standing up, she pulled on her hat and then linked arms with Peter. The dusk had faded into evening, the lamps lit, trams passing and lighting the evening like fireflies. Suddenly Faith felt very adult, very grown up. As though she was on the verge of some great event and had to be composed to face it.

Quietly she walked alongside Peter. The trams passed them, a man whistling as he crossed the road. Faith said good night to Peter at the corner of David Street.

'See you in the morning,' he said, kissing her gently.

Her arms went around his neck, pulling him to her, both of them laughing softly.

'Good night,' she said, smiling and kissing him again. 'Good night, Peter.'

'I don't want to go.'

'You have to!'

'I want to stay here, on this spot, holding you. For ever and ever.'

'What if it rained?'

'We'd get wet,' he replied, laughing.

'And when it snowed?'

'We'd freeze. People would look at us and we'd become famous. They'd talk about the frozen lovers on David Street, locked together for ever.'

Grinning, she pulled back, then tweaked his beard and ran off down David Street.

James was waiting for her when she walked in, his sleeves rolled back, a hammer in his hand.

'I'm not *that* late,' she joked, taking off her coat. 'What are you doing?'

'It's the sign outside,' he explained, walking to the door and looking upwards to the street. 'It's loose again and creaking. I can't stand one more night listening to it.'

'I can't hear it.'

'That's because you sleep in the back room,' James replied, walking out of the door and up the basement steps.

His voice came from outside, muffled. 'I need a hand.'

'What!' she shouted, walking to the door and looking up.

He was standing, precariously balanced, with one foot on the window ledge of Laurence Goldbladt's showroom window, and the other on the top of the street railings. Below him was a fall of fifteen feet to the concrete floor of the basement.

'Oh for God's sake, James, I'll get the ladder!' Faith shouted to him. 'You'll have an accident like that. Wait a minute.'

Hurrying back into the studio, she made for the storeroom, hearing the steady banging of the hammer as James secured the sign. One, twice, three times he hit the nails in. There was a pause, then he began again, Faith just reaching the door as he struck the sign with one last effort.

But he had put too much of a swing into it and, leaning forward, had lost his balance. Shouting, he fell, trying to clutch the railings as he slammed into the basement steps, the noise a sickening thud in the night air.

'James!' screamed Faith, letting the ladder go and running over to him. 'Are you all right? James, talk to me.'

But she could see at once that he was badly hurt. He was lying on the fifth step, his back arched, a pool of blood coming from the back of his head.

Gently, Faith leaned towards him. 'James, can you hear me? James?'

'I can't feel my legs,' he said quietly, his voice rising quickly with panic. 'Jesus, I can't feel my legs.'

They didn't know it then, but James Farnsworth would never walk again.

All my life my brother had protected me. All my life I had known that my handsome, tall brother would be there by my side. It was a given. He was my friend, my support, my Angel James. I knew angels could fly; I didn't think they could break their backs.

It wasn't fair. James wasn't a bad man, no fallen angel, no exiled spirit, turned out by God. But that night – as I held him and people gathered around, calling for help – I thought God had thrown him out. He was bleeding, and yet I knew that his head injury wasn't that serious. I wanted to say to people, it's OK, it's just a bad cut. It's his legs, his legs. But I couldn't say it, because saying it might make it so. And I didn't want to be the one who damned him.

All because of some stupid repair. All because he couldn't wait for the ladder and because the creaking of the sign had kept him awake at night. For such a cruel, trivial reason my brother smashed his spine. I kept wondering, if I had been quicker, if I had got the ladder to him sooner, would it have been different? But it was pointless to think like that. James fell, for whatever reason. And he would never get up again.

For a time he was unconscious and I thought about Ellie coming back to England that night. His darling Ellie . . . Would someone already have told her? Or would I have to do that? And then I thought about my grandparents and wondered what words I could use to break the news. What phrase would hurt them the least . . . For three hours after the accident my brother slept. For three hours I sat beside him in the hospital. I heard the clock ticking, the sounds from the street outside, and far away I imagined I could hear the sign still creaking.

When he awoke, I knew life would never be the same again.

And so began our year of endings.

PART THREE

CHAPTER TWENTY

March 1908

Until the night of James's accident, Faith had thought she could love Peter Dodds, even marry him some day. But he wasn't the best comforter, and he found words hard to come by. For a man who had hoped to earn his living by the power of speech, he failed miserably. It wasn't his fault, Faith understood that only too well. He couldn't hope to say or do anything that would soften the blow of James's accident. And it wasn't as though he wasn't sorry. He was genuinely distressed by the accident, his position at the City Photographic Studio cemented not by the normal retirement of an older generation, but by a cruel stroke of fate.

Faith was distracted with grief. She couldn't understand what had happened, or why. She couldn't make sense of being robbed of her brother, because the James who remained was not the same as the man who had climbed up to mend the creaking sign. Spending as much time at his bedside as she could, she tried to encourage her brother to

231

talk, but nothing helped. James would talk listlessly about the weather and ask about the studio, but he made no reference to his condition. And then, of course, there was Ellie.

'Is she back yet?'

Faith nodded. 'She came to see you, but you were unconscious. She's coming again very soon. Tomorrow, I think.'

She could see the puzzlement in her brother's face and inwardly cursed Ellie Walker.

'You told her what happened?'

'Yes, I told her,' Faith replied, remembering the exact conversation that had taken place. The whole scenario repeated itself in her head, unbidden. Not the conversation with Ellie. Not first. First Faith had spoken to her grandparents. The talk with Ellie had come later . . .

It had been such a terrible night. James had been taken to the Manchester Infirmary, and then Faith had caught the late tram to Oldham, arriving at Hardy Street after eleven. Waiting for a long moment on the doorstep, she finally walked in. A moment later Beryl had come down the stairs in her nightdress.

'Faith! Whatever is it?'

'It's James,' she had begun, her voice faltering, the words thick in her mouth. Upstairs she could hear Sid calling out and wanted to run, to never tell them. To say that it had been a mistake and James was all right. But she couldn't.

'What about him?' Beryl had asked, grabbing hold of Faith by her shoulders.

'He had a fall.'

'A fall?' Beryl had repeated. 'Is he hurt?' But she had known without being told that yes, James was hurt. He was hurt terribly, he was changed. She knew it because she could see her granddaughter's expression, and because Faith would never have come to their house so late at night without there being a good reason.

'Faith,' Beryl had said, fighting panic. 'Is it very bad?'

'He's semi-paralysed, and the doctors don't know if he will ever walk again,' Faith had replied, her voice failing her, her head dropping. Beryl had her arm around her granddaughter and walked her into the kitchen. There had been no hysteria from Faith; she just sat motionless, her hands cold, her gaze unfocused. But in her head all she could hear was the sound of creaking and the sickening thud as her brother's body fell.

'Drink this,' Beryl had urged, passing her a brandy and pouring herself one. 'Drink it up!'

Obediently Faith had done so, the liquor burning her throat as it had gone down, her stomach warming. But there had been no comfort in it.

'Where's your brother now?'

'In the Infirmary. I've just come from there.'

'You should have got them to ring. You should have told them to telephone the pub and ask to speak to us,' Beryl had said, sitting down as her legs weakened under her. Dear God, not James. Not her handsome grandson. 'Why didn't they call?'

233

'I wanted to tell you myself.'

Nodding, Beryl had put her arms around Faith, rocking her. 'Thanks, love. That can't have been easy.'

'No.'

'Is he . . . You say he can't walk?' God, Beryl had wondered, how could she sound so calm? How in God's name could she sound so calm?

Faith had nodded. 'He's broken his back. The doctors say he might never walk again.' She had paused, unable to go on, and then had begun sobbing, long, dry sobs, her grandmother rocking her backwards and forwards.

In that instant Sid had walked in. He had been slow, looking unwell and anxious. He had heard the door and wanted to know what was going on, why they had visitors so late at night. Then, looking from his wife to Faith, he had understood immediately that something dreadful had happened to them.

'What is it?'

Beryl had looked up. 'James has had an accident,' she said, standing up and walking over to her husband. 'You should go back to bed, love. Keep warm.'

But Sid had not been put off. 'How bad is it?'

'We'll talk about it later.'

'Oh Beryl,' he had said helplessly. 'Tell me. How bad is it?'

Only minutes later, or maybe it had been a lot longer, Faith had left her grandparents' house on Hardy Street. Beryl had wanted her to stay, but she had been determined. She had another visit to make. Someone else had to be told about James. Promising that she would return and spend the night at their house, Faith began the walk towards the Walker home. There were only streets to go, only minutes between Ellie not knowing and being told. Only a hundred or so yards between happiness and despair. Moving automatically, Faith had kept walking, thinking of all the plans James and Ellie had made. Their engagement had been a secret; only Faith knew, only she had been made privy to their future. Swearing her to silence, James and Ellie had told her how they would marry, save up, and one day have enough money to buy their own home in Oldham. Ellie had been full of it, reassuring James endlessly that when she returned from Paris the whole dancing nonsense would be over. Sybil, she had decided, would have to get over her disappointment. But then again, Ellie would have made sure she had been rejected, so there was nothing her mother could do about it.

And then she and James would be free to marry, Ellie told Faith, laughing. Free to tell Sybil that they had been secretly engaged for months . . . Walking up to the front door of the Walker home, Faith had knocked softly, then more loudly. She had seen that the gas lamps had been lit, so they had obviously returned from their journey. For a moment Faith had wanted them to be delayed, so that she wouldn't have to pass on the dreadful news – but just as she was thinking it, the door had opened.

'Oh my Lord!' Ellie had said excitedly. 'It's Faith! Faith, come in, come in.'

Her face had been flushed, her hands moving restlessly. And in front of the black-leaded kitchen grate Sybil had stood smiling.

'I have to tell you!' Ellie had gone on. 'You won't believe it! You won't!'

Catching hold of her friend's hands, Faith had tried to slow her down. 'Ellie, I have to tell you something . . .'

But Ellie hadn't been listening; she had been fired up, giddy with her own news. 'Faith, you can't imagine. I mean, I know that I always said I wasn't really interested, but then again . . .' She had smiled brilliantly, her mother laughing behind her. 'How often does anyone get a chance like this?'

'What?'

'The Moulin Rouge, they want me!' she had cried, spinning Faith around the room with her, Sybil covering her mouth to muffle the sound of her own laughter.

'Ellie!' Faith had said, trying to stop herself being twirled around. 'Ellie! You always said you weren't interested in going there.'

'They said I could be a real star. Not as a dancer, but I can act.'

'Ellie!' Faith had cried, catching her friend's hands. 'Listen to me . . .'

'Like Mistinguette . . .'

'What?'

'The famous dancer and singer. She came to the

236

Moulin Rouge last year and she's made a fortune. They said that I would be different, because of the way I look and because I'm English, and that I could triumph. Of course I'll have to learn how to speak French—'

'Ellie, listen to me, please.'

But there was no getting through to her. Faith had finally had to pull her friend out on to the street, away from the watching Sybil. In the cool night air, Ellie had paused, as though coming back to reason, looking at Faith with a child's excitement.

'I know I never wanted it before, but this is the chance of a lifetime.'

Confused by the unexpected volte-face, Faith had stared at her, her mouth opening and closing in an effort to talk. But no words had come out, and Ellie had continued without pause.

'I know you've every right to be angry with me, but I would be crazy to miss out on this chance. You do see that, don't you? It's like Mum said all along, it was meant. I have to do it, I have to go to Paris.'

'What about James and you?'

'Well . . .' Ellie had said distantly, embarrassed and looking away. 'I won't be gone for ever. I'll be coming back, and besides, he should want the best for me. If he really loved me, he would.'

'James couldn't love you any more than he does. You must know that.'

'But anyway,' Ellie had blundered on, 'like everyone's always said, I'm very young to settle down just yet.'

'But not too young to go and work in Paris.'

'It's my dream!'

'It was never your dream!' Faith had reacted fiercely. 'You said you were going over there to fail. To make sure you were rejected. You told James that. You said that when you came back, all this Paris nonsense would be over.'

'It's not nonsense!'

'Not now, obviously,' Faith had snapped back.

Misreading the reason for her friend's anger, Ellie had taken the victim role.

'You can't be cross with me! You can't! I have to make the best out of my life. You might be happy living here, Faith, but I've seen more, and I realise that I want it now.'

Faith's tone had been glacial. 'More than you want James?'

'James will find someone else if he can't wait for me!' Ellie had replied, feeling cornered and knowing she was going back on everything they had planned. 'I'll talk to him, explain.'

'He's in the Manchester Infirmary.'

'What?'

'He had a fall . . . he's broken his back.'

Taking in a shocked breath, Ellie had paled, glancing away, her face losing its excited flush of colour. At any moment Faith had expected her to break down, to turn back, for them to hold and comfort each other. For Ellie to rush to the hospital to see James, to reassure him. But she had not done that. She had remained rigid, unmoving, her expression slowly altering from shock to resignation.

Then, after another protracted pause, she had finally spoken.

'Well that's settled it, hasn't it? I can't marry James now. No one would expect me to.'

And that was when Faith had hit her. Slapped her closest friend, her brother's fiancée, hard across the face. So hard that Ellie had rocked back, her skin still burning as she watched Faith's figure disappear into the night.

CHAPTER TWENTY-ONE

Over the years, no exercise and too much rich food had taken their toll on Laurence's poor circulation, and the downsurge in his business after a hot summer, coupled with the devastating news of James's accident, had hobbled him. Laurence had been a close friend of the Bentley family for years, had welcomed Faith's employment and liked the idea of James resurrecting the photographic studio below, along with Peter Dodds. Young blood, he told Mort often, was what everyone needed. Stopped people getting set in their ways. So close was Laurence to the Bentleys that he visited Sid at home, wondering to himself how long his old friend could survive. It had seemed for a while – with the help of Beryl's adept nursing – that Sid might fully recover. But James's accident had been a crippling blow, and now Sid Bentley kept to his bedroom, Beryl putting on a brave face, but seldom seen at David Street.

Leaning on his cane, Laurence looked out of the window into the basement below, wincing as he imagined the pain of James's fall. For a moment he could almost see James's body lying there, and it took some effort for him not to feel the same despondency that had overtaken Sid. After all, both James and his sister were like children to Laurence. Not wanting to interfere, and just offering support, Laurence had told Faith to take some time off after the accident. But she was back to work within days, visiting her brother in the evenings and helping Peter Dodds out in any spare time she had. Of course the workload told on her, and Laurence soon realised that he would temporarily have to release Faith from his employment and let her take over in the studio. After all, Peter Dodds was a great fellow, but he wasn't family, and Laurence knew only too well that Beryl would want a relative to oversee the place.

In the meantime, he did not ask about James. Whether he would stay in hospital, or return to David Street, where he could still do the accounts for the business, albeit in a wheelchair. What other company would hire him now? From being a handsome, healthy young man, James Farnsworth had been reduced to an unemployable cripple. At least that was how he had described himself to Faith. And she had returned from the hospital after he said it and cried in the stockroom. A week later it had seemed that James was coming to terms with his situation, but then Ellie Walker's rejection had sent him falling backwards into complete despair. His temperament, previously so even, became withdrawn, and far from being impatient to leave hospital, he wanted to remain in the only place he felt accepted and safe.

Laurence could understand that. He was over sixty, but he could imagine being in his twenties and having to face life in a wheelchair. Rubbing his forehead with his left hand, Laurence tried to work out a way to still pay Faith some wage whilst she was working downstairs. God knows, they would need the money even more when James came home – either to David Street or to Hardy Street, which was where Beryl wanted him. Sighing, Laurence had no interest in the customer he was due to see and jumped when he heard a cough behind him.

'Oh, Lennie, it's you.'

'Are you all right, sir?'

'Fine, fine,' Laurence replied. 'Will you see to Mrs Thorp for me today? Tell her . . . just see to her, will you?'

Lennie was more than willing to assist. James Farnsworth's accident had been a shock to him – but in a different way from Laurence. Lennie Hellier did not feel sympathy for James; he was just aware that the event would probably take Faith away from the showroom for a while. The thought was not welcome, but, typically, Lennie found an advantage in it. His rise to the top was not being curtailed; in fact this unfortunate event might further his advance nicely. Surprised by the low spirits of his employer, Lennie had found himself taking over more responsibility, and now that Faith was going to be temporarily absent, he would have a chance to make the showroom more and more his own territory. Laurence's previous love of the good life had left Lennie time to investigate the workings of the Goldbladt studio, and he had mentally stored away any information that could further his cause. And feather his nest.

In fact, whether Laurence Goldbladt realised it or not, Lennie was becoming indispensable. And again without realising it, Laurence had reassured his employee and shored up his fantasy. Over the previous months Laurence had mentioned Peter Dodds and his interest in Faith. He had also mentioned that the pair were going out, a thought that tore into Lennie like a razor blade. But then Laurence had smiled at his employee and raised his eyebrows. A typical gesture, but one that Lennie interpreted to suit himself as *Well, that Peter Dodds might think he has a chance with Faith, but we know better, hey?* It was a code, but Lennie had understood it. So he relaxed and watched. And waited. His master plan was working so smoothly that his employer was shedding responsibility like a snake shedding its hampering skin. The more Lennie improved his appearance and knowledge, the more Laurence leaned on him. The more Lennie offered suggestions and made little improvements, the more Laurence allowed his protégé's influence to expand. Preoccupied, and still seeing Lennie as the faithful old dogsbody, Laurence became careless with accounts and paperwork. His sleight of hand with the furs had never escaped Lennie's attention, but now Lennie also made notes of who had been short-changed. The fact that the traders had often cheated Laurence was of no interest to Lennie. He was only interested in the hold he could increase on his mentor, for use at a later date.

'Will Faith be coming back to work here soon?' Lennie asked his employer. 'It was so sad about her brother. Such a tragedy.'

Laurence was still looking out of the window, thinking about how fast time had passed and how short health and life actually were. 'Faith will be working in the photographic studio for a while, Lennie.' He turned round. 'Can you cope here on your own?'

'You can rely on me, sir.'

'I know that,' Laurence replied, moving to the door and then leaning heavily on his cane. 'Perhaps a little bonus might be in order?'

Smiling, Lennie nodded. 'That would be very welcome.'

'Pay for some new clothes,' Laurence said, pointing with his stick to Lennie's suit. 'You care about your appearance.'

'I do what I can.'

'You do well,' Laurence said distantly. 'Anyway, I'll leave you to run the place for the rest of the day . . . No leaning out of windows, hey?'

'No, sir.'

'There's been one young man's life ruined; we don't want anything to happen to you, Lennie.'

*

'No!' Faith said emphatically, facing her grandmother in the kitchen at Hardy Street.

'You'll not say no to me!' Beryl snapped back. 'Remember, I'm your better.'

'But you're not my wiser in this,' her granddaughter replied. 'You can't have James here.'

'Why not? It wouldn't be too difficult. I have to be here to look after your grandfather.'

'Which is why you can't take James on.'

Annoyed, Beryl studied her granddaughter. She noted the tight line of Faith's mouth, her determination not to cry or show weakness. It reminded Beryl of the time Ivy had died, when Faith had cried at night, never showing her feelings in the daytime.

'It would be too much for you.'

'Bah!' Beryl snorted. 'I've the strength of four women.'

'I don't doubt it,' Faith replied, her tone even. 'But *I'm* going to look after James.'

'Oh aye, where?'

'At David Street.'

Wrong-footed, Beryl stared at her granddaughter. 'I thought . . .'

'He needs to be where he feels safe. A place he knows. Somewhere he can work. Somewhere he feels useful,' Faith went on. 'I've talked to the doctors and they agree. James will never come to terms with what happened whilst he's just sitting around, brooding on it. And he *would* brood here, Gran, you know he would.'

'Faith, you can't take the care of your brother on,' Beryl replied, feeling embarrassed as she took off her apron and sat down. 'I've looked after children and your grandad. I know about washing people and what has to be done for them. And James will need all sorts of care. Things a sister can't do.'

'I know,' Faith said simply. 'The hospital have explained it all to me.'

'They have?'

'James isn't completely paralysed. He has enough movement to use a chamber pot, and to clean himself. God knows, it's not difficult to empty a jerry.' She flushed slightly, but hurried on. 'He has very good upper body strength – that's what they call it at the hospital; he really just needs someone to help lift him in and out of the wheelchair. Which I could do, with Peter's help.' She paused again, showing how much she had investigated the problem. 'If James needed something that I couldn't do for him, Peter would help.'

Beryl sniffed. 'It's a lot to ask of an employee.'

'Peter is a friend too.'

'Of yours, or James?'

Holding her grandmother's look, Faith answered her. 'I'm fond of Peter, but no more. I thought there was something more to it, but he's not very strong. He fell apart when James had his accident.'

Beryl patted the seat next to her, Faith taking it. Then Beryl put her hands flat on the table, looking at them as she spoke.

'Some people are naturally very strong. They need

to be, or they become that way. Some people want to be strong, but they haven't got it in them. Some people are born weak and stay the same all their lives. You can't blame a man for not being able to cope with tragedy.'

Faith nodded, her tone kind. 'I know. I don't blame Peter. I understand it in a friend. But I would need more in a husband.'

Blowing out her cheeks, Beryl stared at the young woman next to her.

'How did you get so wise?'

'I had a good teacher,' Faith replied, touching the back of her grandmother's hand. 'Please, let James come to David Street. Let me take him on, look after him. He's looked after me all my life. He was always there, always ready to stand up for me. I could rely on him a hundred per cent. I could talk to him and he was always there for me . . .'

Faith paused. Now that route was off limits to her, and she knew it. Knew that her beloved brother, her closest ally, needed *her* now. The situation had reversed. Angel James had fallen to earth, and she had to make sure that he fell no further.

'It's a lot to take on, Faith.'

'No,' she replied, turning to her grandmother. 'He would have done it for me without a second's thought.'

In the hospital ward, James sat in his wheelchair, motionless. Around him there was activity, doctors and nurses visiting other patients, one man critically ill, the screens drawn around his bed. It was rumoured that he would die. Lucky man, James thought, glancing at the clock. He wasn't really interested in the time. It meant little to him now. What good was time when you had no structure to your life? There was no need to get up – if you could, which he couldn't any more – and no timetables, no trams to catch, no evening dates to keep. No Ellie . . . He paused, fighting his own self-pity. She hadn't come to see him. Not in all the weeks he had been in hospital. She had sent word, at first, through Faith. But even that had stopped. He thought that she should have had the grace to write to him, then realised that Ellie was very young, and wouldn't know what to write to say goodbye.

His hands gripping the arms of the wheelchair, James thought of his fiancée. Or should that be ex-fiancée? Without anyone telling him, he had guessed what had happened. The trip to Paris had gone well, and if Ellie had felt any guilt, it would have been quickly crushed by the reality of his accident. How could she be tied to a cripple? Sybil would have said. And not just her mother; other people would have said the same. Ellie was pretty, young and full of life. She couldn't sacrifice herself. No one would expect it – least of all him. But James had wanted her to come and see him. Had wanted her to offer, to tell him that she would stand by him. He would never have allowed it, but it would have hurt less if they had pretended. Even if only for a little while.

But she had never come. And now she never

would. James had stopped asking Faith about Ellie and she had stopped mentioning her. Instead, Eleanor Walker, with her pale-skinned, pert little face, had exited their lives without so much as a curtain call. The gap she left was immense. Because not only did he miss Ellie, he missed the future they had planned. With her, there had been a life to come. Now there was only a life that had gone. Nothing to look forward to any longer. Because what kind of life did a cripple have? Frustration welled up in him and made his eyes fill, shame for his weakness compounding his despair. He had been told what was going to happen to him. His grandmother was going to look after him, in Hardy Street. After all, Beryl had said, she was already looking after Sid, and his grandfather would appreciate the company.

But James didn't want his grandfather's company. He wanted to make love to his girl, and walk down David Street. He wanted to feel masculine, and have the local girls give him the eye. At his age, he was entitled to the scurry of attraction and frenzied dreams with Ellie. Entitled to show off in his clothes, and save up for a hat like the one he had seen George Raft wear. It was the time of life when you could be a bit foolish, a bit giddy, a bit reckless, because after that you would settle down and grow old and end up in Hardy Street. But not now, James thought helplessly. Not bloody *now*. He could imagine the years falling past the upstairs bedroom window on Hardy Street, and watching the seasons changing over the roof of the Presbyterian Chapel. People would pass under his window and the newsboy would call out the headlines, and where would he be? In a wheelchair. The very place where he was going to spend the rest of his life. In a wheelchair in Hardy Street, dying in his twenties.

Hearing quick footsteps behind him, James wheeled himself round, surprised to see his sister facing him.

'So, are you ready?'

He frowned. 'Am I going to Hardy Street today?'

'An ambulance is waiting outside. They'll be up in a minute to get you,' Faith went on, looking at him steadily. 'Are you ready to leave here?'

'No.'

She nodded. 'It's time to go.'

'I don't want to go.'

'I don't blame you,' Faith replied.

'I don't want to go to Oldham and have Beryl look after me. I don't want to be a burden on my own grandmother.'

'That's good.'

He frowned again. 'Good?'

'Yes, because you're coming with me. To David Street.'

'I thought . . .'

'Oh, I know what you thought,' she teased him. 'And I know what Beryl thought and what all the doctors thought. But *I* know what's going to happen. And you're coming back to David Street.'

He felt as though someone had opened a window,

as though his lungs had filled with cool air and given him life again.

'I need you, James,' Faith went on firmly. 'I need you to do the books, the accounts, run the place for me. Peter's fine, but he's not got a business head; you've got that, and we have to keep the studio going. It's our business, James. *Our* responsibility.' She could see his eyes filling and hurried on. 'I've spoken to Laurence, and he's agreed that I'll work in the studio for a while. You know, until we get the place running to suit you.'

'To suit me?' he asked, incredulous.

'Yeah, to suit you,' Faith replied. 'There *is* no City Photographic Studio without you.'

'I thought . . .'

'I know what you thought,' she said evenly, waiting for his next words.

'It won't be the same.'

'No. But then nothing stays the same, does it? Apart from you and me. We stick together.'

'I have to ask . . .' James said, wanting to clear the air before he left the hospital. 'Just once. And I won't ask again. Is Ellie . . . she's not . . . I'm not going to see her again, am I?'

'No, love,' Faith told him, after a long pause. 'She got the job in Paris. She left last week.'

He nodded, rubbed his forehead with his left hand and then glanced back to his sister.

'You don't have to do this, you know. It'll be hard work, looking after me. There are some things that . . . might be difficult.'

'Much like everything else in life,' she replied, unfazed.

'What I mean is that you have an opportunity to say no. To live your own life,' he said, his tone genuine. 'You have Peter now, you two could settle down. Everyone expects it.'

'Well, they'll have to live with the disappointment,' she replied deftly. 'Peter is a nice man, but I'm not going to marry him.'

'Not because of me?'

'No. I think the world of you, James, but I can't marry my own brother,' she said, teasing him and laughing. 'Let's just say that Peter isn't husband material.'

'Neither am I.'

'Not for Ellie Walker, no,' she said evenly. 'But then again, she wasn't wife material. Was she?'

Faith was trying to stay calm and not reveal her true feelings. Because in reality she wanted to tell her brother what she thought of Eleanor Walker and how she hoped her old friend would burn in hell. Or at least in Paris. But what would be the point? She might get her own feelings out, but in doing so she would only be hurting James more. He didn't need to feel any lower. What he needed was a purpose. And only she could give him that.

'I think Peter should go out and about taking photographs. You know the kind of thing, go to the seaside and snap the day trippers. We need to get some more money in.'

James nodded, momentarily forgetting that he

was in a wheelchair, his thoughts preoccupied. 'You know, if Peter *did* get some extra work, I could do the paperwork.'

'And help me run the studio.'

'I'm in a wheelchair,' he said, his voice flat.

'Yeah, I know that. But you can still talk to people. God knows, James, people always take to you. More than they take to me, or Peter.'

'The steps . . . the steps down to the basement. How will I get to the studio?'

'The ambulance men will carry you down,' Faith replied, having already checked at the hospital.

'How do I get upstairs again?'

'God, James! For someone in a wheelchair, you aren't half keen on escape.'

He laughed. After all the weeks of people pitying him, after all the commiserating letters, the overheard talk of his life being ruined, the dread of living in Hardy Street, to hear Faith talk to him as she had always done was like being thrown a lifeline. She made him feel as though he was still James, still whole. As though nothing was too bad. As though nothing had really changed . . . His spirits began to rise, but his sense of fair play made him question her one last time.

'Faith, think about what you're offering. I can't lean on you for the rest of my life.'

'Really?' she said, taking the brake off the wheelchair and pushing her brother to the door. 'I was always leaning on you – and I never thought twice about it.'

CHAPTER TWENTY-TWO

Watching from the window above, Lennie Hellier saw the arrival of James Farnsworth and watched as he was carried downstairs. It was a slow and awkward process, but finally they got James into the basement – with Peter Dodds's help – and Lennie heard the door close. A moment later, it opened again, Faith coming back out into the street. A couple of people stopped to talk to her, and Lennie noticed her composure, and the way her hair shone darkly in the sunlight. Always impressive, she seemed very confident, as though responsibility suited her.

Ambling downstairs, Lennie walked into the main hallway just as Faith came inside. Her eyes took a moment to adjust to the light, and then she saw him, nodding curtly and moving over to the side wall to collect the studio post.

'I was pleased to see your brother back,' Lennie said.

Faith kept her face averted. 'Thank you.'

'Mr Goldbladt said you would be working down here for a while, until things got sorted out,' he went on, Faith not responding. 'I'm sure I can speak for myself and Mr Goldbladt when I say that we will miss you.'

'I'm sure you *can't* speak for Laurence,' Faith replied, turning her freezing dislike on him. 'I don't think he'd like to know that you were speaking for him.'

Lennie's face paled. He was suddenly scruffy again, sleeping on rags, a boy without prospects. Someone she had rejected, and now loathed. And Lennie Hellier saw in that instant that whatever his fantasy might be, whatever Laurence Goldbladt had planned for his future, Faith Farnsworth would never be a part of it. Not willingly, at least.

'You have no reason to dislike me so much,' he said finally, trying to sound confident. 'I'm advancing in life.'

'I can see that.'

'I am becoming indispensable.'

Her eyes narrowed. 'Don't let your ambitions get too big, Lennie. You might overreach yourself.'

'Mr Goldbladt is getting older, he needs my help.'

'Your help – not your plotting.'

The words struck home. 'Mr Goldbladt has prospects for me!'

'Not if he knew what you were really like,' Faith replied. 'Don't undermine Mr Goldbladt. He's no fool. And remember, he's a friend of our family. You are his employee. Who d'you think he would believe – you or me?'

'There's nothing you can tell him!'

'Oh, but there is,' she replied. 'You know it, and so do I. So I suggest that you keep your distance, Mr Hellier. I told you once, and I meant it – touch me again and I'll see you on the street.' She turned to go, then turned back. 'And don't try to hurt your employer in any way. Don't think you have any real power over Mr Goldbladt.'

'I have more power than you.'

Her eyes blazed. 'Would you like to take a bet on that?'

Back in the cool darkness of the basement, Faith watched from the doorway as Peter talked to James. But the old camaraderie had gone. It was obvious that Peter wanted to try and act normally, but he couldn't get past the wheelchair. James's accident had opened a chasm between them, decreased their similarities and increased their differences. Faced with a handicapped man, Peter was mortally embarrassed, unable to relax and fearful of saying the wrong thing. And as Faith glanced over to her brother, she realised how hard life was going to be for him. How often the condition would be seen before the man himself.

'Are you hungry? I got some beer in,' she said, walking over to James and watching him pause at the step that led from the studio to the lower seating area. 'Hang on! Can you give me a hand, Peter?'

Nodding, he moved over, the two of them easing the wheelchair down the step.

'We need a ramp,' Faith said simply, turning to Peter. 'Can you build one?'

'I can try.'

Nodding, she turned to James. 'Will you be all right sleeping in the back room?'

'Fine.'

'I mean, you could have my room . . .'

'I said I'd be fine.'

'I don't mind—'

'Jesus!' James exploded. 'Just stop fussing me, will you? Just stop fussing me.'

Red faced, Peter walked out, Faith behind him. They paused outside in the yard. The sign had been rehung soon after the accident. It no longer swung, or squeaked. It was no longer green either; Beryl had insisted that it be repainted, dark red with gold lettering. She had always said that green was unlucky. Mind you, she had never been one for religion either, but she had been to St Anne's church a few times recently. And if she wasn't too keen on all the ritual of the services, she liked the atmosphere, and did the altar flowers when she was asked . . . Staring up at the sign, Peter sighed. If he was honest he had not thought it was a good idea for James to come back to the studio. But he soon realised that Faith had made up her mind, and that his opinion wouldn't be asked for. He had also realised that he had failed her and was suffering for it. It hadn't been intentional, it was just that he had not known how to support her. What words to use, what gestures. He could have acted compassion and sympathy – he certainly felt it – but expressing it was another matter.

And so he lost her. In the first days after James's accident, when Faith was travelling back and forth from the Manchester Infirmary and then calling in at Hardy Street to check on her grandparents, that was the time when another man would have made her his own, the right time to show strength and solidarity. But Peter had lacked the natural responses. He was too hampered by shock to be of use to her. When he did hold her and try to comfort her, his words were automatic, clichéd. And before long, Faith stopped turning to him.

It was a hard time for Faith. She was used to helping people, but now she felt the strain of having to support her grandparents *and* James. Her time was spent careering between Oldham and Manchester. She would see to James first thing in the morning, work at the studio with her brother and Peter, and then leave later to make the tram ride over to Oldham and her grandparents. Aware that Sid was not making any progress, Faith tried to cheer Beryl up. But her grandmother was no fool, and knew only too well what the reality was: that James's accident had been the final blow for Sidney. He might rally some days, but it never lasted long, and he was eating little. Angina attacks occurred with frightening regularity, and the doctor could offer no hope.

'We have to face it,' Beryl told Faith. 'The end's not far off.'

'I don't believe it.'

'Well, believe it or not, it's the truth,' Beryl replied, sitting Faith down to talk. Anxiously she studied her granddaughter. 'You have to rest up a little. Take a bit of time for yourself. You can't keep running from Manchester to Oldham every night.'

'I want to see you.'

'I know,' Beryl replied, 'and I want to see you, but I know what you're really thinking – you don't want to miss your grandad dying.'

Faith hung her head, choked up. 'I want to be with him.'

'You don't understand,' Beryl replied. 'You're where he *wants* you to be. With James, at the studio. He loves that place, you know that. He loves the work and the people, like Mort and Laurence. Your grandad has always been happy there. He'll tell you that, love, he'll tell you about when we first went to work in David Street, just before his daft father keeled over. Tommy Bentley,' she laughed, 'what a womaniser! What a horrible man! He drove your grandad's mother to hell and back, but she loved him for it. Even though the bugger damn near killed her with his running around. I remember when your grandad inherited the City Photographic Studio – he was so proud that day. Went outside and kept walking up and down David Street, telling anyone and everyone that he had just come into a business!'

Smiling, Faith listened to the old stories. She knew that her grandmother wanted to talk, and she wanted to listen. Wanted to pretend that the sickly man upstairs would recover and come back to them.

'Your grandad was going to do all these amazing things when we first went there. But not much came of it. We settled down and made a good life, but didn't hit the big time.' Beryl shook her head. 'I never wanted to, so it was no skin off my nose. I just wanted to be with him, and make sure no other woman got her claws into him. Oh, and I had to watch the accounts. Sid has no head for money. You're lucky, you've got James to run the books for you.'

'Yes, and he's good at that.'

'Are you glad you took him back to David Street?' Beryl asked quietly.

It took Faith a moment to reply.

'I'm glad, yes. But James isn't happy. Not that he's said so, but I can tell, I know him very well. He works on the books, but when he stops and we have something to eat, Peter never seems to know what to say and James ends up either trying too hard to make us laugh, or being silent. And when women come into the studio, they avoid him. I can see the pain in his eyes. I can feel it. Before, they were all over him, but now they dismiss him and it hurts.'

Moved, Beryl stared at her hands. They were dry, veined and wrinkled. By comparison, Faith's hands were still smooth. But for how long? If she carried on working, struggling and worrying, how long before she aged? Before she started to show the anxiety in her face? Jesus, Beryl thought frantically, I don't want that for her. Not now, not ever. Faith had had enough of grief. The deaths of her parents, James's accident and the failure of her romance with Peter Dodds were all body blows. She needed some lightness in her life, some joy, but where was it going to come from? Beryl wondered. Sid's death was imminent, and James's condition wasn't going to get any better. Could she really stand by and watch her granddaughter work and worry herself into the ground? Faith might not have said anything, but Laurence had informed Beryl about the extra time Faith was putting in modelling. Beryl knew it was a kindness on Laurence's part, and on Mort's, but it was still work. More and more work piling up, without any sign of it decreasing. The business was chugging along, but Beryl knew only too well that the summer had been slow for them. Doctors' fees for Sid and then James had eaten into the meagre savings they had, and having to pay Peter Dodds more for his extra work wasn't easing the burden.

'I've been thinking,' Faith said tentatively, 'I could ask Agnes to help . . .'

To Beryl's astonishment, Faith burst out laughing. 'Agnes? Oh, spare me that! She would be useless. Anyway, what would Perry say about his new wife working? Why did they sneak off to get married anyway?'

Beryl pulled a face. 'You know how Agnes lies about how old she is? I reckon she wanted everyone to think she was in the family way.'

Laughing, Faith shook her head. 'Never!'

'Nah, they did it just to save money,' Beryl went on. 'Perry's as tight as a duck's arse and Agnes doesn't ever like to be far away from her purse.'

Laughing, they paused when they heard a sudden sound from upstairs. Glancing at each other, they both ran towards the stairwell, Faith leading her grandmother up the steps. When she reached her grandparents' bedroom, she ran in to find Sid lying half on, half off the bed.

'God!' Beryl exclaimed, running over to her husband. 'Sid, Sid, love! Wake up! Wake up!'

But he wasn't going to wake up, Faith knew that. She knew he was dead, that he had died only moments before. When they had been downstairs talking . . . And she was oddly comforted by the thought. Her grandfather would have died hearing the sound he loved most in all the world – the sound of laughter.

Hesitating, Ellie waited by the post box with the letter in her hand. She had wanted to call by and see Faith, but hadn't dared, and now she was back in Paris, working in the job she had chosen over marrying James Farnsworth. Of course her mother and her friends had backed her up. How could she have sacrificed her whole life to look after a crippled man? No one would expect it of her. Ellie knew that the news of James's accident had come as a relief to her mother. Just as it had to her. Because although Ellie hadn't wanted to go to Paris, when they wanted her, when they fussed her and told her she could be a success – well, then she wanted to. Suddenly Oldham wasn't enough for her. The job at the bakery too lowly. And then Ellie could see what Sybil had been talking about for years – it was a chance to be someone.

Who could blame her? Ellie asked herself often. But she could still remember the sting of Faith's slap and knew she had deserved it. Besides, Ellie missed her old friend, missed their talks and confidences. And she knew that Faith had needed her most at the very time she had turned her back on her friend and her fiancé. Nothing she could do would ever make up for it. She fingered the letter in her hand, remembering what she had written.

> Dear Faith
> Please don't tear this up before you read it. Even though you have every right. What I did was terrible, but I'm too young to marry. Everyone said so. I did love James, but . . . I don't know what to say. Give him my love, if you want to. If not, I understand. If he hates me, I understand. But there was no one else.
>
> Sorry about your grandad. I heard yesterday and wanted to call round, but I thought I might be the last person you wanted to see. Honestly, Faith, I'm so sorry. Sorry about Sid and about the rest.
> Ellie

Could she send it? *Should* she sent it? What good would it do to reopen old wounds? But then again, Ellie had been fond of Sidney Bentley and it would look rude to ignore his death. *Rude*. The word sounded suddenly lame, out of place. She and Faith were long past politeness. In reality, the letter might look as though she was crowing. After all, she had escaped, whilst her friend was struggling with James, the business and all the pressure of her family. Torn, Ellie extended her hand towards the slot in the post box.

Then she paused, screwed up the letter, and walked off.

It was no good, Peter decided, he couldn't get used to the idea. And the atmosphere at the studio was impossible. He was sympathetic, but there was a limit, Peter told himself. Besides, Faith didn't want his sympathy. The real reason for Peter's growing dissatisfaction was the news that Beryl would be coming back to work in David Street. She couldn't stand to be alone in Hardy Street, Faith had said, so would be returning the following week. She had been grief-stricken by Sid's death and it would do her good to work. Faith had been relieved by the thought of her return, but Peter had been horrified. Beryl was a formidable woman, used to running the studio her own way. How long before he was being bossed around? Besides, the business was short of money, and Beryl wouldn't take the salary Peter was being paid. She was perfectly capable of doing the photography too. It might be unusual for a woman, but that wouldn't stop Beryl Bentley filling her dead husband's shoes. Peter realised in that instant that soon he would be a burden. If they didn't want to fire him now, circumstances would soon force them into it.

The glory days were over. The short time the three of them – Peter, James and Faith – had shared. All of them young, all independent for the first times in their lives. Peter thought back fondly, thinking of how James and Ellie would sit chatting on the old sofa in the studio. At the same time he and Faith had been sweethearts . . . Peter started at the word, as though it was a gunshot. *Sweethearts* . . . And then he wondered how odd life was, that love could alter so quickly. Not because of anything that had happened between them, but because of James's accident.

Glancing down at the prints in his hands, Peter began to hang them along the string in the darkroom. He had grown used to the lack of light, to the smell of the chemicals, and had even mused about expanding the business, he and James going off for days to take snaps of the trippers. But now there would be no day trips, no holiday snaps. No jaunts to the seaside. James was marooned in the basement of David Street, and now Peter wanted to get out fast. Get out before he was stuck there too. Before Beryl came, and before the relationship between him and Faith worsened.

Taking off his overalls, he walked into the studio, smiling briefly at James, who was just closing the ledgers.

'I'll be off then.'

'Fine,' James replied. 'Can you turn the sign round?'

Peter nodded, keeping his face averted. He didn't want James to look into his eyes. Didn't want him to guess about the advertisement Peter had read earlier that day for a job in Southport. Walking over to the door, he turned up the gas lights and then moved the sign to CLOSED. Outside, he could hear rain dripping on the cellar steps and thought of James's fall. How he would never be able to look at a basement again without thinking of his crippled friend.

Clearing his throat, James called out, 'See you tomorrow.'

Peter nodded, putting on his hat. 'Yeah, see you tomorrow.'

Something in Peter's voice alerted James, making him call his friend back. 'Are you OK?'

'I'm fine.'

'You seem . . . on edge,' James went on, trying to draw Peter away from the door, trying to stop him leaving. 'I'm sorry it didn't work out between you and Faith. I hope it wasn't my fault. I mean, it can't be easy having me here, hanging around all the time.' James laughed, but the sound was strained, almost desperate. 'I could get out of here for a bit, go over to Hardy Street and keep Beryl occupied. Give you and Faith the place to yourselves. Perhaps I should have done that before now.'

'James . . .'

'The two of you need time to talk.'

Peter's hand was still on the doorknob, his voice distant. 'I don't think it would help.'

James nodded. 'No, maybe not.'

'She's a great girl, your sister.'

'Yeah.'

'And you're a great man,' Peter went on, turning back to his friend and looking at him.

'You're saying goodbye, aren't you?'

Hanging his head, Peter nodded, then turned away. From the studio, from his friend in the wheelchair and from the romantic hopes he had once nurtured. Without answering James, he ran up the cellar steps two at a time, only looking back when he reached the end of David Street. The rain was pelting down, the City Photographic Studio sign dripping water into the dark basement yard below.

CHAPTER TWENTY-THREE

May 1910

Whistling, Samuel Granger crossed St Peter's Square, pausing to light a cigarette. His attention was caught by the headline about the death of Edward VII, and it made him think of his own mortality, something he seldom considered. After all, he had always been fit. A pretty good runner at school, and a fair boxer too. But nothing special, nothing out of the ordinary. Not enough to go on to train as a top-class athlete. Instead Samuel had followed his father into the family business, running a corner shop. Until the shop had burned down in a fire and Samuel had moved to Liverpool to find work.

Always loving the outdoors, he had avoided anything that kept him inside. Soon he was working for the council as a gardener, and then he was promoted to head gardener in charge of three other men. Not bad for a man of twenty-six. But when they wanted to promote him again, he refused. An office job wasn't for him. The pay would have been better, but he had no dependants, and besides, no one on earth was going to keep Samuel Granger tied to some desk. So he kept working the gardens, and in his spare time he went fishing in the Manchester Ship Canal, and later, further afield. Or he went walking, up to Hawkshead Pike or over to the moors. His last girlfriend had been a keen walker too, but her insistence on getting married had finished their romance. Samuel was a free spirit. And by God, he was going to stay that way. He knew that in time he would have to settle down, marry and have kids, but he was going to put it off for as long as he could. One day, he told himself, a woman would come along. A one-off type of girl. A strong, independent, feisty lady would enter his life, take a grab at his heart and make his existence seem colourless without her. And when she arrived, he would snap her up . . . But for the present, he wanted to be free, with nothing to hold him back.

The regular life of his late parents had instilled in Samuel a loathing of routine. Luckily, his older brother had the academic qualifications that had enabled his parents to brag, and Samuel had the brooding good looks that had made up for his lack of ambition. His father might have fretted about his future, but Samuel's mother would always say: 'With a face like that, people will forgive him anything.' What Mrs Granger hadn't realised was that Samuel's real power lay in his sensuality. He was at peace with himself and at ease with the world, relaxed and irresistibly carefree. The fact that he had inherited the Celtic good looks from his father's side and the intensity of his mother's Spanish ancestors only added to his appeal. Whilst other men fretted about their jobs, pay packets and courting, Samuel let the world go on its merry way, giving the impression that at any time he might choose to join in, or leave the party.

Taking a breather on the Manchester street, Samuel inhaled on his cigarette and read a headline about the suffragettes. Good for them, he thought, let women have the vote, why not? Why should men rule the world? But his relaxed manner as he leaned up against the wall had drawn some unexpected attention. After all, it was midday, and most healthy young men were at work.

'Morning.'

Pausing in front of Samuel, a middle-aged policeman looked him up and down.

Samuel smiled back. 'Morning.'

'Can I help you, sir?'

Samuel shook his head. 'No thank you.'

'You work around here?'

'No,' he replied, unfazed. 'I'm new to Manchester.'

'Where d'you live?'

'I haven't decided.'

'Where d'you work?'

'Don't know yet.'

Suspicious, the policeman stared at Samuel hard. 'You just come out of prison?'

'God, no! I've never been in trouble with the law.'

Samuel laughed easily. 'I told you, I've just arrived in Manchester. I'll be getting a job and a place to live soon.'

Normally, idle young men hanging around city centres meant that they were layabouts, or up to no good. But this man seemed different to the policeman. He was well spoken, for one thing, and very presentable. In fact he could have passed for a professional man. Not the usual kind of deadbeat.

'There's always vacancies in the police force,' the officer said, regarding the healthy young specimen in front of him. 'You could do worse.'

Samuel doubted that, but kept up his charm. 'I've been thinking of going to talk to the council, see about some gardening work.'

'You might at that. But then again . . .' The policeman paused, thinking. 'I've just heard about a job going over in St Anne's Square. They want a handyman to help out with the chores in the church, and do the outside plants and flowers.'

Surprised, Samuel nodded. 'Thanks. I'll check that out.'

'You do that,' the officer replied. 'Say I sent you. Officer Tully.'

'You don't know me.'

'I'm usually a good judge of character,' the policeman replied. 'Mind you don't let me down now, you hear? I've friends there and I'll not be too pleased to hear any complaints.'

Finishing his cigarette, Samuel watched the policeman walk off, then followed the directions he had been given, reaching St Anne's Square about fifteen minutes later. The day had dried out, and soon an idle sun was trying to make an impact on the greasy streets. Having seen the squalor of Liverpool, Samuel was glad he had decided to move cities, and was immediately taken by the smart streets in the centre of Manchester. And St Anne's Square was the smartest he had seen so far. Walking up to the church, he paused to admire the large stone urns outside, and the circular stone beds. Good work, Samuel decided, impressed by the geraniums and roses glowing up at him. Gently he touched the leaf of one of the roses, feeling the softness and smiling, his hand trailing over towards a small knotting of lobelia. For a moment he forgot he was in a city, until the sound of a horse-drawn carriage disturbed his thoughts. Turning, Samuel caught a glimpse of an elderly man inside, looking out. His face was pale, without expression, his head rigid and powerful.

Thoughtful, Samuel turned his gaze away from the carriage to the opposite side of the street. There two men in top hats were debating some point, the younger man's hands moving with agitation, the older man bearded and portly. They seemed very much at ease in the city, very busy, very full of business. Smiling, Samuel's scrutiny moved on, past the gossiping men to a group walking towards Deansgate. There was a woman with two children, an older woman – probably the grandmother – walking with them. Their clothes were well cut, the women's skirts long and full, their large, glamorous hats speckled with feathers. Samuel could imagine the feathers on some bird, imagine it winging its way up into the clear blue sky over Hollingwood . . .

'Are yer standing there all bloody day?'

Starting, Samuel turned to see an old man without any teeth staring at him. 'Oh, I was . . .' He recalled the policeman's name. 'Officer Tully said that you needed help here.'

The man was obviously a caretaker, stooped, his arms wiry as he emptied a pail of water down the nearest drain. 'Yer come from round here?'

'No.'

'This is a church.'

'I can see that,' Samuel replied, smiling. The old man shrugged, but his ill temper was fading.

'I'm the caretaker here. I work for the trustees, church council. I don't have anything to do with the religious side.' He spat into the drain. 'From what I've seen of life, religion's a bugger. A right bugger.'

'I wouldn't disagree with that,' Samuel replied, lighting a cigarette and offering the old man one.

Rubbing his hand clean on the side of his overalls, he took it, lighting up and nodding a curt thanks.

'Yer know about flowers and plants?' he asked hoarsely.

'None better. Used to work for the council in Liverpool.'

'So why did yer leave?'

'I got bored,' Samuel answered honestly. 'Officer Tully said you needed a handyman too.'

'Yer can turn your hand to most things, then?' the old man asked, inhaling deeply and enjoying the smoke.

'I'm useful to have around.'

'Yer look healthy,' the old man said, putting out his hand. 'M' name's Ezekiel Horne.'

'Samuel Granger,' he replied, shaking hands. 'Quite a name you've got there, Mr Horne.'

'Ezekiel.' He sniffed. 'My mother was a church woman, put me off for life.'

Together they smoked their cigarettes. Samuel was in no hurry. He never was.

Finally the old man spoke again. 'Pay's not bad. Yer work six days a week. And attend services if yer want to.'

'No, I don't think I'll bother with that.'

'Wise man. The woman yer have to talk to is Mrs Alice Winter. Tough old bird, runs the church council. Nothing gets past her, and if she doesn't like yer, yer've no chance.' Ezekiel pointed one spindly finger towards the back of the church. 'Go to the end of the building, no further or yer'll end up in the Corn Exchange, then take the back door into the church. Inside, there's a room off the entry porch. She'll be in there now.'

Nodding his thanks, Samuel stubbed out his cigarette and followed the directions he had been given. On entering the back of St Anne's church, he felt the chill of the thick stone walls, the heavy wooden door swinging closed behind him. When his eyes adjusted to the light, he could see the aisle in front of him leading towards the altar and, above it, a huge stained-glass window. In the centre of the window was an image of the crucified Christ, various saints around him, the yellow of his crown of thorns catching the sunlight and making a golden orb on the tiled floor. Thoughtfully Samuel walked over to the patch of illumination, putting the tip of his shoe into it, the yellow making a toecap of light.

'Who are you?' a reedy voice said imperiously behind him.

Samuel turned to see a narrow woman staring at him. Her hair was hidden under a black bonnet, tied severely under the chin, her dress long and without colour. She was holding several hymn books, her hands bluish at the fingers.

'I came about the job,' Samuel began. 'Officer Tully sent me. He said you needed help.'

'But who are you?' the woman demanded, putting down the hymn books and looking Samuel up and down. Her manner was autocratic, her face wrinkled deeply around the eyes, her tone already indicating that he was not the kind she wanted around the church.

'My name's Samuel Granger—'

'Which means nothing to me,' the woman snapped back.

He realised then that he had come across this kind of woman before. Judging from her clothes, she was well off, high in the social strata, with a merciless sense of her own importance. A woman who sat on committees and doled out charity like torture. A woman who had never known poverty and despised people who needed help. A woman who was humble in the presence of God but cruel to her fellow man. In short, the type Samuel loathed.

'Never mind, I must have got it wrong,' he said, turning to go.

'Hold on there!' another voice called out, stopping him. 'Just a minute.'

Hurrying from the back of the church came a rotund woman with a full head of hair. She was carrying hymn books and flowers and struggling to keep hold of them, her arms laden, her smile warm as she reached Samuel. He liked her at once. Liked the open face, and the no-nonsense northern accent.

'Mrs Winter, I don't think beggars can be choosers,' she said to the chilling woman, who was pursing her lips with disapproval. 'We need a hand with all that needs doing around here, and if this young man was sent to us by Officer Tully, we should consider him.' Turning to Samuel, she put out her hand, the books dropping to the floor. 'I'm Beryl Bentley,' she said, laughing. 'And we *do* need help. Now.'

He shook her hand, smiling in return, then bent to pick up the fallen hymn books. Mrs Winter had disappeared like a November frost. Beryl dropped her voice and raised her eyebrows.

'Her late husband left a lot of money to the church, so she thinks she owns it. And God too – if she had her way. As for me, I just help out when I have the odd hour. I like to keep busy, stops you thinking.' She put her head on one side, studying the newcomer and taking in the dark eyes and hair, the easy smile. Oh, he was a looker, she thought, but OK. Not one of the bloody Tommy Bentleys of the world. 'So, where did you spring from?'

'I've been in Liverpool, but left.'

'Wise, it's a dump,' Beryl replied crisply. 'When can you start work?'

'Now.'

'Now?'

'Well, I've just arrived in town and I've nothing else to do,' he explained. 'I might as well get started.'

'Only just arrived?'

He nodded. 'Officer Tully asked if I had just got out of prison.'

Beryl laughed. 'Your hair's too long for that!' she teased him. 'Where are you living?'

'I don't know. I thought I'd have a walk round later. There's usually a room to rent in a city centre.'

'Morpeth Street.'

'Sorry?'

Beryl repeated it. 'We have a family business on David Street, and Morpeth Street is nearby. I happen to know that Mr Allen at number 126 is looking for a lodger.' She paused. 'Oh, and whatever he asks, offer half. He's a rogue, but he keeps a clean house.'

'Thanks for that.'

'It's nothing,' Beryl replied, taking to the stranger. 'Tell him I sent you.'

'Is everyone in Manchester so trusting?'

'No, but Mancunians are pretty good judges of people. You learn to be, working with people every day.'

'So what kind of business do you run?'

She puffed herself up, always proud of the family empire. 'We've got the City Photographic Studio, in David Street. Of course, there's all this talk about people having their own cameras and taking their own shots, but there's always room for a professional. And we're real professionals. Three generations now. My grandson runs it with me. I take the photographs.'

Interested, Samuel regarded her. 'That's unusual work for a woman.'

'We're unusual women in our family,' Beryl replied, returning to her previous train of thought. 'When you're ready, we need the window frame of the vestry mending, and the door easing on the east side of the church.' She paused, going through a list in her head. 'Then you can wash down the back wall – some flaming kids have scribbled something on it – and after that the beds need weeding out the front.' Nodding, Samuel took off his coat, Beryl noticing how well built he was, how strong. This was a real worker, she thought, a man who was used to graft. 'You can handle that?'

'Of course, no problem.'

'Good,' Beryl said firmly. 'And when you're finished, come and look for me and I'll pay you. You'll need to give Mr Allen a week's rent in advance. That is, if you're staying for the week.'

He smiled at her. 'Oh, I think I might well be staying for a while.'

Three hours later Samuel had finished the work. Under the inhospitable glare of Mrs Winter he had mended and cleaned and weeded. With his sleeves rolled up and his jacket off, he seemed even larger, a fine figure of a man, Beryl thought, knowing that the dried-up Mrs Winter would find Samuel Granger intimidating. She was perfectly comfortable with the desiccated Ezekiel Horne, but Samuel was a young man, not yet thirty, and very male . . . Smiling to herself, Beryl left for David Street, arriving to find James at work developing some of the prints she had taken earlier in the day.

Over the previous two years times had been hard. The departure of Peter Dodds had been a surprise, but a relief, Beryl returning that week and taking over. At first she had thought about hiring another photographer, but soon realised that the takings would not run to it. So she had done what she had always done: she made the best of it. Having watched Tommy Bentley take photographs for decades, and seen how Sid did it, she was more than capable. But willing as she had been, Beryl found the process arduous. People, she realised, could be a pain in the backside. And children had been the worst. Watching his grandmother's struggle, James had found himself offering to help her. Beryl had scoffed. He had replied that if she wanted them all to end up in penury, she could keep refusing help. He had suggested that life might be easier if she let him assist.

From then onwards, Beryl had taken the photographs and James had developed them. They had the darkroom adjusted, the worktops lowered so that James could move around more easily, and after his wheelchair had got caught in the doorway twice, Beryl had the frame widened. The peculiar teaming of a stout middle-aged widow with her handicapped grandson had drawn some comment around Manchester, some clients attracted to the place because of the novelty value. But it had been touch and go. Faith had returned to work for Laurence Goldbladt and Mort Ruben; after all – as Beryl had said often – they had to know that there was *one* reliable wage coming in.

Time had shifted past the family whilst they had adjusted to James's handicap, Sid's death, and the saving of the business. Taking on as much extra work as she could, Faith had shored up the income. The City Photographic Studio stayed open, despite Kodak and Eastman flooding the market with cameras. Admittedly, it was only a small percentage of the population who could afford them, but before long the prices would start to drop – and instead of a camera being a week's wage, they would soon be within reach for many. The younger generation had been flushed with the thought of taking their own photographs, but many people still relied on the old formal studio portraits. What had seemed to be a hundred weddings had been immortalised. A thousand babies had been put on bearskin rugs and asked to smile. Half of them had puked or screamed. Many of them had wriggled so much that their portraits had to be repeated. The local butcher had come for a portrait before he had been due to become mayor. He had died a week later. Miriam Goldbladt had been snapped with her sister, and Agnes had had her second wedding anniversary commemorated with a photograph. She had bought a silver frame too – and lied about how much it cost, because Perry was mean with money.

A year after Ellie had thrown away her letter to Faith, she had written another one. This time, it had been Faith who had thrown it away. Ellie Walker had never been mentioned in front of James, even though both Beryl and Faith knew that he still missed her. Once Faith had passed Sybil in the street and been amazed when she had been snubbed. As though the fault had been James's, not Ellie's. The damage she had done had been grievous. She had struck the man she had supposedly loved when he was at his lowest ebb. For that, Ellie Walker would never be forgiven. Despite the passing of time, no other woman had caught James's eye and his confidence had gone. Time had sawn away the raw edges of shock, but nothing had prepared him for his fall from manhood. His accident had not only changed his body, it had stunted his mind.

James's sense of humour had returned. He had been able to make jokes, and tease his sister again, but his wheelchair kept him physically and mentally hobbled. He had aged before his time. Talking to Faith and his grandmother about world matters, the making of the first movie in USA and the death of Mark Twain, he could have been a man in his fifties, not his twenties. As for Faith, she had been preoccupied looking after her brother and bringing in a wage. She had never talked to James about Peter Dodds. How could she when romance was always such a painful issue? But she had thought about him often when he first left, with a mixture of regret and relief. And curiosity. If she had married Peter she would have had a home of her own. Been released from David Street, moving into another world – but she knew it would not have been enough. Faith had been right about Peter Dodds: he hadn't been strong. He hadn't been reliable. He hadn't been there for her.

Taking off her hat as she entered the studio, Beryl glanced at the clock, looking into the kitchen for Faith. She was standing in front of the oven, taking out a pie from Sullivan's, one she had collected earlier in the day.

'Smells good,' Beryl commented, turning the hat brim round and round in her hands. 'We got a new handyman at the church today.'

'Oh yes?'

'Good-looking fellow. Strapping man,' Beryl went on admiringly. 'Muscles on him like the strongman at the carnival last year. I told him to go to old Allen's for a room.'

Faith raised her eyebrows. 'It's not like you to recommend a stranger.'

'I like him,' Beryl replied, taking off her coat

and starting to lay the table for supper. 'You'd like him too. Time you were going out and having some fun. You haven't had a boyfriend since Peter Dodds.'

'I've been busy,' Faith replied. 'You know what it's been like here. God knows, if we had another year like the last, we'd have to close down.'

Beryl waved aside the words.

'Well, we're still here. And that's not in small measure down to you. Thank God you've got that job with Laurence.'

Putting down the knives and forks in her hands, Faith turned to her grandmother. 'I'm worried about Laurence.'

'You're always worried about someone.'

'Honestly, I am worried.'

'He has a wife for that.'

'Miriam doesn't know what's going on at the showroom,' Faith replied.

Beryl raised her eyebrows. 'What *is* going on at the showroom?'

'That lizard Lennie Hellier . . .'

'Who gets better dressed every month that passes.'

'. . . is undermining Laurence. And Laurence doesn't see it. He thinks Lennie is a good man, a good help. Laurence isn't as sharp as he used to be. I know he's not well, but he's not seeing Lennie Hellier for what he is.'

'Which is?'

'Dangerous.'

Beryl blew out her cheeks. 'That's quite a word. You never liked Lennie, why is that?'

'He's a creeping toad of a man,' Faith replied, turning away. 'He's sneaked into Laurence's life and business like a worm crawling into an apple. And I think he'll turn it rotten – just like a worm would.'

Surprised, Beryl mulled over the words. 'What's he up to, then?'

'That's the point. It's never anything you can put your finger on. It's just him, creeping around, always into everything. Watching, listening. I hate the man.' Faith paused, trying to rein in her feelings. 'And I'm worried that he might harm Laurence. Laurence has been good to us, Gran. Good to all of us. We should watch out for him.'

At that moment there was a knock on the basement door. Faith put down the pie and hurried to open it. On the doorstep stood a stranger, a well-built man with dark eyes.

Surprised, she asked, 'Can I help you?'

'I wondered if Mrs Bentley was here?' Samuel replied, looking past Faith and watching Beryl approach. 'I'm so sorry for coming uninvited like this, but Mr Allen wants something in writing.'

Sighing, Beryl took a pad off the desk and began to scribble, beckoning for Samuel to come in. Standing to one side, Faith studied the newcomer, finding herself impressed by his appearance and his easy manner. But when Samuel glanced over to her, she looked away, flushing.

'I thought I heard an unfamiliar voice,' James said, wheeling himself out into the studio.

For a moment he looked at the newcomer, and Faith could feel what he was thinking. A man around his own age, healthy and strong as James had once been. A man who reminded him – without saying a word – of his own terrible shortcomings. The instant was electric, until Samuel walked over to James, offered him a cigarette and then took a seat next to him.

'So,' Samuel said easily, 'what happened to you?'

James had never been accepted so immediately. No one had ever asked outright what had happened. Instead everyone had tried to ignore the wheelchair, and made its presence bigger and more offputting by doing so.

'I fell,' James said, smiling as he took the offered cigarette. 'Broke my back.'

'I broke my leg once,' Samuel replied. 'Hurt like hell. Does your back hurt?'

'No, not any more.'

'That's something.'

'Yeah,' James agreed, suddenly light-hearted. 'You're right, that *is* something.'

Watching the exchange between the two men, Faith stood mesmerised. She saw the two of them, both dark, but dissimilar in the details: James fine-featured, Samuel brooding, moody-looking – although nothing could be further from his character, she suspected. She watched the stranger tell James about the work at St Anne's church, and saw her brother respond, talking about the old days for the first time in two years. Enthralled, she watched James laugh as he used to, and felt herself drawn to the sturdy stranger who had brought her brother back to life.

There and then, she fell in love with Samuel Granger.

CHAPTER TWENTY-FOUR

It was the autumn that Dr Crippen was tried for murdering his wife. His attempted escape overseas with his mistress, Ethel le Neve, had been followed by the nation. A telegram had been sent to the vessel to apprehend the couple, the first time that a wireless communication had been used to catch a criminal. They had been brought back to England to stand trial, and now the news was being called out all over Manchester: DR CRIPPEN GUILTY. SENTENCED TO HANG.

It was a time of change. Only months before, Thomas Edison had demonstrated in the USA the first moving film, sound and picture coming together to capture real life.

'Bugger it,' Beryl said angrily. 'Why couldn't he leave well alone? Before long no one will want to have their photograph taken.'

'He says it will take at least two years to come on to the market,' James replied, trying to console his grandmother. 'A lot can happen in two years.'

'A wedding can happen,' Beryl said suddenly, all

thoughts of Edison dismissed. 'I reckon Faith will marry Samuel Granger.'

'They've only known each other for a couple of months!'

'Oh, what difference does that make?' she responded, getting to her feet. 'I knew almost straight away that I would marry your grandad. And look how happy we were.'

James couldn't argue with that. And besides, if Faith was going to marry anyone, he would want it to be Samuel. The two of them had quickly become friends. Samuel had the knack of drawing James out, of making him face the difficulties he had tried to ignore for so long. James had even talked about Ellie Walker with Samuel, the latter not responding the way people usually did, but with rare understanding. Ellie had been very young, he said to James. Too young to cope with such a trauma.

And suddenly James let go of all the resentment he had been harbouring. All the anger he had turned inside, he released. Ellie *had* been too young, too thoughtless, too scared. If she had stayed with him, what could he have offered her? And how would he have judged himself, marrying her when he couldn't be a proper husband or father? In the face of Samuel's calm judgement, James could finally see what he had refused to admit – the romance could never have worked. The moment he fell, it was over. It wasn't Ellie's fault. It wasn't his. It was fate. And that was all there was to it. As simple, and damning, as that.

'How do,' Samuel said, walking in and waving the newspaper above his head. 'Good day for the banks.'

'It's always a good day for the banks,' Beryl replied, turning to him. 'You want to stay for some tea?'

Samuel paused, taking a paper bag out of his jacket pocket. 'Boiled ham,' he said simply. 'Enough for all of us.'

He never came empty-handed.

'So, where's Faith?'

James jerked his head upwards. 'Still in the showroom.'

'With Mr Goldbladt?'

'No, he's off sick. She's holding the fort with Lennie Hellier.'

'I don't like him. He's shifty,' Samuel replied. He turned to James, changing the subject. 'I've got an idea for you. You've been in this basement too long; you have to get out. I thought we could go for a jar later on.'

Bemused, James stared at his friend. 'How do I do that? Levitation?'

'I've been working on a plan,' Samuel continued, putting a drawing down on the table and spreading it smooth. 'It's an improvised pulley system to get you up from the basement on to the road above. We could make it safe, and haul you up so you could get back into the world again.'

'How's it work?'

'With ropes.'

James put his head on one side. 'What if the ropes break?'

'What are you worried about? You've already broken your back.'

Laughing, James stared at the drawing of the device with unexpected excitement. Living and working in the basement had been the perfect excuse not to get back into real life. He couldn't get out, unless several people helped him, and so he had become used to *not* getting out. In time, the basement and the studio had become a refuge. He found them safe, and gradually ceased to resent his captivity. But now Samuel had come into his life, and suddenly all his friend's talk of beer, music hall and pubs seemed irresistible. Now James *wanted* to go out, was no longer afraid of being seen or pitied. Because if a man like Samuel Granger had chosen him for a friend, what was there to pity?

'Are you sure it will work?'

Samuel shrugged. 'I'm sure. Don't you trust me?' He turned as Faith came into the basement. 'Look at this,' he said, guiding her over to the drawing. 'This is the way James is going to get his freedom back.'

She frowned. 'What is it?'

'A pulley system to get him out of the basement.'

'Oh, I'm not sure about that.'

Samuel cut her off at once. He knew how protective she was, and had decided that she needed her brother's independence as much as James did. Just as he had decided – within weeks – that he was falling in love.

'I looked into getting a lift from inside to the ground floor,' Samuel went on, 'but that's too expensive and I can't build it myself. This would do for the time being.'

'But would it be safe?'

'I like the idea,' James cut in suddenly. 'For God's sake, Faith, you know how handy Samuel is. He can build anything within reason. Let's give it a go.'

That weekend, Faith and James watched as Samuel began to build the pulley system. Whilst Beryl struggled with a portrait of a newly engaged couple in the studio beyond, brother and sister stared out of the window. Admiringly, Faith gazed at Samuel's well-muscled arms, and when he took off his jacket and rolled up his sleeves, she flushed. He was, she had to admit, a fine specimen. More appealing than Peter had ever been, and – despite his good looks – not as conceited.

'Are you going to marry him?'

She nodded dreamily. 'Oh yes.'

James laughed loudly. 'Does he know?'

'Not yet.'

'He soon will . . . I thought there was something going on between you two.'

She smiled shyly. The attraction between them was obvious, but they hadn't even been out on a date yet, although Samuel had asked her to go for a walk with him on Sunday. Faith couldn't wait.

'He is very handsome, isn't he?'

James was struggling to keep his face straight. 'If you say so.'

'And very good around the house.'

'That will be useful,' James replied, tongue in cheek. 'Good God, Faith! I thought you had a steady head on your shoulders. I can remember you not being interested in boys when you were younger . . .'

But you didn't know why, thought Faith, glad she had never confided. The whole sordid scenario with Lennie Hellier was in the past, and need not impinge on her future.

'Although you *were* keen on Peter Dodds once.'

She continued to stare out of the window. 'Not like this.'

'Well, he didn't have the muscles, did he?'

Laughing, she turned to her brother. 'I wasn't really in love with Peter.'

'I know.'

'He was safe.'

'And Samuel isn't?'

'No, he's secure, which is a different thing. A safe man is unexciting; a man who offers a woman security is the answer to her dreams.'

Laughing, James nudged his sister. 'God, listen to you! What a romantic!'

'I *like* being romantic,' she replied, flushing again. 'It feels good.'

'I remember.'

She stopped laughing at once, James shaking his head. 'No, it's OK, honestly. It doesn't hurt like it used to. I was mad about Gracie once. Remember her?'

'Could I ever forget?'

'And then there were others.'

'*Plenty* of others, James.'

'And then there was Ellie.' Faith baulked at the name, glancing away as James continued. 'I still think of her, you know. And I've forgiven her.'

'I haven't.'

'You should.'

'After what she did to you? Never.'

A noise outside made them both turn. Samuel was tapping on the window and gesturing to the pulley contraption. Walking to the door, Faith held it open for James to pass through, both of them then looking at the device with open curiosity.

'Are you ready to try it?' Samuel asked James.

'It looks . . .'

'Professional?'

'No, the word I was looking for was strange.'

'Ah,' Samuel said lightly, 'that's what everyone has been saying about the new flying machines.'

'And they've been crashing.'

'This,' Samuel said, holding his confidence, 'will not crash. Now, James, I'm going for a pint. You want to come with me or not?'

It hadn't taken Ellie long to realise her mistake. About a month, actually. At first she had been carried away by the excitement of the Moulin Rouge, by the thrill of living and working abroad. But reality had set in quickly, and hard. For a start, she didn't speak the language and the other girls resented her. When she asked for help from the manager, she was told to fend for herself, the only offer of lodgings being some cheap hotel around the corner. One that housed the dancers and the prostitutes from the surrounding area. By the time Sybil had been gone for a week, Ellie was regretting her decision to stay in Paris. Not that she could complain. She had burned her boats once and for all. There was no going back. Because what was there to go back to?

Homesick, she stared at her reflection in the dressing room mirror. Behind her she could see some of the other girls changing, walking around nude or semi-clothed without any embarrassment. Not respectable girls, none of them. Putting on some rouge, Ellie turned her gaze back to herself. She looked much older than her years, some of the softness gone from her face already, the make-up giving her a hard, worn look. But then again, it was a hard life. A life of dance routines, long nights, and running the gauntlet of the stage-door johnnies who hung around the back of the theatre after every performance. It hadn't taken Ellie long to realise that some of the girls were giving more than their time to their admirers, and when she saw one girl back at her hotel actually taking a man to her room, she had felt adrift, naïve, lost.

It was at such times that she thought of James Farnsworth. Of how happy they had been. Of how she had promised she would ruin her chances at the audition and never leave him. But then temptation had come, and Sybil pressurising her, together with the shock of James's accident, had forced her into moving to Paris. And what a disaster it had turned out to be. Ellie knew that her mother bragged about her in Oldham. Could imagine Sybil telling the customers at the milliner's about her famous daughter starring in Paris. But the truth was far more sordid. Ellie was in the chorus, losing weight and losing interest, and before long losing her job if she didn't watch out. The manager had thrown a scare into her the previous night. Told her to buck up her ideas or she would be fired. If she wanted to throw away her chance, fine with him. Ellie had been determined not to lose her job. Not because she enjoyed it, but because she couldn't go home a failure. Sybil would never forgive her. And anyway, Ellie told herself, any day now she could meet someone. A good man, with money and prospects. A man who would rescue her. Hadn't her mother told her about her own past? Hadn't she constantly reminded Ellie about her lost opportunity? You're a dancer, her mother had told her, reminded her in her frequent letters:

Look after yourself, Ellie, and keep your eyes open. You'll get an opportunity to better yourself and when you do, grab it. Don't make the wrong decision, like I did. Marrying for love is all well and good, but a woman needs to be secure.

Ellie wondered just how secure she would feel

with any of the stage-door johnnies she had met. One look into their leering faces put her off. They were all similar, all after the girls for a good time, nothing else. Young men in packs, middle-aged men with money, old men with beards and walking canes. Music-hall villains, Ellie thought, only they weren't in the music hall. They were in her life. And she hated every one of them. It hadn't helped that Sybil, in trying to protect her daughter, had managed to put Ellie off the whole notion of romance and sex. Ellie had grown up believing that love was a bargaining tool, and that men didn't know how to love, only how to seduce a woman. And always in the back of her mind was the towering image of her mother, strident, warning her of the dangers of being taken in by a look, a word. Don't trust anything a man says, Sybil had told her. Don't drink with them. Don't be alone with them. Don't let them touch you . . . So deep had the indoctrination gone that Ellie now loathed and distrusted all physical contact with men. Her mother might worry that she would go off the rails, but Ellie wasn't even tempted.

The only man with whom she had ever felt safe had been James Farnsworth. He might have been experienced, good-looking, and had all the girls after him, but he had loved her. Had made the notion of loving and making love something tender . . . Ellie bit her lip, fighting emotion. Jesus, why had James fallen? she asked herself, looking away from the mirror and the tawdry reflection of the girls and the dressing room behind. Why hadn't she married him? What a fool she had turned out to be. After all, she had been in two minds about the job from the start. Excited that she had passed the audition, but undecided if she would really go. She had even come to a kind of compromise in her own head. She would go to work in Paris for six months, or a year. Have the experience, and then come back and marry James.

All the way back to England Ellie had practised the words, the explanation. She had known that James would be resistant, but had trusted that he loved her enough to let her have her way. Then, after a while, she would come home again; she would make him that promise. She would have had the experience, satisfied her mother's ambitions for her, and at the same time not missed out . . . Still biting her bottom lip, Ellie remembered the night she had returned. Remembered Faith coming to the door. Remembered telling her that she had passed the audition. Then Faith had told her about James, and suddenly Ellie had panicked. Had known that if she had stayed then, if she had stood by her fiancé then, she would never escape.

So she had taken the coward's way out. If only James hadn't fallen, she thought despairingly. But he *had* fallen. And she had made the decision to turn her back on him. A decision that had stranded her as much as James. She was ashamed of her cruelty; ashamed of her actions.

And she knew she could never make it right.

It was a cool evening when Faith and Samuel took their first walk. Because it was autumn, there were still people about after six o'clock, families with their children, and a number of couples. Some talking, some linking arms, others gazing into each other's eyes as though breaking contact would mean disaster. Having dressed himself in his smartest clothes, Samuel arrived at David Street to find Faith wearing a soft blue dress and jacket, topped off with a small half-veiled hat. She looked spectacular, he thought, mesmerised. Of course he had known from the start that she was good-looking, but this evening she had taken special care with her appearance and he took it as a good sign. After all, if she hadn't been interested in him, she wouldn't have gone to so much trouble.

Offering her his arm, Samuel felt a sense of real pride as they walked down David Street towards St Peter's church. They walked in perfect unison and he was faintly disturbed to see several other men glance at his companion enviously. But apparently Faith hadn't noticed, and when Samuel paused by a bench in St Anne's Square, she was more than happy to sit down next to him. He could feel the warmth from her body and stole a quick look at her profile, the long eyelashes fringing the dark eyes, the nose not too short or too long, the bottom lip slightly fuller than the top one.

Coughing, Samuel took out his cigarettes and lit one. 'You don't mind if I smoke, do you?'

'Oh, no,' she said easily, trying to think of what to say. Did she talk about the weather, or about the business? Maybe she should say something intellectual about politics. Or would that put him off?

'I was—'

'I just—'

They had both started talking in the same instant, and laughed.

'You go first, Faith.'

'I was . . . I was just wondering if you liked Manchester?'

'Yes, it's a nice city.'

She nodded, not knowing how to continue, just knowing that if he turned around, pulled her to him and kissed her she wouldn't object. In fact, looking at his big hands, Faith was *longing* for him to stop talking and touch her.

'Are you all right?'

She flushed, staring ahead.

'Of course. What's it like living at Mr Allen's?'

'Busy,' Samuel replied. 'There must be another ten people in that house. Two old women, a family, and some Chinese man who doesn't speak English.'

'Chinese?'

Samuel nodded.

'We have to queue up to use the bathroom.' He stopped, certain he shouldn't have mentioned bathrooms.

Faith stepped in to rescue him. 'Do you think you'll be staying in Manchester for a while?'

'Oh yes.'

'That's good,' she said, then flushed again. Damn, she shouldn't have said that! Everyone knew that men didn't like a girl to seem keen. 'I mean, it's a nice city.'

Thoughtful, Samuel scratched his cheek. 'I was in Liverpool for a while.'

She relaxed at once. On safe ground. 'I remember you said you'd been there.'

'Before that I was in Preston,' he went on hurriedly, as though it was imperative that he give Faith a résumé of his geographical history, so that she knew all about him from the start. 'I was working for the council there as well, on the parks and gardens. Before that, I worked in my father's shop.'

'Your father had a shop?' she asked, turning to him with interest.

'A corner shop, in Bolton. Nothing grand. Not like the City Photographic Studio.'

'It's not grand!' she replied, relaxing and taking off her gloves. 'We've been lucky to keep it afloat.'

'Your grandmother's an amazing woman.'

Faith laughed. 'Oh yes, she's all of that! The place wouldn't be the same without her. When she was nursing my grandfather, James ran the business with someone called Peter Dodds. He was a decent photographer, but not as good as Beryl. Not that she would ever admit it! She says she hates taking pictures, but she loves it really. She learned from her father-in-law, and from Sid. She's a real professional.'

He could see the genuine affection and warmed to it.

'You're lucky having such a close family.'

'Haven't you got anyone?'

'No, only a brother, and he emigrated a while back.'

Thoughtful, Faith watched a pigeon pecking at something in the gutter. Samuel inhaled on his cigarette languidly.

'Why didn't you go into the family business?' he asked.

'We need a regular wage coming in,' she replied matter-of-factly. 'And besides, I like working for Laurence Goldbladt.'

'I don't like his assistant, though.' Immediately Faith tensed, Samuel noting the reaction as he carried on. 'Odd man. I wouldn't trust him as far as I could throw him.'

'You're a good judge of character.'

'I think so,' Samuel replied. 'I judged you the moment I saw you.'

'Really?'

'Yes. I judged you to be beautiful and good.'

'Samuel!' she said, laughing. 'You don't have to say what you think I want you to say.'

'I never do that,' he replied, perfectly calm. 'I only say what I think. You should know that about me, Faith. I don't flatter or manipulate people. I don't plot or even make many plans. I know where I'm happy and who I want to spend my time with. I'm not a politician and my ambitions are limited.' He paused, stubbing out his cigarette with the toe of his boot. 'I like the outdoors, gardens, and not having to answer to a boss. Or having to clock in at some office every day at eight thirty. My life will never make me a millionaire, but I'm a happy man.'

Surprised by his eloquence, Faith took a moment to reply.

'Not everyone in the world has to be ambitious.'

'It would be hard if everyone was,' he agreed.

'James wanted to do more with his life. Wanted to open things out with the business, but that's over now.'

'No, it's not over,' he contradicted her. 'It's just changed.'

'I'm glad James has got you for a friend,' she said sincerely. 'You've given him a new lease of life. He likes you.'

'I'm glad, I like him. But there's something more important . . .'

'Yes?'

'Does his sister like me?'

Smiling, Faith glanced down again. 'His sister doesn't really know you that well.'

'Do you think she might like to get to know me better?'

'That depends.'

'On what?'

'Well, she wouldn't want to waste time getting to know someone who would then move on.'

He paused, pleased by her answer, but carrying on with the charade.

'What if he thought he had found a place to stay?'

'Then she might be interested in getting to know him,' Faith replied, looking Samuel full in the face.

Gently he touched her cheek, brushing aside a stray hair, her heart rate increasing rapidly. 'I want to get to know you, Miss Farnsworth. I want to know about your past, what matters to you, what you care about. Whether you like animals and hate circuses. Whether you cry at books or read the evening paper. I want to know if you admire the suffragettes. If you think the world is round, or if you believe there's nothing beyond the stars.'

Her voice was muted. 'You have a way with words.'

'I've had a long time to think them up – and no one to say them to, until now,' Samuel replied gently. 'All the time I've worked the gardens, travelled, spent time alone and thinking, I was rehearsing and hoping that one day I'd be sitting next to a beautiful girl. And now I am.' He took Faith's hand, kissing the palm and then closing her fingers over it. 'Are you interested in me? If you are, tell me. If not, I'll leave you alone. Stay friends, but not bother you again.'

'Oh, Samuel,' she said, leaning towards him eagerly. 'Please, *never* stop bothering me!'

CHAPTER TWENTY-FIVE

From that evening onwards, Faith and Samuel spent most of their spare time together. Samuel hadn't lied, he did want to get to know Faith, and she returned the compliment. Sometimes she wondered about Peter Dodds and breathed a sigh of relief that the romance hadn't worked. By contrast to Peter, Samuel was always supportive. He might not always agree with Faith, but he was always one hundred per cent on her side. And woe betide anyone who said anything about his girl. He was loving, but stood up for himself. He was relaxed, but no doormat. He was sensuous, but not crude. The only problem Faith could see with Samuel Granger was his lack of ambition.

Thoughtful, Faith watched her grandmother through the gap in the door. The studio was carefully prepared for the next session. A man with large ears was sitting with his whey-faced wife, who was holding a baby. With big ears. And a cold. Judging from her grandmother's expression, Faith could guess what Beryl was thinking: why bring the

kid when it had a snotty nose? But the couple –
against an English countryside backdrop – seemed
impervious. Patiently they posed. Patiently they
turned their heads on Beryl's commands, and
patiently they waited whilst she flicked away a fly
that had landed on the husband's right ear. Beryl
had just got the photograph nicely lined up when
the baby puked.

After another exhausting ten minutes, she walked
into the back room, and looked at her granddaughter incredulously.

'Did you see that?'

Faith nodded.

'Well, if anyone wants a photograph of vomit in
motion, we can sell them a copy . . . What's up?'

'I don't think Samuel's ambitious.'

'You can't blame him for that,' Beryl said, walking off. A moment later she came out of the darkroom with some recently developed prints. Holding
a magnifying glass over the pictures she sighed, then
marked out three prints she approved of. 'He always
admitted as much. Anyway, you're not ambitious,'
Beryl went on, 'so what's the problem?'

'Nothing,' Faith replied, glancing at the prints
and wondering how her grandmother had managed
to get two of the plainest brothers in Manchester to
look impressive. 'It's just that men *should* have
ambitions, shouldn't they?'

'To be happy, treat their wives and families well,
pay the rent and have a bit left over – that's all the
ambition a man needs.'

'But Samuel's still working as an odd-job man at St Anne's.'

Beryl put down the photographs and her magnifying glass, looking steadily at her grand-daughter. 'Oh, I see.'

'See what?'

'It's serious between you and Samuel. Mind you, I did suspect as much from the start. I thought you two were made for each other.'

Gesturing for Beryl to drop her voice, Faith asked, 'Shouldn't Samuel have a better job, if he's going to get married?'

'Depends on who he's marrying.'

'Gran!'

Beryl laughed. 'OK, let's be serious.'

'It *is* serious.'

'Yes, I can see that. I can also see that you're determined to work out the future for the both of you.'

Faith looked away. 'Is that wrong?'

'God, no!' her grandmother replied. 'Marriages always work out best when the woman does the organising. But Samuel mustn't know that. A man likes to think that he's in charge.'

She paused, looking at her granddaughter with admiration. What a wise head on such young shoulders. But then Faith was twenty years old, old enough to marry – although Beryl had hoped she would have a bit more of a life before she settled down. Then again, Beryl had worried about Faith getting mixed up with the wrong man. She was pretty enough to turn heads, and a flightier girl might have been tempted to go off the rails. Luckily Faith wasn't flighty in the least. And now she had made her choice of husband. Beryl frowned. She liked Samuel, liked him a lot. Thought he was honest and attractive, and knew that he genuinely cared for her granddaughter. There was only one matter on which Beryl had any doubt – was Samuel too easy-going?

Yet there was a big difference between easy-going and easily led. And certainly Samuel was not easily led. He had very clear ideas about his life, what he wanted and how he wanted to live. Ambition did not seem to figure. But then again, Beryl thought, he was a hard worker, not the feckless type. Not one of the Tommy Bentleys of the world . . .

'Does it matter?'

Beryl blinked, turning to her granddaughter. 'Does *what* matter?'

'That Samuel is so content with his lot?'

'I would say that was a rarity in a man. Most are always running after something – or someone.'

Faith nodded. 'He loves me, he tells me all the time. And I believe him. I feel happy with him, and safe.'

'Do you love him?'

'Oh yes,' Faith said easily, smiling at her grandmother. 'I think I fell in love with Samuel pretty quickly. But now I feel something deeper for him. You know, like he's family. I care about him, about how he feels. Like I would care about you, or

James. But in a different way . . .' She frowned, trying to articulate her thoughts. 'He's made me feel something I've never felt before. Like it would be wrong *not* to be with him . . . D'you understand?'

Beryl sighed. 'I do. Sounds to me like Samuel Granger is the man for you.'

'I've never really wanted that much in life,' Faith went on. 'A nice home, enough money, a few treats. But I've never been ambitious myself, so why should I expect it from Samuel? Perhaps it's not a problem; perhaps I'm just making something out of nothing.'

'Perhaps you are, love,' Beryl agreed, adding slyly, 'But then again, better to think about your future before you rush into it.'

'I *have* been thinking about it. About all the practical things, as well as being married to Samuel.' Faith flushed. 'The job he's got now pays enough to cover his rent and take me out. He never seems short – and he always brings something when he comes.'

'But?'

'He's an odd-job man.'

'You really are a snob!' Beryl said, feigning outrage. 'You're just like Agnes after all.'

'I'm not like my aunt!' Faith hissed sharply. 'I'm just trying to work out if it matters that much to me. I know I love Samuel, but do I want more from a husband?'

'Well, you're honest, I'll give you that.'

'All right, I know it sounds horrible – but it's how I feel, and I have to talk about it.'

'Peter Dodds didn't have a proper job until he worked here.'

'But I wasn't thinking of marrying Peter.'

Beryl nodded. 'Has Samuel proposed?'

'Not yet, but he's hinted,' Faith admitted. 'And you know something? Now we've talked this out, I know what to do. When Samuel *does* ask me, I'm going to say yes. Our two jobs would bring in a decent amount, but we'd have to find somewhere to live.'

'What!'

'Well, we would, Gran. We can't live here and I can't live with Samuel at Mr Allen's.'

'God, this *is* serious,' Beryl replied, thinking ahead and suddenly brightening. 'You could live in Hardy Street!'

'That's *your* home.'

'I know, but it's not felt like it since Sid died. In fact, when I'm there at night it's sad, to be honest.' She paused. 'You could take the house on, pay the rent to me. I mean, I'd like to say you could have it for free, but I've not got the money for that.'

'Of course we'd pay!' Faith said, her voice excited. Hurriedly she looked around her, checking that James couldn't overhear their conversation. She wanted to break the news when everything was settled, and not a moment before. 'Do you mean it? Samuel and I could take over Hardy Street?'

'Well, I daresay you'd want to change it a bit, but of course I mean it,' Beryl agreed. 'I'll move back and live here, in your room. James won't be alone and neither will I. To be frank, love, it'll suit me down to the ground. So, are you going to tell Samuel?'

'No!' Faith replied heatedly. 'Not until he proposes – and then I'll let *you* suggest it. I don't want him thinking we've been talking and plotting behind his back.'

Picking up the photographs again, Beryl stared at her granddaughter. 'Are you sure this is the right man for you?'

'Yes.'

'And it's not going to be a problem that he's not ambitious?'

'I said he was the right man,' Faith said archly. 'I didn't say he was perfect.'

Getting to her feet, Faith moved to the door just as Samuel walked in. He was hot from working at the church in St Anne's Square, and out of temper, Mrs Winter having given him the runaround all day. Unusually irritated, he nodded curtly at Beryl and passed her some oranges he had bought off a street vendor. Taking them from him, she had the sense to leave the two of them alone, walking into the back and pretending to be busy. Luckily James was in the darkroom, working on the prints Beryl had taken earlier, and wasn't likely to re-emerge for an hour.

In the studio reception, Samuel was standing, hot and irritated, the skin on his neck sunburned and beginning to blister.

Caught off guard, Faith tried to soothe him.

'D'you want a cold drink?'

'Up on the roof!' Samuel snapped, throwing down his jacket and rolling up his sleeves. 'I was up on that flaming roof for nearly an hour, the sun boiling my brains.' Faith smiled, but it was the wrong thing to do and simply infuriated him further. 'It wasn't funny!' he snapped. 'I can't stand that old woman, always hanging around telling me what to do. She treats me like a child.'

'Sit down,' Faith urged him. 'Come on, put your feet up. You must be tired out.'

But for once he ignored her. 'Where's James?'

'In the darkroom.'

'I wondered if he wanted to go out for a drink.'

'I could go out with you.'

'I can't take you to a pub! What kind of woman goes into a pub? God, Faith, sometimes you talk rubbish!'

Stunned, she stared at him. 'What?'

'As if I would take you to a pub!' he went on, his face colouring, the sunburn looking painful. 'You're impossible sometimes!'

Angry, she turned on him. 'I don't really want to go out with you.'

'Yes you do. You just said you did!'

'I was lying,' she said coldly. 'Why would I want to go out with some half-boiled idiot?'

His eyes blazed. 'Half boiled, hey? I'd like to see what you would look like after an hour on a church roof.'

'Better than you!'

'Really?' he hissed. 'Perhaps you should try it.'

'I was working here.'

'Modelling clothes? Hah!' he snapped. 'Some hard work that is.'

Faith's expression was explosive, her voice rising uncharacteristically high. 'My job is hard work!'

'Well if I could find someone to pay me for just wearing clothes, I would.'

'No one would pay you – you'd put the customers off. Who'd wear anything some oaf modelled?' she hurled back.

Samuel grabbed her arm. 'So now I'm an oaf, am I?'

'Yeah, an oaf with a red face,' Faith retorted.

Samuel stopped short – then pulled her to him and kissed her hungrily.

When he stopped, he was laughing. 'Oaf with a red face, hey?'

'Does it hurt?' Faith asked, touching his sunburn gently.

'Not half as much as all those cruel things you said, Miss Farnsworth,' he teased her. Then he paused, kissing her again. 'Will you marry me? I mean, when I'm not so red-faced?'

Laughing, she kissed him, her lips resting against his sunburned cheek. 'Yes, I'll marry you, you big oaf,' she said. 'And I love your red face, sweetheart. Every sore, burning patch of it.'

CHAPTER TWENTY-SIX

Laurence Goldbladt was trying very hard to concentrate, but the pain in his left leg and his anxiety about Miriam's health were taking their toll. All Laurence's dreams of cruises seemed suddenly out of reach. He wasn't fit, and Miriam was certainly nothing like she had been only a few years before. Sighing, he sat down heavily, his bad leg stretched out before him. He could see that the showroom was running smoothly, but his eye for fashion was failing him. Having missed the Paris and London shows, his latest collection looked tired and uninspired. There was, after all, only so much to be gleaned from catalogues and newsprint. Faith had been invaluable, as ever. In fact Laurence knew that without her his business could possibly be running at a loss. She had a sense of style and was good with the customers. She had kept people coming and buying despite Laurence's absence, charming them into sales that would otherwise have been missed.

The day-to-day administration and maintenance

was still being undertaken – as it had been for years – by Lennie Hellier. He had grown a little plump on good fortune, and obviously regarded the show-room as his own domain, although he was careful not to show it when Laurence was around. One thing Laurence *had* noticed, however, was the increased freeze between Faith and Lennie. Often he had wanted to ask her about it, but the time never seemed right, and Lennie was always around, almost as though he wanted to prevent any confidences passing between his employer and Faith. Wincing, Laurence eased his leg on the stool. The specialist in Rodney Street, Liverpool, had told him it was his circulation. Bloody marvellous, Laurence thought, he had paid ten pounds to be told something he knew already. Miriam's diagnosis was more complicated. The consultants talked about some virus, possibly something they had picked up on one of their trips abroad, but no one had any idea how to treat it. Slowly she was growing worse. And slowly Laurence was cutting back on his hours at the showroom. Money and success were still important to him, but other matters had taken precedence. Health and old age, the fear of being left alone. Of losing Miriam, of being crippled . . .

'Sir?'

Laurence looked up. Lennie was watching him with a sympathetic expression. 'Is there anything I can do for you?'

He waved aside the question. 'No, I'm fine.'

'Perhaps you should go home?'

Laurence was tempted by the idea, but he had to look at the books and keep an eye on the business. He might trust Lennie completely, but *he* was Laurence Goldbladt – it was his business, and his responsibility.

'I have to check the accounts.'

'They're completely in order, sir.'

'I don't doubt it, Lennie, but I want to see them,' Laurence said, wincing again as he reached out and touched his painful leg. 'Business wasn't so good last month.'

'It goes up and down, sir.'

'More down than up at the moment, hey?'

Slowly Lennie approached his employer, looking at him with real concern. 'You should go home and rest, sir. The books will wait for a few more days.'

He could see the pain on Laurence's face, the effort it took for his employer to move, let alone get comfortable.

'How's your wife?'

'Not good. Thanks for asking.'

'Please send her my best regards,' Lennie replied, offering his employer a glass of water. 'I could call your driver, sir. I mean, there's a chill in the air and you should be home. No point catching a cold now, is there? You don't want to make things worse.'

Make things worse . . . The words echoed in Laurence's head, along with the dire warnings about Miriam's health. No, he didn't want to make things worse. He wanted – if he was honest – to take himself home, lay his tall, heavy body on the soft

315

bed next to Miriam, and sleep. Not have to think about furs, Russian traders, customers, showrooms or accounts . . . Heaving himself to his feet, Laurence made his slow, painful way to the door.

'I think I *will* go home. You hold the fort now, Lennie. You hear me?'

'Of course, sir.'

'Faith will help you.' He looked round, suddenly realising she wasn't there. 'Where is Faith?'

An almost imperceptible change came over Lennie's face. 'Oh, you mustn't worry . . .'

'About what?'

'Miss Farnsworth is just as interested in her job as she ever was,' Lennie went on silkily. 'She's just a little preoccupied.'

For a moment, Laurence's mind cleared. 'Preoccupied? With what?'

'Not with what, but with *whom*,' Lennie replied, pretending that he had said too much and was now embarrassed. 'Oh, ignore me, sir, I didn't mean to imply anything. It's just that Miss Farnsworth seems to be seeing the wrong kind of man. And she has been for some time. A roughneck,' he said, his tone damning.

He expected Laurence to be outraged, to insist that he didn't want Faith getting mixed up with any man. After all, hadn't Laurence picked them out for each other a long time ago? Hadn't he said he had plans for the two of them? Hadn't Lennie *lived* for that promise? That intimation of domestic and professional advancement?

'Yes, it's grand news about Samuel, isn't it?' Laurence said, not noticing Lennie's face pale, his mouth opening slightly in confusion. 'Although he's hardly a roughneck, Lennie! Anyway, good for her, I say. Faith deserves a bit of joy in her life.'

'But sir . . .'

'No point getting jealous, Lennie. You'll meet someone one day. Some nice girl. When I'm gone, and you're free of this place, you'll start a new life.'

Lennie was sure his legs would give way under him, that he would drop where he stood. The shock was so great he almost lost control of his bladder. All the years of planning and waiting. All the years of looking after Laurence Goldbladt and his showroom. He had grovelled and crawled his way up from a heap of blankets on the floor to the position of assistant showroom manager, with prospects . . . Only there *weren't* any prospects, were there? They had just been a figment of his imagination. Laurence Goldbladt didn't think of Lennie Hellier as his protégé, or his successor. He thought of him as he had always thought of him – a dogsbody. A glorified, jumped-up dogsbody. And when Laurence gave up the showroom, Lennie Hellier would be a dogsbody without a job and without a home . . . In that instant Lennie Hellier hated Laurence Goldbladt. He hated him so much that he could have knocked the older man over and kicked him into a pulp. There was no future glory, no alliance with Faith Farnsworth; it was all a sham.

Lennie had been cheated, and someone was going to pay for that.

But he wasn't going to show his hand until he was ready.

'As you say, sir, we can't be too hard on Miss Farnsworth,' Lennie went on pleasantly, although he could taste the bile in his mouth. 'Now, would you like me to call your driver, sir? If you hurry, you could be home safe before it gets dark.'

His face impassive, Lennie watched through the window as his employer was helped into his carriage, waiting until he saw the brougham leave David Street. Then he looked down at the pulley mechanism that lifted James Farnsworth from his basement prison on to the street. The lights were on in the City Photographic Studio, and as Lennie watched, he saw the door open and heard voices. Grasping the window ledge, he leaned out, listening. He knew the voices well. Faith was laughing, Samuel running after her as she took the basement steps two at a time. When she reached the street above, she was still laughing. Lennie ducked back into the shadows so that he couldn't be seen. But he could see them. See the way Faith looked at Samuel, and the way he touched her cheek. He could see with blinding clarity what he would never feel. What he would never earn. What he would never have.

And then Lennie Hellier made a promise. That however long it took, whatever it cost him, he would get his own back on Laurence Goldbladt –

and ruin Faith Farnsworth's life. How, he didn't know. When, he didn't know. But as he remembered Laurence's words, and watched the happiness of the couple below, he soured inside. His heart folded, his blood curdled and his thoughts turned to one thing and one thing only: revenge.

Hurrying through the front door on Gladstone Street, Agnes paused to consider the news. Her eyes blinked, as though unfocused, the shock resonating throughout her entire body. Dear God, she thought, feeling her way to a seat, how would she break the news to Perry? Sitting down, Agnes pushed her hair away from her forehead. Thank God marriage had put an end to her disguise and now she was free to show her grey streak. Anyway, she had told herself repeatedly, it was elegant. There was some woman in the *Variety* magazine, who actually showed off her streak – even if Beryl had said that it looked like an old knife scar.

The previous years had been mellow for Agnes. Having at last caught Perry, she had settled down into married life with him with considerable ease. Agnes, house proud and hysterical at the thought of leaving her own home, had managed to convince Perry to come and live under her roof – thereby getting the residential upper hand. Further upper hands followed. Perry's regular visits to the Lion and Bugle were limited, until Agnes realised the advantage of getting her husband out from under her feet. She was more successful with the church, and loved nosing around St Mark's in Oldham. As she said to her mother, watching Perry – recently promoted to usher – working his magic on a Sunday was worth being bored into stupefaction by the vicar's sermon.

Agnes made sure that her marriage was happy, and although she was puzzled by Perry's sense of humour, they were a good pair – even though she had tried his patience with her pretences, and damn near suffocated him with her collection of china dogs. As he had said – not unreasonably – how many pairs of china dogs did one couple need? Agnes was immune to logic. She had read somewhere that china dogs were a sign of breeding, and so she reckoned that four pairs meant four times the breeding. And then there were the window boxes . . . Agnes had heard about the affectation in France and had decided that she would have the first window boxes in Oldham.

The trouble was that Oldham was not rural France, and so the day after her careful planting out, every geranium had been stolen, leaving empty boxes of earth. Outraged, Agnes had insisted that Perry plant some more flowers – with a notice underneath that read, DO NOT TOUCH. The next morning, all the flowers had been removed again, with the sign underneath scrawled out and overwritten with HELP YOURSELF. Determined not to be beaten, Agnes planted more flowers, this time with a notice saying, THIEVES WILL BE PROSECUTED. Relieved that this last threat had done the trick, she was pleased to find her flowers still in place in the morning – but with a pile of cat excreta deposited in amongst them. Beaten, she got Perry to move the window boxes to the back, away from the street – and any vandals or ginger toms.

But *this* news was even worse, Agnes thought, her mind returning to the present. This was a black mark on the whole location; the street would never be the same again. A Chinese laundry had opened around the corner. The thought made Agnes blanch, and she fanned herself with the afternoon paper. What kind of neighbourhood was it coming to when you had Chinamen washing clothes only a few doors away? She wondered fleetingly if there was anyone she could complain to. What about the local MP? Perhaps Perry could write to the House of Commons? Perhaps there had been a mistake and the Chinaman would be moved on. Back to Liverpool or Manchester. To some city where laundries were more commonplace.

'Agnes?' Perry said, his tone concerned as he walked in and saw his distressed wife. 'Whatever's the matter?'

She buried her face in her handkerchief, milking the moment before she spoke again. 'Oh my dear, such a terrible thing has happened.'

'What is it?'

'Some Chinaman's opened a . . . a . . . laundry in Parkway Road.'

Amused, but not daring to show it, he sat down beside her. 'Why?'

'To wash clothes!' she snapped, beside herself. 'A laundry round the corner – what a comedown.'

'Who's running it?'

'I told you, some Chinaman! And there's worse – he's married with four children. Four *yellow* children.'

'But . . .'

'What *are* we going to do?'

'Well, it could be worse, Agnes dear. The Chinese . . .'

She fixed her baleful glance on him.

'. . . are very industrious.'

'Industrious!' bellowed Agnes. 'You can say that again! Four children – and all under six!'

CHAPTER TWENTY-SEVEN

Inside the darkroom, James was staring into the chemical tray in front of him as the image of a man slowly materialised on the print. He had heard the mock argument outside, and had smiled as it came to its conclusion. For nearly six months he had waited for the inevitable proposal, knowing that Samuel would ask, and that Faith would accept. It was, James knew, the perfect match. As perfect as any match could be. And the knowledge that Samuel loved his sister so much was a consolation to James. A consolation, but a blow to his own heart. From now on, everything would be different. When Faith married, she wouldn't live in David Street; she and Samuel would have their own home. Which was the way life went – for most people. But not for him.

James was sensible enough to know that when Faith left, his outings with Samuel would be curtailed. Not over, but lessened. The hand-made pulley that had winched him back into the world would be pressed into service less often. Well, James decided, hanging up the still-developing print, he

would just have to make some more friends . . .
Sighing, he let the print drop back into the chemical,
for once not caring if it was ruined. James was sick
of being agreeable, of being able to cope with his
handicap. He *had* come to terms with it – but not all
the time. At nights he dreamed he was walking
again, making love to Ellie. But in the morning he
woke and struggled to get himself into his
wheelchair.

There had been some improvement in his
condition. As the doctors had hoped, he now had
intermittent feeling in his pelvis and left leg. But it
wasn't enough to enable him to get on his feet and
walk. Or even enough to give him mobility with a
cane. He could look after himself, wash himself and
dress himself, but it wasn't enough for a twenty-six-
year-old man who dreaded the loss of his sister's
company. Especially as he knew that Beryl would
move in as Faith's replacement. It wasn't that he
didn't love his grandmother, it was the fact that he
hated the thought of being dependent again,
grounded in the basement of David Street. After all,
Beryl couldn't get him in and out of the pulley, and
he hadn't the strength to do it for himself.

Fighting despair, James took the print out of the
chemical and realised he had left it in too long and
ruined it. How unlike him, he thought, but then
again, Beryl had taken other prints. If only life
consisted of a series of prints, so if you buggered up
one, you could just develop another . . . Come on,
James told himself, stop the bloody self-pity. Things

could be worse. He could have been put in some home for disabled people. God knows he had heard about such places, where the patients were left for twenty-three hours a day making baskets or weaving bloody paper bins. Living in wards with dozens of other handicapped people, with no access to the outside, apart from weekly visits from relatives.

He had to pull himself together, remember that he had been lucky. He still had a job, a home . . . So why didn't he feel lucky? he wondered, wheeling himself out of the darkroom. He had heard the shop door close as the others had gone out, calling their goodbyes, and had replied saying that he was busy and would see them all later . . . Now he paused and looked upwards, seeing the feet of the passers-by, and the pulley system hitched up against the basement wall. He smiled, remembering how Samuel had built it, and then thought of the letter in his pocket.

Should he open it? No, he thought, no, there was no point. But then again, how did he know for sure that there was no point until he read it? Slowly he took the letter out of his pocket. An apology, he told himself. That was what it would be. An apology, after so long. Years, in fact. So why write now? he thought, curious and afraid of the paper in his hand. Why write now if it was just to say sorry? Wasn't that something she should have said a long time ago, after she had rejected him and gone off to France?

Open it, you ass, he told himself. But his

reluctance was immense. He had got over the worst of losing Ellie, but there had never been a real chance for him to forget her. Unable to live as a normal man, he had been denied the opportunity to find another woman and fall in love again. Instead he had been suspended in an emotional limbo, with only Ellie to remind him of being able-bodied, in love. Open the bloody letter, he told himself. But what if it *was* just an apology? Then again, what else could it be? James thought, wondering what tricks his mind was playing on him. What else could she want, or offer, or ask? He wasn't any good to a pretty young woman, a woman who would want to be loved and bear children. But still he couldn't open the letter. Still he couldn't bring himself to be hurt, or disappointed. It was so long ago; forget it, he told himself, just forget it . . . He stared at the handwriting on the envelope, so childish, so young. Just the same as it had always been, when Ellie had written him notes and hidden them in his jacket pocket for him to find later. Or pinned them in his account books, where he would come across them and smile, longing to see her later that evening. She had been so warm, so yielding, so very young. He thought of the last time he had seen her, in a cream coat, with her soft red hair pinned back from her face, her eyes enormous, full of hope. His girl, his wife to be. Marry me, he had asked her. Marry me . . . and she had said yes. Yes, yes, yes . . .

Making up his mind at last, James ripped the

letter into tiny pieces. Then he put the pieces in an ashtray and put a match to them. He sat in his wheelchair and watched them burn, curl up, turn from words and emotions and ink and paper into ash. Unreadable, undecipherable, safe.

Beside himself with excitement, Mort Ruben danced from foot to foot like a one-eyed pixie. His girl, his beautiful Faith, was getting married. In the chair beside him sat Laurence, his leg raised on a stool, watching Mort with curiosity.

'Faith works for me, she's closer to me than she is to you.'

'Nonsense!' Mort piped up. 'She's always been my girl.'

'Sid and I were friends.'

'You can't pull rank, Laurence, I'm making Faith's wedding dress.' Mort turned away, then pushed a pattern towards his friend. 'You see, this is the latest. A small hat, and a slender silhouette.'

'She could wear a fur . . .'

'In September!' Mort replied, aghast. 'No, Faith will have a proper dress.'

'Beryl said they wanted to keep the wedding a quiet affair,' Laurence went on, trying tactfully to suggest that money was tight and there was no cash for a splashy do. 'Just family and a few friends.'

Holding up some ivory silk, Mort paused, regarding his friend with his one good eye. 'Which means us; we're the only friends Faith has.'

'Well, Samuel's not got any family, except a

brother in Australia,' Laurence went on, rubbing his leg, Mort watching him with anxiety.

Laurence's health had deteriorated rapidly over the preceding months. He was spending a good deal of his time at home with the ailing Miriam, and when he did come to David Street it seemed that he could hardly wait to be gone again. For a while Mort had wanted to talk to his friend, but the time had never seemed right – until now.

'How's Miriam?'

'The doctors aren't sure what's wrong with her.'

Hypochondria, Mort thought, uncharacteristically judgemental. He knew that Laurence had spent a fortune on doctors, and that after Miriam's original illness – from which she had recovered – they had discovered nothing else. Mort also thought that Miriam was enjoying having Laurence dancing attendance on her. Which wouldn't have mattered if Laurence had been well himself. But as it was, a few difficult seasons and his anxiety at home had aged Laurence and taken the lustre out of his life. At one time he would never have been seen without being perfectly and exotically turned out. Now he had discarded his opulent waistcoats and spats, and his jackets were in need of a press and some sponging. Mort had seen the deterioration and had worried about it, but on the occasions he had gone downstairs to talk to Laurence, Lennie Hellier had always been hanging around. Lennie Hellier, smarter by the month, more groomed, seeming to take on Laurence's polish as his employer faded.

'You need to take a holiday,' Mort said, fingering the silk. 'And when you get back, you should have a good look at your business. I mean, I don't want to pry – I never have pried into anyone's life – but you're a friend, Laurence, and I'm worried about you.' Taking in a hurried breath, Mort continued. 'Perhaps you shouldn't let Lennie have too much of his own way. I mean . . . I mean, well, when Faith is on her honeymoon, Lennie will be in the showroom on his own.'

'He was alone when Faith had to help out in the studio,' Laurence replied, his voice lacking its usual vigour. 'I trust Lennie.'

'Well, yes . . . yes . . .' Mort moved from foot to foot again. 'But . . . but . . . but *should* you?'

Slowly Laurence turned to his old friend. He was exhausted, mentally and physically, and the showroom didn't matter to him any longer. He knew it should, knew that when he was better he would be angry with his lethargy, but his life was so difficult, and he couldn't think as clearly as he once could. Rubbing his forehead, Laurence gazed into Mort's face and found himself momentarily emotional.

'I can't live without her . . .' he said at last. 'Not my Miriam. I couldn't live without her.'

'Sssh, sssh,' Mort said consolingly, sitting beside his old friend. 'This is tiredness talking. Go away, Laurence, have a trip, both of you. When you get back you'll see everything so much more clearly. You will, you will.' He paused, then added, 'And close up the showroom while you're away.'

'But I've never closed it before, not in twenty-three years.'

'All the more reason why you should close it now,' Mort replied, his tone sympathetic. 'Laurence, my dear Laurence, close the place and then come back to it with fresh eyes. You can, you can.'

'Close it?' Laurence repeated, his mind wandering. Well, why not? If he did it when Faith was on her honeymoon, it would be the perfect time. Lennie had never taken a holiday, he could have a break himself. Yes, Laurence thought, why not? Close up, take Miriam off and have some time by the sea. Get some sun, some sleep, then come back with his appetite for work restored.

'Close up shop . . .'

'Yes,' Mort said, nodding. 'It would be so good for you, Laurence.'

'What about Lennie?'

Mort was unusually abrupt. 'Lennie can look after himself for a while.'

'He could stay in the showroom.'

'No!' Mort said, then tempered his tone. 'No, if I were you, I'd pay for Lennie to have a little holiday too. Close up the showroom, Laurence. Don't let anyone have access – not even Lennie.'

'But where would he go?'

'To the seaside,' Mort replied, encouraging Laurence. 'Most young men would like to take a break, all expenses paid.'

He knew that Laurence would have to pay for

Lennie, otherwise he would plead poverty and stay in David Street.

'You think about it. What a treat. A treat for him!' Mort repeated eagerly.

He didn't fully understand why he wanted Lennie Hellier out of the way, only that he did. He wanted his cloying influence out of the Goldbladt showroom, because in the time Lennie Hellier had been working – and advancing – there, Mort had seen Laurence deteriorate. Had seen Lennie take on more and more, assuming insidious control as he urged his employer to lean on him. And gradually the power had shifted, their positions reversing over the years. If anyone had walked into the Goldbladt showroom now, they would have thought that Lennie was the owner.

Mort was no politician, but he was a good man, and a caring one. All he knew for certain was that he wanted to break the hold Lennie Hellier had over his friend. Once there was some distance between them – once Hellier was barred from the territory he had made his own – Mort believed that Laurence would come to his senses.

'You think Lennie would go on a trip?' Laurence asked.

Mort nodded, for once lying. 'He would love it. Love it. Lennie will be grateful to you, Laurence, you'll see. Mark my words, you'll see.'

It was almost half an hour later when Laurence made his way downstairs, grunting with the effort as he limped into his showroom. A new delivery had been made of Canadian furs, the bales piled in the outer room. Faith was upstairs at a fitting with Mort, the day overcast as Lennie ushered in another delivery. Surprised, Laurence made his way over to the new arrivals. Russian sable, best quality – not something he had ordered, or could afford after the last indifferent season.

'What are these?'

Spinning round, Lennie seemed surprised to see his employer. Usually Laurence told him when he was coming in, but not this time.

Covering his dislike, Lennie made a slight inclination of his head. 'Russian sable, sir.'

Had he forgotten he had ordered it? Laurence wondered, trying to clear his thoughts, then noticing the name on the label: SKELINKERKI. He had stopped doing business with the firm a while back. They had cheated him, and although Laurence had made a good profit from them in the past, he was nervous of the new generation of thugs who now seemed to be bringing in the furs.

'We don't use Skelinkerki any more, Lennie.'

'I thought . . .'

'You know we don't.'

'But I thought you wanted to give them another try, sir,' Lennie replied, not looking at his employer, because if he did so, he would want to lash out. It was still so vivid what Laurence had said. How the flat-footed, heavy bastard had ground his dreams underfoot. 'You did say they had the best furs – and that Mrs Ford might like to see them.'

Laurence couldn't remember the conversation at all. Only that he hated the Skelinkerki people, and as for Mrs Ford, had he risked doing business with the Russians just to appease one customer? God, Laurence thought, Mort was right. He needed to take some time off. Needed to get his balance back, get fit again, on the ball. Slowly he turned to Lennie.

'I've got a surprise for you, Lennie. A thank-you.'

'But you treat me so well already, sir,' replied Lennie, his tone unctuous.

'I'm going on a trip with Mrs Goldbladt,' Laurence went on. 'For a little while.'

His heart shifting, Lennie could visualise the opportunity he would have to wreak havoc. Oh, he had started to undermine Laurence already, but a few weeks left to his own devices would suit him admirably.

'I hope you have a good rest, sir.'

'*You'll* be having a good rest too,' Laurence replied. 'I'm going to close up the showroom and send you on holiday.'

'But . . .'

'No buts, Lennie. You've worked for me for years without taking a break. You need a holiday; we all do. I'll pay for you to go away.'

Leave the showroom, Lennie thought, his head swimming. How could he? Where would he go? What would he do? He stared at Laurence, wondering if his employer had guessed. Wondering if he would investigate the books once Lennie was out of the way, find out what his assistant had been doing over the last few months. Breathing quickly, Lennie thought back. He had been determined to get his revenge on Laurence for leading him on. For making a workhorse out of him, dangling hints and promises, when secretly he was laughing behind Lennie's back. Thwarted, Lennie had chosen to get revenge. As the days passed, he had plotted, and when he heard about Faith's coming marriage, he had set his plans in motion. Only now Laurence Goldbladt was banning him from the showroom.

'I can't go away, sir!'

'Of course you can, Lennie,' Laurence replied, taking Lennie's reluctance as professional devotion. 'Have a good time, find yourself a girlfriend.'

Certain now that he was being mocked, Lennie found breathing difficult.

'Where shall I go?'

'A hotel,' Laurence replied. 'Let someone look after you for a change.'

'But . . .'

'Enough, Lennie! We're closing up the showroom and you're going on holiday.'

His attention wandering from his employee, Laurence touched the sable pile in front of him. He remembered the Russians and their reputation and felt distinctly uneasy.

'Tell them to take the furs back.'

Having ordered the skins himself to sell off privately, Lennie did not take the suggestion well. Oh, his employer was losing his grip all right, but apparently he had made an unexpected, if temporary, recovery. Damn him, Lennie thought, he had to turn the situation around, and fast.

'I don't think we *can* send the furs back, sir.'

'Yes you can!' Laurence replied, suddenly irritated to have his instructions challenged. He didn't like the Russians and he couldn't afford the furs. And if he had slipped up by ordering them, then they had to go back. 'Send them back!'

'I can't.'

'*You* can't?' Laurence replied, suddenly coming alive. His mind might have been foggy with worry lately, but he wasn't about to risk his business with dodgy dealings. And he wasn't about to be told what to do by his assistant. 'You would do well to remember that this is *my* showroom, Lennie. I say what goes here. I want you to send the furs back.'

'I don't think they'll take them, sir,' Lennie replied, his tone acid.

Laurence noticed the shift and felt suddenly anxious. 'Why not?'

'You owe them money.'

Blinking, Laurence stared at his employee. 'What?'

'I don't want to remind you, sir, but you did have a few . . . suspect dealings with them in the past.'

'That wasn't with them!' Laurence blundered. 'That was the traders before them. And they weren't suspect dealings, it was trade.'

'Skelinkerki don't see it that way, sir,' Lennie replied, his tone glacial. 'In fact, I don't think they would take it at all well if you went back on this order.'

Confused, Laurence tried to understand, but he couldn't. Had he made a bad business error? Had he offended someone and forgotten it?

'Lennie, what *are* you talking about?'

Taking in a calm breath, Lennie sounded utterly reasonable. 'Mr Goldbladt, why don't you leave me to run the business? After all, I have done so for years now. And lately, you and your business would have gone under if it hadn't been for me.' His bitterness threatened to choke him, and Laurence stared at him, stunned. 'Go on your holiday, sir, and don't worry about a thing.'

'You're telling me what to do!' Laurence said finally, when he found his voice. 'You upstart, you bloody—'

'Watch what you say, sir,' Lennie replied, backing away. 'I can do you harm, if I choose to.'

'Do me harm!' Laurence repeated, aghast. 'Why would you want to? What did I ever do to you that you would want to harm me?'

'You lied to me.'

'About what?' Laurence asked, his expression incredulous. 'I gave you a home, a job—'

Lennie cut him off, his anger too far gone to control. 'You made a fool out of me. You let me think that I was going to inherit this place.'

'What!'

'And that I was going to marry Faith Farnsworth.'

Laurence stared at the white-faced man in front of him.

'Marry Faith! I never said anything about that. How could I influence who she married? As for being my successor, I never promised you that.'

'You all *but* promised it!' Lennie replied, jabbing Laurence with his forefinger. 'You owe me!'

'I owe you nothing!' Laurence hurled back. 'I want you out of here now! Get out, Hellier, get out and never come back!'

'If I do, I'll bring you down with me!' screamed Lennie, seeing his plans destroyed before his very eyes. 'I'll ruin you!'

'GET OUT!' Laurence repeated, pushing Lennie towards the door, his anger overwhelming.

Always a coward, Lennie shrank away from his employer – then suddenly turned back to him.

'I'll get you! I'll get my own back on all of you. On you and Faith Farnsworth. I'll ruin you all.' He was terrifying in his rage. 'You hear me? All of you!'

Two weeks later I married Samuel in St Anne's church, Manchester. I remember reminding him of how he had got sunburn repairing the roof only the previous summer. True to his word, Mort designed a wedding dress so beautiful it made me gasp. God knows we could never have afforded to buy it, but he insisted that there was no charge. Typical. As for Laurence, even though business had been erratic for a while, he paid for us to have a weekend in Lytham. A honeymoon, he said. We had all heard about his argument with Lennie Hellier, and I wasn't the only person to be glad to see the back of him.

That autumn there was a brief warm spell, just when we went away. Mort told me that Laurence had gone on holiday too, with Miriam. He also told me that the showroom had been closed for a while. Empty for the first time in decades . . . I think about it now and shudder. But then I was going on my honeymoon, and if I spared one thought for Lennie Hellier, it was fleeting. Instead I gave myself to my new husband, and he adored me and teased me and made me feel complete. Comfortable, desired, loved.

On the second day we were away, we decided we would go for a swim. Embarrassed, I remember hiding in the beach hut as Samuel called for me – and then I thought of the woman I had seen all those years before. The beautiful woman who had been so elegant and so effortlessly cruel. Remembering her, I walked out of the hut, my new husband wolf-whistling and grabbing my hand as we ran to the sea. The water clung to my body and I could taste the salt on Samuel's skin as we lay on the sand afterwards. When the light began to fade, we were left alone on the beach. With his arms around me, Samuel told me about the future. He looked up at the darkening night sky and pointed out the North Star. He said no man could ever get lost if he followed that star. That it was put there by some good spirit, to guide the lost back home.

He said that he loved me. That I made his life worthwhile, and that he would never be alone again. That I would be his North Star. That wherever he was, he would be safe: able to look into the heavens and know that as long as the star was burning he could follow its light and know it would bring him back to me.

PART FOUR

CHAPTER TWENTY-EIGHT

The argument was the talk of the building, James having overheard it downstairs and telling Faith, then Faith passing it on to Mort. Who had already heard, thanks to the internal gossip of his workforce. What they didn't know, however, was the real reason behind Lennie's sacking. That Laurence revealed later – but only to a handful of his closest, oldest friends. People who knew Hellier and his history.

Hurrying downstairs to see Laurence, Mort immediately found himself pulled over to the window by his old friend, both of them staring down into the empty street below.

'I've fired the bastard.'

'I know,' Mort replied reassuringly. 'Come on, my old friend. Come on, Laurence, relax. He's gone now.'

'Bastard . . .'

But as the word left his lips Laurence faltered, slumping into one of the salon's chairs, colour draining from his face. Hurrying for the brandy,

Mort gave him a drink, urging Laurence to finish it. If the truth be known, Mort was terrified that his friend was going to have a stroke. But the brandy did the trick, Laurence coming round and staring at Mort with incomprehension.

'That snake said that I had promised he was going to take over the showroom one day.'

'Good Lord.'

'And that I intended for him to marry Faith.'

Mort's eyebrows rose dramatically. 'Marry Faith? Whatever gave him that idea?'

'The man's mad,' Laurence went on, the argument coming back to him in detail. Urgently he clutched Mort's sleeve. 'He tried to blackmail me.'

Stunned, Mort poured himself a brandy and sank it in one. 'Blackmail you? How could he, Laurence?'

'I don't know. He was talking about the fur traders.' Laurence heaved himself to his feet, moving into the workroom and pointing to the bales of Russian sable. 'He had been doing business with Skelinkerki.'

'But you'd stopped dealing with them!'

Laurence nodded. '*I* had – but obviously Hellier hadn't.' He moved into the back room, took out the account books and then sat down heavily at the showroom table. 'I have to go through these with a fine-toothed comb, Mort. God knows what I'll find, but I have to do it. Will you stay with me?'

Nodding, Mort sat with his old friend whilst Laurence went over the account books, entry by entry. As the hours passed, Mort listened to his friend sigh, click his tongue and curse. Finally, Laurence asked him to recheck the books, and both men came to the unpleasant conclusion that Lennie Hellier had been defrauding the business for the previous six months. Before that, he had simply kept a check of every sale Laurence had ever made. As midnight passed, Laurence slumped back in his seat, Mort offering him a Turkish cigarette, both of them too stunned to speak for a while. Mort knew what Laurence was thinking – what a fool he had been, what an imbecile to trust Hellier with his business. Mort was thinking the same, but he would never say it.

'What d'you think he'll do?'

Laurence sighed. 'He can't do anything really. I threw him out before he had time to get his things together. He left with nothing. Not my books, his notes, nothing.'

'Which was how he came,' Mort said, adding more quietly, 'I'd change the locks.'

'Yes,' Laurence agreed. 'And I'll sleep here tonight. Just in case the bugger comes back.'

Turning over in bed, Faith stirred, wondering what had woken her. Her hand automatically went out for Samuel, then she realised that he was staying the night at Hardy Street, doing some decorating. Confused, she opened her eyes, trying to place a sound she couldn't recognise. Then, startled, she sat up, glancing over to the window. Beyond the glass she could hear the ominous sound of crackling, the glowing red light and the smell of smoke alerting her. Jumping out of bed, she hurried from the bedroom into the studio, calling out to James and then running out into the street and shouting:

'FIRE! FIRE!'

At once the lights went on in the building next door, someone answering her immediately. 'We've seen the smoke. We've called the fire brigade!'

'There are people inside!' Faith shouted back. 'My brother's in the basement and there are people upstairs! Get help!'

Running back inside, she called frantically up the stairs to Laurence, but the smoke was getting thicker by the instant, and realising that she wasn't being heard, she began to ring the intercom buzzers on all the upstairs floors. Persistently she pressed the buzzers to warn Mort and Laurence, then saw to her relief that lights were going on overhead. Moments later she could hear footsteps on the stairs and people coughing. Without thinking of her own safety, Faith ran back down into the basement. Through the window of the bedroom where she had just been sleeping she could see flames rising against the glass. She closed the door to try and contain the fire, then moved into the back room and shook James awake.

'There's a fire!' she said. James sat up immediately on the couch. 'Come on, we have to get out!'

'You go!' he urged her, smelling the smoke and knowing that by helping him she might well endanger herself. 'GO!'

'I'm not leaving without you!' Faith snapped back, putting her brother's arms around her neck.

With an almighty heave she lifted him, James using his arms to steady himself as they both began to cough violently in the thickening smoke. Staggering forward, struggling with her brother's weight, Faith realised to her horror that his grip was beginning to fail. She also knew that if he fell, she wouldn't be able to lift him again.

As though he could read her thoughts, James pushed her away. 'GO! Faith, get out of here!'

But instead of leaving him, she clung on to him more fiercely and began to half carry, half drag him across the studio, making her way through the smoke towards the basement door. Exhausted, she was finding it difficult to breathe when suddenly someone took James's weight and helped them both out of the studio and into the cold air outside. Once on the street, Faith doubled up, coughing hoarsely, her mouth dry as ash, the taste of smoke still burning her lips and tongue.

The fireman who had helped her had put James down on the front steps of the building, Mort running out into the street where a crowd had gathered. As she looked up, Faith could see smoke at the top of the building, and then smelled the cold water and heard the slow fizzling out of the fire.

Exhausted, she turned to Mort. 'What about Laurence?'

'He's out – but they're going to check on him in

hospital,' Mort replied, his eyes empty with shock, his hands shaking as he slumped down on the front steps next to James.

'It could have been fatal,' one of the firemen said, walking over and looking at Faith. 'You were lucky . . . and brave.'

She nodded, not trusting her voice.

'Apparently it broke out in some boxes in the back yard,' the fireman went on, glancing at the building. 'It looks bad, but it's not really. Only superficial, nothing that redecorating won't fix. We stopped it before any real damage was done. Mind you, if you hadn't woke up, miss, it might have been another story.' The man paused before continuing. 'The smoke would have killed all of you – even before the fire would have done.'

Numb, Faith sat down on the steps next to Mort and her brother. Her voice was barely more than a whisper when she finally spoke.

'You know who did this, don't you?'

James nodded. 'Hellier . . . But we can't say anything; we have no proof.'

'If we did say anything, the whole argument with Laurence would come out,' Mort added, his tone wavering. 'And if anyone mentioned the blackmail, it would expose Laurence as much as Hellier.'

James sighed. 'So the bastard's going to get away with it?'

'For now,' Faith replied, her tone hard. 'But not for ever.'

*

In the dressing room, Ellie was sitting alone, huddled into a silk gown, her make-up heavy, her exotic costume cutting into her flesh. She had tried to do what her mother had asked. After she let James down so brutally, she had tried to put him out of her mind. Even attempted to emulate the dancers where she worked, accepting a date with one of the stage-door regulars. A middle-aged man who was rich and much sought after by the other girls. Balding, and very smart, he took her to a restaurant and showed her off, touching her bare arms repeatedly and talking about how Frenchmen all had mistresses. And whilst he talked, Ellie had felt as though her insides were a vacuum, her body emptied of emotion. She didn't want this kind of attention. The man's groping repulsed her, and when the time for dessert came, she excused herself and made for the powder room.

Once inside, Ellie locked herself in a cubicle and stared at the painted pink walls. She felt as though she was drowning, lost under water. As though there was nothing – and no one – who could save her. Leaning against the door, she thought of James the night he had first started to court her.

I want to get to know you, Ellie. I mean properly get to know you . . . I mean to make it my duty to find out about you . . . We'll just take this nice and slow, shall we? See how we get to like each other? No rushing about; just be friends first and then see how we go. How's that?

Such kindness, such gentleness. And she had

thrown it away. Thrown a handsome, good man away – for what? For the Moulin Rouge? For middle-aged rich men who wanted to sleep with her? For sex? Dear God, Ellie thought desperately, this wasn't what she wanted. It never had been. All she had ever really desired was a man who loved and understood her.

And James Farnsworth had done both.

Turning, Mort glanced away from the smoke-stained walls, making a mental note that when he had some extra money coming in he would have them repainted. Then he thought of Faith, and realised that if she hadn't raised the alarm, no one would be alive to be worrying about paint.

'Hello down there!' he called, looking down the stairwell as he heard footsteps in the hall below.

Faith looked up, waving. 'Hello up there.'

'How's married life treating you?'

'Horribly,' she replied, smiling and moving up the staircase towards him. When she reached Mort's floor, she kissed him on his cheek. 'You look well.'

'I had a little nap.'

'After a little sherry?'

'Faith!' he said, acting shocked. 'I never drink. I mean, oh, how could you tease me so?'

She squeezed his arm. 'How's Laurence? I know you saw him this morning.'

Mort took in a short breath. How was Laurence? he wondered, thinking about his friend and how much he had changed in only a few months. Mort put Laurence's heart attack down to Lennie Hellier. He knew that Laurence had been under pressure for a long time, but Hellier had delivered the *coup de grâce*. Not only had Laurence been duped, cheated and damn near burned alive, he had lost his appetite for living.

'Not too good,' Mort replied, putting his head on one side. 'But Miriam's better than she was.'

'Miriam wasn't ill.'

'No, no, my dear,' Mort agreed reluctantly.

'A person can recover from an illness they never had.'

He nodded. If only the same could be said about his friend.

'Laurence was talking about you, about how he could trust you to run the place whilst he was away. Not like . . . well, not like he had trusted someone else and been so badly treated.'

They both knew who he meant.

'In fact, he was chatting about reopening the showroom.'

Faith smiled broadly.

'He was?' she said, her tone delighted. 'God, he must be getting better if he's talking about the business again.'

Mort interrupted her at once. No point giving anyone false hopes.

'Well, my dear, you don't want to get too excited. I mean . . .' He paused, fidgeting from one foot to the other. 'The doctors don't think Laurence will ever be able to go back to work.'

She paused, stunned. 'But I thought he was recovering! I thought he'd get better after a while. Especially now that Miriam's looking after him. I thought he would come back to David Street. He loved the business so much, he was so good at it.' She stopped, glancing away. 'That man as good as killed him! I hate Lennie Hellier. I always hated him. I knew he was no good.'

'We all thought that.'

'But I *knew* it,' she replied curtly. 'I should have talked to Laurence. Told him . . .'

Surprised, Mort saw her colour and touched her arm gently. 'Told him what?'

'Nothing, nothing.'

'I think perhaps it is something *very* important,' Mort went on. 'Tell me, Faith. Please, please, my dear, tell me.'

'It's really nothing.'

His voice was encouraging, kindly. 'Tell me.'

'A long time ago Lennie Hellier made a . . . I don't know what you call it . . . a pass at me. I was eleven . . .'

Mort took in his breath, shocked.

'Why didn't you tell someone? Oh my God, how terrible. But you *worked* with the man! How could you stand to be anywhere near to him?'

'Sssh,' Faith urged him. 'I didn't tell anyone, and when the job came up with Laurence I couldn't refuse to take it, because I would have had to explain why. Beryl was so pleased that I was going to be working there, and we needed the wage.

Besides, she didn't know the position she was putting me in with Hellier. Oh, come on, Mort, don't look so shocked, it's all history now.'

Stunned, he shook his head. 'You should have told someone.'

'I couldn't,' she said simply. 'Anyway, it's over. Hellier's gone. He's done his worst and with luck we'll never see him again.'

'Laurence said he was obsessed with you.'

'I loathed him. And I showed it. That's why he hated me so much,' Faith replied. 'He hated everyone. Even Laurence, who had done so much for him. And you; think what you did for him, Mort. That hateful man set a fire wanting to kill us all.' She paused, shrugging her shoulders. 'I can't talk about Lennie Hellier any more. I can't even think about him. He was evil, and he's gone.'

'But . . .'

'He's gone,' Faith said gently, 'out of our lives. And you have to forget what I told you. Hellier was the past; the future is what matters now.'

CHAPTER TWENTY-NINE

Sybil had been ill for some time, but she hadn't confessed the extent of her illness in her letters, and when news came that she had died, Ellie went into shock. She was told just after a rehearsal, the manager breaking the news and offering his condolences. Ellie sat down on a stool and wrapped her arms around herself. What on earth would she do now? she wondered. How could she live without her mother? Without Sybil telling her what to do, to think, how to act, to behave, how to make her way in the world? How could she exist without the letters from England? Letters that seemed either poignant or sad, depending on Ellie's mood, because surely her mother had realised that by now there was never going to be a rich suitor. A glossy wedding. A fabulous partner. Surely Sybil would have realised that the chance she had missed was never going to present itself in her daughter's life?

It wasn't her mother's fault, Ellie had realised after the first year. Sybil was a woman with limited intelligence and education; she had had one chance at bettering herself and had passed that information on. If it hadn't worked out for her, it would for Ellie. But although similar in appearance, the two women were very different in personality. Sybil was a fighter; Ellie a realist. The years in Paris had taught her how to survive. She was an indifferent dancer who held on to her place in the chorus line because of her looks. When they faded, she would be shunted to the back, and then through the back door. It was reality, it was life. Ellie knew there wasn't going to be a rich rescuer. She could easily have found one – but she had never played the seduction game.

Blinking, Ellie stared at the bare boards of the stage. Everyone had moved off, gone for their break; only she remained, sitting on the stool in her dancing costume, looking like a broken doll, all china white, her red hair gathered back with feathers. Slowly she felt the tears begin, making indentations in the heavy make-up. One by one they fell from her cheeks on to the front of her costume, marking the pale silk. Silk that looked so lovely from the audience's viewpoint, but was stained and stale in reality. Silk that had been worn by other girls who had danced, got older, got married, got out.

Her mother was dead. Ellie thought of the words and decided that it wasn't true, that there had been a mistake. She also decided that she would have to go home. Despite what she had here, she would have to go back to Oldham and sort out the blunder.

She would walk up to her house and see the lights on, and Sybil would be in the kitchen, working on one of the hats for Riley's Milliner's. All her life her mother had worked on hats. All her life, sewing, mending, putting in feathers, nets, ribbons, every stitch earning money to pay for the trip to Paris. All those hats, Ellie thought, all those hats to get me the chance to succeed.

Then she thought of the day Sybil had won the prize. How her mother had told her over and over that it was destined, that God wanted it . . . Was this really what God wanted? Ellie wondered. If it was, He was cruel; no wonder she had never believed in Him. What was the point of believing in someone who let you down? Sliding off the stool, Ellie stood for a moment in her costume and then slowly took off her headdress. She would go home and find her mother, and when she was sure that everything was all right, she would come back. In fact, Ellie told herself, she would bring her mother back with her. Sybil would like that, would like to see her on stage again.

Slowly Ellie walked across the bare stage. Past the painted backdrops, past the wings, into the dressing room behind. When she walked in, all the girls fell silent. Ellie picked up her things and left without a word. She had no one in life and the thought terrified her. Her mother's dream had been fulfilled in part. Eleanor Walker *had* made it to the Moulin Rouge, but the second half of that destiny – the happy marriage, the secure future – had been a sham.

Alone, Ellie walked back to her lodgings. And alone she prepared for the long trip home.

Listless, Faith looked out of the showroom window, wondering if Laurence would call by. She had thought the same every day, but her employer and friend hadn't visited for over six weeks. Business had gone on as usual, Faith apologising for Laurence's absence and explaining that he was ill. Regular customers came to see the new stock, but as Laurence hadn't been buying, there was precious little to see.

Having made sure that the locks had been changed, Faith wasn't nervous about the place being unsafe, and besides, she enjoyed having full responsibility. Messages came from Miriam about Laurence's wishes, but when Faith visited she was warned not to talk about the business. Even if she brought up the subject with Miriam herself, it was brushed aside as though it was of no importance. But before too long someone would have to either start trading again at Goldbladt's, or close up shop permanently. Of course Faith hoped it was the former. She was fond of Laurence and enjoyed her work, especially now that Lennie Hellier had gone. But she had to face up to the fact that her job might not last for much longer. And she couldn't, in all honesty, drag it out for ever. She wasn't doing enough to earn the wage, and although she had tidied out the storerooms, cleaned the showroom, reorganised the furniture and rehung the furs endlessly, she was now underemployed.

But she wasn't going to suggest that she became manager. Memories of Lennie Hellier prevented that course of action, and besides, if Laurence wanted to promote her, he would when he was good and ready . . . Getting to her feet, Faith looked down into the street below, watching as a tram passed and two kids kicked a ball down into the basement. She could imagine how it would sound, echoing in the yard, and how James would look up, seeing the children's feet as they ran past.

Her own personal happiness was complete. Samuel was a kind man, a good lover, attentive and hard-working. They laughed a lot. But every time Faith thought about her life, she couldn't help but compare it to her brother's and remember how promising James's future had once been. It was true that he had seemed to adjust to his handicap, and although Faith had been worried about Beryl moving back in, it had worked out well. Her grandmother was busy running the studio, and James was becoming more interested in the new developing techniques. He talked about the painters like Picasso and described how Degas had used photographs to help with his paintings. He even mentioned wanting to visit an exhibition in London, but then he had trailed off, realising that he couldn't get there. At least not without help.

Having always liked James, Samuel still spent time with him, the pulley system pressed into service, but it was obvious to both Faith and her husband that James's life was limited. Too empty for a young man . . . Glancing down into the street again, Faith watched the city pigeons landing on a window ledge opposite, and heard the clatter of typewriters coming from the secretarial college three doors down. Then she noticed a figure standing on the corner, a small figure that seemed familiar. Leaning further out of the window, Faith kept staring. The figure seemed anxious, nervous, the face shielded by a veil. Her clothes were simple but stylish, fashionable even on David Street. Curious, Faith studied the woman, watching as she turned, and noticing the pale amber hair . . .

It couldn't be! Faith thought, dumbfounded. It couldn't be Ellie Walker. After so long. And then she remembered hearing about Sybil's death the previous month. She had wondered then if her daughter would return, but she had never expected to see Ellie on David Street. Moving to the door, Faith was about to go down, and then stopped herself. Was Ellie coming to see her? She doubted it. More likely that her old friend was coming to visit James. The thought confused Faith. What would such a visit do to her brother? What point was there to it? If Ellie had wanted to apologise, she should have come sooner. Years sooner. So why now?

Faith knew the reason: Sybil was dead, and Ellie had no one. But was that enough of a reason to come back home? Or maybe, Faith decided, it was the best reason. Hovering by the window, Faith fought her anger and the temptation to interfere. What business was it of hers? Ellie had been engaged to her brother; it was their relationship. She should stay out of it. But then again, Faith had been protective of James for years and was desperate not to see him slip back into depression. Because even if he was pleased to see Ellie again, what could she offer him? And, more importantly, what could he offer her? Wouldn't any reminder of their love only serve to underline what he had lost?

'God,' Faith said out loud, turning away. 'What do I do? What do I do?'

Then she turned back and looked out of the window again. But this time the lonely little figure on the corner had gone.

Moving carefully down the basement steps, Ellie paused and thought for a moment that she should backtrack, leave before she made a fool of herself or did any further damage to James. Pausing, she read the sign over her head – City Photographic Studio – and thought of the times she had kissed James under it. *All* the times they had kissed under it. Then she realised that she was standing where her fiancé had fallen, and, shaken, she ran down the remaining steps, pausing at the bottom. Her hand went to the knocker, then dropped back to her side. What would she say? she thought, trying to build up her courage. A moment passed, then another. What if Faith opened the door? God, Ellie thought, she couldn't face her old friend. Faith would be angry, and rightly so.

Indecisive, Ellie stared at the knocker, then glanced back to the steps, and thought suddenly how easy it would be to retreat. But then again, what would she retreat to? Back to Oldham, her mother's empty house? Back to the bakery? Back to her old life, empty without Sybil and James? But then again, this wasn't the old James. This was the James she had never seen, the James she had rejected out of hand. Her courage failed her at that moment. Turning, she saw the pulley mechanism that had been strung up against the basement wall and walked over to it, puzzled. Then she realised what it was. A way to lift James – her beloved James – from the basement out on to the street. Suddenly it seemed so poignant that she buried her face in the canvas straps and drew in the smell of fresh air, and another scent, of a man. A man she had once loved. And let down . . . In that instant, she knew she had no right to return.

Taking a deep breath, Ellie moved back up the steps and walked away from David Street.

'Of course, my dear, if you want to write to the newspaper I am sure they would be only too pleased to print your letter,' Perry said evenly, secretly amused that Agnes actually thought she could change the roosting habits of the Oldham pigeons. 'A well-written letter always impresses.'

Brushing her hair vigorously, Agnes took some satisfaction in pinning it back from her face, letting the grey streak – which Perry had never noticed –

finally show. After all, a woman could only walk around looking like a pirate for so long.

'Couldn't they shoot them?' she asked.

'With what?'

'Guns!' Agnes replied heatedly. 'Think about it, Perry; there must be hundreds of guns left over from the war. Doing nothing, just hanging about. Well, those guns could be pressed into service again.'

'Agnes, my dear, I think that blasting a pigeon off a roof with a machine gun might be overreacting a little.'

'Why? If you think about it, pigeons aren't too different from Boers.'

Enthralled, Perry laid down his paper. 'In what way, my dear?'

'They're both dirty, don't speak English, and invade other people's territory.'

'Did you see her?' Faith asked, walking into the studio and looking at James.

'See who?' he replied, putting down the ledger and glancing at his sister. He could see at once that Faith was unnerved, and obviously regretting the words that had come out of her mouth. 'Who are you talking about?'

'Oh, no one.'

'Must be someone, Faith,' James said calmly. 'I know when you're lying. Come on, tell me – who was I supposed to have seen?'

'Ellie . . . She was heading this way. I thought she was coming to see you.'

The name took a swing at both of them. James wheeled himself over to the door and turned the sign to CLOSED. It was a complete and total rejection of Ellie Walker. The only way he could physically block her from his life.

'We're not due to close for another hour,' Faith said simply, moving over to the couch and sitting down. 'Do you want to talk?'

'No.'

She nodded. 'James . . .'

'No, Faith, I *don't* want to talk about Ellie.'

'I'm sorry, I didn't mean to upset you.'

'It's over,' James said flatly. 'She made her decision and it was final. She made her choice.'

'She was cruel.'

'I don't blame her,' James said suddenly. Faith noticed how – when she had made a criticism of Ellie – he had immediately jumped to her defence. He still loved her, she realised. He might try and pretend otherwise, but he did . . . The thought unnerved her. If Ellie came back, would she go off again? And besides, what could James offer a pretty young woman? A woman who was fit, a woman who would want a normal life and children?

Irritated, Faith began to tap her foot, her brother glancing over at her.

'What is it?'

'Ellie. I hope we never see her again.' Faith could see the flicker in James's eyes and decided to push him, to really test his feelings. 'I hope she goes back to Paris and never comes back to Oldham. We're better off without her. She was bad luck.'

He flinched. 'She wasn't bad luck!'

'She was! She broke your heart, James; you want to forget about her once and for all and find another girl.'

'And who'd have me?' he responded tartly. 'I'm in a bloody wheelchair! What kind of woman would want to saddle herself with me? I'm no catch any more. Think about it, Faith, my choice is pretty limited. Besides,' he said, his tone softening, 'I loved Ellie. Whatever she did after my accident, a part of me still loves her. And always will.'

Minutes after Faith had ended her conversation with James, she left the studio on David Street and began to look for Ellie in the surrounding streets. What her brother had said had been enough to lay to rest any doubts she might have had. He still loved Ellie Walker – but did Ellie love him? Or was she just alone, wanting to get some security back into her life? Faith had to know the answer. And the only way to find out was to talk to Ellie directly. Hurriedly she moved along, glancing from left to right, looking for the delicate little figure on the city streets. But after an hour had passed, Faith realised that she had missed her chance. Ellie had gone.

Suddenly all Faith's previous anger and bitterness towards her old friend disappeared, and panic took its place. She *had* to talk to Ellie. Ellie might be the last chance of happiness for James. But where had she gone? And then Faith realised that she would have returned to Oldham and her mother's house. Going back to David Street, she told James that she had to visit a client to deliver a photograph, and that she would be back later. Deep in thought, he hardly responded as Faith left the photographic studio and made her way over to Oldham.

The journey seemed to take longer than ever, Faith's hopes fading mile by mile. When she had set out, she had thought she might be lucky and find Ellie on the train – but it wasn't going to be that easy. Instead she sat out the long, uncomfortable ride, getting out at Oldham station and walking up Union Street alone. A couple of times she wondered if she would be too late; worried she would find the house empty and hear that Ellie had already left. But when she arrived outside the Walker home she saw, with intense relief, that there was a light burning.

Hurriedly she moved to the front door and knocked.

'Faith?' Ellie said nervously, seeing her old friend and expecting an argument. 'I didn't see James! I was going to, but I didn't.'

Walking in, Faith paused, unsure of what to say next. Ellie looked fragile, diminished by life and the death of her mother. In fact she seemed tiny, a world away from the hard-faced dancers of the Moulin Rouge.

'Why,' Faith asked evenly, 'why *didn't* you go and see James?'

'I thought I could face him. But I couldn't . . . Do you still hate me?'

'I don't hate you, Ellie, I just need to know what you want,' Faith said, her tone guarded. 'You can't see James if you're planning on going off again. I can't let that happen. You can't use him.'

'I love him.'

'You say that.'

'I do love him,' she repeated, close to tears. 'I've never stopped loving him and thinking about him – and about the wrong decision I made. About how I ruined his life and my own. I haven't lived one day and not regretted what I did.'

'Ellie,' Faith said warningly. 'Don't lie to me now. Not now. I want to know – are you telling me the truth?'

'Why would I lie!' Ellie replied desperately. 'I'm never going to see James again. I'm going away, back to a life I hate. I won't bother you or him again. It was the past. A chance I should have taken. An opportunity for happiness I missed. I loved James and he loved me, and he understood me. Dear God, Faith! I know what I've lost – why would I lie now?'

'Oh, Ellie . . .' Faith said suddenly, reaching out and putting her arms around her old friend.

Sobbing, Ellie clung to her. 'I miss him so much,' she cried, her voice desperate. 'And I miss you.'

'Then come back and talk to James. Come back with me. Don't leave, Ellie. Don't *ever* leave again.'

When they arrived back on David Street, it was dark and the street was quiet. They had already agreed that Faith would enter, unseen, by the back door, while Ellie was to go in and talk to James alone. Walking down into the basement, Ellie moved to the door and knocked. There was no answer. Opening the door she entered, looking round. But there was no one sitting behind the reception desk, and when she walked over to the kitchen area, it was also empty. Surprised, she glanced round, pleased that the studio had changed so little. The same photographs were on the wall, albeit with some new ones, and on the shelf over the desk was a picture of Sid, taken when he was a young man.

A sudden noise made Ellie jump. Moving back, she saw the darkroom door open and watched as a pair of feet appeared, followed by the rest of the person, sitting in a wheelchair. James had rolled up his sleeves, his forearms well developed from getting himself around, and his head was turned, so that for an instant he didn't see her. But when he glanced round, he stared at her, startled, as though he was looking at something forbidden.

'Ellie?' he asked, as if she was some hallucination. Slowly he wheeled himself a little closer. 'Ellie, is that you?'

She nodded, but couldn't move. This was her James, the man she had loved so much. But he wasn't the same. He was crippled, but stronger than she remembered. And that was what puzzled her, almost upset her. She had expected – hoped – to see a man as worn down by living as she had been. But James looked vital, healthy, young.

'I shouldn't have come,' she began, stepping back towards the door. 'I shouldn't—'

'I'm sorry,' he said simply.

'What for?'

'I never replied to your letter.'

She smiled, her eyes blank, her face fragile. 'What I did to you . . . it was so wrong.'

He nodded. Once.

'I should go,' Ellie said again, standing in the middle of the room, not knowing what to do or say. Not wanting to leave, and longing for James to welcome her. To want her back. 'My mother died.'

'I heard. I'm sorry,' he said, his tone gentle.

'Thank you.'

'Are you going back to Paris?'

She paused, hardly able to move her head. Exhaustion dragged on her, a weariness of spirit.

'I suppose . . . Yes, I think I will.'

'Are you happy there?'

She paused again, her hands clasping and unclasping, then she looked at him. 'Do I seem happy?'

'I don't know,' he replied. 'Do I?'

'You seem at peace.'

James smiled faintly. 'My face is lying.'

'Do you hate me?'

'I did, for a while . . . Why did you come?'

'To see you, James.'

'But why?' he asked her.

She gazed around her, then shook her head. 'Because you're the only thing left that I love.'

Sighing, he studied her. 'I'm crippled, Ellie. I've made some progress, but I can't be a proper husband or father. I'm half a man. Half the man you knew. And I'll never be what I was.'

Her head was bowed, her eyes lowered. 'Don't you love me any more?'

'Love doesn't come into this,' James replied.

Ellie's head snapped up. 'Love *is* this,' she said fiercely. 'I've never stopped loving you, James. Never. I thought I would, but I never did. And seeing you now hasn't changed anything.'

He put up his hands to stop her. 'Ellie, no!'

'Ellie, yes!' she said softly, moving over to him and dropping to her knees beside his wheelchair. 'James, love me again, please love me. I don't care about the accident, I only care about being with you.'

His heart was breaking as he looked at her. 'You need a real man.'

'You *are* a real man,' she told him, catching his hand and clinging on to it as he tried to pull it away. 'James, I'm not like I was. I've learned about life, about myself. I don't want to be anywhere but here, with anyone but you. Please, don't send me away.'

'I have to, Ellie. It's over for us.'

Shocked, she stepped back, her hand over her mouth. Her whole body shaking, she moved towards the door. He wouldn't have her back. It was over. She might love him, but she had hurt him too much and couldn't repair the damage. Desperately, she turned the handle, fighting tears, a rush of cold air coming through the doorway.

'Sorry.'

Her head rested against the door jamb. 'I can't leave you.'

'You have to, Ellie.'

'No,' she said brokenly, turning round. 'I *won't* leave you again. I'll *never* leave you again.'

'I'm in a bloody wheelchair, Ellie! Get out of here. Go away and make a new life. I'm doing this for you.'

She winced, her expression defiant. 'No. You're doing it because you're a coward.'

'A coward!'

'Yes, because you think you can't love me enough, and that worries you. But you're being selfish – because it *doesn't* worry me.' She shook her head. 'I know, I know, *I* was the selfish one before. But not now. I don't want to martyr myself, I don't want to make things right between us by looking after you, by being your carer. I want to be your wife. I want you, James. I love you. I love you more than anything on earth,' she cried desperately. 'Out of a wheelchair, in a wheelchair, I love you and I *want* you.'

Closing his eyes, James reached for her, and Ellie ran over and clung to him, sobbing as though she would never be able to stop.

CHAPTER THIRTY

August 1914

On 4 August 1914, Faith was finally certain that she
was pregnant. That morning she had been about to
tell Samuel, but he had left in a hurry. So instead
Faith had opened up the Goldbladt showroom after
the Bank Holiday. The showroom smelled musty as
she threw open the windows and picked up the post,
her excitement almost unbearable as she tried to
compose herself. An old customer, Mrs Hardy, was
coming in, and Faith would have to serve her before
she could go downstairs and tell everyone the good
news. Or should she wait and tell Samuel first? But
then again, how could she face everyone and *not* tell
them?

Impatiently she tapped her foot, waiting for Mrs
Hardy to arrive. True to her word, Beryl had passed
her house over to the newly-weds and Faith had
immediately gone to the market and bought
material for new curtains. She had also invested in a
new bed and a pair of best chairs for the sitting
room. Although money was tight, as always, her

buys at Tommyfields Market had transformed the tired terraced house into a brighter environment, and when she had cleaned out the second bedroom it had crossed her mind that it would, one day, make a fine nursery. It wasn't big, but it was certainly bigger than James's old bedroom at Gladstone Street and plenty big enough for a cot. Perhaps they could paper the walls with something a bit lighter than Anaglypta. She had never liked that, or the dark colours that were fashionable. A baby should have a bright room, full of colour . . . Faith smiled to herself. Perhaps she and Samuel hadn't thought of having a baby quite so soon, but then again, they had made love so often it was hardly surprising. She smiled again, then tried to be practical. Of course she would have to give up work when she was six or seven months on, but perhaps she could still work part time. As for Samuel, he was still employed at St Anne's church, but news had travelled fast, and now he had more work than he could handle. It wasn't highly paid, because he wasn't skilled labour, but it was reliable. And they were going to need as much money as they could find now . . . Listening for the doorbell, Faith drummed her fingers on the desk, planning ahead whilst waiting for Mrs Hardy to arrive.

Samuel would be ecstatic. Hadn't he said repeatedly that he wanted a family? And, unusually, that he wanted a little girl rather than a son as his firstborn. Faith could already imagine how much he would spoil a daughter, how he would brag about her as he bragged about his wife. Leaning back, she let her hands rest on her corseted stomach and wondered how long it would be before her pregnancy showed. How long before people started congratulating her. She could see herself walking with Samuel down the street. He would have his arm through hers, smiling at everyone. And later they would push the baby out in its pram together . . . Faith sighed contentedly. She had been so lucky, and she knew it. Lucky with her husband, lucky that he loved her and looked after her. Lucky that he wasn't like Tommy Bentley or Lennie Hellier.

Surprised, Faith wondered why she had thought of her old enemy, and then wondered why Mrs Hardy was so late. A sudden commotion outside the window, followed by the sound of cheering and shouts, made her jump. Getting to her feet, she was about to look out into the street when the door opened and Beryl walked in.

'My God,' she said simply. 'I've just heard the news.'

Thinking that somehow Beryl already knew and was talking about her pregnancy, Faith smiled. 'I know. Isn't it amazing!'

'Amazing isn't the word I would have used,' Beryl countered, looking her granddaughter up and down. 'War's been declared, and sure as hell that's nothing to smile about.'

Slumping back into her seat, Faith could feel the colour leave her cheeks. Beryl hurried over to her and rubbed her hands.

'I thought you knew! I thought you'd heard the news . . .'

'Not *that* news,' Faith replied. '*My* news.'

'Your news?' Beryl echoed, then stepped back, understanding immediately. 'You're having a baby!'

'Yes,' Faith said dully. 'I'm having a baby – and war's broken out.'

Jumping on to the tram back to Oldham, Samuel read the headlines over the shoulder of another man. War, damn it, he thought. And all because some archduke had been shot. Nothing to do with England. Well, not directly, Samuel thought, wondering how long it would be before he was called up. Or perhaps he should volunteer. He would have done before, but now things were different. He was a married man and that made volunteering more problematic.

'It'll be over by Christmas,' a man said suddenly.

Samuel turned to him. 'You reckon?'

'Oh aye,' the older man went on. 'It's just sabre-rattling. You watch, it'll be a storm in a tea cup.' He looked Samuel up and down. 'Mind you, I'm too old to fight, but they can't say the same about you, mate, can they?'

Turning away, Samuel gazed out of the tram window. He wasn't afraid of a fight; he'd been an amateur boxer and could handle himself. But now he had lost his desire to fight – or wander. Samuel liked being married, with his own home and his own way of living and his good-looking wife. The excitement of war was stimulating, true enough, but he had good reason to stay home. But then again . . . His mind turned over the possibilities. What kind of man could shirk from fighting? He was tough, well built, strong, just the type to make a good soldier. If he was called up, he'd go with a good heart. War with Germany had been on the cards for some time, and teaching the Huns a lesson was long overdue. He wasn't going to complain; what the hell was there to fight for if you couldn't fight for your country? As he kept thinking, Samuel realised that in a way he liked the idea of being a soldier, of going abroad, seeing a different life and living a different way. After all, he would be doing something worthwhile, something of which he could be proud.

Still thinking, Samuel got off the tram. He would be a soldier. He would make his wife proud by doing the right thing. Anyway, he consoled himself, it would only last a few months. The British Army would go in, flatten the enemy, and then be home for Christmas.

Nothing to worry about really. Nothing at all.

Thoughtful, James looked up from the paper and glanced over to Ellie. She would be one of the women who didn't have to worry about her man being injured or killed. At least that was something, but what about all the able-bodied men who would have to go and fight? Men like Samuel . . . James sighed. At times he had to pinch himself because his good fortune was too much like a dream. But

375

however hard he tried to wake himself up, his luck remained real. Ellie was back. And within a few short, hurried weeks, they had been married. The news had come as a shock to everyone, Beryl's anger only evaporating when Faith calmed her down. Facing up to her previous actions, Ellie pleaded forgiveness from everyone, and when some criticised her, she took it on the chin. A fact that impressed Beryl and won Ellie an unexpected supporter. And so Ellie had been taken in. A pretty outcast who had come back and been absorbed into the family.

Despite all of James's protestations, Ellie did love him. He wasn't able to have proper sex with her, but they made their own kind of love, and became tender with each other, making allowances for each other's failings and anxieties. He understood then that Ellie wasn't particularly interested in sex, but craved closeness. And as that was what he could offer, their marriage seemed hopeful from the start.

James looked back at the paper, his thoughts turning to the war. Fighting, bloodshed, death. Then he thought of Samuel again, and wondered how Faith would manage when he was called up. It would be lonely for her living in Hardy Street by herself. After all, Beryl was now ensconced in David Street again, and although Agnes was living around the corner in Gladstone Street, she and Perry kept themselves pretty much to themselves.

He stopped musing as the door opened and Beryl ushered her granddaughter in.

'Faith's having a baby!' she announced.

Smiling, Ellie came out of the kitchen, walking over to Faith and kissing her cheek. 'That's wonderful news.'

'Samuel doesn't know yet; don't breathe a word of it until I've told him, will you?' Faith asked, glancing over to James. 'You're going to be an uncle.'

'Lucky kid,' he replied, winking, noticing that his sister's gaze moved over to the paper.

'Bad day for such news.'

'Any day you hear of a baby coming is a good day,' James reassured her.

Faith sat down on the sofa next to his chair, Beryl and Ellie moving off to the kitchen together.

'Answer me honestly,' Faith asked her brother. 'Samuel will be called up, won't he?'

'If the war goes on for a while, yes,' James replied. 'But there's talk that it might be over by Christmas. Some of our lads will go in there, help out the French, and come home.' He tapped her on the knee sympathetically. 'Samuel might not have to go.'

'He'll want to,' Faith replied, sighing. 'I know him, Samuel never backs down from a fight. He'll want to get stuck in there, prove himself.'

'Not now he's going to be a father.'

'But he doesn't know that, does he?' Faith replied, dropping her voice. 'I've only just found out and I was thinking that perhaps I shouldn't tell him for a while.'

'You can't do that!' James replied, shaken.

'Samuel has always said that if there was a war – and there's been talk of it for months now – he would volunteer, sign up. He thinks it's his duty.'

'When he was a single man, it was. But he's married now, that makes things different.'

'I know,' Faith replied. 'He's married. And he's going be a father . . . I wish I hadn't got pregnant now.'

James looked at her incredulously. 'What *are* you talking about?'

'About war. About my husband volunteering or being called up. About worrying about his safety, about being widowed.' She paused, shaking her head, surprised and annoyed at her own unease. 'Oh, listen to me! I'm getting all worked up and war's just been declared hours ago.'

'Faith—'

She cut him off. 'They *will* take the men away, James. You know that and so do I. Funny, only this morning I was thinking about how happy I was, how lucky I've been. And now this, a war.' She sighed. 'I was planning to work in the showroom until I was six or seven months gone, until early spring next year, then I wondered if I could work part time. But it will all be different now, won't it? God knows where any of us will be then.'

'This doesn't sound like you,' James said, surprised by his sister's anxiety.

She nodded, trying to shake herself out of her mood. 'You're right, I'm being morbid. And like you say, the war will probably be over before Christmas.

Samuel will never have to go away and we can all look forward to the baby coming.' She paused, the helpless expression in her eyes giving her away. 'They won't take my husband away from me, will they?'

'Who?'

'The army. Or God, who knows? You see,' she fought to keep her voice steady, 'I need him, James. I love him and want him with me. I've got used to feeling safe and being his wife. I need him. We need him now. Me and the baby. That's selfish, isn't it? I should say that the country comes first, but England can get men from anywhere. I want Samuel with me. I want my husband and my child's father to stay safe, to stay home.'

She stopped talking as the door opened and Samuel walked in, throwing down his jacket and kissing her. 'Have you heard the news?'

James could see his sister's hesitation, the momentary pause. 'About the war?'

'What else?' Samuel replied. 'They say it'll be a short fight. Those bloody Germans, we need to teach them a lesson.'

Faith flinched. 'I suppose most of the single men will volunteer?'

Bending down to retie his shoelace, Samuel answered her. 'Single men, married men. The army doesn't care what you are.'

Alerted, she exchanged a glance with James, then looked back to her husband. 'You're not thinking of volunteering, surely?'

'I wouldn't mind,' Samuel replied, full of excitement.

And then Faith saw something ominous in his face, something she remembered from their first meetings. That urge to live, to be on the go, in on a fight. Samuel had proved a wonderful husband, but she knew that married life was quiet and that it had curtailed his wanderings. Not that he had been eager to resume his erratic lifestyle. On the contrary, he had assured Faith that he was content, settled. But the news of war had relit some ember inside him, and she could see that he was already dreaming of being a soldier. His expression and the excitement in his voice told her so without the need for words.

'You're not *really* thinking of volunteering, are you?'

He turned to her, hugging her. 'No, love. But in time, if they need more men, then we'll talk about it. You wouldn't want to be married to a coward, would you?'

'I'm pregnant.'

He stopped dead, staring at her. 'What did you say? You're pregnant?'

Nodding, she stared at him. Her eyes searched his face, reading his emotions, dreading any reluctance, any irritation. But there was none. Relieved when he wrapped his arms around her, Faith clung to him, Samuel's voice now full of another kind of excitement. The promise of fatherhood, not war.

That night, they lay together in bed and talked until the early hours. Samuel wanted to pick a name for the baby, but Faith said they should wait until it was born and they knew whether it was a boy or a girl.

'Unless we call it Francis; that's a boy or a girl's name . . .'

Faith rested her head on his chest. 'It should be a pretty name, if it's a girl.'

'. . . or Lyn. That's a name for girls and boys.'

'Only if you live in Wales,' Faith replied. 'What about Milly?'

'He'd be teased at school.'

She dug him in the ribs, laughing. 'When the baby's born, we'll be a *real* family, Samuel. A husband, wife and baby. I've wanted this all my life.'

'And I never wanted it – until I met you,' he said, kissing her tenderly.

Sighing, Faith's thoughts turned momentarily from the baby. 'What about the war?'

'It won't last long.'

'But with the baby coming . . .'

'Don't worry,' he reassured her. 'It'll be over soon. A storm in a tea cup.'

But it wasn't. As Faith's pregnancy advanced, there was constant talk of fighting and of the German aggression, and the news turned more and more towards the subject of more men being called up. Of course the eager, single young men had already volunteered, but Samuel had decided against it. If he was called up, he would go and fight, but otherwise he would stay home. Do his work, look after his wife, and the baby that was coming. He was going to be a father. His first responsibility was to his family.

The war had other ideas. As it ground on, it seemed that it wasn't going to end early – and that there was a real chance it wasn't going to let husbands off the hook, or new fathers. And as the Germans upped their hostilities, Faith went unexpectedly into labour, a month early. Luckily it was a Saturday and Beryl was home, Faith trying not to panic as Beryl hurried Samuel out of the bedroom and ordered him to stay downstairs. Taken aback, he sat in the kitchen below for the rest of the day as the noise of feet reverberated overhead, Faith crying out intermittently as the hours wore on. All his enquiries were met with brisk efficiency by Beryl, and when the doctor arrived he was told little more than 'Your wife is doing very well. Don't worry.'

But Samuel did worry, and the arrival of Agnes didn't help. As Faith let out another cry upstairs, her aunt threw the kitchen towel over her head and began to sob dramatically against Perry. By this time completely unnerved, Samuel ran to the bottom of the stairs just in time to see the doctor descend, smiling.

'Congratulations, you've got a daughter.'

Samuel nodded, his expression tight. 'But Faith? How's Faith?'

'Doing very well,' the doctor replied. 'She wants to see you.'

*

From the moment of her birth, Milly was petted and fussed, Beryl doting on her, Agnes bringing presents and Perry spending long minutes staring at the infant.

'What's he trying to do, hypnotise her?' Samuel asked.

Faith shushed him. 'He never had children of his own. He's fascinated.'

'Wait until she starts crying again,' Samuel said drily, 'then we'll see how fascinated he stays.'

Long broken nights took their toll on the couple, Faith rising to feed the baby in the early hours, Samuel staggering downstairs to make them some tea. To Faith's surprise, he was patient, and nursed the baby back to sleep often, at times even getting up to soothe her himself and let Faith catch some sleep. Although the birth had been relatively trouble-free, Milly was a small baby, prone to colds, Beryl buying endless blankets and coverlets. As for Samuel, he had a theory that Milly should spend as little time as possible in her cot. He said it was good for her lungs to be carried, but the whole family knew that he was just making it an excuse to nurse his daughter. His affection was unlimited, his pride inexhaustible. He really did love his home and family, and he let everyone know it.

From being a happy-go-lucky wanderer, Samuel Granger had become a committed family man. Nothing was too good for Faith, or for Milly. As he had always known, it had taken a rare woman to catch him – and now that astonishing woman had presented him with a mini version of herself. Samuel Granger – albeit exhausted from lack of sleep – was a happy man. In fact, he couldn't believe his luck. Nothing on earth would make him utter one word of criticism of his family. No one could prise him away from them for long. Time spent at work was filled with thoughts of home. He was protective, indulgent and ambitious for his family's happiness. In short, he was a family man – and proud of it.

He didn't realise how quickly his contentment would be over.

CHAPTER THIRTY-ONE

France, 1916

Sleeping upright, Samuel felt the mud seeping through his trousers, his feet wet, deathly cold, even in the summer heat. He knew that if he took off his boots, some of the skin would come with them, and so he left them on. Beside him, he saw another private sleeping, and further along the trench two men lay motionless, gazing upwards into the dull sky. The silence was unsettling. Day after day, night after night, for weeks the bombardment had sounded. The German line, behind its barbed-wire fencing, was being incessantly targeted. In the end, the soldiers were told, the enemy would all be killed. Soon the British Army would be running into trenches to fight corpses.

But not yet. And so the bombardment continued. So long had the firing gone on, some men had gone mad, even the trench rats losing their minds. Samuel had seen one ripping its own tail apart, driven insane by the guns. The noise thundered around them, rattling the planks and reverberating in the men's chests. Samuel knew that the news had not reached home of the slaughter of so many men. Men who had stormed the German line only to be mown down by their guns, or left suspended on the barbed wire. Bodies hung there motionless, or worse, wriggling and crying out for help. He had lost friends already. Lost one of the men who had signed up with him, a young lad from Brompton Street.

It had all been so different when Samuel had been called up in May 1915. To be honest, he was glad to fight, even though he was a husband and father. There had been no choice, and Faith had been stoical about it. Like so many other wives. Full of hope, the soldiers had been drafted into France, and for a while it had seemed like a game, a man's game of drilling and preparation. Of big talk about bringing the Krauts down a peg or two. *They started the bloody war*, was the common theme. *Time they got their comeuppance*. At first the soldiers had been bored when they were sent to France. And although there were some intense pockets of fighting, in other places the men played football to relieve the monotony.

Surely there's more to it than this? they asked each other. Is this why we came to bloody fight?

Samuel asked the same questions. And then the army moved them on, further inland. Gossip skittered along the lines like woodlice, word of heavy artillery, of a dogfight coming up. News from home came and went, Faith telling Samuel about their daughter, Milly, who was now a year old.

*She looks like you. She's cheeky, full of zip. I tell
her all about you. Tell her about her father, and she
sends her love . . .*

Samuel wrote back: *I'll see you soon. I love you,
I love my two girls.*

Short leaves came and went, visits passing too
quickly, hurried. Sometimes, when he was in the
trenches, Samuel dreamed of making love to Faith,
but on the third visit home he just lay in her arms,
in their bed, listening to the silence. Trying to give
husband and wife some time together, Beryl had
taken Milly over to Manchester, but there was no
need for privacy. Faith and Samuel just lay together,
holding each other and listening to the clock
chiming downstairs. He told her snippets of his
experiences, censoring the worst aspects and
describing the trivia. The pointless, everyday
minutiae of French life, which was still – incredibly
– going on in places. Like the little village his
company had once been stationed in, Verdane, and
the boarding house with faded blue shutters and a
creaking gate. He talked about chickens running
free down the middle of the village lane, and a
stream that turned into a river over the hill. And
then he would pause, remembering other things,
other experiences too terrible to describe.

When Faith talked, she told her husband about
how she was doing part-time factory work. They
had asked for women to help out making
armaments and she had volunteered, and every time
she made a piece for a gun, she blessed it, thinking

that it might come into Samuel's hands. Thinking that it might protect him. That her love might reach him via the metal. She smiled when she told him, pretending to laugh although she was choked up, then hurriedly went on to describe her days. How she would leave Milly with Agnes every morning, returning home to collect her from Gladstone Street around three. Nodding, he listened, then asked about David Street. The City Photographic Studio was chugging along, Faith reassured him, telling him about the soldiers who came to have their photographs taken. Pictures they left with families and girlfriends. She teased him then, telling him that she hadn't got a photograph of him, and that Beryl would do a fine job. And only charge him half price.

Laughing, he had held on to her, but only hours later he had to return to France, leaving her again. And taking a photograph of Faith and Milly with him.

I'll be back soon, the war has to be over soon . . .
And Faith had nodded, as though she believed it.

Shifting his position in the trench, Samuel wondered how long the unaccustomed silence would last. For a moment he wanted to jump to his feet and shout, plead for them to begin again. Because the anticipation of noise was worse than the guns themselves. He was sick of the filth, of the smell of piss and shit. Of the mud that seeped into his skin, grime deep in the palms of his hands, his hair tacky with muck and sweat. And then he realised how hungry he was. How hungry he had been for a couple of days. He doubted that anyone back in England knew about the lack of food. Doubted that the politicians and the generals would tell the British public that their soldiers hadn't been fed for two days. Fight, yes. Fight until there wasn't a man left. But on an empty belly ... All the promises had come to nothing. When the war started out, there had been cheerful propaganda, footage of hundreds of bed sheets, tinned produce, sides of beef, all bound for the soldiers. The reality was something else. As the fighting had continued, there were few blankets to sleep on, no clean water, no change of clothes. In the cold, no one washed themselves until it became unbearable, until their skin itched and crawled with lice. Helmets discarded in the trenches were soon smeared with mud, and thick with vermin. After one scuffle with the enemy, several wounded soldiers – too weak to help themselves – fell off the makeshift stretchers and drowned in the mud, which was now eighteen inches deep. Dirt was everywhere, making walking difficult. Mud clinging to clothing, to coats, to tired legs. Foul, stinking mud, sucking the life out of everything. Mud and hunger, mud and the guns. Mud and madness.

Tell them about that back home! Tell them fucking that!

Samuel screamed inwardly, looking up into the darkening sky as the guns began again. Putting his hands over his ears, he slumped back against the side of the trench. It was 30 June, on the battlefield of the Somme. They had been prepared for the advance, each man taking with him two gas helmets, wire-cutters, a water bottle and a haversack – weighing almost seventy pounds in all. Loaded up with this burden, the soldiers were told that they had to 'push forward at a steady pace in successive lines'. No one told them that the persistent artillery bombardment had done little to break through the German barbed-wire defences. No one knew that then . . . That night they were told that the morrow would bring victory.

The following morning, at seven thirty, the British troops were going to go over the top.

With Milly in her arms, Faith left the house on Hardy Street and walked over to her aunt's. It had come as a welcome surprise that Perry had taken to Milly so readily. As ever, Agnes had not been particularly maternal, but Perry had discovered an unexpected indulgent side. Smiling, he took hold of the baby as Faith put her bag on the table.

'Her food is in there, and a few nappies. I've changed her, so she should be all right for a while.' Faith paused, watching the little girl and touching her hair gently. 'Are you sure you don't mind looking after her?'

Perry pulled a face. 'She's a beauty,' he replied. 'No trouble at all . . . Have you heard from Samuel?'

'No, not lately.'

Sitting down, Faith poured herself some tea and

studied her daughter. Having inherited dark hair and eyes from both her parents, Milly was a striking child. She had had a bad run of colic when she was tiny, but after that she had proved to be a docile baby. Thinking back, Faith couldn't imagine that she had once regretted her pregnancy. Even though it had been a bad day when she had discovered she was carrying Milly, the thought of life without her child was intolerable. How would she have managed to live without her? Without having to look after her? Worry about her? Tend to her? Without her child, Faith would have spent all her time worrying about Samuel, and what good would that have done? But with Milly she was always occupied. With her well-being, her feeding, her first word – which Samuel hadn't been around to hear.

Faith knew that she wasn't the only woman left without her man. Half the town was gone, only older men and those unfit to serve left behind. Like James. Unexpectedly, the memory of Lennie Hellier came back to Faith. He wouldn't be called on to fight, she thought bitterly. He was a coward, and besides, he was handicapped. She wondered fleetingly what had happened to him, especially now that the Goldbladt showroom was boarded up. CLOSED FOR THE DURATION OF THE WAR, the notice said. No one had expected the sign to remain there for so long. But the war had been going on for nearly two years now, and it didn't look like the notice was coming down any time soon.

For the first time in her life, Faith was living

alone. True, she had her child, but Milly was dependent on her. Before, she had always lived with someone else – her aunt, her brother, her husband. Family had always been around, offering support and company. But when Samuel had been called up, Faith had realised that she was going to have to cope alone. At first the thought had panicked her, but then her strength kicked in. She would manage, of course she would. It helped that she was living in her grandparents' old house. The place was familiar, known to her. Even though she had made changes with Samuel, and the second bedroom had become a nursery as she had once hoped – it was still comforting. The old black range in the kitchen still heated up the water, the outside lavatory still stood with its corrugated roof, and although Faith didn't know the new neighbours who had moved in next to her, she made friends with some of the younger women in the street who had also been left alone. And Ellie came to visit, the two of them close again, Ellie bringing pies from Sullivan's and walking Milly out in the pram, eager to give Faith a break when she needed it. Not that Faith rested. She wrote to Samuel instead, or did odd jobs around the house, or her accounts, relying on Samuel's army wage and her own from the factory to cover the rent and buy food. She liked to tell Samuel how well they were, how she was coping. Wanted to reassure him, and herself. Whistling in the dark as the war ground on.

If she was honest, Faith missed her life on David Street. Missed Beryl, but knew that her grandmother was doing her damnedest to keep the studio open. And they would succeed between them, Faith had promised her that. War or no war, City Photographic Studio was not closing. All of them worked to keep the business afloat, Faith and Ellie helping out part time. Beryl assured Faith that they didn't really need her and that she could stay at home, but Faith looked forward to her trips to Manchester with Milly, even though the trams ran intermittently and sometimes not at all. Her visits to Manchester made the time at Hardy Street pass more quickly, and seem less lonely. Sometimes, when Faith was in David Street, she went upstairs to check on the Goldbladt showroom, walking around and remembering – but Laurence's health was deteriorating and it was unlikely that the place would reopen under his charge. As for Mort, he was chugging along but had lost most of his workers, the women going to work for the war effort. Undeterred, Mort sewed many of the clothes himself, selling cheaper garments on to Tommyfields Market direct.

'People need clothes; only Adam and Eve could walk around naked,' he told Faith 'You have to cut your coat according to your cloth. I'll get by, you'll see. I've come through hard times before.'

But for all his bravado, the trade wasn't there, and before long Mort moved into the showroom and lived there, giving up his rooms in Macclesfield because he couldn't pay the rent. Circumstances were a little easier downstairs. Because the City Photographic Studio was a family business, no one took wages. Instead they paid the rent with whatever they made, and Ellie, making gun shells in a Manchester factory, added what little money she could to the pot. As for James, he kept the books and managed to convince a Jewish family over in Lloyd Street that they needed to have their daughter's wedding photographed for posterity. They agreed to a studio session, and then ordered prints. Those prints covered the family's needs for two months. Then James had another good idea, getting Ellie to put notices up saying that the City Photographic Studio would take photographs of soldiers half price. He was, Beryl told Faith, turning into a real businessman.

The situation was difficult, but as no one expected it to last, it was a question of making do. Even when July of 1916 came, no one expected the full horror of the news from the Somme. The details came through late, and very slowly.

It was Beryl who broke the news to Faith, walking into the studio and looking at her granddaughter.

At once Faith picked up on her sombre mood. 'What is it?'

'There's been a bloodbath, on the Somme,' Beryl replied, taking Faith's hands. 'News coming in now, bits and bobs.'

'What is it?' Faith repeated, her voice steady although her heart had started to speed up. 'Is it Samuel?'

'It might be, no one knows for sure. There have been a lot of casualties.'

'Samuel?' she whispered. 'Is he dead?'

Beryl hurried to reassure her. 'No, no. We don't know, love.'

'But he could be?'

'He could be – but he could still be alive. We don't know,' Beryl said, her tone even. 'We have to wait for news—'

Faith cut her grandmother off. 'How bad is it?'

'Over sixty thousand of our men have been killed.'

Grabbing the nearest seat, Faith slumped into it, Beryl sitting down beside her. 'We don't know that Samuel is dead.'

'If he is . . . when will we know?'

'When they tell us,' Beryl replied. 'They say they'll print the names by the end of the week. But I don't know how reliable that is.'

Faith took in a sharp breath. 'He might not be dead.'

'No, love.'

'He could be fine. He could have been lucky.' Faith looked at her grandmother desperately. 'Or he might have been injured. If he was injured they would send him home, wouldn't they? He wouldn't have to go back to fight?'

'No, love.'

'He could stay out of the war, stay safe,' Faith said helplessly. 'I could nurse him. *We* could nurse him. I could look after him at Hardy Street, and Milly could sit with him, keep him company. I mean, even if he was seriously ill, I could get him better. We looked after James, didn't we? We looked after James and he's fine now.' She stopped talking, taking in a breath. Slowly her panic subsided, an unshakeable belief filling her. 'My husband is not dead.'

'You go on believing that, love.'

'I'm right, you'll see,' Faith replied emphatically. 'Samuel's not dead. I know it, I can feel it.'

'That's right, love, we have to hope.'

Faith stared at her grandmother. 'I don't care what anyone tells me. Samuel is alive, and one day I'll see him again.'

CHAPTER THIRTY-TWO

March 1918

It was Milly's birthday, and they were celebrating in the basement of David Street. The war was still not over, and even though there was talk of great progress by the Allies, no end was in sight. Despite Faith's belief, a month after the carnage of the Somme, Samuel Granger had been posted Missing, Presumed Dead. When details came through about the battle, everyone was stunned that anyone had survived. The losses had been indescribable. The soldiers had gone over the top in waves, advancing into no-man's-land, and in the first few devastating minutes thousands of husbands, sons and fathers had been killed by the German guns. Even the capture of the enemy's first and second lines afforded little progress, and the Germans' ceaseless machine-gun fire dropped man after man until the soldiers were walking over the dead and wounded to advance. So intense was the carnage that from noon on that first day until four in the afternoon the Germans permitted stretcher-bearers to collect the injured from the blood-soaked no-man's-land. The cries of the injured and the dying echoed over the scorched earth, some soldiers screaming in pain through the dark hours. Shaken by what they had experienced and seen, the surviving soldiers were urged on by their superiors, who told them that it had been a day of 'great success'. The following morning it all began again. It took three days for the wounded to be collected, between bouts of fighting and against the clamour of the guns. When the Somme campaign finished, nearly a hundred thousand French and British soldiers had been killed. Where fields had once stood was a bare mud wallow. Trees had been killed and stripped of leaves, only jagged stumps remaining after the barrage of gunfire. There was no grass, no intimation of life; nothing was left but the ghosts of the dead and the missing. And amongst the missing was Samuel Granger.

The whole family had hoped that he would return, but only Faith believed it, and even she was beginning to doubt. They would have found him by now, she told herself. Surely, after all these months, they would have found him.

'Mummy!' cried Milly tugging at Faith's sleeve. 'Look, Mummy, a cake.'

Smiling, Faith kissed her daughter on the top of her head. Beryl watched them both. She had not been surprised by her granddaughter's fortitude, but if she was honest, she would have preferred knowledge to hope. The chance that Samuel was still alive was becoming very remote. His death would have been a calamity for Faith, but it would have been easier than this limbo, this protracted half-life. This place of waiting for the news that might never come. Or might prove to be bad. And all the hoping would be in vain.

'She's getting tall,' Beryl said to her granddaughter, trying to bring her thoughts round to the present.

'She's getting more like her daddy every day,' Faith replied. 'When Samuel sees her, he'll be amazed.'

Unusually irritated, Beryl wanted to grab her granddaughter's arm and shake her. To make Faith see that her husband might never come back. It had been too long, there would have been news before now if he was still alive. The notification from the army had said, Missing, Presumed Dead, but Faith hadn't accepted those last two words. Instead she had fixed on the all-important first one. In her mind, it meant Samuel could be found. To everyone else, the reality was evident, though not to Faith . . . But Beryl hadn't the heart to shatter her granddaughter's dream. Even though she wondered how long she could hold out before insisting that Faith stopped living on false hope.

'Milly's very like you, love,' she said, carefully nudging the reference of Samuel to the background. Dear God, she thought, it was like living with a ghost. With someone who was ever present, but not seen. For a woman as sensible and strong as Faith, she was proving remarkably blinkered.

'Oh, she's like both of us,' Faith replied. 'You'll see, when Samuel gets home.'

'I'm sure you're right, love.'

'Samuel said he would come home and I believe him. One day he will come back, you'll see.'

The summer limped past, and still there was no news, then the autumn brought hope of an end to fighting. Was it possible? everyone asked, Mort visiting Laurence and telling him the good news. Temporarily bedridden, Laurence cheered up at the thought, surprising Mort by talking about his showroom again. Maybe he could reopen it when he was better?

'I was talking to Miriam about the fashions,' he said, leaning against his pillows and breathing rather more rapidly than was good for him. 'Women won't be dressing like they did before. Not now, not after this war. I mean, they've been doing the work of men, they'll not want to go back to long dresses and big hats.' He laughed, thinking of the old days. 'Remember how some of those hats were too big to get through a narrow doorway?'

Mort nodded. 'I was reading about the women who are delivering coal.'

'No!'

He nodded again. 'Young women, with great sacks on their backs. Hair scraped back, overalls, you'd not believe it, Laurence. And many of them are cutting their hair and raising their skirts. You know Ellie, James's wife?' Laurence nodded. 'She worked as a clippie on the trams for a while.'

'Never! That's a bit of a rum job, isn't it?'

'Well, she did it. Bonny little thing in her uniform and hat. She looked like a doll. Worked the Oldham to Manchester line, and then the Piccadilly. I tell you, Laurence, women have changed. They didn't know how capable they were until the men went away, and now there'll be no stopping them. The tide's turned.'

'Especially as so many of the men will never come back.'

Mort sighed. 'Faith still thinks that Samuel will return.'

'I was thinking,' Laurence hurried on, 'after the war I could ask Faith to run the showroom for me. There'll be a chance to make a killing, with women wanting new clothes and all those designs coming from Europe now. I know women, and they'll want cheering up after having to act like men for years.'

'You might be right there,' Mort agreed. 'But there's hardly any money about. Who'll be buying furs?'

'Oh, there might not be money now, but there will be. You'll see, Mort, when peace comes, prosperity will follow. Women like to look good, that much will never change. And Faith could help me out there, and do herself a good turn at the same time. She was always charming with people, but now she's older and I reckon she could run that showroom.'

Mort frowned. 'She's also married and a mother.'

'She's a *widow*,' Laurence said sadly. 'How many soldiers turn up after being posted Missing, Presumed Dead?'

'A few.'

'Yes, a few do. But not after so long.' Laurence sighed. 'In time, Faith will have to come to terms with Samuel being gone. And when she does, she will be glad of a good job. She's the intelligence to run a business, and she's got a few ready-made baby-sitters downstairs.'

'You've been thinking about this a lot, haven't you, old friend?' Mort asked, realising that although it wasn't likely Laurence would return to David Street, the reopening of his business might well give him the lifeline he needed.

'I have, yes. I like Faith, I trust her – even though sometimes I've trusted the wrong people.'

They both thought of Lennie Hellier in the same instant.

'Faith's life's not over. Not by a long chalk,' Laurence said firmly. 'If the war is going to end, we have to think of a new world, Mort. All of us. I know I'm not what I was, but the young have a chance – a good chance – to make a fresh start. People are tired, worn down, exhausted by the war, they'll want to enjoy themselves, make money, have fun again.' He stared at his friend, smiling. 'We have to put the past behind us. It's the only way if any of us want to survive.'

*

Pausing at the corner of David Street, the man stood watching. He could see the light from the basement shining up and illuminating the steps where James Farnsworth had fallen. And the sign was still hanging straight, the words City Photographic Studio writ large. It jogged memories in him, of the pulley system that had winched James from the basement, and the smell of the chemicals coming from the darkroom. Old memories, poignant memories, which had come back slowly, but achingly clear. His injuries had been so intense that for months he had been medicated, suspended between two worlds. Not dead, not alive. No one had been able to identify him, because his dog tag had been lost. No one knew who he was. So the unnamed soldier was christened Jimmy, and Samuel Granger stayed missing.

The doctors had given him little chance of survival, but although his heart had arrested several times, Samuel had come back to life. From the battlefield of the Somme, he had been taken to a military hospital. From there he was transported to a specialist hospital back in England, and although no one had expected him to survive the journey, his burned body, with its gunshot wounds and head injury, somehow managed to hold on to life. Sedation prevented him from feeling the worst of his burns, but his head injury had caused his brain to swell. The pressure affected his memory and his movement. When it became too great, it was released by boring a hole into his skull, and allowing the excess blood to be drained off. The surgeon who undertook the operation gave Samuel a ten per cent chance of life.

It was all he needed. It gave him back his life – though not his memory. And as he had been found without any papers or means of identification, he was the patient without a name, a home or a family. No one claimed him. His burns healed slowly, but although they had been serious, they were not as severe as first thought. His legs below the knee were affected, and his left forearm; otherwise the damage was limited and after a while the burns healed, only the worst leaving angry red scars. They set his broken leg and wrist, and waited. But although his wounds were healing, Samuel had not recovered from his experiences. And free from medication for the first time in months, he went into limbo. Shell-shocked, he backed off from reality and was shipped to Spike Island, the psychiatric hospital in Southampton. There he was given medication to ease his tremors. His mind was damaged and the doctors feared that when he regained full mental alertness – *if* he ever did – he would be unbalanced. Unstable at best.

What they didn't understand was *how* Samuel was still alive. After all, they had expected him to die within the first few weeks. His burns would kill him, or his brain injury, or his heart would give out. But against all the odds, he had kept his grip on the world, and held on with the tenacity of a dog locking its teeth into a bone. Deeply traumatised, unable to move, he still kept that hold. His body might not be responsive, his mind might be unreachable, but Samuel Granger was still there. Somewhere.

Some things did get through to him. Dreams that were more real than life. Times when Faith came to visit him and brought him letters, letters he couldn't read, but that he knew were important. At other times she whispered in his ear, and then he heard her laughing and was suddenly back in bed with her in Hardy Street. Then there were the other dreams, of the gunfire, the incessant pounding, the thumping of the earth under their feet, shaking their bodies and making the trenches weep with noise. And the rats, gone mad with the noise, screaming and running around in the thickening mud. When finally Samuel came out of his stupor, he was still partially drugged, unable to remember who he was, or what had happened to him. The amnesia didn't last long, but it was still another six weeks before he came fully back to life.

The realisation that he had been posted Missing, Presumed Dead struck him as oddly accurate. He *had* been missing, in his own head. Cut off from the war, from battle, from health, from living. And it took him a little while to come around. His first instinct was to head home straightaway, but then he decided that it would be better for everyone if he took a little time to come to terms with his injuries first. The scarring wasn't too bad, and he no longer walked with a limp, but the shell shock – although

405

it hadn't completely turned his brain – had left him mentally fragile.

So it was a different, much-altered Samuel Granger who stood on the corner and looked over to the basement of the City Photographic Studio, twenty-one months after that fateful day on the Somme. A man who had chosen to come back from the dead and was no longer certain if he had made the right decision . . .

'Samuel?' a voice said suddenly. An incredulous Ellie approached him slowly and looked into his face. 'Is it you?'

He nodded, but couldn't find the words.

'Faith knew you'd come back!' Ellie went on, her excitement making her breathless. 'Oh God, Samuel, she always knew. She never gave up on you.' She touched his shoulder, surprised to feel him flinch. 'Come on,' she said gently. 'Time to go home.'

Led by Ellie, Samuel walked down the basement steps towards the studio. He could hear voices, and recognised James, and Beryl laughing. *Laughing*. The thought struck him with unease. They were happy, happy without him. Would they want him back? Pausing, he stopped in the basement yard, looking through the window. The studio was hardly changed, but times had obviously been hard during the war. The photographs on the wall were the same, the old sofa barely disguised under a paisley shawl. Nervously he hesitated. Perhaps he shouldn't go in, perhaps it was too late to come back. A ghost returning to life. Was that possible? Then Samuel saw his wife enter, a small child walking beside her. His heart folded, shifted, the memory of her, the love of her making his feet move again. Slowly he turned the door handle. When he opened the door, when he walked in, nothing would ever be the same again. He would have come back, to life, to living. Back to a family. And although he knew how much Faith had loved his old self, would she love or want this new version?

Breathing quickly, he pushed open the door. A long moment seemed to pass before anyone reacted, then Faith looked up and put her hand to her mouth, momentarily too stunned to move. Urgently she searched his face, then she moved, running over to him and burying her face against his neck.

'I knew you'd come home,' she sobbed, clinging on to him. 'I knew you'd come home.'

*

He was home. He had returned. At last. My husband, the father of my child, my Samuel. The man I had prayed for, waited for, longed for. He had come back. Just as I had always believed he would. And I felt – in that first instant of seeing him – that my whole body relaxed. Every pore, every inch of skin, each pulse and shifting of the blood seemed to speed up, to renew itself. I was reborn.

So was Samuel.

And that was the problem. The man who had left to go to the war was not the man who returned. The Samuel who had paused and waved one last time before leaving was gone. He had gone with all the other men who had fought. He had gone with the fighting and the guns and the foreign dawns . . . Oh, he was still Samuel. I could recognise his face, his voice, his mannerisms – but it wasn't *really* him.

And the thought terrified me.

CHAPTER THIRTY-THREE

November 1919

'People can say what they like,' commented Alice Winter shortly, 'but that Samuel Granger's not the man he was.'

Snorting under his breath, Ezekiel Horne avoided her gaze. 'He's all right.'

'He's changed completely,' she retorted, lowering her voice and looking down the aisle to where Samuel was cleaning the stained-glass window behind the altar. 'He's moody now. He was never moody before. I can't understand it. The war's been over for months, he should have settled down by now.'

'Leave the man alone. He's suffered enough.'

'Many men suffered in the war,' Mrs Winter retorted. 'Samuel should count himself lucky that he didn't lose a limb.'

Just his mind, Ezekiel thought to himself. Just his mind . . . He liked Samuel, always had, and understood more than the sour Mrs Winter what war could do. At first their employer had been sympathetic about Samuel's injuries; then she heard about his shell shock. That, she had decided, was weakness. Mental illness was just a lapse in character, everyone knew that.

'He doesn't seem to have the same interest, or work as hard as he did before,' Mrs Winter went on, the old man letting out his breath with exasperation.

'Give him time to come round.'

'That's the point. Samuel Granger can come round on his own time, not mine.'

Up on the ladder, Samuel could hear the voices, but didn't bother to listen to what they were saying. He had no interest in Mrs Winter, Ezekiel Horne, or anything else for that matter. He had no interest in St Anne's Square, Manchester, or the rest of the world. The only things that interested him were his wife and daughter. In his home on Hardy Street Samuel was safe. For a while it had seemed to him that beyond the confines of those walls the rest of life was threatening. Then no longer threatening, just boring. Dull, grindingly dull. He didn't miss the army, or the fighting. He didn't miss the twenty-one months of half-life he had endured. But he still found himself longing to escape the city streets, or the enclosed terrace of Hardy Street.

Returning to work as an odd-job man, he soon discovered that there was less to do than there had been before the war. Money was scarce, and many people had learned to undertake the minor jobs themselves. Women had become particularly practical whilst their men had been away at the war.

The light-heartedness of the pre-war years had altered to something more intense. There was a sense of relief, but also a sense of uncertainty, and all the sermons in St Anne's church couldn't take away the brooding overhang of loss. Having earned money easily before, Samuel found himself embarrassed by the small amount he could contribute, constantly making excuses to Faith.

'Don't worry,' she would tell him, smiling. 'It'll pick up. You're home, that's all that matters.'

Climbing down the ladder, Samuel put it on the back of his cart and wheeled it over to David Street. Walking along, he had a sudden urge to leave it on the pavement, to catch the first tram and make for the country. Go up to Hawkshead Pike, watch the birds. Or go fishing. If they still *had* fish in the Manchester Ship Canal . . .

'Oi, watch out!' shouted a man, tooting the horn of his car.

Cars seemed to have become a more regular feature in the centre of Manchester. Stepping back, Samuel watched the well-dressed man drive past, then pushed his cart onwards. He had never been an ambitious man, but suddenly he felt a despair about his situation, a despair that had been growing steadily for months. Where was he going? Was this the whole of his existence, his life? Was this all he could offer Faith and his daughter? He was an odd-job man, a war casualty, pushing a bloody cart around the city centre like a down-and-out.

Stopping, he lit a cigarette, then noticed his

hands. Workman's hands. It had never occurred to him before, but he wasn't much of a catch. His previous light-heartedness seemed irritating now. His easy, drifting manner an embarrassment. He had gone through a war, had fought for his life – but for what? To push a bloody cart around for the rest of his days? And what about Faith? Samuel knew that there had been talk of her running the Goldbladt showroom when it reopened, but he had forbidden her to take the job on. How would it look, he thought, his wife a manageress, whilst he was an odd-job man? Inhaling smoke, Samuel realised that his hand was shaking and tried to steady himself. Faith loved him; she had never asked anything of him. And his daughter loved him too. But was it enough? he thought desperately. Was *he* enough? Or should he have stayed Missing, Presumed Dead? If he had, Faith could have married again, married someone with more about him. Milly would have had a better father. Not a man who could hardly meet the rent on Hardy Street. Angry, Samuel ground out his cigarette, looking across the city square.

Failure, violent as a gunshot, tore up his insides.

'We have to do it, Gran,' Faith said, taking the note out of Beryl's hands and putting it back in the front window of Hardy Street. 'Other people take in lodgers.'

'Not in our family, we don't,' Beryl replied.

Just then Agnes walked in and pointed to the

sign. 'Oh my God, it *is* true! Perry said he just saw a notice in your window.' She turned to Faith, her voice pleading. 'You're not serious?'

'We need the money.'

Agnes turned to her mother imploringly. 'Tell her! She can't do that. I mean, it's all right for the likes of Mrs Hardcastle, but she's widowed and got three kids to feed.' She glanced back to Faith. 'Your man came home; he should provide for you. You can't take in a lodger – you could be housing a murderer.'

'I was in more danger during the war, living here on my own,' her niece replied dismissively. 'It's only temporary.'

'Like the Chinese laundry round the corner!' Agnes countered. 'They said *that* would be temporary, but it's still there. And they've got another two kiddies. Breeding like flies, they are.'

Irritated by her daughter, Beryl brushed her words aside. 'If Faith and Samuel need to get a lodger, then so be it.'

'We can manage,' Faith replied. 'The lodger would have Gran's old room.'

'None of this would be necessary if Samuel got a proper job.'

'Shut up!' Beryl hissed. 'You've a mouth like a bakehouse oven.'

'Look who's talking!' Agnes snapped back. 'I can remember how vocal you were on the subject of lodgers once upon a time.'

Ignoring her, Beryl turned back to Faith. 'There's no shame in it.'

'No shame!' Agnes exploded. 'That's not what Perry said.'

'Oh, bugger bloody Perry!' her mother retorted. 'Just because he's got a pension, he can do no wrong.'

'He's my husband!'

'And Samuel is mine,' Faith replied coldly, looking from her aunt to her grandmother. 'We're getting a lodger to help with the money until things get a bit better. I'm sorry if you don't like it, but that's the way it is.'

When Agnes had left, Beryl sat down, looking at Faith enquiringly. 'Mort told me that Laurence was talking about reopening his showroom. And that he might like to make you the manager.'

Stiffly, Faith nodded. 'There was some talk about it.'

'So what d'you think?'

'Laurence isn't well.'

'That's why he'd need a manager,' Beryl replied evenly. 'Someone he could really trust. Not like that bastard Lennie Hellier.'

Wincing, Faith kept her face averted. 'Samuel doesn't want me to take the job.'

'Why ever not?'

'He wants to be the main breadwinner.'

'But an opportunity like that . . .'

'I can't do it,' Faith replied, a little more heatedly than she meant to. 'I can't shake his confidence like that. He's very . . . He's not settled down properly.'

'He's changed.'

Sighing, Faith sat down at the kitchen table. 'He's not the Samuel I remember,' she admitted softly. 'I still love him, that's never changed. He's always been – and always will be – the only man I could ever really love. But he's lost somewhere, and I can't reach him. He was never moody, never bad-tempered. But now the slightest thing sets him off. He even shouted at Milly the other day – and I know how much he loves her. He's so unhappy, Gran.' She paused, shaking her head, fighting confusion. 'I always knew he would come back. I always knew that. I just didn't realise that he would come back changed.'

Taking her granddaughter's hand, Beryl blew out her cheeks. 'You have to give him time.'

'I'd give him my life if it would help him,' Faith replied. 'But we can't go on this way.' She paused again, then hurried on. 'I wanted to ask you something.'

'You can ask me anything, love, you know that.'

'Samuel's lost because he feels like a failure. He's embarrassed that he hasn't got on in life.' Faith smiled wanly. 'Strange, he was never ambitious before, but now it seems as though he needs to feel like he's got a position in life.'

Beryl prompted her. 'Get to the point, love.'

'You know how you signed over the business to James? So that he owned it?' Faith asked, her voice timid. 'I know if I asked him he would agree to it – but I wondered what you thought. Could half of the

415

business be signed over to Samuel?' she hurried on. 'I know, I know, he's not a businessman, but he could manage it, with my help. After he settled in, then I could take Laurence's job and bring in some good money. And Samuel wouldn't feel inferior.'

Taken aback, Beryl glanced down. 'Well, I can see you've been thinking about it.'

'I have. For a while now.' Faith paused, trying to read her grandmother's expression. 'Samuel's an honest man. He might have his faults, but he would never harm any of us. You know that.'

Sighing, Beryl leaned back in her seat. 'But half the business . . . Oh, I don't know, love.'

'James wouldn't mind, and it would give you a break if Samuel took over some of the work. You've been saying how tired you are, how much you want to work part time. Samuel could take the photographs, you could teach him. He's got an eye for beauty, always has had. Oh Gran, please think about it. If Samuel could share the business with James, if he could say he was joint owner of the City Photographic Studio, it would give him confidence.'

'It's just a studio in a basement.'

'It's not, and you know it. It's Tommy Bentley and Sid, and all the old stories. It's a family business that has roots. And that's the point – it's *family*, Gran, and Samuel is family. I know he would work at it, I know he would. And I know how much I'm asking, but please give him a chance. He needs that so much . . .'

*

Against her better instincts, Beryl agreed to the arrangement. James was willing to share the business with his brother-in-law because he would have done anything to make life easier for Faith. Ellie was all for it too. Her relationship with Faith had reverted to their old closeness, and she was a doting aunt to Milly. Realising that she and James would never have children of their own, she was eager to spend any time she could with the little girl – and equally eager to make life easier for Faith and Samuel.

Suitably reassured, Faith told Laurence that before too long she might be in a position to consider his job offer and then went with her grandmother to draw up the legal papers, ready for James to sign. Within the month, Samuel Granger became the joint owner of the City Photographic Studio.

The rise in Samuel's status had been unexpected and seemed to have the desired effect. He was eager to begin, putting aside his work overalls for a start, and listening carefully to James as he taught him the rudiments of photography. Delighted by the upsurge in her husband's future and temperament, Faith watched the two old friends working together, James laughing about the pulley system Samuel had built so long before. Keen to learn, Samuel listened to Beryl and watched her take photographs, repeating the process afterwards. Using Faith as his model, and sometimes Milly, he discovered an interest, although Beryl pulled him up repeatedly about his positioning.

'You've got the subject too far over to the left,' she said, closing one eye and looking through the lens. 'Why d'you do that, Samuel?'

'I didn't know I was,' he replied, taking another picture, Faith pulling a face at him through the lens.

'Better,' Beryl said, then sniffed. 'But you can't let your subject get bored. They take a lousy picture if they get bored. You have to be quick, get the shot while they're still relaxed.'

They had made an arrangement that while Samuel was learning the business, he would live in David Street. As Beryl said privately to Faith, it would be better if her husband was on site, concentrating one hundred per cent – as his attention could sometimes drift. If he was tied down to David Street, he would get a grasp of the business more quickly. At first unwilling, Faith finally agreed to the scheme, realising that it would make learning easier for Samuel. And, as she said, it was only temporary. Meanwhile, Beryl would live at Hardy Street with Faith, travelling to Manchester every day. The respite every evening from Beryl's tutelage was welcome for Samuel and for James. Ellie would make a meal for the three of them, and would then go to bed early in the back room, leaving her husband and Samuel to talk. Slowly Samuel relaxed. He talked about future plans, James joining in and confiding his own ideas for the business, realising that his brother-in-law would, in all likelihood, prove to be an asset. It was good for James to have a business partner and someone he could talk to, but he realised early on that Samuel was not the same easy-going person he had once been. In fact he could get carried away. His ideas were clever, but not financially sound. And he didn't take criticism well, falling into a mood quickly if he was challenged. It wasn't long before James realised that while he himself was crippled, Samuel was just as handicapped – but in a different way. His concentration was shaky, his attention wandering off to some private realm, somewhere vague and, at times, disturbing.

Surprised and worried that their partnership might prove to be more difficult than he had anticipated, James gave his brother-in-law a long leash. He would find his feet, James said later to Ellie. It was all so new for him; he was just trying to run before he could walk. Curious, James watched over Samuel's tutoring during the next three weeks, and encouraged him when Beryl was critical, advising him to take her nagging with a pinch of salt, but listen to what she told him about photography. She had learned from a master. Two masters, in fact.

'But don't you find it difficult taking orders from a woman?'

James turned to look at his brother-in-law, surprised and laughing. 'That's no woman, that's my grandmother.'

'She's still a woman,' Samuel responded, moving back to the camera.

Bloody hell, thought James, this wasn't going to be as easy as anyone had thought.

At Hardy Street, Faith was looking after Milly and wondering if anyone would ever answer the notice in the front room window. While Samuel was finding his feet, she knew that he didn't want her to take on a job. But as money was tight, she also knew how much they still needed the lodger and longed for the knock on the door. For three weeks no one enquired about the room to rent, and Agnes complained that Faith had only put the note in the window to spite her. Then, at the beginning of November, someone finally answered.

Smoothing back her hair to tidy herself, Faith walked to the door to find an uncertain, rather nervous woman standing there, holding a child of about two years old.

'I was wondering,' the woman said, with a faint foreign accent, 'about the room to rent.'

'Oh yes,' Faith replied, glancing at the child. 'It's a single room, but . . . Well, come in.' She smiled, showing the woman into the front room and noticing that her clothes were worn but clean, and that she was wearing a wedding ring.

'I need somewhere to stay,' the woman began, taking the seat Faith offered her.

She was in her early twenties, and underweight, but her hair was wavy and her face – although tired – had the distinct promise of good looks. Uneasy, she kept her deep grey eyes averted, as though fearing rejection; but her hands were delicate and told of better times. This wasn't a woman who was used to poverty, Faith realised. She was a woman who had fallen on hardship.

'What's your daughter's name?' Faith asked.

The woman smiled, a flash of beauty coming and going in an instant. 'Her name's Suzette.'

'Pretty name,' Faith said sincerely. 'Pretty child . . . But to be honest, Mrs . . .'

'Bonnard. But please call me Leonie.'

'We were looking for one person only. Just one lodger. We only have two bedrooms and a box room; it would be a squeeze.'

'I'm widowed,' Leonie said simply, her voice falling. Faith immediately sympathised with her.

'I'm so sorry.'

'My husband was killed at Passchendaele.'

'Are you French?'

'Yes, and so was my husband.'

'You speak English very well.'

'My mother was bilingual,' Leonie explained.

'Where's your mother now?'

'Dead. She died in the war. And I have no one else. No one left.' She took in a breath, then hurried on. 'I should have stayed in my own country, but there was nothing left there after the war. And I heard so much talk of jobs in England, well paid jobs, enough to support me and my child. I thought we had a chance to make something of our lives here. I was sure that it was right to move on, to a different country, a different life. But when I got here . . .' She paused, her voice wavering. 'I can't even go home. I sold what I had when we left. My savings are the only money I have in the world. I have no family apart from Suzette, and no husband.'

'My own husband fought in France,' Faith replied, adding quietly, 'But I was one of the lucky ones; he came home.'

Silent, Leonie held on to her child, the little girl staring at Faith. It seemed to Faith that even the child was weary, that she and her mother had been through a great deal and desperately needed a place to call home. Unwilling to turn them away, Faith hesitated, wondering what to do. She had hoped that a single man would knock on the door, asking to rent the room. Someone who was out at work in the day, someone who would be no trouble. A woman and child would be asking for problems. A child cried, needed tending; her mother would have to be with her most of the day. The house was small, perhaps too small for all of them. And in a few weeks Samuel would be moving back home. How would he take it? God, he wasn't the old easy-going Samuel; he was difficult now, his reactions hard to predict . . . Faith sighed inwardly. They needed the money because of Samuel's reluctance to let her work, so how *could* he be choosy? If Faith was honest, she also realised that she might like to have company. Two mothers, with children around the same age, could be good friends. And Leonie certainly looked like she could use a friend.

'I can pay!' Leonie said, aware that the decision was hanging in the balance. In the very air between them. 'I can pay, and I can help you in the house, if you want. Suzette's a good child, and she knows to keep quiet.'

'I don't expect a child to keep quiet!'

'But your husband might,' Leonie replied quickly, her voice failing. 'I can see we're not what you want. But we've been knocking on doors for two days and no one will have us. No one wants a child, you see.' She paused, trying to stay tough, composed. 'I don't know what else to say to convince you. I have some savings. Not much, but I can pay for the room. I know the normal rate, I can pay.'

'I'm not worried about that,' Faith replied sympathetically.

Undecided, she studied Leonie, wondering if she could be hard enough to turn her away. After all, times had been difficult for Faith, but she had always had her family to support her. And then, against the odds, Samuel had come home. She could only too easily imagine herself in the French-woman's place, relying on the good will of others, desperate to keep herself and her child safe. It was an unpleasant thought. How would *she* have fared alone, in a foreign country, with Milly to care for?

'How long would you want to stay?'

'You'll take us!'

Faith put up her hands. 'Just a moment, we have to talk this out. You see, I mean to go back to work before too long. And then we wouldn't need to have a lodger. I don't want to give you the wrong idea. My husband's got a business in Manchester. He's learning the ropes now, and . . . well, when he's settled, I have a job to go back to.' She paused again. For all her talk, Faith wasn't sure *when* she could go back to work, or how long they would need a lodger's rental. What if no one else came to take the room? Could she really afford to turn the Frenchwoman down? They needed money and Leonie Bonnard needed a roof over her head. 'All right, you can have the room . . .'

'Thank you, thank you!'

'. . . but we'll talk again in a few weeks, all right? I can't promise that the situation won't have changed by then and I want to be honest with you.'

Leonie took in a breath, as though drawing in hope. 'Whatever you say.' She seemed close to tears. 'I'll be a good lodger, I promise. You won't regret this. You'll see, you won't regret your kindness.'

Walking into the kitchen at Gladstone Street, Perry smiled at his wife. At once Agnes put down the evening paper and glanced at him.

'What are *you* smiling at?'

'Good news, my dear.'

'The Chinese laundry burned down?'

'No, no, Agnes,' Perry admonished her. 'But the notice has gone out of Faith's window. No more ROOM TO RENT sign, my dear. I think your niece has come to her senses. I think the world of her, as you know, and Milly, but a person has to keep up appearances.'

'She told me that she was hoping a man would answer!' Agnes thought about it and shuddered. '*A man*. And what would people think about that? She could be taking anyone in. You don't know who'd be under your roof. A villain, some kind of . . . pervert . . . If you ask me, my niece isn't as clever as she thinks. Obviously she can't handle the housekeeping money. *I* never had to have a lodger . . .'

Nudged by the unfairness of the remark, Perry wanted to say that Agnes had never been as poor as Faith.

'. . . and I had to look after her and her brother. And children don't come cheap, you know.'

'To be fair, love, your sister *did* leave some money to help out.'

Agnes's face set. 'I see, I see! You're like the rest, Perry, you think of everything in terms of money. How much something costs. But I gave my niece and nephew more than money, I cared for them, fed them, was like a second mother to them.' Agnes paused, censoring her memory. 'They confided in me about everything. We were *that* close. Nobody knows what I did for those children.'

'I know, Agnes,' her husband said, as always ready to console his difficult – but amusing – wife. 'I used to admire you for your selflessness . . .'

She wondered for a fleeting moment if he was being sarcastic, but Perry was all genuine admiration.

'You set them a wonderful example.'

'Of course my mother should have taken them on,' Agnes moaned, reliving her old grievance. 'But

425

she's a law unto herself. More interested in the business. Left me to take the burden on. And nothing's changed . . .'

Perry blinked.

'Look at us, baby-sitting Milly every day! I mean, by our time of life we should have some peace and quiet.'

This was too much for Perry. He was very fond of Milly and could only take so much from his wife.

'It's a pleasure to look after that little girl.'

'Hah!' Agnes replied. 'It's clear to see that you never had children of your own, Perry Braithwaite.'

The tram journey from St Anne's Square to Oldham Mumps had taken longer than usual, Beryl nodding off until she was two stops away from home. Waking stiffly, she sat up in her seat and raised her eyebrows at the conductor in recognition. Same man who'd been working the buses for years before the war, she thought. And now he was back to his old job. Funny how some parts of life seemed to go in circles. Reaching into her handbag, Beryl took out her door key. She had a little walk before she got back to Hardy Street, but it paid to be prepared. The thought of a cup of tea and a sit-down by the kitchen fire cheered her after an exhausting day. Samuel wasn't without talent, but he was proving to be a difficult pupil. He had ability, but he wanted everything too fast and had no patience. Was that because of the war? Beryl wondered. Or because of his injuries? Certainly he wasn't the man she had known, and she realised suddenly that if Faith had brought Samuel to meet her now, she would have advised her granddaughter against marrying him.

Good God, Beryl told herself, shocked by her own thoughts. But it was true. Samuel was still a good man, but now he had corners to his personality. The lightness of touch, the easy-going, unambitious person had been replaced by someone overeager to be important. Beryl sighed, wondering for the hundredth time if she had done the right thing signing over her half of the City Photographic Studio. James had been more than happy to please his sister, or was he just wanting to repay Faith for all her loyalty? Either way, her grandson had accepted his partnership with Samuel. Perhaps she was the only one who was having second thoughts.

Not for the first time, Beryl wondered about Samuel's illness. He had told them about his condition – what he remembered. But there were chunks of time missing, parts of his life off limits. To his family – and even to him, it seemed. Beryl had asked their doctor if he could give her some insight, but he had only repeated what she already knew. Shell shock and trauma affected soldiers in different ways. Samuel had been lucky to get his senses back. And if there were some portions of his life missing, that was amnesia, and maybe it had been a mercy . . .

Oh Sid, Beryl thought suddenly, I miss you. If you'd still been alive we would have talked about this. I would have told you I was worried, and you would have said that I was being silly. That Samuel would settle down, get back on his feet . . . Without wanting to, Beryl's thoughts slid back to the previous afternoon at the studio.

'I can't think with you standing over me!' Samuel had snapped, then apologised. But Beryl had seen a real anger in his face, something unexpected and unpleasant.

'I have to tell you when you're wrong.'

'I know. You just don't have to tell me that I'm wrong all the time,' Samuel had replied. Beryl had caught James's eye and bitten her tongue.

Rising from her seat, she moved down the tram, ready to get off at her stop. She would have a word with Faith when she got back home, see if anything was troubling Samuel. And then tomorrow she would pretend that nothing was wrong and they would all start afresh at David Street. Liking the idea, she left the tram and moved over Mumps Bridge, turning towards home. Next month would be December, and that meant Christmas coming. Beryl made a clicking sound with her tongue. She had already started to see if she could put a bit away. Otherwise there wasn't going to be much money in the kitty for presents. But enough to get something small for everyone. And besides, when Samuel started going out and about looking for work, the money would improve. She sighed, trying to lift her own spirits by singing a popular song under her breath.

My old man said follow the van,
And don't dilly dally on the way . . .

But her thoughts kept returning to David Street, and her voice petered out. Samuel hadn't liked it one bit when she and James had told him about their plans. As they said, the business wasn't coming to them, so he would have to get out and find it. Go to the seaside – there were always people there wanting their photographs taken. Even off season, he could go to the boarding houses and drum up some Christmas work. And then in the spring and summer, even autumn – if the weather was kind – he could work the coast. There was Lytham St Anne's, Fleetwood, Morecambe, Southport and, of course, Blackpool. But instead of being fired up about the idea, Samuel had muttered about wanting to stay in the studio. He was a professional photographer, he told an astonished James, not some amateur snapper. And besides, he wasn't an odd-job man any more, going cap in hand, touting for work.

Dear God, Beryl thought as she turned into Hardy Street, it was a difficult situation. And it didn't look like it was going to be easy to solve. Samuel wasn't an employee, he was a partner. He couldn't be sidelined or fired; they were stuck with him. And anyway, he was family, married to Faith, who loved him. He had power now . . . Beryl stopped dead, key in her hand, replaying the thought in her head: *Samuel had power now* – and she didn't like it one bit.

'I'm home. Faith, I'm home!' she called out, walking into the kitchen and then stopping at the sight of the young woman sitting on the floor playing with Milly and another little girl. Faith glanced over to her grandmother and smiled over their heads.

'I want you to meet our lodger, Gran,' she said lightly. 'Leonie, this is my grandmother. And this is Suzette, Milly's new friend.'

CHAPTER THIRTY-FOUR

Afterwards Beryl had to admit that it was worth getting a lodger just to break the news to Agnes. That they had a woman, a mother, and a *foreigner* living with them at Hardy Street. Beryl had hardly had time to get acquainted with Leonie herself when she was grabbed walking out of the back door into the yard.

'God!' she snapped, as she saw Agnes's face illuminated by the light from the kitchen window. 'What the hell are you doing creeping around in the dark?'

'It's a woman!'

'What?'

'The lodger is a woman.'

Beryl couldn't resist. 'Yes, and she's a widow – and a foreigner.'

Agnes reeled back as though she had been pushed. '*A foreigner*. Oh my God. Whatever is Faith thinking of?'

'She needs the money,' Beryl replied, moving over to the coal shed and passing Agnes a shovel. 'Here, you might as well do something useful whilst you're here.'

'I've got a bad back!' Agnes wailed. 'Perry won't let me do anything that means heavy lifting.'

'So you've given up cooking, then?' Beryl replied smartly, turning back to her daughter. 'Are you coming in, or what?'

'You can't have two women in one house!' Agnes went on, ignoring the question. 'It causes problems. There can only be one boss.'

'Leonie Bonnard is the lodger, Agnes. She's paying for her room, and most of the time she'll be busy looking after her daughter.'

'There's a child!' Agnes said, aghast.

'A little girl,' Beryl told her. If she had had misgivings herself, she was losing them in the face of Agnes's overt bigotry. 'Think about it. Faith needs the money until Samuel's earning more. And it might be nice for her to have someone of her own age around. Especially since they both have daughters.'

'What about Samuel?' Agnes asked, desperate to keep her outrage going. 'What's he going to say?'

'He's going to welcome the money, and if he's any sense, he'll hold back on the objections,' Beryl said sensibly. 'After all, Samuel's the one who doesn't want Faith to go back to work, and he's the reason they're feeling the pinch. Money has to be got somehow.' Pushing her daughter to one side, Beryl took the shovel and rested it against the coal shed door. 'So, are you coming in for a cuppa, or not?'

Snorting under her breath, Agnes left. Beryl put some coal into the scuttle and then paused on the back steps. Above her the sky was dark and clear, but the air was cool, cutting through the clouds and chilling her. Shivering, she glanced up, seeing the light go off in the back bedroom, which was now Leonie's room. She waited for an instant, but there wasn't a sound. No voices, no cries from the little girl . . . Deep in thought, Agnes moved back into the kitchen and tackled Faith.

'I thought you didn't want to have a woman lodger?' she asked her granddaughter.

Faith shrugged, folding some laundry. 'Yes, I know. But no one was interested in the room, and when Leonie came, I . . .'

'Felt sorry for her?'

'Yeah.'

'You *are* a chump!' Beryl replied. 'You never change. Can she pay?'

'Oh yes, she's got some savings.'

'So why did she come to Oldham?' Beryl asked, picking up a sheet and folding it.

'Apparently she heard there were jobs over here.'

'In England, perhaps. But why here? Why Oldham?'

'When we were talking, she said that her father had once stayed here. Well, not here, in Manchester, but he'd visited the town. So when she left her own country, she thought she'd try her luck in the place her father had been happy.'

'Oh, I see,' Beryl replied, taking another sheet.

Hurriedly, Faith changed the subject. 'How's Samuel getting on? I miss him.'

'He's . . . he's learning the ropes,' Beryl said tactfully. 'How are you going to break it to him about the lodger?'

'I've written him a note. Can you give it to him tomorrow when you see him?' Faith glanced over to her grandmother. 'Will he make a go of the business?'

'If he buckles down,' Beryl said honestly, then added, 'I still say that you would have been better taking that job at Laurence's, rather than having a lodger. You like working. And you could bring Milly with you.'

'Samuel doesn't want me to work.'

'Samuel can't run your life!' snapped Beryl, suddenly irritated. 'He's your husband, not your jailor.'

'Oh Gran, that's a bit harsh,' Faith replied, shaken. 'Why are you angry with him all of a sudden?'

Fighting to hold her temper, Beryl paused. Now wasn't the time to confide her anxieties, to confess that she was worried. Faith loved Samuel, so she had to give her granddaughter's husband some more leeway. Besides, Samuel owned half the business. He was in charge now.

'I'm tired, love,' Beryl said, yawning expansively. 'Forgive me. I just need a good night's sleep.'

'Well you'll have to bunk up with Milly and me,' Faith reminded her, pulling a face. 'We've got a lodger now, remember?'

While Beryl was busy in the studio taking a photograph of a sickly baby with its over-weight mother, James was watching Samuel, who was reading Faith's note with concentration. Noticing that James was watching him, he tossed it on to the table between them. He was fully aware of the bond between brother and sister, and couldn't grumble about the lodger, even though he wanted to. In fact, he had hoped that no one would answer the advertisement, that they would not be intruded upon. But apparently some woman had answered, and without telling him, Faith had taken her in.

'A lodger.'

James nodded. 'Well, it's regular money and it'll be a help.' He could sense the reluctance on Samuel's part and tried to lessen it. 'Besides, it won't be for long. Once the business is doing well again . . .'

'So it's all down to me, is it?'

Sighing, James looked up, seeing Ellie in the kitchen door, watching the exchange. 'Samuel, stop taking everything so personally.'

'Why not?' he replied curtly. 'It seems to me that everyone is putting the success of this place squarely on my shoulders. I'm going to be the workhorse – go here, go there . . .' He paused, suddenly aware of how he was sounding. Sighing, he slumped into a chair. 'Jesus, listen to me. Sorry, James, sorry. Sometimes I just get so het up, you know? Things that would never have bothered me in the past now drive me crazy.'

James stared at his friend sympathetically. 'You went through a lot.'

'I don't remember *all* of what I went through,' Samuel admitted, leaning his head back against the chair.

His thoughts returned to the last time he and Faith had made love. She had traced the scars of his burns with her fingers so tenderly, then, kissing them, told him how much she loved him. How she had never given up hope when he was missing. How she had always known he would come back.

'There are gaps in my memory, James. Not so many as there used to be, but gaps when I don't know what I did. Even who I was.'

Relieved that Samuel was finally opening up about his feelings, James encouraged him to talk. 'I imagine it'll all come back in time. When you're ready.'

Nodding, Samuel glanced down. 'I can remember the guns. I can remember the villages in France. Sometimes I remember every detail, like the civilians watching us as we passed by. Then suddenly my memory shuts down. Slams a door on itself and I can't go any further.' He took in a breath, embarrassed. 'I know I can be bloody difficult. I don't mean to be like that; I can't seem to stop myself.'

'Give yourself time,' James replied, tactfully changing the subject. 'A lodger will be company for

Faith while you're at work. She's been on her own for a couple of weeks now. She'll be glad to go back to Hardy Street. She loves you very much, you know that, don't you?'

Nodding, Samuel rose to his feet. 'Oh, I know that, James. When I get all worked up, it's what keeps me going. Without Faith believing in me, I'd have given up long ago.'

While Samuel was talking to James, Faith was in the kitchen of Hardy Street, putting on her hat, Milly standing beside her, holding the old toy monkey Faith had had as a child. The housework had been done and Faith was going to take her daughter in to Oldham to look at the shops. Money was tight, but that was no reason to avoid the shops. Milly would love to see the windows with their displays, and if she was careful, Faith might be able to buy her the doll's pram she had been asking for as a Christmas present. Smiling, she glanced at Milly, amazed that her daughter was so interested in dolls, something Faith herself had never liked as a child. But then she had been a tomboy, growing up with James, her maternal instinct only coming to the fore when Milly was born.

Checking her purse for change, Faith paused when she heard footsteps on the stairs. She hesitated and hurried out, just as Leonie was walking towards the door.

'How did you sleep?' Faith asked her, wondering why the Frenchwoman hadn't eaten breakfast with them and hoping that she hadn't overheard the argument last night with Beryl and thought that she was the cause.

'We overslept,' Leonie admitted, smiling. 'The bed was comfortable and both of us were tired.'

'D'you want some breakfast? It's included in the rent for your room; you've paid for it.'

Pausing, Leonie looked at Suzette, then glanced back to Faith. 'I had some sandwiches left over from yesterday. We ate those.'

'Good,' Faith replied, turning, then turning back. 'Look, I'm taking Milly into town. Would you like to come with Suzette? We could all go together.'

Obviously taken aback, Leonie paused, Faith realising that she was moved and struggling not to be emotional. It must be so hard for her, Faith thought, her first Christmas widowed. Hadn't she gone through hell herself when Samuel was missing? Only it was a thousand times worse for Leonie. She knew her husband was never coming home.

'I'd like that,' the Frenchwoman said at last. 'I was wondering what to do with the day.'

Taking their time, they walked into town, passing the town hall, Leonie pointing out the library and art gallery. Grasping Milly's hand as Leonie pushed Suzette in her pushchair, they then went into a café, ordering tea and cheap cakes, Milly leaving half of hers, Suzette taking the remainder. Faith pretended that she hadn't seen, but wondered if Leonie and her daughter had actually gone hungry. Slowly the Frenchwoman sipped her tea, colour coming to her cheeks and giving her an unexpected prettiness.

'It must be very bleak for you,' Faith said, glancing at the thin coat Leonie was wearing. 'I have another coat you could have. It's not much, but I think Oldham might turn out to be colder than you thought.' She hurried on, not wanting to appear as though she was being a Lady Bountiful. 'Mort Ruben – someone I used to model for – let me have some clothes cheap.'

'You're a model?' Leonie asked, hurrying on. 'Yes, you could easily be. You're tall enough and pretty enough.'

Faith laughed. 'Thanks for the compliment, but I just helped out. I worked in the rag trade on David Street; my family has a business there.'

'You said something about it last night,' Leonie said, interested. 'Is that where your husband works?'

Faith nodded. 'Samuel was very seriously injured in the war. He had burns and shell shock. He was posted Missing, Presumed Dead.'

Frowning, Leonie looked at her. 'What does that mean?'

'At the Somme, they knew who was dead, and they had a pretty good idea of the injured, because they knew most of the soldiers who had been hospitalised, but others they couldn't find any trace of. Or, as in Samuel's case, they were too sick to tell anyone who they were.'

Leonie's eyes widened. 'He didn't know who he was?'

Passing Milly her glass of milk, Faith sighed. 'He had amnesia and shell shock. In fact, I think he had a nervous breakdown. But you must never say that when you meet him!' she added hurriedly. 'I don't want Samuel to think that we've been discussing him. And besides . . .'

'Yes?'

'He's finding normal life very hard. Can't seem to adjust.' Faith paused, suddenly ashamed. 'Dear God, here am I moaning about my husband, and you lost yours. I'm sorry. Had you been married for long?'

Leonie shook her head, Suzette on her lap, picking at the edging on her mother's collar. 'No, only a year.'

'What was he like?'

Taking in a breath, Leonie glanced over to Faith. The café was very ordinary, the cakes cheap, the tea weak. But it was warm and busy, and seemed very safe to her. And as for Faith . . . Leonie hadn't expected to like her so much. But almost by the time they had walked into town, the two of them had struck up an easy friendship. Their similarity made them easy companions. They were virtually the same age, both mothers with toddlers. And if Leonie had expected her new landlady to be standoffish, Faith had been at pains to make her feel at home.

Putting her hands around her tea cup, Leonie felt the warmth soak into her skin, the steam rising.

'He was very handsome. Is your husband handsome?'

'I think so,' Faith replied. 'Was he dark?'

'No, blond. He had big shoulders, and blue eyes.'

'What did he do for a living?'

Leonie paused. Faith could see that it was obviously difficult for her to talk about her late husband, but she could also sense that Leonie wanted to talk. And that she had loved this man very much.

'He was a carpenter.'

'Really? Samuel can turn his hand to anything. He could fix anything. You name it,' Faith went on. 'Though not so much now. Now he's different . . . What was his name?'

Leonie blinked. 'What?'

'Your husband, what was his name?'

'Yves. Yves Bonnard.'

'How old was he?'

Leonie paused, suddenly almost tearful. 'I can't talk about him any more.'

'Oh, sorry, I didn't . . .'

'No, no,' Leonie reassured her. 'You're very kind and I want to talk about him. But no more today, is that all right?'

'Whenever you're ready.'

'I've been very afraid, but not now,' Leonie went on quietly. 'Now I think I was very lucky to come to Hardy Street.'

Faith had not had a close friend since Ellie, and even though they kept in touch, Ellie was preoccupied with James in Manchester. It felt good to have a companion, Faith thought; she had been getting isolated in Hardy Street.

'You said that your husband was living in the city at the moment?'

Faith nodded. 'Yes, Samuel needed to learn the business fast, and frankly it was easier for him to concentrate if he stayed there for a little while. I know my grandmother's going back and forth every day, but James can carry on teaching Samuel in the evenings when she's gone.'

Leonie thought back, recalling an earlier conversation. 'James is your brother?'

'He certainly is, and he's known Samuel for years.'

'It's lucky they get on,' Leonie mused. 'If they didn't, it would be difficult, working together.'

'Frankly I think Samuel finds it harder working with my grandmother.'

They both laughed, Leonie leaning across the table.

'Your grandmother *is* very frightening.'

'So people tell me,' Faith replied, still smiling. 'I suppose she can be very scary, when she's a mind to be.'

'I can imagine.'

'Not the kind of person you cross, my grandmother,' Faith went on. 'Not if you want to stay healthy.'

They spent the rest of the morning walking around the shops in Oldham, stopping when Milly saw a doll's pram, although Suzette had fallen asleep in her pushchair. The pushchair was battered, obviously well used, and probably not new when

Leonie had bought it. Faith had been lucky that way: the family had provided, clubbing together to make sure Milly had everything she needed. And all of it new . . . During the war there had been little money and no cause for celebration, even at Christmas, but this year Faith knew that every shop would make an effort at decoration. As they walked along, she told Leonie about the fruit, how it was laid out in rows at Christmas time, in silver foil, or blue tissue paper. How game and turkeys hung from steel hooks, rocking gently in the winter breeze and lit by the outside lamps. And the chemist's window was decorated with fake snow, the huge medicine bottles garlanded with cotton wool.

'It'll be a good Christmas this year,' she said, but was suddenly interrupted by her daughter.

'Look, Mummy!' Milly cried out, as she stared into the toy shop window. 'Dolly, dolly!'

It was the same doll she had been looking at for the last two weeks. A beautiful concoction of lace and velvet, but expensive. Far too expensive.

'I see the doll, sweetheart, but we have to move on.'

But Milly wasn't going anywhere. 'I want it! I want it. Please, Mummy, please   '

'Milly,' Faith said patiently, aware that some passers-by were watching her child work herself into a tantrum. 'Now come on, stop this silliness. You can't have the doll, little one. I'm sorry.'

Letting out a howl of protest, Milly started to cry. Glancing over to check that she hadn't woken the

443

sleeping Suzette, Faith bent down to her little daughter. 'Milly, stop crying. We don't have enough money for the doll.'

'But—'

'No, sweetheart, you can't have it today. Maybe in a while.'

Gently touching her cheek, Faith tried to soothe her, but Milly was crying openly as they moved on. Surprised that her usually pliant child was proving to be so troublesome, Faith tried to pick her up. But Milly wasn't having any of it, and only the intervention of Leonie stopped her crying.

'Milly, can you do something for me?' she asked the child. 'Can you help me to push Suzette?'

Thoughtful, Milly considered the request, then took the handle of Suzette's pushchair, walking next to Leonie.

A flicker of jealousy flared inside Faith. It was unexpected and mean-minded, and it shook her. What had she to be jealous of? Here was someone who understood children, someone who would help her. Perry was an excellent baby-sitter, but Faith didn't really want Milly to spend too much time with the bigoted Agnes.

'You have a way with her,' Faith said, as they moved on.

Leonie shrugged. 'I like children. I had two sisters myself when I was growing up. We were a very close family.'

Smiling, Leonie walked on, Milly pushing the pram happily, Suzette fast asleep. Chatting easily,

Faith watched her new friend, and then realised that something was nagging at her. Surprised, she went back to wondering how she could raise enough money to buy the doll for Milly for Christmas. It was expensive, she knew that only too well. After all, she had priced it the week before. It would take a lot of saving up for . . . Faith stopped, pretending to look into a haberdashery window. In the glass she could see Leonie talking to Milly – and then she realised what it was that was making her uneasy. It had been something Leonie had said only minutes earlier: *I had two sisters myself when I was growing up*. It had been a simple remark, hardly worth thinking about. Apart from the fact that Leonie had told Faith an entirely different story the previous night when she had been talking about her past. Then she had said: *I have no one else. No one left*.

Unnerved, Faith tried to shrug the matter off. Maybe Leonie *had* had two sisters. Maybe they had been killed in the war. Maybe they were no longer friends . . . But then again, it was quite something to ignore the existence of two siblings. Two members of a family. Taking in a breath, Faith told herself to relax. She was overreacting. Everyone had secrets. You couldn't know anyone in one day. Leonie was a godsend, and she liked her. No point making something out of nothing. And yet as they walked on down the Oldham streets, Faith felt herself running over everything else Leonie had told her. Picking into the words, wondering if there had been other lies . . .

'I miss him.'

Surprised, Faith stopped walking, staring into Leonie's shy, lost face. 'Who?'

'My husband. It's going to be Christmas next month and he's . . .' She paused, brokenly, her hands clinging tightly to the handle of the pushchair. 'I can't imagine never seeing him again.'

At once all doubts left Faith's mind. Instead she was moved to pity, remembering how she had felt, waiting for news. Waiting for her husband to come home. But this woman's man didn't get home. Yves Bonnard was dead. Leonie Bonnard was a widow. She had lost her man. He was never coming back.

CHAPTER THIRTY-FIVE

Three weeks later, Samuel broke a bottle of processing fluid in the darkroom. Swearing, he jumped back, wrenching open the door and letting in the light. As he did so, the developing photographs inside were ruined, Beryl running out from the kitchen when she heard the commotion.

Seeing the door of the darkroom open, she turned on Samuel. 'You bloody fool!' she snapped. 'You've gone and wrecked those prints.'

'It was an accident!'

'You know not to open the darkroom door when we're developing film,' Beryl went on, beside herself. The photographs had been a good order, enough to ensure presents for everyone and a damn good Christmas dinner. But now Samuel's carelessness had ruined everything.

'I broke the bottle. What was I supposed to do? Let the chemicals get into my clothes?'

'You were supposed to keep the door closed!' Beryl shouted. 'The processing fluid won't kill you. It didn't go on your face! God, you're so stupid,' she went on, desperate because she knew she would have to do the photographs again. For free. And more than that, they had been of Lionel Duckworth, an Oldham councillor. A good customer who would have sent others. The kind of customer they needed, and hadn't been around for years. 'You bloody fool!' she said, beside herself. 'You've learned nothing. Not one thing in all these weeks.'

'Gran, calm down—'

She turned to James, cutting him off immediately. 'Keep out of this! This is between me and your brother-in-law.' Infuriated, she spun back to Samuel. 'I signed over half of this business to you because I love my granddaughter and because she asked me to. I thought – we both thought – it would be the making of you.'

Stung, Samuel raised his voice. 'Don't talk to me like that!'

'I'll talk to you any way I please! Remember, I knew you when you were doing odd jobs, and you were a damn sight happier then. You come back from the war and we've all pussy-footed around you ever since. I know you had a bad time, but for God's sake, Samuel, when are you going to pull yourself out of it?'

'Gran,' James said warningly, 'you've said enough. It was an accident.'

'It was carelessness! It was lack of thought.'

'You never wanted me here,' Samuel said, standing up to her. 'You never liked me.'

'I liked you plenty – when you were likeable.'

'You should count yourself lucky I wanted to work here!' Samuel replied, beside himself and saying more than he meant to. 'I hate it here. I hate working with you, you old bat.'

'How dare you!'

'How dare *you*!' he snapped back, both of them losing their tempers, Ellie watching timidly from the kitchen door.

Trying to intercede and break up what was turning out to be a violent row, James turned to Samuel. 'Let it go.'

'But she's always on at me!' Samuel hissed, his face pale with anger, his voice raised.

'Bloody man doesn't know he's got it made,' Beryl replied, striking out verbally. 'If Faith had any sense, she'd leave you.'

She had said too much, not even meant it, but in the heat of the moment she had struck Samuel where it hurt him most: Faith's love for him. Suddenly he looked at Beryl and loathed her. Loathed her for nagging him, berating him, rubbing his nose in how lucky he was. His advance had been costly. The City Photographic Studio was struggling, and he had been bullied and badgered by Beryl into being grateful. But he *wasn't* grateful, Samuel thought, his brain burning with fury. He was sick of the place, sick of her. Sick of bloody life. There was nothing to look forward to, only the years of work ahead. All that kept him going was Faith's love – and now Beryl had tried to undermine that.

His rage was uncontrollable. 'I loathe you!' he

shouted at her. 'I loathe your face, your voice, the way you nag at me. I hate the fact that this is your place. Always was and always will be.'

'Samuel,' warned James, 'cut it out.'

But he was too far gone to hear anyone. 'I'll tell you why this business is failing, Beryl – it's because you're old. You're past it. You're a fossil, a widow woman trying to keep busy.'

'Right!' she roared. 'That does it.' Moving to the door, she took up her hat and coat. 'You want this place, you have it, you bastard. *You* run it. I've had enough worries to last me a lifetime. You sort your own life out, but I'm not going to be your whipping boy. You wanted the business – you've got it.'

With that she walked out, slamming the door shut, James watching his grandmother's feet move up the basement steps as she made for the street.

'Well done!' he snapped, turning back to Samuel. 'Go after her and apologise. She'll make you work for it, but she'll come round in time. Go on, go after her.'

Samuel didn't move. He wasn't going to run after Beryl. In fact he was glad she had gone. Now he could run the business and show her how wrong she was about him.

'Let her go.'

James's voice hardened. 'You said a lot of bitter things, Samuel, and so did she. But my grandmother's getting on, she's worked hard all her life, she deserves to be treated with some respect.'

'*I* deserve respect!'

'You had respect, you bloody ass!' James shouted back, thinking that if he was able-bodied he would have got out of his wheelchair and punched Samuel. Knocked some sense into him. 'You blew it yourself. We all gave you a chance, and you've ruined it.'

'It's not easy trying to fit in.'

'Tell me all about it,' James responded coldly. 'It's not easy living in a bloody wheelchair either. Go after Beryl and make your peace with her, Samuel. Don't let your pride get in the way. We know you've been through a lot. We've all made allowances for you, but you went too far today. You never used to be difficult or arrogant. The old Samuel would have understood. He would have known that ruining those prints meant money, not just for him, but for all of us. Beryl wasn't just striking out at you – she was upset, you fool. She was worried about the loss of money, the fact that she'd have to redo the sitting. She was thinking about next month, about Christmas coming.'

'Who cares what she thought?' Samuel replied, his tone flat. 'She's gone. And about time. She's too old.'

'Are you serious?' James asked, his voice deadly.

'Yeah, I'm serious.'

'Without Beryl there wouldn't *be* a business. My family made this place what it is.'

'A run-down studio in a basement?' Samuel sneered, moving towards the door.

He knew he had gone too far, and for a moment he wanted to apologise, but he couldn't back down.

He willed himself to turn around, make his peace with James and then go after Beryl, but something stopped him. Rubbing his forehead with his fingers, Samuel slowly turned, James looking at him with an expression of intense dislike.

'Do you *really* think I can work with you after what you've just said?'

Samuel shrugged. 'If you can't, you can leave too. Go on, get out! Get out!'

Horrified, Ellie shrank away from the kitchen door. James watched her go and then studied his brother-in-law warily. Was he crazy? Or just angry, beyond reason? Pacing the floor, Samuel kept moving, James cursing his handicap, his limitations. He was helpless, unable to defend his grandmother or his wife – except verbally, and he didn't know if that would be enough. The old James would have pitched Samuel out of the door. But James wasn't capable of being a hero any more. If he wanted to protect his family and the business, he had to be more cunning. He had to calm Samuel, not antagonise him.

'Sit down, let's have a drink.'

'I don't want a drink.'

'Shut up, Samuel, and sit down,' James said firmly. 'You need a drink.'

A moment sizzled between them, then finally Samuel slumped into a chair next to James. He was breathing quickly, but after another few moments he began to calm himself, taking the beer offered to him.

Finally he spoke again. 'Sorry, I lost my temper.'

James smiled, as though the matter was of little importance. 'We all do now and again.'

'But I still hope Beryl doesn't come back,' Samuel went on. 'What she said about Faith – about how if she had any sense she'd leave me – it just made me so angry. Without Faith, I couldn't go on. There would be no point to anything without her.'

James realised then that Samuel wasn't insane. He was walking a mental knife-edge. The only real security he had in his life was Faith. As long as he had her, he would get through. Without her, James realised, Samuel would self-destruct. She was his lifeline, his hold on the world. She was his saviour.

Tossing her hat aside as she came through the door, Beryl looked from her granddaughter to the lodger, giving Leonie such a hard stare that she retreated upstairs without uttering a word. Waiting until she was sure the Frenchwoman was out of earshot, Beryl sat down heavily in front of the kitchen fire, Faith watching her curiously.

'Don't tell me – you've been visiting Agnes.'

Snorting, Beryl shook her head. 'Your bloody husband threw me out of my own business.'

'What!'

'Well, he didn't throw me out, I left.' Beryl filled her granddaughter in on the details, adding curtly, 'Your husband doesn't like being told what to do. And especially not by me. He thinks he knows everything. I can't talk to the man.'

Faith stared at her grandmother. 'Why didn't you tell me about this before it all blew up?'

'Because I wanted it to work!' Beryl said firmly. 'I know how much you love your husband, and I wanted to train Samuel up and then leave him to it. I thought when he was working with James it would all be all right. I thought he just saw me as some irritating old bat who was nagging him.' She paused, her voice rising. 'But I *had* to nag him! Photography is a skill; if you want to be good at it, you have to listen and learn from people. I learned from your grandad and that bloody awful Tommy Bentley. But there's no teaching Samuel. Oh no, he knows it all.'

Sighing, Faith reached for her coat. 'If you keep an eye on Milly, I'll go over to Manchester and talk to Samuel.'

'No, love,' Beryl said simply. 'Bless you for wanting to make it work out, but I can't go back to David Street.'

'Gran, come on,' Faith urged her. 'Don't be silly.'

'I'm not going back!' Beryl shouted. 'It's not the way I'd have planned it, but maybe this is all for the best. I've had enough of Oldham and Manchester anyway. It's not just the young who need to alter things.'

Unnerved, Faith stared at her. 'What *are* you talking about?'

'I'm getting older. Times have changed, we've all changed. I was thinking that I'd like to slow down, but now it's been forced on me.'

Shaken, Faith touched her grandmother's arm.

'Look, I'll talk to Samuel. We can solve this.'

'No, it's too far gone! We don't get on, Samuel and me, we couldn't work together now. Not after what we both said. He might be all right with James, his own age and all . . .' Beryl paused, fighting bitterness. 'I should never have signed the business over to him.'

Faith winced. 'That was my fault.'

'No, no, love!' Beryl said, sighing. 'Like I said, I've been thinking about things for a while. About the situation. I mean, when I'd finished training up Samuel, where would I have lived then? James and Ellie need the bedroom at the studio, and you and Samuel have this place.'

'Oh no, Hardy Street is *your* home,' Faith said hurriedly. 'We'll find somewhere else.'

'You can't afford it, love. You've no money, or you wouldn't need to get in a lodger.'

Unsettled, Faith could feel her world shifting under her feet. First Samuel had changed, then their home life, and now her grandmother – the woman who had been a constant supportive influence in her life – was threatening to move on. To leave Oldham, Manchester. It was unthinkable, impossible . . .

'Gran, we have to sort this out.'

'I'm going to my sister's.'

Faith stared at her, incredulous. 'Your sister's. She lives in London.'

'Well, it's not the end of the world,' Beryl

responded. 'And to be honest, I need to put some space between your husband and me.'

Numb, Faith gripped her grandmother's hand. 'What exactly did Samuel say to you?'

'It's too late . . .'

'It's *not* too late!' Faith snapped back. 'You're not being run out of your own business and home. Don't be daft, Gran, Samuel can't say what he likes and get away with it. You've done so much for him, he owes you. I know he's been difficult, but he can't break up the family.'

'I think he already has,' Beryl replied coldly, giving her granddaughter a quick hug and then drawing back. 'I'm not doing this to create a scene, honestly I'm not. But your grandfather and I had some good times in David Street and I can't – even for your sake – stay there with such a bad feeling going on. I'll just get some things together and I'll be off.'

She moved towards the door.

Faith ran after her, tears in her eyes. 'You can't go!'

Pausing, Beryl gave her granddaughter a stern look. 'I'm not saying I'm going for ever, love, but I need to have a think. You've got your life and your man; you're happy. And if there are a few problems, maybe having an old woman around isn't helping them, I understand that. But now I have to work out what I want to do with the rest of *my* life – and staying at my sister's will help with that.'

'You two don't get on!' Faith retorted. 'I hate to

think of you so far away. Why don't you stay with Agnes instead?'

Beryl rolled her eyes. 'Oh no, love. Not Agnes and Perry! I said I wanted to clear my mind, not lose it.'

CHAPTER THIRTY-SIX

Intertwining her fingers with her husband's, Ellie listened until Samuel's footsteps had faded down David Street. When she was sure he had gone, she looked into James's face. Her expression was more eloquent than words, James squeezing her hand tightly.

'He'll cool off.'

She nodded. 'Do you think Beryl's really gone for good?'

'God knows, but I doubt it,' James replied, touching his wife's hair and wishing that Samuel Granger would never descend the basement steps again. 'I think she's been getting sick of Samuel for a while and she's glad to have an excuse to get away from him.'

'But it's not like Beryl to back down from a fight.'

'Maybe she hasn't backed down,' James replied. Ellie rested her head on his shoulder. He could smell soap and developing chemicals coming off her skin, that peculiar mixture that clung to her clothes, just like it had always clung to Beryl's. 'My grandmother's a tough woman; she stormed off because she knew she couldn't get through to Samuel. She'll not leave it like this, you mark my words. This won't be the last we see of Beryl.'

'But Samuel said so many harsh things!' Ellie said incredulously. 'That she was too old – he as good as threw her out. Maybe that's what he wanted – to get rid of her. After all, she's signed over half the business to him. Cut herself out by doing so. Samuel has power now, he has the upper hand.'

'He only has *half* of the business,' James reminded her. 'I have the other half.'

'And he told you to get out,' Ellie said quietly, feeling her husband's grip press on her hand. 'How could he? This is *your* family, *your* business. He has no right coming here and trying to take over.'

Amused, James smiled at her. 'What a little fighter I have for a wife!'

'But I don't *trust* him.'

'Samuel can't do anything.'

'You say that, but he's managed to get Beryl to leave.'

Irritated, James looked away.

'Leave it to me, Ellie, I'll sort this out. I'll finish training Samuel and then get him out and about, away from David Street. I told him he's got to find work on the coast; he won't be under our feet for much longer. And besides, he'll be moving back to Hardy Street soon.'

'Can't be soon enough,' Ellie replied. 'I used to like Samuel. But this is not the same man. I don't know what happened to him, but he's unpredictable, James. And the way he was going on today, he sounded a bit crazy.'

'Samuel's just bluster,' he reassured her, wondering how he could make sure that the cuckoo *wasn't* going to throw them all out of the nest. 'When he's having to go out and find work, he'll burn all that temper out of his system. A few months travelling around, touting for business, should cool him down.'

'Unless he refuses to go,' Ellie countered, her tone quiet. 'After all, we can't make him do it, can we? And if he refuses to find work, or make work, the business will come down around all our ears.'

Troubled, Faith put Milly to bed later that night, and then sat down in the kitchen, hoping that Leonie would come down and talk. But apparently the lodger had retired early, and before long the house was silent. In the front room, Faith could hear the faint ticking of the old clock – the one and only heirloom passed down from Tommy Bentley. The clock had sounded throughout her childhood. On the night she and James were told about their mother's death, on the day Faith had been dragged back home to Agnes's, Beryl unable to resist a lecture in the front room of Hardy Street. The clock had ticked on the dreadful days after James's accident, then chimed down the months of Sid's slow death. Throughout the long war Faith had wound the clock, keeping the routine going, keeping life sane and measured in the eye of the maelstrom.

Getting to her feet, she moved into the front room, checking the time and then winding the clock. The thought that Beryl was no longer around was like an ache to her, a stitch in her side. By now, she realised, her grandmother would be on her way to London, on her way to Lambeth and her sister's home. Purposeful, Beryl would stamp down the street and then ring the bell of that old-fashioned terraced house, Margaret opening up and showing her in, hurriedly making room amongst the grandchildren and the clutter. They would be at loggerheads within a week, if not before . . .

Faith moved to the window, holding back the net and looking out. Her first instinct had been to rush over to Manchester, but James had forestalled her. Phoning the studio from the pub on the corner of Hardy Street, Faith had put her hand over her ear as she strained to hear her brother above the sounds of the drinkers.

'Where's Samuel now?'

'Gone out,' James had replied. 'He'll be round at the pub in St Peter's Square, drowning his sorrows.'

'Not getting drunk?'

'No, he doesn't get drunk,' James said truthfully. 'He just has a few jars and comes back.'

She blew out her cheeks. 'I saw Gran, she's gone to London, to her sister's. What in God's name did Samuel say to her?'

'It was a bad argument,' James admitted. 'I don't blame Gran for walking out.'

'I blame myself,' Faith said, straining to hear above the pub noise. 'I should never have asked Gran to sign over her half of the business. I was wrong there, stupid.'

'You thought it was right.'

'But it wasn't, was it?' she replied. 'It was bad for her, and for you.'

'All families have arguments—'

She cut him off in mid-sentence. 'Gran never said a word about how difficult Samuel was being.' She paused, then asked, 'Can you work with him?'

'I'll do my best.'

'Sorry,' she said quietly. 'I should never have got him involved in the business. What are we going to do?'

'Ellie and I were just talking about that. Samuel's nearly trained up. He knows how to take a studio shot, and by next week he'll be ready to go out and find business. Frankly, he's no good to us here – I can run the studio and take the photographs. I think he should move into the city centre and the coast. Get in some work. It's Christmas next month; if Samuel buckled down he might get a few people wanting photographs for the holidays. Ellie and I got some cards made, only cheap, but they'll do the job. Samuel could pass them out on his travels, get some custom that way. What d'you think?'

'It sounds good.'

'There's just one thing.'

'Yes?' she asked, her tone wary.

'Will he do it?'

Frowning, Faith held the receiver even closer to her ear. 'What d'you mean, will he do it?'

'He doesn't want to. He thinks that going out touting for business is demeaning.'

'But the business is half his!'

'I know, but he says that working the coast would be like going cap in hand.'

'What the hell has got into him?' Faith asked, shaken.

'He said it was beneath him.'

'Really?' she replied, her tone cold. 'But taking in a lodger and throwing out Beryl is all right?'

She paused, turning away from the bar, her face averted. God, why hadn't she kept a closer eye on events? Why hadn't she insisted that she work for Laurence? That way she would have known what was going on at David Street. Might even have prevented her grandmother leaving. Certainly she could have kept a closer eye on her husband. But instead she had obeyed Samuel, desperate to please him and anxious not to upset him. And what had her compliance cost her? What had it cost everyone?

Faith's voice was metallic when she spoke again. 'I'm coming back to work in David Street.'

'You're what!'

'Beryl's gone. You can't run the place on your own when we get Samuel on the road. I can take the job in the Goldbladt showroom and get a decent wage – Laurence wrote to me only last month to say he still wants me back. It's Christmas next month, James, I can earn money at this time.'

'We certainly need it.'

'That bad?'

'Not good. And Samuel wrecking those prints will cost us.'

She sighed. 'Mort might want me to fill in too; he always has customers at Christmas time, his non-Jewish clients. And besides, when I'm at David Street I'll be on tap to help you out.'

'You know Samuel doesn't want you to work.'

'I don't care!' she said simply. 'I love him, I love my husband with all my heart, James, you know that. I swear I couldn't love any man more. But Samuel is *not* going to break apart my family and ruin our business, or we'll end up with nothing. I can't let that happen. I can't stand by and let him do that.' She paused. 'I'll ask Agnes and Perry to baby-sit Milly for me.'

'And travel from Hardy Street every day?'

'Yes,' she agreed, thinking of her grandparents and feeling oddly comforted by the idea. 'Just like Beryl and Sid used to do. I'll be over on Wednesday.'

There was a pause before James spoke again. 'D'you want me to tell Samuel that you're coming?'

'No,' she said simply. 'This time I want the upper hand.'

Putting down the receiver, Faith hurried out of the back door of the pub, nodding quickly to one of Sid's old drinking pals. Moving out on to the street, she walked the four doors home, then paused, surprised to find that her heart was thumping and she was breathing rapidly. As she closed her eyes momentarily, James's words came back to her with the force of a rock fall: . . . *like going cap in hand . . . it was beneath him* . . . Pushing her hands deep in her pockets, Faith looked down the street, thinking back to the time she and Samuel had been courting. How easy he had been then, funny, unambitious . . . The thought was bitter to her. It had been Samuel's easy-going way that had worried her, made her wonder if he was the right man for her. But now that he had discovered his arrogance and achieved some status, he was becoming unbearable.

Of course Faith had been worried for a long time about his change in character. Had spoken to his doctor and even written to the hospital where he had been treated. But she had got the same answers as Beryl and no one had any real advice to offer her. Just that these things happened when people had suffered shell shock and a mental collapse. No, they said, Samuel probably wasn't the same man he had been. But it wasn't his fault; it was because of the war and his injuries. And Faith had accepted that. Made allowances – too many allowances. Being too indulgent, giving way instead of giving guidance. She had been a fool, *a fool* . . .

Well, she told herself, she had better do something to stop the rot. And fast . . . Her gaze moved down the street, her eyes moving upwards to the light in the front bedroom of Hardy Street. So Leonie was awake, probably reading or nursing Suzette. Faith thought about her lodger. She would stand by her word, but in the spring Leonie Bonnard would have to move on. When Faith was working too, they wouldn't need a lodger's rent. But that was in the future, she decided; what she had to do was to sort out the present. And that began with Wednesday, when she went back to David Street.

More settled in her mind, Faith moved back to the house – then had the oddest sensation that someone was watching her. Turning round, she glanced back just in time to see a figure moving quickly into the ginnel at the end of Hardy Street. A figure whose gait was clumsy, who ran with their body tipped to one side. It was familiar. And unwelcome. Unnerved, Faith ran towards the ginnel and looked down the alleyway to catch another glimpse.

The figure had disappeared. But the memory hadn't. Lennie Hellier was back.

CHAPTER THIRTY-SEVEN

Shaken, Faith hurried into her house and locked the door behind her. After another moment she moved into the kitchen, relieved to see Leonie putting the kettle on to the stove.

'Do you mind if I make a cup of tea?' Leonie asked, then paused, looking at Faith. 'Are you all right? You look shocked.'

Shaking her head, Faith sat down. It couldn't have been Lennie Hellier, she thought. He had been gone for years, and no one had clapped eyes on him. Besides, what would Hellier want in Oldham? Convincing herself that she had been mistaken, Faith glanced over to her lodger.

'I'm fine. A cuppa sounds like a good idea,' she said, moving on hurriedly. 'And I've got something to tell you – I'm going back to work in Manchester.'

Surprised, Leonie made the tea, then sat down at the table. Her face was losing its pinched, exhausted look, her eyes intelligent.

'Back to work? I thought you were talking about going back in the spring.'

'I was, but things have changed,' Faith replied.

She didn't know Leonie well, and although she liked her, she was finding it difficult having to share so much personal information with a relative stranger. But then again, she had to explain Beryl's sudden absence and her return to Manchester.

'I start work again on Wednesday. You'll be on your own from then on.'

'I've had no luck finding a job yet.'

'Ask at the factory,' Faith said, her tone encouraging. 'They sometimes have the odd vacancy.'

Leonie nodded. 'Good idea. Then, when I've got a wage coming in, I can get someone to watch over Suzette for me. To be honest, I could do with some time on my own.'

'I was just thinking how much I'll miss Milly when I go back to work. And Suzette,' Faith admitted. 'I'm getting fond of your little girl.'

'Oh, I love her too, I love them both – but I still wouldn't mind a chance to go out for an evening. Like when I was younger . . . Still, no point daydreaming.' Leonie paused, then turned back to Faith, her spirits lifting. 'Can I do anything to help? I mean, you can't take Milly to work with you. Whilst I'm at home, I could look after her.'

'Oh, she'll stay at my aunt's in the daytime,' Faith replied. 'We had the same arrangement before.'

'But wouldn't it be easier for you to leave her with me?' Leonie countered. 'I mean, she'd be in her own home and she'd have a friend to play with. Suzette would like it too. I'm not a stranger to Milly; she's grown to know me over the last few weeks and we get on.' She paused, then flushed. 'I'm sorry, of course it was a stupid idea. I'm not family . . .'

Embarrassed herself, Faith hurried to reassure her. 'No, it's not that. It's just that Agnes and her husband took care of Milly when I was working during the war . . . Of course it *would* be easier for her to stay here, but I can't ask you to take care of her.'

'I came a long way, on my own, with a little child,' Leonie said, her voice quiet. 'It was hard, but I survived and I'm safe here. For the first time in a while I can relax, and so can my daughter. Listen to me, Faith, please. If you're in trouble, let me make it easier for you. We women have to stick together. And besides, I don't forget that you were the only person who took me in when everyone else turned me away.' She smiled, her hair tied back off her face, her expression earnest. 'I owe you so much, Faith. Please let me repay you now.'

'You're paying me rent.'

'Not much for a room.'

'It's not much *of* a room,' Faith replied drily. 'And there's something else I should tell you. My grandmother's gone to stay with her sister in London. She might be gone for a while.' In silence, Leonie stared at her, Faith shrugging. 'Apparently my husband and Beryl had a real argument and my grandmother walked out. She's gone off to London.' She paused, trying to sound optimistic. 'She'll be back, but for a while I should go back to work. You know, get some more money in and keep an eye on the business.'

'Oh dear,' Leonie said softly. 'I don't seem to be bringing you much luck.'

'It's not you. This row was on the cards – only I didn't see it coming until it was too late. I told you, my husband's changed a good deal since he came back from the war. He's not easy-going like he used to be, and Beryl isn't exactly placid. I should have realised that those two working together would never be a success. But it was the only way I could think of making Samuel feel secure.' She paused, glad of someone to talk to. 'I thought that if he had a position, responsibility, he would settle down again.'

'Working for your grandmother?'

'Not just working. James signed half of the business over to my husband.' Faith sighed. 'I shouldn't have asked him to do that; it was a stupid move on my part.'

'But you wanted to make Samuel feel like he belonged.'

'Yes, that's it,' Faith agreed. 'I wanted him to feel secure, but look what happened. Apparently he was impossible, and now my grandmother's walked out and James can't cope on his own.'

'But he wouldn't *be* on his own,' Leonie said, puzzled. 'Your husband would be with him.'

'My brother can take the photographs and run the studio with his wife, but Samuel will have to get out and drum up some more work, or we're in trouble.' Faith was suddenly annoyed with herself. 'God, listen to me! As if you needed to hear all this after what you've been through.'

'Let me help you.'

'I don't think—'

'I can look after Milly,' Leonie insisted. 'What's one more little girl to care for? It would be nothing to me and it would make life a lot easier for you. Please accept,' she said imploringly. 'There's no shame in taking help when it's offered – I did. And it was the best thing that's happened to me for years. Think how much easier it would be for you, knowing that Milly is home with me. You wouldn't have to worry about the time, or getting back if you needed to work a bit later. It would give you a chance to sort things out, Faith. To talk to your husband, your brother, get some money in – and the business on track again.' She paused, suddenly leaning back in her seat. 'I'm sorry, I'm not trying to interfere. God, you must think so badly of me.'

'No, I don't!' Faith assured her. 'I think you've been talking a lot of sense. And I think I *would* like you to look after Milly for me. Agnes didn't really want her around.' She was liking the idea more and more. 'And Milly *would* be company for Suzette. I love to see them play together, they're like sisters already. Besides, it will only be in the daytime, I'll be back in the evening. And so will Samuel.' She smiled, relieved. 'So yes, Leonie, I *will* take you up on your offer.'

'Good. Does your husband know you are going back to work?'

'No,' Faith admitted. 'I want to surprise him.'

'You love him a great deal, don't you?' Leonie said, her voice understanding.

'Oh yes, I love him,' Faith agreed. 'Perhaps too much; perhaps it makes me blind to his faults sometimes. I don't see what's going on under my nose.'

'Does he love you?'

'Yes,' Faith said firmly, 'I might not be sure of many things in life, but I know Samuel loves me. I have never doubted that for an instant.'

'Oh my God, my God, my God!' Mort said, jiggling his foot excitedly. 'Faith is coming back—'

'Now then, Mort,' Laurence warned him. 'Keep your voice down, Samuel doesn't know.'

Mort put his finger to his mouth in a childlike gesture of silence and stared at his old friend. Laurence had recovered some of his strength, but he wasn't the ebullient, loud character he had once been. Instead he hobbled around with the help of a walking stick, and his frame – once decked out in velvet and the best serge – was now hunched and thin. But he had found a new lease of life – something that had surprised Miriam and his doctors – in deciding to reopen the Goldbladt showroom. And in the fact that Faith was going to run it for him. Laurence was no fool; he knew he wasn't strong enough to spend more than twenty hours a week in the place, but he had a hunch that Faith could make a go of the business, and although he was sorry to hear about the upheaval downstairs, he was more than delighted to have her back.

'Like old times, hey, friend?' Mort asked him, twinkling with pleasure.

'Like old times,' Laurence agreed, even though he knew full well that Mort was struggling to keep his head above water. His showroom was half empty, his seamstresses having been called up for war work long ago. And now the fighting was over, most of them had sorted out better-paid and less strenuous work in offices and shops. Only two of the originals had returned – the young widow and the cobra-tongued Honour. Except that the young widow wasn't so young any more, and Honour was getting too old to be disruptive.

'You watch, our luck will turn now,' Mort went on. 'Now that Faith is coming back.'

Laurence nodded. 'I never asked what you thought of Samuel Granger, did I?'

Mort shook his head. 'No.'

'So what *do* you think of him?'

Shifting his feet – still in their fashionable spats – Mort struggled for an answer. 'I liked him at first. But he's changed. Not that I don't still like him.'

Laurence smiled. 'You like everyone, Mort.'

'No, no,' he said firmly. 'I didn't like Lennie Hellier. I never liked him. Not a bit. Not at all.'

'What about Beryl?'

'I've always liked Beryl.'

'No, Mort,' Laurence sighed. 'I mean, do you think she'll ever come back?'

'I think,' the little man replied thoughtfully, 'that she left for good reasons. Some we might not even know. And I also think that it would take something very important to bring Mrs Bentley back here.'

Glancing over to James, Ellie kept her other eye on the entrance door of the studio. In the darkroom Samuel was developing the prints that had had to be retaken of Lionel Duckworth, prints James had done for free. Mr Duckworth had not been best pleased to have to redo his sitting, and complained that he was being kept from important council work, although James knew only too well he was on his way home. His displeasure was cemented by the fact that it was James, not Beryl, who took the photographs.

'So where is Mrs Bentley?' Lionel Duckworth had asked.

'My grandmother is having some time with her sister in London.'

'Oh aye,' Duckworth had replied, his moustache quivering as he scented a bit of scandal. 'I heard there had been a bit of a do.'

'Keep your head up, please,' James had asked, hoping it would shut the sitter up. But it hadn't.

'I heard that she flounced out, saying she were never coming back here. And all because of Samuel laying down the law. I said it were a mistake Mrs

Bentley signing over half the business to that man. He weren't up to it.'

Incensed, James interrupted him. 'Mr Duckworth, I don't know what you're talking about.'

'I'm talking about what your brother-in-law were saying in the pub the other night. It's common knowledge that there were a falling-out and that he's got half the business.' Duckworth leaned forward towards James. 'It were bad enough about your accident, young man. You don't want to have the rug pulled out from under your feet a second time. I mean, anyone can tell from listening to Samuel for a couple of minutes that he's not cut out for business and might turn out to be a liability.'

Reliving the conversation, James shook his head to try and dislodge the unpleasant words. Then he glanced over to the darkroom. Samuel was still busy, sullenly doing the prints, although he had been less bullish that morning. Suddenly James heard footsteps, Ellie smiling at him and running out of the door. From where he was sitting in the wheelchair, James could see his wife's feet and his sister's in the street above, and watched with relief as Faith walked in.

'God,' he said, as she bent to kiss his cheek, 'it's good to see you.'

'And you,' she replied, looking round. 'So, where is Samuel?'

'Developing some prints. He should be out soon.'

Nodding, Faith took off her hat and coat and then sat down at the table with her brother and

Ellie. She felt surprisingly nervous, her heart beating rapidly, her mouth dry. Why? she asked herself. This was her second home and she was about to see her husband. Why should she be nervous?

'Hey, James,' Samuel said suddenly, walking out and then stopping in his tracks.

For an ugly moment Faith thought he was going to make a scene, but instead he moved over to her and picked her up, swinging her round and kissing her repeatedly.

'My God! What a surprise!' he said, genuinely glad to see her, Faith wriggling in his grip and laughing. Surely everyone had been wrong, she thought. This was the old Samuel, easy-going, loving, relaxed. 'What are you doing here?' he asked.

'I came to help.'

His expression darkened. 'Help? Why do we need help?' He sighed. 'Of course, Beryl's gone. But she chose to go, Faith; whatever your grandmother told you, it was her choice.'

'Well, she's visiting her sister in London . . .'

'Where's Milly?' Samuel asked, looking round.

'I didn't think it was the right thing bringing her with me. After all, I'm going to be busy.'

He didn't get it. 'Busy? Why?'

'Well, James said you were trained up now, and soon you'd be free to get out and about and find some more work. You know how much you always hated to be cooped up. It will do you good.'

'Oh, I see,' Samuel said coldly. 'You're checking up on me.'

476

'No. I don't have to check up on you, do I?'

He blinked, slowly turning from his wife to James and Ellie. Then he took hold of Faith's arm and steered her towards the kitchen at the back of the shop. Once there, he closed the door and folded his arms.

'What's this all about?'

'Don't try and bully me, Samuel,' replied Faith. 'You know what it's all about. Gran's gone, James can't get out and about, so you have to, or we'll not keep the business going. We need to get some more work. As for me – I've accepted Laurence's offer.'

'Without discussing it with me?'

'There seems to have been a lot going on that you haven't discussed with me!' Faith countered. 'Like how bad relations were between you and my grandmother. I had to find that out when Gran told me she was leaving Oldham.'

'She never stopped nagging me.'

'She gave you a chance in a million!' Faith snapped back, breaking her resolution not to fight with her husband. 'She gave you a half-share – *her* share – in this business. The least you could have done, Samuel, was to respect what she was trying to teach you.'

'You have no idea how difficult it's been.'

'So why didn't you tell me?'

'You would have taken her side. You *always* side with your family, Faith.'

'That's not true!' she replied heatedly. 'My family is your family, Samuel. We don't take sides.'

'Well we do now,' he replied curtly, turning away.

Angrily she moved over to him and took his arm, pulling him round to face her. 'Look at me, Samuel! Look into my eyes and then tell me that I put *anyone* before you. I love you. I believe in you. I knew you weren't dead when everyone else said you were. I knew you would come back – and you did.' She touched his cheek, stroking it tenderly. 'I've never given up on you, and I never will.'

Taking in a deep breath, he took hold of her, resting his head on her shoulder.

'God, Faith, I've made another bloody mess of things.'

'No, not really. It's nothing we can't salvage.'

'Why do you want me?' he asked, his breath against her neck. 'Why do you bother with me?'

'Because I know your heart. And it's good, that's why.'

Gently he took her face in his hands and kissed her. 'How would I live without you?'

'You'd survive,' she said gently. 'You had to once, remember?'

It was past one the following afternoon when Faith finally finished clearing up the Goldbladt showroom, standing back to assess the result. The old mirror – the slimming mirror – looked back at her, the sofa and chairs invitingly soft, now that the dust had been knocked out of them. As for the curtains, they had had to come down. Years of being closed and catching the light had rotted the linings.

Faith had made a mental note to order new ones. That morning she and Laurence had gone over their plans for the showroom, Faith realising early on that her employer had lost his edge. Laurence was excited about her return, but the reopening of the showroom was more a grab at life than a grasp at a fortune. Obviously Laurence's illness and his exile with Miriam had been claustrophobic, and although work might be exhausting for him, it was better than being buried alive in Macclesfield.

Making herself some tea, Faith stared out of the window down into the street below. The view was familiar and comforting. She had, she realised, missed David Street. But the war had done its damage: the buildings had changed, some businesses closed, some trading under new management. A few, like Mort's, were still running – old-fashioned against the tide of change. From this same window, Faith thought, she had seen Ellie's return. She had watched Beryl leave to do her shopping, Laurence hail his carriage and the newsboy call out the headlines about Mussolini founding his fascist party. From this same window she had stared down at Lennie Hellier, hating him as she watched him cross the street, and from this spot she had seen Samuel Granger coming round the corner and known that she was in love for the first time.

So many years she had watched the world pass by David Street – and now she was back. And, Faith thought, she was going to make a success of her return. The City Photographic Studio would survive because she would *make* it survive. Samuel would prove himself, Beryl would come back, and there would be enough money to make the future secure for all of them . . . Sighing, Faith walked into the stockroom and stood, staring, at the piles of old skins. Some she knew were too old to use, some moth-ridden, others dried out and split. Walking to the back of the workshop, she opened the old cedar cupboard that Laurence had had installed before the war. Now, Faith thought, this was more like it . . . Before her eyes she saw the rows of his best furs, hanging pristine and expensive. Skins that could be made up, or sold on. Her thoughts moved back, trying to remember the dealers Laurence had respected. If she did her research, she could sell some of the furs and make a profit. As for finding a designer, that would be more difficult, but not impossible.

The day wound on in the same manner. Faith, only stopping for a few minutes to grab a bite to eat or make a drink, carried on listing all the furs in stock. A couple of times she heard Mort's feet rapping on the floor above, and the third time she went out on to the landing to look up. He was standing looking at her and holding a bottle of sherry aloft.

'Hello, down there!'

'Hello, up there!' she called back.

'Fancy a tipple?'

'Mort, you're dreadful! I have to work.'

'Just a little one, my dear,' he called down the stairwell. 'Just a little drink to keep out the cold.'

She pulled a face at him. 'Maybe when I've finished. I want to get everything done before Christmas, and that's only a couple of weeks away now. I told Laurence I would, I promised.'

He sighed extravagantly. 'Maybe tomorrow.'

Smiling, Faith walked back inside, moving back into the stockroom and closing the door. Then she stopped, her mouth drying. The corner was empty, no bundle of blankets left there, but she could remember only too clearly the huddled figure of Lennie Hellier when he used to sleep there. Annoyed with herself, Faith dragged a filing cabinet over and pushed it into the space, rubbing her hands on her apron when she had finished. Now she could walk past without thinking of Hellier. At four, Faith finished the inventory of the furs in stock. At five, she began on the last set of accounts before Laurence had closed up the showroom. But by five thirty she was fighting tiredness, her eyes going in and out of focus.

Pleased with the day's work, she locked up and went downstairs. In the studio, James was taking a shot of someone's baby, Ellie cooking in the back. Smiling, Faith walked over to the kitchen door and looked at her old friend.

'How's things?'

Turning, Ellie smiled. 'I can't tell you how glad I am to see you back,' she said, her tone earnest. 'I was getting a bit worried after Beryl left.'

'We'll sort it out,' Faith assured her, looking round. 'I'm taking Samuel home tonight.'

481

Grinning, Ellie raised her eyebrows. 'Does he know?'

'Oh yes, he's been looking forward to it all day,' Faith responded, laughing. 'I told him that the lodger goes to bed early.'

'That's what you two need, some closeness, some time on your own,' Ellie said, keeping her voice low. 'Samuel's missed you. I know he wanted to stay here to learn everything quickly, but I think he was missing home.'

Faith leaned against the door. 'Are you happy with James?'

'Oh yes,' Ellie answered, surprised that she had been asked. 'I've never been happier.'

'But . . . you know . . .'

Ellie nodded, understanding immediately.

'I know what you mean, but no, it doesn't matter to me. I love him, and that's what I wanted from life. We can be close, not like most couples, but then most couples aren't us. I didn't compromise, Faith, I got lucky.'

Returning home that night on the tram from St Peter's Square to Oldham Faith thought about Ellie's words, sitting next to Samuel and feeling the warmth of his body against hers. She had always wanted him, and desired him, and their sex life had been important. Without it, they would both have felt cheated, unsatisfied. Sliding her arm through her husband's, Faith leaned her head on his shoulder. She felt closer to him than she had done for years. Everything was going to work out, she knew suddenly, a weight lifting from her. Everything was going to be fine. They would survive. The business would survive. Their marriage would flourish.

Still arm in arm, they got off the tram at Mumps Station and began the walk home.

'Look,' Samuel said teasingly, pointing upwards to the night sky. 'Venus.'

'You don't know one star from another!' she replied, pinching his arm. 'That's the North Star.'

'You're my star. You've always been the star in my life, the light to guide me. You've always been there to lead me home,' he said, kissing her on the railway bridge, a train passing underneath, their bodies suddenly shrouded with steam.

It was another half an hour before they finally got back to Hardy Street. On the way home they had acted like teenagers, stopping frequently, kissing each other and making murmured plans. The old excitement had returned, Faith flirtatious, Samuel relaxed and loving. At one point he had even picked her up and carried her until she wriggled free, her hat falling off, both of them running after it as a winter wind blew it along the street. Finally, laughing, they turned into Hardy Street, Faith reaching for the front door key and opening up.

Together they walked in, Samuel keeping his voice low.

'Are you *sure* the lodger's gone to bed?'

'She always goes to bed early,' Faith replied, then, noticing a light coming from under the kitchen door, she pulled a face at her husband. 'Maybe not tonight . . . Oh well, time you two met anyway.'

Opening the door, Faith smiled and walked in, followed by Samuel. She was so busy noticing Milly fast asleep on the kitchen sofa that she didn't see the jolt that went through her husband. As Faith bent down to kiss their child, Samuel stared at the Frenchwoman and felt his life turn to dust in his hands.

CHAPTER THIRTY-EIGHT

Waiting until he was sure Faith was asleep, Samuel climbed into bed and stared into the dark. Memory came back intermittent and sketchy. The trenches, the gunfire, the cold and the hunger. Then the marches. The marches . . . He struggled with his recall, but when it came, he cursed himself for remembering. It had been just before he was injured, before the battle of the Somme. There had been a young woman who had lived in a village nearby, whose family had been kind to the soldiers. She had been called Eloise, Eloise Lempar. Not Leonie Bonnard . . . As the time wore on, she had become close to the soldiers, picking out Samuel for special attention. She hadn't slept around, she had just been fascinated by the men, and the so-called glamour of the fighting.

Samuel stared upwards blindly, remembering. He had missed home and his wife, and one night, alone and afraid of dying, he had slept with the young Frenchwoman. Made love to her quickly and furtively, feeling shame afterwards. Shame for himself and for her. Shame that he had acted so out of character and led a woman on. Not that he had lied to her; he had told her from the start that he was married with a child. But she had been persistent, saying that it was wartime, and that it would mean nothing. Asking him for comfort, when he was asking the same from her. Afterwards, he had only been able to think of Faith. Of his wife, his adored wife. He couldn't believe what he had done. Nothing would excuse it. He had cheated on his wife. He had told the woman the following day that it could never happen again. She had been angry with him, but then the company had been moved on. On to the Somme, to the thousands of dead and dying. And the injured, the shell-shocked. The ones who couldn't remember . . .

Oh, but he could remember it all now. He could remember the Frenchwoman's face, because he had just seen it again. A little older, a little more strained, but the same face, the same woman. The same lover he had wiped out of his mind because he had been so ashamed . . . Sighing, Samuel rolled over, almost imagining that he could sense the woman sleeping in the room next door. This was no accident, he told himself. She had traced him, found out where he lived. She had moved into his house whilst he was away. Moved in with his wife and child . . . His mind replayed what Faith had told him about the new lodger, details that he hadn't really taken on board until now. Like how helpful she was. How good with Milly. How she had been widowed and left with a child to raise after the war. So why come here? Samuel asked himself desperately. Why, after so long? Why, after one slip of judgement, the one and only time he had ever committed adultery, had it come back to haunt him now?

Finally, Samuel got up. In her sleep, Milly stirred and rolled over, lying against Faith. Samuel left the bedroom and moved downstairs. He had wanted a smoke, but as he reached the kitchen he realised he wasn't the only person awake. The Frenchwoman was sitting at the table, her hands around a cup of tea.

He couldn't hold back the shock in his voice.

'What are you doing here?' he said, his tone harsher than he meant. 'What do you want?'

She turned her face up to him, her expression losing its sadness and becoming hard instead.

'Well, the hero returns. I spent a long time looking for you, Mr Granger.'

Hurriedly taking her arm, Samuel led her out into the back yard, terrified that Faith would awaken and overhear them talking. In the cold of the winter night, Leonie shivered, pulling her dressing gown around her, her hair blown loose about her shoulders. Above them, a half moon grinned like a gargoyle, the brick walls of the terrace surrounding them on all sides.

'Why have you come here?' Samuel asked again, his tone helpless. 'I told you, it was nothing. It was a mistake. You said yourself that you didn't want anything from me. We agreed it was of no importance.' He tried to calm himself. 'What I did was wrong, I know that.'

'Hah!' she said coolly. 'It was certainly wrong.'

'But I told you I was married and had a child. You knew nothing could come of it, Eloise.'

'You remembered my name,' she replied, without emotion. 'Only it's not my name any more. I'm Leonie now, Leonie Bonnard. Widowed, with a little daughter.'

'You married?'

She laughed, the sound light as a bat's wing.

'No, I never married. But I had a child, so I had to *say* I had been married, otherwise life would have been even more difficult than it has been.'

'Life's been difficult for all of us.'

She looked him up and down, studying him.

'You've got older, put on weight. Not the soldier I remember and fell in love with.'

'You never fell in love with me!' Samuel retorted. 'You and I agreed that we'd made a mistake and that we'd never see each other again. So what changed?'

'I had your child.'

He took in a breath, so sharp it tore at his throat.

'What?'

'The little girl asleep upstairs – in the next room from your wife and child – is yours.'

He didn't know what to say, how to respond. He wanted to say that she was lying, but knew that she wasn't. Her face, framed with the heavy fall of hair, looked at him impassively. She was neither

488

aggressive nor pleading, just determined. And terrifying in her implacability.

'You owe me,' Leonie went on, her voice low. 'It took me so long to find you. Your wife said that she was told you were Missing, Presumed Dead. That's what I heard too, when I made enquiries. Private Samuel Granger, of Oldham, Lancashire, was presumed dead.' Her eyes were expressionless. 'I thought it was all over, then I wondered about it. Were you *really* dead? Or were you only missing? If you were missing, I could find you. And I did. It wasn't that difficult, I had a lucky break.' Smiling, Leonie leaned against the shed, silhouetted by the moonlight.

'What d'you want from me?'

'What d'you think, Samuel?' she countered. 'I have no family.'

'You had family in France, when I knew you.'

'Yes,' she said scornfully, 'but they didn't take too kindly to my having some soldier's bastard. They threw me out. I went to Paris with my baby, waited on tables, anything I could to make money and pay for someone to sit with Suzette. I can't tell you how many bars I've tended for your child.'

'Keep your voice down!' Samuel said warningly. 'Why have you come here? You want to ruin my marriage, is that it? You want money?' He paused, desperate. 'I don't have any money.'

'So make some,' she replied deftly. 'After all, if you want me to keep quiet, you have to reward me for my silence. It's only reasonable; most men care for their families.'

'You aren't my family!' Samuel said, his tone trapped. 'Faith and Milly are my family.'

'And if you don't want them to find out that their tenant and friend is actually your old lover – along with your illegitimate child – I suggest you find ways of looking after us. I had to do it for long enough. I'm tired, I need some help, some support.' She moved towards him, looking into his face without pity. 'You poor fool, did you really think you could get away with it?'

'I didn't even remember you,' he replied, honestly. 'I was injured in battle. I had a breakdown. Jesus, I hardly remember you.'

'Although I don't think that will matter to Faith when she hears the truth.'

'You can't tell her!'

'I can, and I will – unless you do as I say.'

She smiled distantly, walking around him under the half-moon. Her sweetness and shyness – which had so duped Faith, and Samuel himself once – were gone. Now she was cold and determined to get what she wanted. To barter, to get recompense for having to struggle, for humiliation and for the loss of her own family.

'You left me.'

He was blundering with confusion. 'We agreed never to see each other again! It was a joint decision.'

'I was pregnant!'

'But I didn't know that,' Samuel replied. 'I didn't know.'

'You know now,' she countered. 'That little girl is yours. Suzette is your child, just as Milly is. And you can't favour one over the other. It wouldn't be fair. Of course, I haven't told Suzette, but if she knew the truth, that you were her daddy . . .'

'You mustn't tell her.'

'In case she lets something slip?' Leonie paused, pretending to be thinking. 'I see how difficult that could be for you. How inconvenient to have a wife, an ex-lover and *two* of your children under one roof. It would be very hurtful to Faith and she's such a lovely woman. Lovely to look at, and very genuine. You were lucky there, Samuel, to find someone like that. I think if I had had such a nice husband I wouldn't have cheated on him.'

Glancing away, Samuel raked his hands through his hair, trying to control his panic. The shock of seeing the Frenchwoman had all but paralysed him. She had come like some vicious ghost from a past he could only half remember, bringing destruction with her. If she told Faith . . . He couldn't bring himself to think of it, because he knew what his deception would mean. Faith would leave him. She would take their child and leave him. The woman who had loved him, waited for him, prayed for him, never given up on him would not forgive a betrayal like this.

Desperate, he turned to Leonie. 'You have to keep quiet.'

'I will, for a price.'

'I don't have any money.'

'I told you, find some,' she replied, looking up at the bedroom window where Faith and Milly were asleep. 'Remember, I'm letting you off lightly. I could demand that you leave her and come back to France with me. If your wife knew the truth, she would probably kick you out anyway.' She touched his chest lightly. 'I still care about you, Samuel. Funny, but I do. We could have been happy, we still might be . . .'

'I don't want you!'

'You didn't want your wife when you were with me!' Leonie snapped back, humiliated. 'You have to start making amends, Samuel. Your past has well and truly caught up with you, and now you have to sort it out. Either you look after me and your child – or I'll tell your wife everything.'

The following morning Samuel was up early, making breakfast for Faith and Milly and flinching every time he heard a noise overhead. Sleep had not come to him. After the altercation in the back yard, he had lain awake, trying to piece together what he had been told. Wondering how one incident of sex had resulted in this hideous situation. He didn't know if the Frenchwoman had deliberately tricked him, and decided that she probably hadn't. From what he *did* remember of her, she had been shy and close to her family. A simple girl who had got herself into trouble. After all, a more worldly woman would have got rid of the child . . . His mind baulked at the idea. That was *his* child;

however she had come into the world, she was his daughter.

'Morning,' Faith said, walking into the kitchen and kissing him on the cheek. Surprised, she stared at him. 'You look exhausted.'

He smiled distantly, sure his guilt was written on his face. 'I didn't sleep well.' Then he turned and bent down to pick up Milly.

Pleased, Faith watched her husband, deciding that time at home with his family would settle him down. All he needed was to feel secure.

'I'm glad you're back at Hardy Street,' she said, glancing upwards. 'Has Leonie come down yet?'

He couldn't trust his voice and shook his head.

'Oh, well, sometimes she does come down later,' Faith went on. 'You can meet her properly tonight. If I have time later, I'll get a pie from Sullivan's and we'll eat together when we get home.'

'I might have to stay on at the studio,' Samuel said hurricdly. 'James wanted to talk about some new plans, you know. And I thought I'd go over to Blackpool today, see if I can get some photographs for the Christmas season. We've only got a bit longer and I thought going round the hotels might pay off.'

Surprised but pleased, Faith nodded. 'Oh, fine, love. Well, you come home when you can. We'll eat early, though, it's better for the girls.'

Pausing, it took him a moment to phrase the next words.

'How old is the lodger's baby?'

Tying on her apron, Faith thought for a moment. 'A little over two, I think.'

'What's her name?'

'Suzette. She's a tiny, pretty little thing with dark hair, and she and Milly get on so well. Like they've been together for years. To be honest, I've become very fond of Suzette. I've baby-sat her a few times for Leonie and she was adorable.' Faith paused, thinking aloud. 'Leonie needs some time to herself now and then. She said she likes to walk and think. Anyway, I never mind watching over the little one. Suzette's no trouble at all. In fact, I think Milly could be a bad influence on her, make her mischievous . . .'

Unnerved, Samuel walked to the door. He couldn't bear to hear his wife talking about the child for a moment longer.

'I have to get off, love.'

She turned, surprised. 'But aren't we going into Manchester together?'

'I want to look enthusiastic,' he said hurriedly. 'After the row with Beryl and all the trouble I've caused, I have to get things on an even keel again. And we need more money, like you said. The sooner I start earning, the better.'

Moving over to her husband, Faith kissed him, her mouth feeling his cool lips, and wanting for a moment to drag him back upstairs into their double bed. Everything *was* going to be all right, she thought with relief; after all her worrying, things *were* going to work out.

'In that case, go to work, Mr Granger,' she said, teasing him. 'I'll see you tonight. But don't be too late, you hear?'

From the window upstairs Leonie watched as Samuel left the house, waiting until he had rounded the corner of Hardy Street before she turned back to the mirror and began to brush her hair. Tying it back from her face, she buttoned up the modest blouse she was wearing and then picked up Suzette, walking downstairs with her child.

'Morning.'

Looking up, Faith smiled. 'Morning. Did you sleep well?'

'Very well, thank you,' Leonie replied, putting Suzette next to Milly on the old horsehair sofa. 'Can I help you make breakfast?'

'Samuel started it off,' Faith replied, looking at the bread he had sliced. 'Then he rushed away, saying he had to get to work. Honestly, he's keen. Really keen. Said he looked forward to meeting you properly tonight, even though he'll probably be late.' She laid down a pot of jam and brought the teapot from the range over to the table. 'I'm going to get the next tram in.'

'We're all going to the park today,' Leonie told her, glancing at the two little girls and passing them some bread and jam. 'We're having an outing.'

'Well, they say it might rain, and it'll certainly be cold,' Faith replied, dropping her voice to a whisper. 'That coat I was telling you about – it's in my wardrobe, at the back. Take it, you'll need it.'

Even Leonie had the grace to blush. Faith misread the situation and changed the subject.

'I can see a change in Samuel already,' she confided. 'He's unsettled, but he's full of ideas. He wants to make the business work out, thank God.'

'I look forward to meeting him,' Leonie replied, her tone light. 'Perhaps I could make dinner for us tonight?'

'Well, I *was* going to bring a pie from Sullivan's . . .'

'Oh no, you have more than enough to do!' Leonie replied eagerly. 'You can't worry about bringing in food too. I'll make something for all of us. And if your husband's delayed, I can leave it in the oven for him to have later. Whenever he gets in.'

Faith glanced at her tenant gratefully.

'Thanks for that, Leonie. There's money in the tea caddy on the top shelf. Take what you need.'

Smiling, the Frenchwoman nodded. Faith reached for her hat and coat and made for the door. There she turned.

'Bye for now, Milly, and you, Suzette. See you later, babies. Have a nice day, all of you.' She glanced back to Leonie. 'You know something? I don't know how I managed without you.'

CHAPTER THIRTY-NINE

It was Ellie who heard the door open just after eight that morning. She walked out into the studio and looked at Samuel with surprise.

'You're early.'

He nodded, uncomfortable and avoiding her eyes. 'I thought I'd get started as soon as I could.' Turning, he saw James coming in from the back. 'Look, I've been a bastard, sorry about that. But I want to try and make things better. So I was thinking I'd go over to Blackpool today, see if I could find some work in the hotels.'

This was good news, but James had enough sense not to seem too surprised. If Samuel wanted to make amends, it was all right with him, but there was no point rubbing his nose in it.

'Well, you could get lucky at the Metropole, or you could go over to the Winter Garden.'

'Yeah, I was thinking about that,' Samuel went on, turning his hat round in his hands. 'All those people coming to watch the pantos, and there's a matinee every afternoon.' He moved over to the back of the studio and picked up the lightest camera, folding up the portable tripod and slipping it into its canvas case.

'You got enough plates?'

'Oh yes, film . . .' Samuel said, reaching for several and putting them into his coat pocket.

'See what you can do, and good luck,' James went on, encouraging him and yet uneasy about the change in Samuel's demeanour. Was he unwell? Or genuinely sorry for the unsettled atmosphere he had caused? Certainly it seemed as though the steam had gone out of him. Then James remembered that Samuel had spent the previous evening at Hardy Street, and decided that his sister had probably effected the change.

'I'll be off then.'

James nodded. 'Well, have a go, Samuel, you might get lucky.'

'Usual rates for the photographs?'

James thought for a moment. 'Yeah, for the Winter Garden. But if you get any interest at the big hotels, put a bit on the cost.' He rubbed his hands together, smiling. 'My God, we might have a good Christmas yet.'

Nodding, Samuel left. In silence, Ellie and James watched his feet as they moved up the basement steps and then out on to the street above. Taking his wife's hand, James looked at Ellie.

'He's a totally different man today.'

'A nicer man.'

James nodded. 'It's hard work out there, though,

touting for business. I hope Samuel keeps his head and doesn't throw in the towel too soon.'

Catching the train over to Blackpool, Samuel sat with the camera on his lap, the folded tripod next to him. Outside the window, the streets dissolved, the city giving way to countryside as they moved out towards the coast. It was a bitter day, cold to the bone, the sky heavy with snow. But Samuel hardly felt the cold; he felt so numbed by shock that nothing could touch him. Handing the inspector his ticket, he continued to stare out of the window, his thoughts sliding backwards to the time he went off to fight. To the trip across the Channel, the excitement of war, then the reality of the trenches and the gunfire. Closing his eyes, he could hear again the screams of the rats, gone mad with the artillery noise, and the splash of their bodies falling backwards into the mud as they scrabbled to leave the trenches. His mind slipped forward in time, to the pain of his burns, to the dreams he had had when he was unconscious. The half-life between worlds, the space he had occupied whilst they posted him Missing, Presumed Dead.

And somewhere, in amongst the gunfire, the shell shocks and the rats, was another image, of a shy young woman lying in his arms . . . It was such a small image, something snatched, out of place amongst all the brutality. But it was real. Tiny, but real. Fleeting, but damning. Samuel and the woman who now called herself Leonie Bonnard. Only she had been a sweet girl then, living with her family. And now she was back, bursting into his mind, changed. Hard, demanding, abandoned by her family and with his child. Out for revenge.

Sighing, Samuel realised that the train was drawing into Blackpool station, and he picked up his belongings. Without enthusiasm he walked from the station on Vance Road towards the sea front. The winter was throwing its worst at the resort, the wind buffeting the posters advertising the pantomime, *Aladdin*, at the Winter Garden. Moving beneath the jerking placards, he kept his head down, feeling isolated and depressed beyond measure. He knew then that he had to make money. If he didn't, Leonie would expose him, tell Faith everything. And he would lose his wife. He would lose his anchor, his North Star. His hope.

Steadily Samuel trudged on, moving up the grand front steps of a classy hotel and pausing in the foyer. In the restaurant beyond he could see wealthy customers drinking tea and talking, the women's furs over the back of their chairs, the men's fine suits and pomaded hair glossy under the lamplight. His stupidity hit him at that moment. If he had been a proper husband he would have worked hard for three months just to bring Faith to a place like this. She would have been the best-looking woman present, and he would have felt wealthy with pride. But instead he was a cheat, a liar, creeping around his own home to avoid his old lover. And now desperate to do anything to make enough money to keep the Frenchwoman quiet.

Walking further into the lobby, Samuel suddenly caught sight of an image of himself and stared. The attractive, straight-backed, healthy young man had gone, and had been replaced by some furtive, down-at-heel stranger.

'Can I help you, sir?'

He started, faced by the manager, then tried to sound confident.

'I was wondering if any of your guests might like to have their photographs taken?'

The manager gave him a slow smile. 'We have an in-house photographer, sir. I must ask you to leave.'

Back on the sea front, Samuel stared up at the white wedding cake of a hotel, then turned and made his way along the promenade. The first Christmas trees grinned out from shop and hotel windows, one spruce being buffeted by the North Sea wind. But there were hardly any people about. No one wanting photographs. Walking along, Samuel moved into the Winter Garden, stopping people randomly.

'Do you want your picture taken?'

'Do you want a snapshot?'

No, no, no, came back the reply. No one wanted their photograph taken, and Samuel's feet slowed down, his breathing becoming more laboured as he moved around, desperate for trade. If he could just get three customers. No, two. Or even one would do. One would do . . . Finally, he stopped, leaning against an ornate pillar, his mouth dry, the clock overhead reading four thirty. He had spent a whole day looking for work. A whole day trying to get together enough money to keep Leonie Bonnard silent. Only it hadn't worked. Helpless, Samuel searched the faces in front of him. If he didn't give her money, it was all over. She would tell Faith. Faith would leave him . . .

'Photograph?'

'Photograph, sir?'

Samuel asked again and again, then suddenly a woman stopped. She was with an older man, linked arms, the man flabby and red-faced.

'How about it, luvvie?' she asked her companion. 'How about a memento of you and me?'

Eagerly, Samuel put up the tripod and fixed the camera into position, the woman posing extravagantly, leaning on the man's shoulder. Clicking away, Samuel took the photographs and then gave the woman his card, asking for her address so that he could send the prints on to her. Grinning, she wrote the details down.

'How long?'

'You should receive them the day after tomorrow,' Samuel assured her, adding, 'I need a deposit.'

'I pay when I see,' the woman replied. 'How do I know you won't rob me? Run off with my man's money and never send the pictures?'

It was a fair point, but Samuel was desperate.

'Look,' he said, his voice low, 'I won't cheat you. You've got my card and the address of my business.

We're honest. You'll get good pictures, I swear . . .
but I have to go home with something. Please, just a
small deposit.'

Having been on hard times herself, the woman
gave Samuel half a crown.

'Make sure they *are* good, hey?' she said, then
winked. 'And Happy Christmas, luv. You look like
you need some luck.'

'Call this money?' Leonie asked, staring into
Samuel's face, her tone cool. 'You work all week and
bring back *this*?'

He signalled for her to lower her voice. The ten
shillings were all he had raised that week, and even
that he couldn't put into the kitty. Instead he had
returned from Blackpool and told Faith that the
day had been fruitless. Her disappointment had
wounded him, but her encouragement had been
worse. Whilst he lied to her, the money burning
through the lining of his pocket, his wife had tried to
raise his spirits. There would be other days; he would
be lucky tomorrow. Or the day after. In Morecambe,
in Southport. He was good, the money would come.
The work would come to him . . . And all the time
she had been encouraging him, Samuel had felt the
coins in his pocket, knowing that he was going to
have to take the money out of his wife and child's
mouths and put it into Leonie's hand.

His voice low, he stared at the Frenchwoman.
They were in the back yard, Faith and Milly asleep
upstairs, the moon beginning its slow dying.

'I tell you, that's all there is.'

'It's not enough!'

'It's all I can get!' Samuel replied, his tone hopeless. 'Look, there isn't that much money around. People are still getting over the war; they don't splash out like they used to.'

'So get another job.'

He stared at her, blinking. 'What are you talking about? How can I get another job?'

'Find a way.'

'And how would I explain it?'

'Find a way,' she repeated.

'Why don't *you* get a job?'

Her expression was flinty. 'Mind your mouth, Samuel. Remember, I don't owe you, you owe *me*.'

Leonie had been nagging him all week. She knew she had the trump card, that at any moment she could bring the whole façade down around their heads. She had, as she repeated often, nothing to lose. And he knew it. If Samuel didn't give her what she wanted, she would ruin him. He couldn't call Leonie's bluff, he couldn't risk it. His family was the most important thing in his life; he would do anything to keep Faith in ignorance.

But Faith was no fool, and aware that there was a simmering animosity between her husband and Leonie, she had tackled Samuel the previous night. She had been sitting on the bed beside him, her arm around his shoulder, her tone relaxed.

'Why don't you like Leonie?' She had felt him

504

wince and repeated the question. 'Why don't you like her?'

'She's . . . she's . . .' He had struggled to find words; to organise a convincing lie, hating himself as it left his lips. 'Look, I know this sounds childish, Faith, but I don't like having her in the house. I don't like having *anyone* in the house. I was happier when it was just us.'

Tenderly Faith had kissed his cheek, smiling. 'You silly thing! It won't be for ever, Samuel. When things improve and there's a bit more money coming in, we can manage without a lodger's rent. Leonie knows that; I told her when she first came. Don't worry, my love, things will change. Honestly, they will.'

Dumbly, Samuel had nodded. But he had known that Leonie was never going to leave. Not until she got what she wanted . . .

His thoughts returned to the present as he stared at her, standing defiant in the back yard.

'So, what *are* you going to do?' she asked him, her hair loose, her arms folded. Upstairs Suzette was asleep, only just across the landing from Milly and Faith. 'If you can't provide for me here, we'll have to move.'

'What?' he asked, baffled.

'We have to leave here.'

The words sent a physical shock through him, rocking him back on to his heels. 'I'm not leaving my family.'

'You have *two* families,' Leonie replied. 'So

505

choose. If you can't provide for both, choose the one you *can* provide for.'

'Faith is my wife and Milly's mother.'

'Yes, and I am the mother of your other child,' Leonie countered, her tone bitter. 'I've been very reasonable with you, Samuel. If you were half a man, you'd have come up with money, you would have been able to take care of us both. But you can't.'

'You have to give me time.'

'Time!' she snorted. 'You think time will do it? I think you're stalling, Samuel, that's what I think. I think you'll say anything to keep me quiet and protect your wife's feelings. But what about *my* feelings? What about Suzette?'

'I can raise money, it just takes more time.'

'I'm not hanging around this place for ever!' she replied. 'I miss home. Miss my own country. And as you can't make enough money to provide a life here, then you'll have to provide one over there.'

'You can't mean that!' he replied, horror-struck. 'We don't even care about each other.'

'I care about being provided for,' Leonie replied, 'and my child having food to eat and clothes on her back. I want the best for her – and as you're her father, I think you should provide it. If not here, in France.'

'I can't leave Faith!'

'Oh, I wouldn't worry about that. When she finds out about us, she'll throw you out. You won't have a choice.'

He stepped back, leaning against the coal shed, Leonie watching him. He knew she was right. If Faith found out, their marriage was over. It was imperative that she remain in ignorance. He wanted for a moment to strike out at Leonie, even to kill her. Anything to get this Frenchwoman out of his life. But he knew he couldn't do anything so drastic. He had to be sensible, control himself. There had to be another way to escape her. There *had* to be . . .

Cautious, Samuel played for time. 'Give me a bit longer. Please, just a bit longer.'

'You have until New Year,' Leonie replied, moving back to the house and pausing by the back door. 'New Year, Samuel. Not one day more. You either find the money, or you leave with me and take the coward's way out. At least that way you won't have to face your wife and tell her about her lodger – and the lodger's bastard.'

'You're a bitch!'

'I was made that way,' she said simply, her tone even. 'There *is* one other route out of this mess. If you were man enough, enough of a gambler, you could simply tell Faith the truth.'

'No!'

'I thought not,' Leonie said calmly. 'So sort this mess out, Samuel. Or I will.'

Counting the takings for the second time, Faith pushed them across the table to her brother for him to tot up. Business at the City Photographic Studio wasn't looking good. It was the day before

Christmas Eve, and Faith realised that there was no way she could buy the doll for Milly. Samuel had managed to get only a small amount of work, and both of them were wondering what kind of a holiday they would have. True to form, Faith had told him only the previous night that they would cope. They were going to spend Christmas Day in David Street with Ellie and James.

Unfortunately Beryl wasn't going to come home, but they had been in touch by letter, her grandmother asking repeatedly how Samuel was getting on. Faith wrote back:

> *Not bad, he's trying. Honestly, he's really sorry about the argument you two had and he's doing his best to make a go of things. He talks about you often, Gran.*
>
> *As for Milly, she's growing up fast and I can't tell you how much help Leonie has been. Without her looking after Milly for me, it would have been difficult going back to work. But she's glad to help me and as she's nowhere to go for Christmas, I've invited her to spend it with us at David Street. Please say you'll join us, Gran, please come home.*
>
> *Missing you, Faith*

The reply was short, but affectionate.

> *My dear girl,*
> *I love you very much, always will, but I*

*don't want to come back to Manchester just
yet. Still have to work out what I want to do
for the future. But I'll be up on a visit soon, to
see everyone. I'm glad that lodger's helping
out, make sure she still pays rent though. You
know these foreigners! As for me, I've
managed to get some savings together – you
never know when you'll need them.*

   Your loving Gran

'It doesn't tot up,' James said suddenly, looking over
to Faith as they hunched over the account books.
'The takings, they seem short.'

'I thought that,' Faith replied, calling over her
shoulder to Ellie, 'Have you taken out any cash for
housekeeping?'

Ellie came to the kitchen door, wiping her hands
on a towel. 'No, I never do without telling you, or
leaving a note in the till. Why, are we short?'

'Not by much,' Faith replied, looking over at her
brother. 'But it's going to be a lean Christmas again
– and I invited Leonie to spend it with all of us here.'

Ellie shrugged. 'I can scrape together a good meal,
stop worrying,' she said cheerfully. 'We've enough
money for that. As for presents, that's another
matter.'

'I'm not bothered myself,' Faith replied, leaning
back in her seat. 'I just wanted to get that doll for
Milly. I was hoping that Samuel might drum up
some business. But he's not got much, has he?'

'Bad time of year.'

'You said Christmas could be profitable,' Faith replied drily.

'Not like the summer. Loads of day trippers in the summer.'

Faith held her brother's look. 'If we *last* until summer. Which we won't, unless we get more business . . . Thank God I took that job at Laurence's. I mean, don't say a word to Samuel, but without that and the lodger, we'd all be in a hell of a mess.' Stretching, she got to her feet. 'Still, it'll be New Year soon, and that's always good. A fresh start. I like New Year; it brings a clean slate.'

Knowing how much it irritated Samuel, Leonie cuddled Milly, then put her down and began to play with both of the little girls on the floor of the photographic studio. Suddenly aware that someone was watching her, she glanced up to see Ellie standing in the doorway.

'The children like you a lot,' Ellie said. Her face was as delicate as ever, but her eyes were perceptive and missed nothing. 'I'm so sorry you lost your husband.'

'It was terrible,' Leonie replied. 'I loved him very much.'

Hardly hearing what James was saying to him, Samuel was listening in on the conversation between Ellie and Leonie. His body was tight with nerves, his ears straining for any off-hand comment that might bring disaster.

By contrast, Leonie was perfectly at ease. She had

been patient long enough, and the Christmas Day festivities had tried her endurance. Obviously Samuel wasn't going to be able to support her and their child, so she would have to take action. What Leonie *hadn't* been prepared for was the affection she still felt for Samuel. And seeing him so obviously in love with Faith and so desperate to protect his marriage made her envious. She had hoped – albeit faintly – that their reunion might rekindle something of their brief affair. But Samuel had all but forgotten her. He might say it was mainly due to his illness, but she knew that if she had been important, he would have recalled her without effort. In reality their fling had been just that, a fling. A coming together of two lonely, frightened people in the middle of a war.

And if Suzette hadn't been the result of that union, Leonie would never have bothered to track Samuel down. But pregnancy, humiliation and abandonment by her family had hardened her, and as time passed she had convinced herself that Samuel was to blame for her troubled life. She might love Suzette, but Leonie admitted to herself that if she could live her life again, she would never have had this baby. Instead she would have carried on her existence in France, in the safety of her family, marrying some man from the village. Not wandering across the Channel to try and prise away another woman's husband.

But then that was the way it was, Leonie told herself, setting aside her momentary weakness. This was reality and she had to make the best of it. Samuel might not love her, but she was sure he would be forced to run away with her. He couldn't face telling Faith what he had done. Although he wasn't a coward, he couldn't look his wife in the eye and rip her world into pieces.

'What did he do for a living?' Ellie asked, breaking into Leonie's thoughts.

'Pardon?'

'Your husband. What did he do for a living?'

'Oh, he was a grocer,' Leonie replied, turning back to the little girls and tickling Milly.

But at the table Faith paused, wondering. A grocer, she thought; hadn't Leonie said her husband was a carpenter? Hurriedly she ran what she knew through her mind, and realised that Leonie had – for some reason – told an untruth. Faith paused. Maybe she had thought carpenter didn't sound like much. That being a grocer seemed more important. But then again, none of them were rich; it was hardly the place to try and make an impression. Uneasy, Faith studied the Frenchwoman. She liked her, had done from the first, and had grown to depend on her. In fact Leonie had been a comfort to Faith, and in return she had welcomed her into her own family, anxious that her friend should not feel alone in a strange country. Even though it was obvious that Leonie and Samuel did not get on, Faith had tried to make allowances. After all, it was difficult for her husband to tolerate a lodger and another child in the house, knowing that their presence was vital, as he wasn't able to provide enough to support the family otherwise. Faith also knew that Leonie had seen Samuel come home late, had heard him explain about the lack of work. Humiliation was hard for anyone to bear – but for a man like Samuel it was intolerable.

And yet Leonie's lie unnerved Faith, coming as it did so unnecessarily. Surprised to catch her friend out again, Faith tried to put the matter to the back of her mind, but as the evening wore on the lie nudged at her. It tickled her, tapped at the windows and came down the chimney, lodged in her head and unnerved her heart.

CHAPTER FORTY

Deeply asleep, Faith seemed to hear a knocking in her dream and stirred, turning over. Her hand went out to Samuel and found an empty bed, and she opened her eyes to realise that the knocking was coming from the front door. Someone was trying to raise her. Pulling on her dressing gown, Faith hurried downstairs, not wanting to make any noise that would waken the children.

Opening the door half an inch, she flinched. Staring into a face she had hoped never to see again.

'Lennie Hellier . . .'

'Yes, it's me,' he said, shifting his feet in the freezing early morning. 'Happy New Year.'

Blinking, Faith remembered that it was New Year's Day. So she *had* been right, she had seen him hanging around.

'What d'you want?'

'What, no Happy New Year for me?'

She ignored him. 'What d'you want, Hellier?'

Standing defiantly, Faith faced the man she had loathed and feared since she was eleven years old.

Shivering in the cold, Lennie Hellier could hardly contain his excitement, blowing on his big, raw-boned hands to warm them. Time had not been good to him. Without the smart clothes, he was reduced to a shambling, ill-nourished outcast. His eyes were the only bright thing about his whole appearance, and those were quick with malice. At last his patience had been rewarded. Lennie Hellier had been determined to get his revenge on Faith, and eventually it had fallen into his lap. All the days and weeks of watching the Grangers; all the hanging around, eavesdropping on neighbours, listening at doors, asking questions. All the standing on street corners, watching and waiting, had finally paid off.

'I'm surprised you dare show your face around here,' Faith went on. 'I know what you did at David Street. You're lucky the police didn't get you for setting that fire. You could have killed all of us.'

'I didn't set any fire,' he said smoothly. 'And from what I heard, no one was hurt.'

'No thanks to you.'

'You know, Faith—'

'Mrs Granger.'

He smirked unpleasantly 'You know, *Mrs Granger*, you could get in trouble going around saying things like that about a person. It's slander, that's what it is. I could be very angry.'

Her patience snapped. 'What d'you want?'

'I've a message for you. I've waited a long time to see you get what you deserve.'

'I never did anything to you!' Faith replied heatedly.

'You led me on.'

'You're crazy!' she snapped. 'You know the truth as well as I do. I spent all my time avoiding you, Hellier. There was nothing between us, it was all in your mind.' Her voice hardened. 'Laurence told me about the argument, about what you said.'

'Goldbladt's a liar and a Jew.'

Faith began to close the door, but Hellier stopped her, putting his foot between the door and the frame, his voice menacing.

'You really should be more polite.'

'Go away!' Faith said warningly.

'No chance.'

'You've been hanging around here for a while, haven't you?' she asked him, trying to keep her voice steady. 'I thought I saw you the other week, but I wasn't sure.'

'I go where I please.'

'I'm sure you do.'

'Life's funny sometimes, isn't it?' Lennie said, his tone suspiciously pleasant. 'The way things work out. I mean, I have to admit that I *have* been hanging around for a while. Well, what else was there to do? No one was going to offer me a job, were they? You ruined my chances at David Street.'

'*I* ruined your chances!' Faith repeated, staggered. 'What happened to you was not my fault.'

He was immune to logic. Revenge was the only emotion left to Lennie Hellier.

'Thing is, if you listen and watch long enough, you see and hear what you've been waiting for. It just takes time and patience, that's all.' He ran his tongue over his dry lips. 'Only a month or so ago I was on a tram coming over this way – something I've been doing a lot recently – and I heard a Frenchwoman talking. She was telling this other woman about how she wanted to trace a man who lived in Oldham called Samuel Granger.' He could see Faith wince and pressed on. 'Well, I had to listen, didn't I? Seeing as how they were talking about an old friend. Then, when the Frenchwoman got off, I followed her . . .' He paused again, relishing his spite. 'I've got very good at following people. It's quite an art, but then I've been doing it for a while now.'

Faith could feel the colour leave her face, her legs shaking as she stared at him.

'Anyway, I stopped this Frenchwoman and told her that I knew Samuel Granger, knew where he lived, and she told me about how she'd been looking for him and how she'd known him in France during the war. She didn't say anything more – I don't think she trusted me – but she was certainly pleased enough to pay me for his address.' He paused. 'She didn't like parting with her money, but, like I said, I was making her life easier. Anyway, she got her money's worth; I even came here with her, pointed out your house. And as luck would have it, you had a Room for Rent sign in the window.' Lennie paused again, savouring his triumph. 'Like I said to her, it

517

was meant to be. Of course, she didn't want me to tell you, and I didn't. Well, why would I? We're not friends any more. I think the Frenchwoman thought she'd got rid of me that night, but you know how I like a mystery, Faith. So I hung around a bit. I mean, I'd invested a lot of time here, I couldn't just walk away without seeing what was going to happen next. Over the next weeks I watched her comings and goings – I don't suppose you realise that she left her kid and yours alone sometimes?'

'She did what!'

'No, I didn't think you knew that. The Frenchwoman might have fooled you, but she's a lousy mother,' Hellier went on. 'And I don't suppose you know about all those little chats she has with your husband in the back yard in the middle of the night either.'

Faith was hardly able to move, the shock was so great. And then slowly little instances came back to her. The way Samuel and Leonie didn't seem to get on. The way her husband tried to avoid Leonie, saying he didn't want anyone else in the house. The strained feeling between them, which Faith had put down to her husband's resentment at having to take in a lodger . . . Jesus, she thought desperately, there couldn't be anything going on between Samuel and that woman, that lying, scheming, conniving woman . . .

'Get away from here!' she hissed, pushing against the door. 'You're lying!'

'I thought you wanted to know why I was here.'

'Then get on with it.' She bluffed. 'Tell me, or I'll call Samuel.'

To her shock, he laughed.

'Really? You'll need to call long and hard, Mrs Granger. Your Samuel's long gone.'

Behind her, Faith could hear the clock striking in the front room.

'Samuel's in bed upstairs!' But he wasn't – and she knew it.

Hellier wasn't fooled either.

'I think you're mistaken, Faith. In fact, I'd go so far as to say that you should have another look. You see, I happen to know that Samuel left early this morning – with your lodger. And I know why. I eavesdropped on their night-time chats, and gradually – I had to be patient, but it paid off – I pieced it all together. Heard all about it. About their . . . love affair. Oh, you look surprised. Didn't you know that Leonie Bonnard and your husband knew each other during the war?' He paused, waiting to deliver the final blow. 'In fact, they were very close. Leonie Bonnard was his lover, Faith – and your husband is the father of her kid.'

With one violent shove, Faith pushed Hellier away, the man overbalancing and falling into the gutter as she slammed the door shut. Resting against it, she thought of what she had just been told. Her husband had gone, run off with another woman. Samuel had gone . . . Her breathing accelerated as she ran upstairs. Milly was sleeping in her own bed at the foot of the main bed, but where Samuel had lain there was only an indentation. Panicked, Faith moved over to the wardrobe and wrenched open the door. Samuel's few clothes and shoes were gone. Gasping, she ran into Leonie's room and stopped dead in the doorway. The space was empty. No clothes, no books, no toys. Just a small empty room, with only a damp towel left behind to indicate that the Frenchwoman had been there that morning.

Letting out a scream of rage, Faith lunged towards the bed, stripping off the blankets and ripping up the sheet. Beside herself, she felt the tears burn her cheeks and only stopped when she noticed Milly at the door.

The little girl had woken and was watching her fearfully. 'Where's Daddy?'

Shaking, Faith sank on to the bed.

'He . . . had to go to work in Manchester, love. He'll be there for a while.'

'But we were going out today,' Milly replied, looking round. 'Where's Suzette?'

Pulling her daughter on to her knee, Faith tried to keep her voice steady. 'Suzette and her mummy have had to go back to France.'

'But . . .'

'They had to go during the night, sweetheart,' she went on. 'I know you'll miss Suzette, but . . .'

'She didn't say goodbye!' Milly wailed, suddenly bereft at the loss of her friend.

'She did say goodbye! She did,' Faith said hurriedly. 'And she said she would see you soon.'

'How soon?'

'When everything's all sorted out,' Faith replied, taking her daughter's hand and walking her back into their bedroom. 'We have to get dressed now, sweetheart. I think we'll go and see your uncle James.'

At once Milly brightened up, running ahead of her mother. Struggling to steady herself, Faith leaned against the door frame. She would go and talk to Angel James, the one man she had always, and *could* always, trust. He would advise her. He might even tell her that Lennie Hellier was lying, that it was just a cruel joke. Faith took in a breath, suddenly brightening. Samuel might be at David Street now. He might have gone in early, or just got up and gone off to the coast to find work. Yes, she told herself, that was it. Hellier was just lying, just trying to hurt her . . . But then Faith remembered that Leonie Bonnard was missing too. Leonie and her daughter. Her daughter, and Samuel's . . .

Slumping on to the top step of the stairs, Faith stared ahead. What a bloody fool she had been. Feeling sorry for the Frenchwoman, thinking herself lucky that Leonie was helping her – when really she was trying to prise Samuel away. And she had succeeded. Bile stuck in Faith's throat. What was the point of it all? she asked herself, baffled. What was the point of loving Samuel so much? Of trusting him, believing in him? Almost *willing* him to come home when everyone else had given him up for dead? And whilst she had worked and waited in Hardy Street, her beloved husband had been sleeping with Leonie Bonnard. He had given the Frenchwoman a child. A child who had been sneaked into her house, a child who had played with Milly. Humiliation and betrayal made Faith gasp, her hand going over her mouth. Had they been laughing at her behind her back? Taking her for a fool? How *could* Samuel let his bastard play with his daughter and not tell her? Not own up? If he had admitted the affair it would have been heartbreaking, but this was worse. This was treachery.

Standing up, Faith wiped the tears from her cheeks, her eyes suddenly clearing. She could imagine how soon the news would be all over Oldham, and Manchester. Could imagine how difficult it would be for her to face people, and have to explain to Milly why her father had gone. And that he wouldn't be coming back. Oh no, Faith thought, her anger rising. Oh no, they might think they could run away in the middle of the night. They might believe they could dodge her and their responsibilities, but she wasn't going to let them get off so lightly.

And then Faith knew what she was going to do. She was going to search for her husband and the Frenchwoman; she was going to find them and face them. And God help them when she did.

CHAPTER FORTY-ONE

'He did what!' Agnes said, lapsing into a fit of the vapours as Perry broke the news of Samuel's departure with the lodger. 'Oh my God, my God.'

'Now be calm, my dear,' he said pointlessly. 'We have to be calm.'

'The lodger!' Agnes wailed. 'I always said from day one that it was folly to take in a woman. With a child, as well. There was bound to be trouble. Mind you, Samuel's been acting strange for a while – no wonder, with two women on the go.'

Enviously Perry thought of Faith and the Frenchwoman, wondering how it was that a man like Samuel Granger had managed not one good-looking woman, but two.

'Are you listening to me?' Agnes snapped, dragging her husband's thoughts back to the present. 'I've said it before and I'll say it again – no decent family takes in lodgers. It's a recipe for disaster, every time. Well, there's only one thing for it . . .'

'Yes, dear?'

'We'll have to make up some story. Say Samuel's gone funny in the head again. That he's in an institution somewhere.'

Perry's eyebrows rose. 'That's better than the truth?'

'Better to be mad than bad!' Agnes replied hotly. 'Of course Faith will have to take some of the blame for this. She was always too indulgent with Samuel. I mean, he was injured in the war, but obviously he wasn't injured *that* much.'

Sensibly Perry decided that now was not the time to tell Agnes the other half of the story. That Samuel was the father of the lodger's child. Somehow Perry knew that it would be too much for his wife to cope with.

'Faith was so in love with Samuel. And he loved her,' Agnes said, sympathetic and angry by turns. 'You can't trust a man, that's a fact. You just can't trust them.'

'I'm a man, dear.'

'No, Perry,' she said dismissively. 'I mean a real man. And as for lodgers . . . Well, you put a notice in your front window and you never know what you'll attract.'

As the news about the Grangers spread across Oldham, Faith took the tram over to Manchester with Milly. Hurrying along David Street, she arrived in the studio and explained to James and Ellie what had happened. Ellie took Milly into the kitchen and gave her something to eat, then returned to the studio and stood beside her husband.

'Lennie Hellier's a villain, he could be lying. Or playing some sick joke.'

'No, it's no joke,' Faith replied, turning back to her brother.

James knew the look of old: Faith was in no mood for compromise. 'What can we do to help?'

'Can you look after Milly for me?'

'You know we will.'

'And explain to Laurence that I've had to go away for a little while?'

Hesitating, James nodded. 'OK, Ellie can sort that out, she's more than capable . . . but where are you going?'

'France.'

'*France!*' Ellie echoed. 'You can't go over there on your own.'

'You did.'

'I went with my mother,' she replied, 'and besides, I knew the place, I was working there. You can't just go off on your own. God knows what could happen to you. You don't even know where they've gone.'

'I've a good idea,' Faith replied. 'I know where Samuel was stationed once, and there's a village there, not more than thirty miles from Paris. I remember he told me about it. Didn't mention Leonie Bonnard, though, he never wrote about her.' The bitterness in her tone was crushing. 'Anyway, I reread his letters and I thought back and remembered everything he told me about the village. About the chickens walking down the lane, about a boarding house with blue shutters and a creaking gate. And a river over the hill . . .' Her voice hardened. 'I'm going there.'

Keeping his voice calm, James asked: 'What for?'

'What d'you think? I want to find them. I want to get my own back on them – especially that French bitch.'

Shaken, James tried to calm the situation down. 'Listen, love, I know this is a terrible shock, but there has to be some misunderstanding. It's just not like Samuel to up and go. He loves you, Faith, you're his life. God knows how many times he's told me that.'

'Maybe he was telling Leonie Bonnard the same thing.'

He winced, but pressed on. 'I can't believe he'd leave you for her.'

'Well he has,' Faith replied, turning to Ellie and fighting an impulse to break down. If she did that, she would never have the courage to follow her plan through. She would give in, let them win. And she wasn't going to let that happen.

'And what happens if you *do* find them?'

'I'll worry about that then,' she replied coolly.

James frowned. 'You want Samuel back?'

'I don't know,' Faith said honestly. 'But I can't leave it like this. I can't just let them ruin my life and move on, leaving me with Milly and with the whole world laughing at me. It's not fair, on me or my daughter.' She paused, glancing down. 'You know something? It's that little child that bothers me. I can't believe Samuel's daughter was in our house and I didn't know. I don't remember him spending any time with her, or giving her any special attention. And Suzette is his flesh and blood.' She shook her head, fighting confusion. 'As for Leonie Bonnard, pretending to be my friend . . . I confided in her, told her all about Samuel, and all the time she must have been smirking behind my back.'

'Faith,' Ellie said softly, moving over to her friend and putting her arms around her. 'Stay here with us for a while. Let the dust settle, don't go running off.'

'I have to!' Faith replied brokenly. 'I can't just sit here. I can't. I have to see him, look into his face and ask him why. I have to understand, or I'll never be able to live with it.'

'But to go in search of him . . .'

'Samuel isn't hiding from me. He knows that I'll guess where he's gone, he knows that much. He isn't hiding . . .' Faith said distantly. 'He just doesn't think I'll go after him. You see, I know my husband, I know what he's thinking. That I'll be too proud, too shocked to follow. He thinks I'll hate him, loathe him for his betrayal, think him beneath contempt. He'll believe that I won't want him any more. That I'll wash my hands of him. He thinks I'll let him go. That I'll have too much pride to follow him.'

Ellie's voice was steady. 'Maybe he's right. Maybe you *shouldn't* go after him.'

Resolute, Faith refused to be dissuaded. 'I have to go to France.'

'But you can't go alone,' James said flatly. 'It's not safe – and frankly, you're in no condition to think clearly. You need some support, you need someone with you. You can't do this alone.'

'It's all right,' Faith replied firmly. 'I'm not going alone.'

Bored, Beryl was staring up at the sky and wondering if it was going to rain again. New Year, she hated it. Hated all that long, winding expanse of days, weeks and months to fill. To be frank, she was happier when it got to March. The year had been broken in a bit then. Like a new chair that had lost its first stiffness, the spring months had shed the shiny newness of January. Yes, Beryl thought, she would look forward to spring. There wasn't that much more *to* look forward to. It was boring living with her sister, and after cleaning the house from top to bottom, sorting out every drawer and having several noisy arguments, Beryl was beginning to realise that she had damn near exhausted the potential for amusement in London.

The only thing that really pleased her was that she had managed to get some money together, having taken a part-time job at the local news-agent's. When they realised how dependable she was, they had increased her hours and she was even asked to help out over the weekends. So – even after she had paid her sister rent – Beryl had managed to put a nice bit of money aside. A *very* nice little sum, she thought with pride. In fact, she hadn't had such a pretty nest egg for years. Not that she knew what she was going to do with it. That didn't matter. Just having it made her feel more secure.

But lately Beryl had been thinking about the City Photographic Studio and wondering if Samuel was really pulling his weight and making a go of it. She wanted that – but she wouldn't have minded a letter from Faith saying that they needed help. After all, Beryl had made her point, and a grudge could only go on for so long, Besides, Samuel was spending most of the time out and about trying to find work. If she did go back, they wouldn't be under each other's feet the way they had been. Longingly she thought of Hardy Street and wondered if Faith remembered to wind the clock in the front room. And if she had replaced the meat safe in the cupboard under the stairs. Beryl had been thinking of replacing that when the argument had blown up and she had left. Perhaps it was time to mention the meat safe in a letter to Faith . . . Just to show that she was still interested in what was going on in Oldham.

Damned meat safe! Beryl thought impatiently. Who was she kidding? She was bored and wanted to go home. Wanted to see David Street. James, Ellie, Faith and Milly, Mort Ruben, Laurence Goldbladt. Even Samuel. She wanted to see her family and friends again. Longed to see the northern streets, the smutty buildings of Manchester, the red-brick terraces and sooty chimneys, and the black iron gates of Alexandra Park. Bloody hell, she thought, picking up some washing and hanging it on the line in the back yard, what she wouldn't give to see home again. Idly, she pegged out the pillowcases, knowing that it wasn't likely they would dry in the cold air, then picked up the laundry basket and walked back into the kitchen.

As usual, her sister was having an afternoon nap upstairs, so Beryl was surprised to hear footsteps approach the front door.

'Hello there?' she called out, opening the door then staring at Faith in open astonishment. 'What on earth!' Hurriedly she grabbed her granddaughter and hugged her, then ushered Faith into the kitchen. 'I was just thinking about you. Did you come down by train? Where's Milly? Are you staying? You should have let me know you were coming . . .' She trailed off suddenly, noticing the lost expression on her granddaughter's face. 'What's up?'

'Samuel's left.'

'What?'

'Samuel's gone. He ran away with Leonie Bonnard.'

Beryl stared at her granddaughter, understanding coming slowly. 'Samuel and Leonie Bonnard?'

'There's more,' Faith said quietly. 'Suzette is Samuel's child.'

'Oh, bugger,' Beryl said, flopping into a seat and gesturing for Faith to sit down. 'When did he leave?'

'First thing this morning. Lennie Hellier came to tell me.'

'Hellier?' Beryl said, shocked. 'I imagine that pleased him, delivering bad news.'

'I couldn't believe it – then I saw that Samuel's clothes were gone, and the Frenchwoman had emptied her room and gone too. With Suzette.' She took in a breath. 'So I took Milly over to James and Ellie, and came for you.'

'Came for me?' Beryl echoed. 'Not that I won't help you in any way I can, love, but why did you come for me?'

'We're going to France.'

'Really?'

'I think they'll be at the village where Samuel was once posted. A place called Verdane. In fact I *know* they'll be there.'

'And we're going there?'

'Yes. We're going to find them.'

'All right,' Beryl said calmly. 'Why are we going to do that?'

'Because I have to, Gran,' Faith said brokenly. 'I have to – or nothing makes sense any more. I have to see Samuel. I have to hear him tell me that he doesn't love me and explain why he ran off. Why he kept it all a secret, why it was easier running away than facing me. Because if I don't find them and get him to explain, nothing makes any sense. *Nothing.* What's the point of loving anyone? Of struggling? Or having hardships, good times? Of bearing children and planning a future? None of that makes any sense if you can't believe in it. There's no sense to the world unless you can trust what you know

531

and feel. I *knew* Samuel wasn't dead, I *knew* he would come home. And he did. I felt it in my heart, just as I felt the love for him. But I never felt this, Gran,' she said, her voice wavering. 'I never suspected anything. Oh, there was a strained feeling between Samuel and that woman, but he told me it was because he didn't like having anyone in the house. Didn't like having to share me – God, and I *believed* him! How stupid was I? I never once looked at that woman and wondered. I never saw my husband in her little girl. I never looked at her and *knew* my husband loved her and not me. I took her as a friend, and now . . . now I want to kill her.'

'I can understand that, love,' Beryl replied, 'but you can't.'

'I know . . . but I can find her. Then I can look her in the eye and tell her what I think of her.'

'And Samuel?' Beryl asked. 'Do you really want to go after him for answers – or because you want him back?'

Faith paused for a long moment, then lifted her head, staring her grandmother full in the face.

'I want him to tell me that he doesn't love me. If he does that, I'll walk away. But he has to tell me, Gran. He has to tell me that he wants her more than he wants me.'

Sighing, Beryl glanced round, then stood up.

'Well, I've pegged out the washing and made some dinner, so when you're ready, what say we get off?'

Faith stood up, hardly believing what she had just heard.

'You mean it? You'll go with me?'

'Oh yes, love,' Beryl agreed. 'Life was getting very boring here, I've been needing a change. Luckily enough, I've got some savings together.'

'And I've brought all the money I have.'

Beryl nodded. 'Good, because we're going to need it. Crossing the Channel costs money, and then there'll be train fares and boarding houses.'

'I love you,' Faith said suddenly, reaching for her grandmother's hand. 'I couldn't do this without you.'

'Oh you could, love, you're strong enough,' Beryl replied. 'But that's not the point – I don't want you coming across that French bint and doing something you'll regret.' She paused. 'If anyone gets to kill Leonie Bonnard, it'll be me.'

CHAPTER FORTY-TWO

The weather broke on the journey across the Channel. Faith and her grandmother huddled against each other on the top deck of the boat, Beryl's hat pinned down firmly on her head.

'Did I ever tell you how much Sid disliked boating?' Faith murmured something incomprehensible as her grandmother continued. 'Oh yes, your grandfather took me on the park lake more times than I choose to remember, but he hated it. Got us stuck once on that little island in the middle. Daft sod.' The boat lurched suddenly, Beryl gripping her granddaughter's hand. 'He was always showing off. Flirting too, always flirting. Not that he ran around with women; I would have maimed him for that.'

Another lurch made Faith wince. 'I was thinking . . . we don't speak French.'

'Yes, I know,' Beryl replied matter-of-factly. 'That had occurred to me as well. But someone will speak English, they can't all be foreigners.' The boat rolled unpleasantly on the waves, Beryl impervious. 'We can't use English money.'

'We'll have to change it,' Faith said dimly.

Beryl nodded. 'And we'll need to get some food. Can't eat their stuff, we'll have to make our own.'

Grateful, Faith held on to her grandmother's arm. She wanted, for the first time in forty-eight hours, to laugh. Here she was – the wronged wife – crossing the Channel with her grandmother, who was talking about making something to eat. In the distance, the coast of England was disappearing under the clogging of mist, France coming closer every minute – and with it, the showdown between her and Samuel. Faith's memory turned back to the time she had gone abroad with Ellie and Sybil. How different their lives had been then. Before James's accident and Ellie's return, before Sybil's death and long before Faith married Samuel and bore his child. She would never have believed – back when she was a teenager – that the next time she visited France it would be as an abandoned wife.

Faith shivered suddenly, unease making her cold, the sea churning darkly beneath the boat. Unable to eat or sleep, only her anger was driving her on, forcing her to confront the people who had hurt her so much.

'I don't suppose they have trams in France, do they?'

'Some, in Paris,' Faith answered, glad that she had visited the country before and wasn't a complete stranger. 'And they have carriages, some kind of buses.'

'But how do we get from Paris into the

countryside? To this village you're talking about?'

'I suppose we'll get a train, or have to pay someone to take us,' Faith said uncertainly. 'Someone will have a horse and cart.'

'How far is it from Paris?'

'About thirty miles. The village is called Verdane,' Faith said, glancing at the paper she had written the name on. 'It's east of Paris.'

'Hmm,' Beryl said impassively.

Faith was thinking ahead. 'They'll be there, won't they?'

'If they aren't, we'll find them,' Beryl replied steadily.

'I want to see Leonie Bonnard's face again,' Faith said, her tone bleak. 'I never thought she was pretty. Never noticed that.'

'She wasn't pretty to a woman.'

'But to a man?'

'I think so,' Beryl went on, adjusting her hat again, the wind blowing around her ankles. 'She had a vulnerable look about her. That could take a man in.'

'It must have fooled Samuel.'

'Maybe, but then again, some women are very clever, they act a part. I wouldn't be surprised if she didn't chase him.'

Faith nodded, thinking of Suzette. 'And catch him.'

'Thing is,' Beryl said, staring ahead, 'catching is all right; it's the keeping that's difficult.'

*

Samuel knew he had made the biggest mistake of his life. And he knew there was no way back from it. He thought back, remembering New Year's Day, the way he had sneaked – because that was the word for it – out of his marital bed and met Leonie on the street outside. Suzette had been wrapped up in a blanket, still sleeping, Leonie standing there questioningly, as though – for a moment – she had not expected Samuel to come. But he had *had* to leave. He could never have confessed to Faith what he had done. Could never have borne the look of injury and disappointment that would follow; the shock at his betrayal of her trust. Because he loved her so much, he could not inflict the blow that would hobble her – that he had cheated on her, that he had made love to another woman. And, worse, that she had borne his child.

He couldn't tell Faith the truth, couldn't look into her face and drive a knife into her heart. Better to run off, let his wife think he was a bastard. The confession of his adultery would have been devastating on its own. So how could he explain the fact that his ex-lover and their child had been living under their roof on Hardy Street? Pretending to be strangers. Sleeping only yards away, Leonie making herself invaluable. Faith's friend and confidante who helped out looking after Milly. While all the time he said nothing . . . How *could* he explain that away? Say he was trying to buy Leonie's silence, trying to find work to pay for her to keep quiet? Even taking money from the till on David Street when her demands became too much? Jesus, Samuel thought desperately, he hated the woman. Hated her for breaking up his marriage, and taking him away from the one person he loved above all else. Faith. The woman who would now despise him, loathe him, wish him dead. The loving, trusting wife he had betrayed. The woman he had given up – for what?

It was obvious to Samuel within twenty-four hours that he couldn't live without Faith. As they left England, he missed her, missed his child, his home. And as the miles wore on, his heart closed down. Returning to the French village where he had been temporarily stationed with the army, Samuel found the place poor from war damage. The people suspicious. Only a little way away, Leonie's family still worked the land on their farm, but she wasn't interested in any reunion. She had not managed to get money out of him, but Samuel knew she had triumphed. What better way to get revenge than to break up a man's marriage and steal him for yourself? He wondered then if Leonie knew how much he loathed her; and realised that in a way it didn't matter. All that mattered was that she had him back, a man to provide for her. And for their child.

Samuel closed his eyes, moving out of the village boarding house into the scrubby yard outside. He remembered the first time he had seen the place, and remembered describing it to Faith. But its rural charm had long faded. Now the building was neglected, the walls mottled with water damage and damp, the old blue shutters hanging listlessly, the gate creaking in the heavy air. Taunted by the memory, Samuel looked down the same lane where he had first come with his army companions: before his adultery, before his injuries, before he had changed irrevocably. He saw in his mind's eye the chickens picking at the dirt, and remembered telling Faith about Verdane when he came home on leave. He had been alive then. A man still believing in a future with the only woman he had ever truly loved. But now all that was gone. He would never see Faith again, never hold her again, never watch their daughter grow up. In that instant Samuel could see the ruin of his life and the ashes of his future.

Leonie had told him that there was always work going in the fields, or at the farms. After all, she said, he liked working outdoors, he should be pleased at the change in his fortunes. But he didn't like the French countryside and never had. It reminded him too much of the war and the gunfire, of loss and longing for home. He knew he would never find peace in this place. And besides, it was January, with little land work needed until the spring. There were Frenchmen looking for work; what chance did he have?

When he mentioned it to Leonie, she shrugged and told him he could find work as a labourer. From odd-job man to businessman to labourer. From family man to outcast. How long before Leonie turned into a shrew? How long before looking at her was intolerable? She had tried to instigate lovemaking, but he had cringed from her, making her angry, explosive. The only woman he wanted to touch was Faith. And somehow the supposition that Leonie could take his wife's place was worse than murder. How could she imagine she could slide into Faith's position? Dismiss her rival, block her out as though she no longer existed? Sighing, Samuel lit a smoke, noticing that his hands were shaking. He felt a helplessness that unnerved him, along with a crippling sense of loss. Leonie had told him that in time he would forget his old life. That he had better forget it, now that he had another family to provide for. Another child to love . . .

It wasn't Suzette's fault, but every time Samuel looked at her, he thought of Milly. It wasn't that he didn't care for Suzette – but he felt that if he allowed himself to love this child, he would be denying the other. As for Leonie, she looked after her daughter, and seemed to care for her, but Samuel was beginning to suspect that from the beginning the child had primarily been a bargaining tool.

Far away, an owl hooted in a cold winter tree. There was no moon, nothing moving about, no lights in the distance, no late-night trams, no noises coming from a riotous English pub. Here the silence was dense with nothingness; it spoke of segregation and regret. It was a landscape that told Samuel he was a stranger, a labourer on soil he would never cherish, with a woman he would never love. And the thought that he was trapped there, that his bones would one day be laid to rot in this foreign soil, tore at his heart like a razor.

Finally reaching Paris, Beryl and Faith stood in the railway station, momentarily fazed by the noise and hustle around them. Voices raised in a language they didn't know echoed around them. Men and women hurried from platforms on to the concourse, a couple of children wearing large sailor hats being chivvied by their nanny. Fascinated, Beryl looked at the younger women's clothes, noticing the shorter skirts, the leaner silhouettes. Sid would have liked to see *her* in those, when they were young. But her thoughts soon turned to more practical matters when she noticed Faith trying to engage a middle-aged stationmaster in conversation. She was showing the man the piece of paper with the name of the village written on it, and it was obvious – even from where Beryl was standing – that her granddaughter was trying to find out how to get there.

The stationmaster looked at the paper and said something. Then he shrugged. Faith pointed to the paper again, Beryl wondering where she could buy a phrase book. But Faith was nothing if not persistent, and after another couple of minutes, she moved back to her grandmother.

Her face was pinched from lack of sleep, but her eyes were determined.

'We have to get another train out of here, which

will take us near to the village. There's one in about an hour. At least I think that was what he meant.' She looked round, picking up Beryl's suitcase and her own.

'Hey, I can carry that!'

'No you can't, you look tired,' Faith replied, moving ahead, Beryl dropping into step beside her as she made for the furthest platform. 'We'll have to ask if this is the right one when the train comes,' Faith went on, sitting down on a bench. Beryl joined her, and Faith opened a paper bag she was carrying and took out a bottle of milk and some bread and cheese, passing half to her grandmother.

'We're going to eat here?'

Faith nodded. 'We have to be careful with the money,' she said, then paused, biting her lip.

'What is it?'

'I shouldn't have dragged you here. It was selfish. I just expected you'd come with me. And now you look worn out, and I've already spent half of our money,' Faith said hurriedly. 'It was selfish of me. I shouldn't have done it, made you run around with me. It wasn't fair on you.'

'Oh, be quiet, I'm enjoying myself,' Beryl said emphatically, beginning to chew on her bread and cheese. 'Wouldn't have missed it for the world.'

Grateful, Faith changed the subject.

'We could stay in Paris tonight, if you're tired.'

'And how much would that cost?' Beryl answered. 'No, we'll get the train to this village, even if it's late. There must be a pub or something to stay in when we get there. I mean, they might be French, but they must sleep somewhere.'

'They have places like our boarding houses,' Faith explained. 'So Samuel told me once.'

'Like Brussels,' Beryl said, her tone flat. 'So that's decided. When we get there, we'll go to one of those. Get a good night's sleep. Things will look different when we're rested.'

'Samuel will still be gone, and I'll still want to kill that bitch,' Faith said coldly, drinking some of the milk and ignoring the curious glances from passers-by. 'Sneaking around in my house, under my very nose. Pretending she was so caring. That's what upsets me the most. That she made *friends* with me. I would have preferred it if she'd been straight from the start.'

'She couldn't risk that.'

Faith turned to her grandmother. 'How d'you mean?'

'I guess that she wanted to test the water first, see if she had any influence over Samuel.'

'We know she did now.'

'But why did it take so long?' Beryl countered. 'Why didn't he just up and leave when she first came to Hardy Street? If he'd really cared about her, that's what he would have done. I think she pressurised him, forced him to go with her.'

'Maybe,' Faith replied, unconvinced. Whatever Beryl said, it made no difference to Faith. Samuel had been a coward and deserted her without giving her an explanation. Leonie had betrayed her. No excuses in the world could make their actions right.

Or even understandable. 'I want to see that woman's face again.'

'You will, soon.'

'I want to see it, and I want to hurt her.' Faith stopped, close to tears. 'Jesus, I want to pay them both back for this! I want them to feel like I feel, I want them to know how much it hurts . . .' She trailed off, crumpling the paper bag in her hand. 'I am going to make that woman wish she had never come to Hardy Street. I'm going to make her wish she had never come under my roof or eaten at my table.'

Startled by the vehemence of her granddaughter's tone, Beryl put out her hand to touch Faith, but she moved away. She was putting distance between them, afraid that if she accepted comfort she would relent.

That night, after a slow, protracted train journey, they arrived at the next village to Verdane, getting lodgings in a cheap hotel that had no other guests. The bedroom was cold, the fire unlit. Chilled, Beryl slept in her coat, Faith staring out of the window across the flat expanse of land to the horizon beyond. Numbed with shock and anger, she slept sitting up, waking often, and finally rising when the cock crowed. Splashing water on her face, she bathed as well as she could in the freezing and primitive conditions, then redressed and pinned up her hair. Beryl was still sleeping, her arms folded, regular breaths coming from her half-opened lips.

Tentatively Faith moved over towards her grandmother. She was going to rouse her, then decided against it. Beryl was getting on; perhaps it was too much to wake her when she needed her sleep so much. Turning away, Faith wrote a quick note to explain where she was going, then moved to the door, pulling on her coat and hat. Alone, she descended the boarding house stairs and crept out into the first light of morning. The cold had begun to lessen, a weak sun crawling up into the mottled clouds, frost on the grass making her boots wet as she walked along. After a few yards she paused to read a signpost, weathered with age, but stating clearly *VERDANE – 1 kilometre.*

Taking in a breath, Faith turned in the direction of the village, her footsteps even and regular, her breathing slow. As she walked, she thought of Leonie Bonnard, of how she had felt sorry for her and believed the sob story of her life. Then she thought of Samuel, and ached for what she had lost, bitter and angry that another woman had stolen what she had most prized. Her fury drove her on. Down the country lane towards the inescapable and inevitable climax of her journey. Towards her husband and his lover. Towards the family he had chosen over her and their daughter. In a land she didn't know, far away from Hardy Street and the safety of home. Her feet beat out an even rhythm on the ground. She took off her hat. Walking through the chill air, she felt the coldness around her head, making her eyes smart, her skin burn.

I loved you, Samuel, she thought desperately, I loved you so much. I wanted you, I believed in you. I knew you were alive when everyone else said you were dead. Why wasn't that love enough? Why wasn't *I* enough? Determined, she walked on, the horizon becoming visible through the morning mist, the village signpost rearing up in front of her like a startled horse. She was there. She had arrived. Soon, if she was right, she would find them. In bed, probably, making love . . . Taking in a slow breath, Faith moved into the village, a dog coming out from a nearby farm and barking at her. But she didn't stop; in fact she walked quicker, unfastening the top button of her blouse as she felt her throat tighten with nerves.

Looking round, she suddenly realised that she had no idea where they would be staying. She stopped dead, almost panicking at the thought that her journey might have brought her so close, only to hold her up now. Then, slowly, she began to walk down the village street, and saw how small Verdane actually was. Little more than a hamlet, some out-of-the-way, forgotten patch of earth. Surprised, she moved on, seeing old carts standing outside barns and houses, the village pump dripping water intermittently. It was, she realised, a depressing place. Most of the houses were in desperate need of repair, and the road wasn't much more than a lane, a dirt track. In the distance she could hear the sound of a horse neighing, but otherwise the place was quiet, the early morning sun sullen. The two village shops still had their blinds drawn, and as she passed, she noticed a small cutting between a row of houses.

And then she saw it. Saw a narrow, ill-kept boarding house, tucked behind several cottages, its sign barely readable. But it had blue shutters, and an old gate . . . Glancing round, she walked up the pathway, noting the weeds and dried flowers, dead where they had been left to rot. Above her head, an old apple tree – bark peeling and the trunk split with ivy – creaked in the breeze. Walking towards the front door, she paused, then pushed it open. The cramped hallway was dusty and empty, but then again, it was early and obviously no one was up yet. No smells of breakfast came from the back as, slowly, Faith walked around into the yard. A scuttle of hens clucked at her feet, a cockerel crowing, but there was no one in the shed, and she turned, retracing her footsteps into the hotel.

As she entered, Faith listened, then moved to the bottom of the stairs and looked upwards. From what she had seen of the village, she knew that this was the only boarding house. She also knew, instinctively, that this was where her husband was. Climbing the stairs, she paused. Three doors faced her as she arrived at the landing, three closed doors with numbers on them, a chipped washing bowl left on the scratched landing windowsill. Her mouth dried, fright suddenly overtaking her. What if Samuel threw her out? What if he refused to answer her questions? What if he told her he didn't want her, and that he wanted Leonie instead? Moving over to the first bedroom door, Faith opened it and looked in. It was empty. Likewise the second. When she came to the third door, she swallowed, hardly able to catch her breath. Then she turned the handle.

CHAPTER FORTY-THREE

Always a heavy sleeper, Leonie was lying in the middle of the old double bed, Suzette beside her. Her heart hammering, Faith moved closer and looked down at her rival. With her hair loose, her eyes closed, the Frenchwoman had a completely different look, a confidence even in her sleep. She reminded Faith of someone – and then the image of the bathing woman came back. The woman Faith had seen so long ago. The woman who had been so casually cruel. They both had the same look, that sensuality and selfishness that marked them out and made them dangerous.

Anger made Faith shake uncontrollably, her hand reaching out towards the sleeping woman, her fingers trembling only inches from Leonie's throat. For a moment she was unsure what she was going to do – but the woman who had injured her so badly was now the vulnerable one. Her gaze moved to the pulse in Leonie's neck, and she watched her breathing, watched the rise and fall of her chest. Leaning down, Faith's hand hovered over the sleeping woman, then suddenly Suzette awoke and began to cry.

Startled, Leonie sat up, staring with disbelief at the woman standing beside the bed.

'What are you doing here?' she asked, rising and pulling on a robe. 'What do you want?'

'Where's Samuel?' Faith asked, trying to keep her voice steady. 'I want to talk to him. I'll deal with you later.'

Looking round, as though expecting to see Samuel in the room, Leonie frowned, then noticed a letter on the bedside table. Before she had time to reach it, Faith had picked it up, pushing it deep into her pocket.

'That's mine!'

'Well now I've got something of yours,' Faith said coldly. Hearing footsteps outside, she glanced down the stairwell, but instead of seeing Samuel approach, it was Beryl moving along the gravel path and then puffing her way up the stairs. When she reached them, she looked at Leonie and then at Faith.

'So you found her, then?'

Faith nodded. 'But not Samuel.'

Turning her gaze back to Leonie, Beryl pointed to the little girl crying behind the Frenchwoman. 'Shouldn't you see to your child?'

Unsettled, Leonie picked Suzette up, then looked over to Faith.

'You can't do anything. Samuel left you for me. He doesn't want you.'

'*He* can tell me that,' Faith replied, moving over to Leonie and looking at her with hatred. 'You were such a good liar. Although you did slip up now and again. Trouble was, I wanted to believe you, so I pushed any doubts to the back of my mind.'

'Samuel doesn't want you!' Leonie snapped dismissively. 'Why are you making a fool of yourself? You should have more pride!'

'Maybe I should break up a marriage instead, like you,' Faith retorted. 'You must have a lot of pride in what you've done.'

'I did what most women would have done – I wanted to provide for my daughter. Samuel is her father, he should support her. He should support us both.' She paused. 'Trouble was, he was so useless, he couldn't make enough money. I told him that I'd have kept quiet if he'd just supported me. I didn't really want him, Faith. But when I told him I would tell you, he couldn't face it. He ran off with me rather than admit what he'd done.'

'Shut up!' Faith snapped, Beryl jumping. 'Where is he now?'

'I don't know,' Leonie replied, adding, 'But he'll be back. And you're going to look very foolish when he tells you that you've had a wasted journey.'

'Where is he?' Faith repeated. 'Where is my husband?'

The Frenchwoman said nothing, just smiled at her rival, her expression triumphant.

Turning to her grandmother, Faith kept her voice steady. 'Stay with her. I'll come back.'

Hurrying out of the boarding house, she paused in the lane, looking around blindly, her head thumping. She had lost. The great climax had been a non-event. Her speeches, her impassioned pleas to Samuel had not been uttered. She hadn't even seen him. All she had found was her despised rival, who was crowing with triumph. Walking towards the footpath, Faith sat down on a large upturned stone, then took the letter out of her pocket and stared at it. The handwriting was Samuel's. She knew it so well, from all the letters he had written her from the war, from the notes he had scribbled, the love letters he had left for her to find on the night table. Just like he had left this letter. Only it wasn't on Faith's night table, it was on Leonie's.

For a moment she wanted to tear the note into pieces, but she resisted. She had come so far. She had to know the whole truth. When she read the love letter to Leonie, she would know that her marriage was over. When she saw words she had believed Samuel had only ever written to her, had only ever *felt* for her, she would know. She might not have the chance to see or speak to her husband; she might not need it. After she read the note, she would know the truth. The letter would be her answer.

With trembling hands, Faith tore open the envelope, the handwriting blurring for an instant before her eyes. Then, slowly, she began to read.

Eloise
I cannot live with you. I cannot stay with you for another minute. I don't love you and I never did. If I had been a better, braver man, I

would have had the courage to tell Faith the truth. As it was, I let you blackmail me into leaving her. You made me leave my family, thinking that you and Suzette could replace them.

She is my child, I know that now. But I can't stay with her mother. The little money I have is in this envelope. Hardly anything, I know. But all I have. Consider our account closed.

When you read this, I will have left. I can't go home because I did the best of women such a bad turn. I threw away love that was greater than I deserved. I humiliated a woman who had only ever loved me and supported me. Being with you made me realise even more how honourable my wife is. Faith did not deserve what I did to her. She does not deserve any more pain. But I deserve everything that happens to me.

Although Faith will never read this letter and never know why I left, I still write – here and now – that I love her. I love her. I love her. And I will love her for ever. My Faith, my wife, my love. My North Star who guided me home. But not this time. Maybe in another time, another place. Maybe then, my love . . .

As for you, Eloise, you were nothing to me. Remember that. Read this letter and know that. Know that you lost.

But I lost more.
Samuel

Shaken, Faith reread the letter, then stood up. She finally understood what had happened, and why Samuel had really left. He didn't love Leonie; he loved her. Loved her so much that he couldn't face her and break her heart. So instead he had gone away, out of Faith's life, believing that she would never forgive him and grow to hate him instead. Faith stared at the letter, her thoughts scrambling. She could imagine how torn her husband would have felt. Still unsteady from the war, uncertain of his place in life, his confidence shattered, he had been an easy man to blackmail, she thought helplessly. A simple target for a manipulative woman. In his prime, Samuel Granger would have confronted the Frenchwoman head on, and fought for his happiness – but time and experience had changed him. His greatest mistake was not in committing adultery, but in doubting the depth of his wife's love.

Faith tried to piece together the sequence of events. For a little while Samuel had thought he could live with what he had done. But he had soon realised he couldn't. He couldn't live without his wife, his family, his home. So he had left Leonie. He would never return to England, so where had he gone? Confused, she looked around, searching the landscape, looking for any sign of her husband. Then she felt a chill come over her. The letter had not been a love letter. It had been a goodbye.

Desperate, her breathing quickened as she began to run down the lane towards the wood. Where would Samuel have gone? she asked herself. Where?

It seemed incredible to her that he would have given up – but apparently he had. His conscience and his sense of loss had been too much. He could not live without her. Crying out, Faith kept running, fighting panic. Where would he go? Where would he go? And then she remembered the Samuel of old, the young, easy-going Samuel, who had loved the outdoors. Walking. And fishing. And she remembered the descriptions of the village, of the dirt road, the fields and the river over the hill . . . But which hill? Which one? she asked herself, stopping and turning round blindly. North or south? Panting, she ran on, seeing a figure on horseback and running over to the man.

'Stop, please!' she said, moving her hands around to make him understand. 'Where is the river?'

The man shrugged, unable to understand her. Desperate, Faith mimicked the action of swimming, and smiling, the man nodded, then pointed over to his right.

Then Faith really began to run. She ran through empty fields hard with frost, the wind clawing at her face as she held up her skirt and raced on. Once or twice she paused, looking round, searching for some sign, then hurried on further. Her chest felt as though it was on fire, her breathing ragged as she ran past another bank of trees and stopped. She could hear water. Panting, she looked round, then spotted a bridge. And someone standing on it.

'Samuel!' she shouted, running towards him. 'SAMUEL!'

He didn't hear her; he was just standing, looking down into the water.

'Samuel!' she called again.

But he still didn't hear her. His thoughts were concentrated on nothing, his eyes staring blankly ahead. His expression seemed devoid of feeling, wiped of hope.

'SAMUEL!'

This time he heard her. Turning, he stared, incredulous, at his wife as she ran over to him and grabbed his hands tightly.

'Come on, it's time to go home.'

'No,' he stammered. 'I can't . . . I can't . . .'

'Samuel, come home with me.' Incredulous, Faith followed his gaze into the depths of the river. 'You weren't really thinking of jumping, were you?'

He stared at her, lost, as though he didn't know the answer himself.

'Because if you jump, I jump. And you don't want that, Samuel. We have a life to live, you and I. We have a child who needs us. Milly needs her parents. She needs *us*,' Faith said firmly. 'And I need you.'

He stared at her, shaking his head. 'I can't come back. I can't make it up to you. What I did . . . Jesus, what I did to you . . .'

'It's over.'

'It'll never be over!' he replied hoarsely. 'You'll always look at me and remember what I did. You'll never forgive me.'

Tightly, she squeezed her husband's hands. 'Yes I will! If you come home with me now, we'll put all this behind us and I'll forgive you. Because I love you . . . But if you give in, Samuel, if you give up, I swear I will *never* forgive you for that.'

He turned to her, hardly daring to hope. 'You want to try again? We can be together again?'

'Come home now and we'll work this out, darling. The bad times are over. *All* the bad times are over. We're going home, my love. We're going to make a new start, a new life. We're going to be happy again.' She stared deep into his eyes. 'I read the letter. I read what you felt. I read how much you loved me. Samuel, listen to me – *I read the letter*.'

He gazed at her, then buried his face in her neck and clung to her as though he would never let go again.

CHAPTER FORTY-FOUR

Smiling grimly, Beryl sat down in the chair opposite Leonie. Her face sullen, the Frenchwoman watched as Suzette ran towards Beryl and climbed on her knee, remembering her. Humming under her breath, Beryl tickled the little girl, then glanced over to Leonie, her expression deadly. She had come across women like Leonie Bonnard before, and had dealt with them; the Frenchwoman did not intimidate her in the least. In fact, unbeknown to Faith, Beryl had been plotting her own revenge and was about to put it into action.

'Your little girl has grown,' she said lightly. 'Children are very expensive, aren't they? I mean, Suzette is not much more than a baby, but soon she'll need to go to school, and then she'll need more toys and clothes – which you'll have to pay for. And of course a child takes up a lot of time. You live for them, put your own life on hold. Especially if you're on your own.'

'I'm not on my own!' Leonie snarled. 'I have Samuel.'

'Not for long. When Faith finds him, Samuel will leave you,' Beryl replied coldly. 'Then you'll have your work cut out. Lack of money and time gets to everyone in the end. Before long you lose your looks and turn round and realise that you're not young any more. And that your daughter's getting all the attention you once had. The attention you could *still* have, Leonie.'

Leonie's eyes narrowed as she studied the doughty Englishwoman. 'What are you talking about?'

'This little mite,' Beryl replied, watching as Suzette climbed off her lap and moved back on to the bed. 'Your daughter deserves a good life. She's not going to get it with you.'

'Really?'

'Leonie, think about it,' Beryl said, her tone composed. 'You need to be free to catch another man. You need to get out of this dump and back to the city. You don't need a child hanging on to your coat tails. I mean, Suzette was a bargaining tool for you, but it didn't work out. Faith and Samuel were meant to be together. He's not your man. So if I were you, I'd grab the opportunity I'm about to give you. Because otherwise you'll live to regret it.'

'What opportunity?'

Beryl reached into the bottom of her bag and brought out an envelope. In it were her savings, every penny she had collected together whilst she had been in London. 'If we do a deal . . .'

'A deal! With you!' Leonie said scornfully.

'You want to change the tone of your voice, young lady. I'm going to give you a chance no one else would give you.' Beryl paused. 'Hand over Suzette and let Faith and Samuel bring her up. There's enough money in this envelope to see you right for a little while.'

Leonie was genuinely taken aback. 'You want me to sell you my child?'

'We love Suzette, and you need to be free. I don't like seeing a child used as a poker chip,' Beryl replied curtly. 'You know as well as I do that Suzette will be doted on with us. She already has a sister and a home – give her up, and give yourself a chance.'

'Samuel—'

'Will not stay with you,' Beryl interrupted emphatically. She could see that the Frenchwoman was thinking about her offer – but was she tempted?

'You've got some nerve,' Leonie said, her tone cool. 'You're nothing but an interfering old woman.'

'Maybe I am,' Beryl agreed, holding out the envelope to the Frenchwoman. 'I'm offering your child security and happiness – and you an escape route.'

'Maybe I don't want your escape route,' Leonie replied, folding her arms and leaning back.

'Don't be a fool and refuse! You'll have your freedom, and some cash. I ask only one condition – that you *never* say that I gave you any money. And you stay away from Faith and Samuel.'

'Stay away from Samuel?'

Beryl made a dismissive clicking sound with her

tongue. 'It hardly seems too much to ask – for what I'm offering.'

Leonie's eyes narrowed. 'Maybe I don't like the offer.'

Beryl could feel her pulse thumping, but kept her voice steady. Slowly she extended her hand, waving the envelope in front of the Frenchwoman.

'Do we have a deal?'

Leonie shrugged.

Beryl waved the envelope again 'Do we have a deal?'

Ten minutes later, Samuel and Faith walked back into the bedroom in the boarding house. Holding Samuel's hand tightly, Faith stared at the Frenchwoman, then glanced over to Beryl.

'We've been having a lovely chat while you two were out,' Beryl said lightly. Leonie was sitting on the bed, now fully dressed, Suzette playing on the floor at her feet. The Frenchwoman seemed oddly relaxed, Faith thought, turning back to her grandmother.

'What's going on?'

Taking in a deep breath, Beryl smiled. She had thought for an instant that Leonie would refuse her offer, but after another moment's hesitation the Frenchwoman had finally taken the money. The relief had been immense.

'Miss Bonnard,' Beryl explained, 'isn't really cut out for family life. I mean, some people marry and settle down young, but others don't suit it. They like their freedom, and let's face it, once you've lost your freedom, you don't often get it back.'

Faith was watching her grandmother with curiosity. She was a wily old woman, and clever. But what the hell was she up to?

'So we thought that seeing as how Suzette is Milly's half-sister, and seeing as how Miss Bonnard would be able to get on with her life more easily without a child around, I said that we'd take her on.'

Dumbstruck, Faith looked at the Frenchwoman.

'You want to give up your child?'

Leonie shrugged. 'I'm not giving her up. She'll be going to her father and her half-sister. She'll have a proper home in England.'

'And you'll be free of the responsibility of her?' Faith asked, her tone acid.

'Look, you're married, you've already got one child. Suzette is half yours,' Leonie replied, smoothing down her skirt. 'If you look after her, I'll move on. Give up any claim to her.'

Faith glanced at her grandmother. 'You believe her?'

'Oh yes,' Beryl said lightly. 'I mean, us bringing up her little girl in return for her independence is a pretty good deal, I'd say.' She turned back to Leonie. 'Don't you agree?'

The Frenchwoman nodded briefly. She made no reference to the money Beryl had given her.

'Take good care of my daughter.'

'Oh yes,' Beryl assured her, 'Suzette will be one of the family. *Our* family.'

'What about you?' Leonie said, looking over to Faith, her eyes hostile. 'You got your husband back; well done. So how d'you feel about taking my child on? I mean, it's a very noble act, but won't you look at her every day and see me? Won't you remember whose daughter she is every moment she's around? Won't you remember constantly that she might be with you, but she's half mine? That whatever you do, however you treat her, she'll *always* be half mine.'

'And half mine . . .' Samuel said, putting his arm around his wife protectively. 'And half mine.'

Two years later, Laurence died. Because Miriam had died four years before and he had no children, he left the Goldbladt showroom to me. My God, that was the talk of David Street! Well, Samuel and I sold the business on for a fair sum – although nothing like as much as people thought – and put the money into the City Photographic Studio. Because it was the family business, and we were a family. James and Ellie carried on working and living in Manchester, but Beryl lived with me, Samuel and our two daughters in Hardy Street until the day she died.

That climactic day in Verdane marked a changing point in our lives. From then onwards, Samuel seemed slowly to regain his confidence, and as time passed he grew into a stronger and happier man. Content with his family and his lot in life, he became a reliable, loving partner to me, and an affectionate father. I never again doubted that he loved us. He never gave me reason to.

Mort Ruben carried on at David Street, working

until he was past eighty-five, still wearing spats long after they were fashionable. And in 1923 he married the shy little widow – when she wasn't so shy or so little any more. Against all the odds, Agnes and Perry had a happy marriage, my aunt becoming a professional complainer. As she got older, she wrote to the papers about everything. Politics, short skirts and Chinese laundries. She was particularly vocal on that subject . . . As for Lennie Hellier . . . Oh yes, I heard about him again. Long after he came to my door to ruin my life I heard that he had died of septicaemia. Died alone and shabby in the worst part of Salford. Which was exactly what he deserved.

David Street began to change in the twenties, and when the thirties came around the Depression hit. But that was long after this story finishes. Another one will follow and take you there. But not with me.

Sometimes I think back to when Angel James and I used to talk about romance. How little I knew then. And yet I was so passionate, even as a child, so sure that I would be loved. That I would be a soldier's woman. Someone tried to steal that title away from me. She succeeded for a little while, but only temporarily. We received letters from Leonie Bonnard for nearly a year after we made our agreement, but then they stopped. Almost six years later she wrote to say that she was getting married, and that she was giving up all rights to her first child. She was never a woman who could hold on to anything for long.

But I kept my soldier, long after he stopped being a soldier, and the only fighting he still did was with me. I kept him. He kept me. We kept our children. And most of all I kept the belief that whatever happens – war, want, treachery, even death – love survives. It survives in the human spirit, in every woman and every man who has ever believed in fate. Who has ever believed in hope.

And in the triumph and bravery of their affection over the world's deceit.